THE
LOST AND FOUND

To Hoar unt Kris /
I hope you enjoy all the
you stay at the
(as) ma frund).
with gratitude,
Jami ober gan

JAMI OBER GAN

ISBN-13: 9781794389366

For my three greatest masterpieces.
For Maddison, my daughter and, Noah and Max, my sons.
You inspire me and you teach me, every day.
I am a very blessed mama.
And grateful, every single day, that you are mine.

For my Immah, who shared with me her tulips and windmills.
And so much more.
And for my Abbah, who flew to Phoenix to talk to my
baby brother before his first vacation.
And so much more.
You were such big people.
So big that all who knew you were better for it.
There is much of you in these pages. I miss you.

Acknowledgments and Gratitude

To my early proofers: Susie H., Gail O., Eddie O., Gail G. and Scott G. I would like to thank you for your critiques and suggestions. I truly appreciate the encouragement, the support and the honesty.

To Dorian Rolston, my creative writing editor. You were a cheerleader, a challenger and an intuitive editor who has great ability to see the words through the lens of the writer. Your creative guidance helped my story grow up. Thank you for helping me to "stick the landing". I am so grateful that we met. Truly.

To Nancy Ozeri, my friend and final line proof editor. You are my comma queen, grammar guard and catcher of many oopse's. Thank you.

To Lauren Grossman, a fellow author, who kindly advised and shared what she knew to help me get to the last part of my "birthing book" journey. And for sharing Debora Lewis with me.

To Julie Stein, who designed my cover. I am honored that my book gets to wear one of your creations.

To Debora Lewis, who put my pieces together to look like a book. *Finally!* So you get two thank you's.

To Marty Johnston, for more than you will ever know.

I want to thank Dr. Sereta Robinson, Ph. D., who so graciously shared her time, her vast knowledge of Dissociative Identity Disorder (DID) and her enthusiasm for my "project". You helped me stay true to my story AND this disorder. Something that was important to me from the start.

And thank you (always), Susie Hallowell, for pointing me in Dr. Robinson's direction. And more importantly, for being my very own Lost and Found.

The mention of specific songs, places or events are all made as a loving fan and I thank those who helped make them possible. Some characters and events in my story were inspired by different things or people that happened to me. And some were inspired from dreaming. The rest are from somewhere in between.

P.S. Noah, come out and (word) play. You are a much greater writer than I am.

Prologue

I didn't want tomorrow to come. Thank God the sun didn't need my permission to rise. I never would have given it. I didn't want to tell him I was leaving. But, even more, I didn't want to stay. Dean was lying. I had no proof or confession; only denials. But I was as sure he was lying, as I was the sun would rise. He would be returning and I would be leaving. He'd been away on business for almost a week. I had spent much of that time sitting, numb and pained at the same time. I relived events and conversations, arguments and promises made and broken. And, occasionally, I found lucid moments that pushed me forward. It was during one of these times that I decided that I didn't want this life. It was time to stop.

It was strange, I thought, that my first reaction when I first truly knew, was relief that I hadn't planned more for the wedding. We had been together for almost five years. It was only in the last year that we got engaged, but we hadn't really finalized anything, other than to decide on a fall wedding. While I thought about it, I went and got my pen and a notebook. I grabbed them and climbed back into bed, where I had spent most of the last three days. Writing had always been my therapy. When I was sad, I opened my heart and put it on paper. Tear stained collections to revisit later. When I felt anger, I screamed at the pages and they held my rage. And when I was happy, I thanked with my pen. Words to remind me when I forgot to be grateful. I had notebooks full of beginnings, middles and ends of poems, songs and tales.

I got out my journal. I stared at it for a few minutes, not sure what to do. I opened it and looked at the page waiting for me. After a few more minutes, with a purpose I did not know I had, I began:

I don't want to write about Dean tonight. I want to not write about him. And since I have nothing else inside me, I will write about writing. I've never said it out loud but, for too long, I felt like I had a story inside of me. What's strange is that I can't remember a time when I didn't feel this way. But I never knew what to do with it. I still don't. I don't know if I can string my words together well enough to grab anyone. I don't know if I can decorate my thoughts enough to lure anyone in. But, I know enough to understand that the words that first greet the reader are some of the most important. They must give the reader a desire to turn the page to see what is on the other side. Unfortunately, that's all I know… about writing, that is.

Part I: Lost

Goodbye

Jesse greeted me as I approached the table where he was waiting. He came in for a big oversized hug. Sometimes it even surprises me that we're twins. He's tall and solid with brown wavy hair and deep green eyes. I'm petite, a bit thin, with wavy long brown hair and brown eyes. His arms enveloped me and held me slightly longer than his usual bear hugs. I think this hug was telling me he was sorry that I was going through this. And that he was there for me. And that Dean was a prick. That's what twins did. They possessed unconditional love, solidarity and the ability to know what the other was thinking.

My mother was gone. Again. She was somewhere other than home, which was usually the case since our father died almost 20 years ago. Phone calls or, more often, voice messages were our preferred mode of communication. My mother never quite comprehended our thorny relationship. A voice message letting her know my plans worked well for me.

Jesse and I sat down and fell into "twin mode." It was comfortable and easy. I was leaving the next day and I wanted to see him before I left. I didn't really have a plan other than to be away from here. Jesse just accepted this and trusted me. My mother wouldn't have.

Because he is four minutes older, Jesse is my self-declared protector, my best friend and my confidant. He is so much better at handling things than I am. He is pragmatic. I, according to my mother, am problematic. He jumps in. I watch from the side. He got the calm. I got the chaos. We are very different. Jesse has a much better relationship with our mother. It was always that way. I never blamed Jesse. I did blame my mother. As far back as I can remember, she'd always been supportive and attentive to Jesse, while absent and impatient with me. And while we both see this, neither of us understands why. So he acts as my buffer and I love him even more for it.

I had broken off my engagement with Dean. Feeling broken felt unbearable. It hurt so big, but I was sure it was right. He protested at first, but when he saw my resolve, he confirmed what I already knew. It was over. Somewhere between my 50th and 60th hour of soul searching, I realized I needed to get away. Having no man was preferable to having this one. An old college friend, Deb, had called recently and reminded me that I had an open invitation to visit her in New Mexico.

"You want a drink?" Jesse interrupted my wandering mind.

"Sure."

Jesse grabbed the waiter and ordered drinks. We sat for hours, drinking and eating, and going backwards, doing the "remember when…?" thing. We began with one memory and it triggered another. And it led us far from where we began. Our favorite cartoons and summer camps. School pranks and museum mishaps. Favorite movies from childhood through last week. And the day we went off to different colleges. Maybe playing Memory Lane was his plan. It was a small distraction from Dean. And it made me happy for a little bit. Our memories mostly were about the two of us. Not our parents. It was as if they visited some of our memories. But most were just Jesse and me. We were almost all we had for family. I would miss Jesse.

It was time to say goodnight. And goodbye.

"You know I don't like goodbyes," I reminded him.

"I know. That's why I'll just tell you that I'll see you later." He walked me to my car and gave me another big bear hug, reminded me of brotherly things and that he loved me. I told him I loved him back, pulled away and got in my car before I got teary. I drove away, already missing him.

On the Road... and Then Not So Much

The bad thing about bad things is that they have the power to spillover, so the damage, really, is immeasurable. A broken heart does that. Lies do that too. Especially the kind that make you feel like a fool and scare the trust out of you. This seemed like Dean's favorite kind of lie. Whatever distraction I found only served as a tether to the grief. Fortunately, the pain was so big that I was becoming numb. Unfortunately, it was so big that I knew that it was going wherever I was. So I packed my car, pointed it east and drove. I didn't plan out the trip. I had a reservation in Arizona, at a quaint inn for the night. Tomorrow I would plan the next leg.

The drive was a long one, but it went fast. When your mind can't stop thinking, an hour goes by like a minute and before you know it, you have 500 miles behind you.

"Long ago, and so far away. I fell in love with you..." I punched the radio off.

"Is every song on the radio about this crap?" I screamed. Song after song was filled with love and happiness. I never realized how many there were. I sulked for a minute before noticing the flashing lights.

"God damn it!" I hissed, slowly pulling off the road.

"Do you know why I stopped you?" the officer asked through the open window. On any other day, my heart would have skipped a beat. Looking through the window was a Greek god in a patrolman's uniform. But today I hated men.

"No, sir."

"Well, you were going a little fast." Exhaustion swept over me.

"I'm sorry. I didn't realize that I was going so fast."

"Something on your mind distracting you?" He seemed to actually want an answer. What to say? Do I start with the way Dean used to look at me a certain way before stroking my cheek? Or how we had planned a future? Or how he betrayed my trust?

And so it came. I didn't plan it, but it came anyway. Tears and sobs. The officer stepped back for a second, genuinely surprised, and then came in a bit closer.

"You OK, miss?"

"No," I almost yelled. "I'm not." He looked like he was sorry he had asked. "My fiancé cheated on me," I cried, "and I don't know how this happened and…" I stopped to blow my nose while the tears kept falling. He waited for me to finish my defense.

"Listen, my divorce just became final a couple months ago. I kind of understand. I'm just going to give you a warning. But you have to slow down. You don't want this guy doing more damage than he already has. OK?"

"Yes, sir. Thank you." The Greek god walked back to his car and I rolled up the window, cried some more, blew my nose and then pulled back on to the highway. I took a deep breath and punched the radio on.

"*Aaaah, let's get this party started…*" Pink screamed, invitingly.

"Well, that's an improvement, Carlos." I called my Jeep Carlos.

I believed in signs. My brother said I found them, whether they wanted to be found or not. But I didn't care that he didn't believe. I did. When I bought my Jeep, the first time I turned on the radio, the D.J. said, "This is Carlos at 97.3 FM." I changed the station and heard an advertisement for Carlos Diego's Taco Shop, which I love, but punched another station, looking for music. Then I heard, "This is Carlos Santana. Enjoy." Needless to say, *Black Magic Woman* was our song. I didn't have a song with Dean, but I had one with my car. It was just as well. It would have been one more thing poisoned for me.

So Carlos and I hit the road again. A little bit calmer and a lot slower.

The sun was a little warmer now and the day was perfectly clear. You could see for miles. The music didn't bother me as much. I resolved not to take it personally. Soon the trees mingled with cactus and the landscape began to change.

I thought that once I left, the healing would slowly begin and the thinking would calm a bit. But the healing couldn't begin because the thinking never stopped. I was on a hamster wheel of tantrums and broken promises. And holding hands, not ever wanting to let go. I wasn't quite sure when things had changed. It happened so slowly that I didn't see it. And then I remembered the waiting. So much time spent waiting to see if the next time would be different.

I tried to think of something else. I focused my attention on the signs approaching. "Tucson 23 Miles." I kept driving. The Arizona desert was magnificent. So much nicer than California's. It had a synergy about it. It seemed that all of the parts connected somehow.

As I approached the city, pubs and shops escorted me into town off the highway. I decided to take one of the major streets across the city to where I planned on sleeping through some of my broken heart. The reservation I had was for a small inn on the east side of town. The street was a tunnel of signs asking me to put my future in Boyd's hands at Pima Realty or reminding me that seat belts save lives and offering me 50 percent off car detailing with any car wash at Tucson Speedy Wash and Detailing. Soon, the signs began to fade and the mountains that came into view again were majestic, peppered in grays and greens and browns that almost surrounded the city. I followed my GPS to the base of one of the mountains and found the Catalina Inn.

After checking in, I ordered a salad that I didn't want. The last thing I had eaten was a bagel for breakfast. I knew I should eat something. Even the blues could not detract from the view from my patio. I sat out there and slowly ate what I could of my dinner, taking in the beauty of the mountains as the sun began to set. If I squinted, I could see the details of the colorful landscape. The trees and shrubs that made up the greens. The rocks and rims that made up the browns and grays. All different shades and hues. When I turned to look at the sun setting, I was stunned by the colors in the sky. I had only seen this kind of sunset in pictures or movies. I always thought it took the magic of the photographer to take a picture like this. I stood in awe, trying to catch the last glimpse of the peaches and lavenders that began to hide behind the top of the roof.

Suddenly, I felt drained. I had just enough energy to reserve a room for my next stop and take a hot shower before falling into bed.

When I woke, I remembered where I was. Dread and pain hit me. Tears welled up in my eyes. And so another morning came that I had to will myself to shower and dress, get up and out. I relied on muscle memory to do this. My mind felt like mush. I checked out and gassed up before turning my Jeep towards the highway that would lead me to New Mexico. I stopped at a quaint cafe for a coffee and muffin to go, and then got in the car and drove. I headed east and navigated some hills and turns before the road opened and I could see miles ahead. I took out the muffin and carefully opened the flap on the coffee cup. I was so engrossed in my muffin that I didn't notice the ping from underneath the hood until the engine light came on.

"This is not good," I said to myself. I pulled over, stopped and turned off the car. And then the worry came. What if I got stuck here? What if Carlos is broken? Why did Dean do this to me? As if the engine light was in cahoots with my ex. I turned on the engine to see if the light would come on again, but it didn't start. I tried again. Still nothing. I took a few deep breaths and then took out my phone, but I had no signal.

"Damn you, Dean!" I screamed to the cacti, the trees and the oh-so-cute cottontail bunny that hopped away, startled at my outburst. I stopped my rant and it was quiet. About five seconds later, the panic arrived. I knew myself enough to know that the lack of reception coupled with my imagination was a dangerous combination. I stopped myself and went out to raise the hood. I hoped this, along with my hazard lights, would alert a passing motorist that I was in need of some help. I went back and sat in the Jeep, waiting for my unknown rescuer, armed with a nail file in one hand and a rape whistle in the other. Just in case.

I sat for an hour before the first car passed. It kept going. I checked my phone and car again. Still nothing. So I sat some more. At least it was a beautiful, cool, clear day. But after a little while, the blues kicked in so the panic wouldn't feel so alone. I replayed how I told Dean that I was leaving. Questioning how things could have been different. It didn't take long to get right back on that track of questions and condemnations.

I was thinking about this when I heard a tap on the window. I jumped and turned to see a man looking in. He smiled apologetically. His smile was disarming, but I grabbed my nail file anyway.

"Need some help?" he offered through the window. Unsure what to do, I nodded. He waited a few seconds before adding, "Maybe you should tell me what the problem is."

I was nervous, but I didn't really have much of a choice. I looked at the man on the other side of the window. He looked nice. But so did some of the serial killers I had seen on TV. This man, I thought, didn't look crazy. In fact, he looked as though he were the one looking at a crazy person. I made a mental note not to look crazy. He was around my mom's age, mid-50s or 60s, somewhere. He was tall, tanned and wore jeans and a button-down shirt. And he had on a wedding ring. I opened the door slowly and got out.

"My car is dead," I started. "I was driving and heard a ping and then the engine light came on and I stopped and now it won't start again." As he listened to me, he made no sudden moves for a weapon. I relaxed a tiny bit.

"Let's take a look." He glanced over his shoulder and added, "I'm Barry." I followed him.

"Nice to meet you, Barry. I'm Jade." He looked at me as I spoke.

"Nice to meet you, too. Sorry you're having car trouble. I doubt I can figure out what's wrong, but let me take a look and if not, then I can point you in the right direction." He lifted the hood and tickled around, pulling, tapping and tugging various parts. While he did this, I explained that my phone had no service, probably because of the mountains, so I couldn't call for help. As he unscrewed some cap, he explained that most phones don't work on this stretch. He reassured me that his did.

"If your engine light was on, and it won't start, I think we should have it towed to a garage. I have a friend, close by, with a garage. Want me to call him?" He looked at me as if we knew each other. He recognized my worry and remembered that we didn't. "Or you can use my phone to call a friend or another garage. Whatever you want to do." I didn't really know what to do or who I would call. I didn't know anything about Tucson except that it had beautiful mountains and desert and delicious coffee and muffins.

"I'd appreciate that. I don't live here and wouldn't know where I would take it." It occurred to me that I could be providing information to the enemy. He appeared genuinely sympathetic. So, I explained how I was from L.A. and passing through on my way to New Mexico.

"Well, this sure is a glitch in your plan. But, hopefully, just a little one. Let me call my friend. I'm sure that he can help, but not sure how soon. "He dialed his friend's number and waited. Someone answered on the other end. Barry's face brightened.

"Hey, Ace. How ya doin', my friend?" I listened to him explain my situation. He kept smiling so I thought this might be good. I heard him make arrangements and then he hung up.

"Looks like we lucked out. Ace said that Joe's already out with the truck and he would call him to come get your car. He should be here in about 15 or so. The shop isn't far. I can drive you over and we'll see what Ace thinks." He waited, patiently, while I thought about what to do. He then added, "Or, if you prefer, you can ride with Joe." He didn't say this with any malice. "Listen Jade. This probably seems unsettling. You don't know me. I'll do whatever you want. But I'm one of the good guys. I'll only take you over to the garage. I won't try anything." I looked up at him, a bit startled by his word choice. "That would be foolish of me while you are armed with a nail file and a whistle." He offered that same disarming smile that greeted me in the window just a short while ago. It made me feel a little better. I took a deep breath, then told him that I would appreciate the ride.

"I like seeing Ace anyway. He's a good friend. He'll know exactly what's wrong. Like I said, cars are his thing." I felt slightly better than I did before Barry stopped.

"Is there someone you need to call?" I thought about it for a second. Who would I call and what would I say? My car is broken.

"No, but thank you. I'll call later when I know what my situation is." Jesse knew I was in Tucson today and that I would check in with him later. We both leaned on my car and waited.

"So, New Mexico? Have you been there before?" Barry was trying to put me at ease.

"Nope."

"And you've never been to Tucson before, right?"

"Right." Barry waited again. "First time," I added. There was too much quiet. "So how long have you lived in Tucson?"

"Almost 19 years." I waited. So did Barry.

"And you have a wife?"

"Yes."

"Any kids?" Barry looked away.

"We had a daughter. She's gone now." So was his smile. I felt terrible for asking.

"I'm so sorry. I shouldn't have been so nosey. I'm really sorry."

Barry didn't smile, but he was relaxed when he turned back to me and spoke. "Don't worry about it, Jade. You didn't know."

I didn't know what to say after that, so I didn't say anything. Barry saw my discomfort.

"Really, it's OK. It comes up now and then. It's just hard to talk about. What else do you want to know about me?"

I thought about it for a few seconds. What could I ask that was safe? What did I even want to know? Then I heard a dog bark. I startled.

"Do you like dogs? He's a sweet one." I didn't realize that there was a dog in his truck. It was parked behind the Jeep and I hadn't really paid attention to it.

"I love dogs."

Barry whistled and a German Shepherd jumped out of the cab window and came running to Barry with his tail wagging.

"Jade, this is Shasta. Shasta, this is Jade." He introduced us. "Shasta, where are your manners? Shake Jade's hand." The dog walked over to me and actually put his paw up as if he was waiting for me to shake hand. So I did.

"Nice to meet you, Shasta. He's beautiful," I told Barry.

"Thanks. He's a good dog. Do you have any?" he asked. I bent down to pet Shasta.

"No. I thought about it. But, no. No pets." Shasta nudged my hand. He wanted me to pet him some more.

"Shasta," Barry said with a stern voice, "don't bother Jade."

"It's OK. He's no bother. I knelt down and scratched Shasta some more. "So does Shasta know other tricks?"

"Ask him!" I was surprised. But I did.

"Shasta, do you know any other tricks?" Nothing. "Should I take that as a 'no'?" I asked Barry.

"Hey, Shasta? Do you know other tricks? Tell Jade." Shasta barked. I looked at Barry.

"So he only listens to you?"

"No, he'll listen to you, too. Tell him to tell you something. You gotta use the world 'tell.'"

"Shasta, tell me if Barry is a good guy."

Shasta barked. I looked at Barry.

"See? I'm a good guy! Watch... Shasta, tell Jade I'm here to help."

Shasta barked.

"That's right, boy. Tell her more." Shasta barked again. "Lilly and Shasta have conversations that can last for 15 minutes. It's kind of funny."

"Who's Lilly?" Barry looked at me and it seemed like he was searching for an answer when the tow truck pulled over in front of my car. The driver got out and greeted Barry.

"Hey, Barry. How the hell are ya? This the car Ace was talking about?" He greeted Barry with one of those man handshake hug combos. Shasta snuggled between them.

"Hey, Shasta, boy. How ya doin?" Joe gushed while scratching the sides of Shasta's head.

"Yeah, this is the car. Joe, meet Jade. Jade, Joe," he introduced us. "Jade's car engine light came on, she pulled over and now it won't start. Ace is gonna look at it for her."

"Nice to meet you, Joe. Thanks for coming out. I appreciate it."

"Hey, no problemo. Any friend of Barry's is a friend of mine. Glad we could help. Wanna give me the keys or are you just gonna go to the shop too?" We explained that we were going to head there too and he told us that we could take off. We thanked him again and told him we would meet him there. Shasta, Barry and I headed back towards town in Barry's truck.

"I lied," Barry said. I looked at him, a little startled.

"I said I'd take you straight to the shop. But do you mind making one stop? We're gonna have to wait for your Jeep anyway. I just need to stop and get some honey for my wife. It's on the way, at a roadside stand. Do you mind?" I relaxed again.

"No problemo."

He smiled. We drove just a bit before Barry pulled over to a makeshift tent by a van on the side of the road. A big wooden sign said, "Local Honey." Barry told Shasta to stay and kept the car running while he got out and walked up to the guy under the tent. They talked for just a minute, shook hands and then the man got a bag out and filled it for Barry. He paid the man and came back to the car. He put the bag in his glove compartment.

"Honey sticks. My wife loves them," he said, as if I knew what a honey stick was. We got back on the road and headed in the same direction as we had before. I was going to ask what a honey stick was but Barry spoke first.

"So, if Ace needs to keep your car for repairs, where do you plan to stay until it's fixed?" I thought about it for a second.

"I don't know yet. Like I said, I don't know Tucson and I was heading out. Any suggestions on where to stay? Maybe I can get a room again at the Catalina Inn."

With a reassuring tone, he told me that he would help me figure it out. "It won't be a problem finding someplace nearby. There's a bunch of places. I'm gonna offer an alternative. You can take it or leave it." He looked over to see me waiting for him to continue.

"You could come stay at the ranch. My family has a place just a few miles from here. We have a lot of property with lots of extra rooms. People come and go a lot at the ranch. You can stay there 'til your car's fixed. You can't beat the rates. You help out.... we feed you and house you. That's the way the ranch works." He looked over at me and saw that I wasn't sure what to say.

"I know this is weird. Some strange guy comes to the rescue and then wants to take you home. But really, it's not like that. We just have a unique situation going on there and, like I said, we always have people coming and going. I'm just trying to help. Think about it. Hopefully, you'll luck out and Ace can fix it today. And if not, I can easily help you find another place to stay if you want." We kept driving.

I was thinking about this when we pulled off the road into the parking lot of an auto shop. The big faded wooden sign announced that we had arrived at "Ace's Auto Works." We parked near the building and Barry turned off his truck.

"I'm gonna just holler for Ace. Want to come with or wait here?" We both walked up to the garage entrance, after he told Shasta to stay in the truck. From underneath a white El Camino came a booming manly voice, "Yo, Barry. That you?"

"Yeah, it's me buddy. You gonna be awhile?"

"Nah. Just finishing up. I'll be right out."

"This Xavier's car?"

"Yeah. He's coming to get it... about an hour ago!" Ace laughed at his own joke. Clearly, he thought he was funny. "He wanted me to customize something. That's not really his thing. He's more into fixing, not making, so I told him I'd take care of it. Just double-checking while I'm waiting on him. Be right with you."

"We're gonna wait outside for you. Do what you gotta do."

Barry and I headed out of the garage when another car pulled up and honked. Barry looked closer and smiled. The car parked and a man and a woman got out of the car with big smiles that now matched Barry's. They walked over to us and they exchanged hugs and slaps on the back with Barry.

"Xavier, buddy. Long time, man. Too long." Barry was talking to this classically, tall, dark and handsome man. Any other day I would appreciate him longer than a few fleeting seconds.

"I know. It's so funny. Charlie and I were just talking about you guys. Como estas? How's everyone doing? Lilly, Nonnie and

Poppie?" The raven-haired woman looked like she was waiting for an answer, too.

"She's doin' fine. She's still Lilly." The Lilly from earlier, I guessed. "Don't know what that means, but she's good." I didn't know what that meant, either. "And Poppie's doin' alright. He's slowly fading. I think he's tired. I don't know. But you both should come on over and see them." Barry looked over to me.

"Jade, I want you to meet two really good friends of ours, Xavier and Charlie." He turned to them. "This is Jade. She was passing through Tucson until her car broke down. Ace is gonna look at it."

Xavier reached out to shake hands. He used both hands to cover my hand. It was endearing. Charlie reached out her hand too. Kind of a quick double-shake-then-done kind of handshake. Xavier and Charlie looked like they could be family. He was very tall, muscular, olive-skinned with black hair. She was petite, olive skinned, too, with beautiful long, jet-black hair.

"Nice to meet you," I told them. The tow truck was just pulling up when Ace came out. After big hellos again, I was introduced to Ace. And then I introduced him to Carlos. While he was looking at the Jeep, Charlie, Xavier, Barry and I chatted about some of the things one can do while stuck in Tucson. Charlie asked where I was staying.

"I'm not sure. Barry offered me to stay at his ranch, but I don't know. I don't want to intrude."

Barry reminded me, "Like I said before, people come and go so it's no problem. But whatever you want to do. No pressure."

Charlie chimed in, "Well, if I were you…" she kind of sung, "I would stay at the Lost and Found. It's a great place. Full of really nice people. Very unique." I thought that an odd word choice. And the name caught my attention.

"The Lost and Found?"

"Yeah, that's the name of their ranch. The Lost and Found. It's a great place. Nothing else like it." Xavier clearly liked the ranch, too.

"And Charlie is right. The ranch gang is cool. So are the others who visit all the time. Maya visits, she's Charlie's partner. They live in the next property just east of the ranch. And you'll meet Barry's family, and Huey." he added. "You'd love Huey." You could tell he thought highly of all these people.

"Let's see what Ace says about my car. I don't even know how long it will take to fix." I still wasn't sure what to do. I hoped that the fix would be easy.

Ace, as if on cue, interjected, "About 10 days." Ace explained that there were a few things that were wrong, and how he would have to get a part from Phoenix. With the weekend and a big repair ahead of me, it would take a little while.

"But if you don't want to wait I can make a call and see if my friend across town can get to it quicker. You might get it a couple days sooner, if you want." Ace broke down the price and said he'd give me the "family discount," explaining that he would do it cheaper than any other shop, but I was free to get a second opinion. All I knew was that I had a very broken car, was stuck in a city where I knew no one and was emotionally exhausted. A plan had been offered and I didn't have a better one.

"No, go ahead and order the parts. A few days won't make a difference and the car is already here." Being at a disadvantage, I hoped this would turn out all right.

"I appreciate your help." I added.

"I'll wait while Ace takes your info. Then we can figure out what you want to do." Barry waited with Charlie and Xavier while I went inside with Ace. He wrote up the estimate and list of repairs, got my contact information and told me he would keep in touch. Then he offered a little advice.

"The ranch really is a cool place. Great people live there. It's a safe place. Really." This big, bearded, grease covered man had a sympathy in his voice and a softness on his face that I found both bemusing and comforting.

"Thanks. I appreciate it." I went out to where Barry was waiting for me.

"All set?" he asked. Xavier and Charlie told me that they hoped to see me again and then they went inside. Barry and I were alone.

"I'm just not sure what to do."

Barry could see my discomfort. "I guess before you decide anything, I should tell you a little about Diana, my wife." I looked hard for a clue in Barry's face. Nothing. Maybe distress? His explanation, the way he delivered it, was worn, it seemed, from use.

"My wife has had a very hard life. The past five years have been particularly difficult. It's pushed Diana down in a big way. We lost our daughter and when that happened she sort of broke. She's still healing with the help of her doctors, but for now, she's childlike. It's her way of coping. She is absolutely harmless, but my 58-year-old wife, Diana, is now known as Lilly, a lovely young 12-year-old girl with a wonderful innocence. It's a long story." He paused, clearly wondering how much to share.

"She is like an alter personality. That's who she has become and you might not meet Diana. But you, for sure, will meet Lilly." he said, confidently. "It's safe, it's interesting and it's weird. And only fair to say so, if you're going to be around her." Barry looked slightly relieved. Sort of like having to do something unpleasant and getting it over with. It made me wonder how often he had to explain this situation. And now I knew who the Lilly was that talks with Shasta. Barry explained that his in-laws lived there with a bunch of friends who helped watch over Diana and the ranch. I guess the word "unique" was not that curious after all. "Totally your call, Jade. No worries about offending me. I get it."

Barry gave me a few minutes to think about it while he went inside and said goodbye to everyone. When I actually gave it thought, I found that I didn't really have any options other than to take a chance on my own. The combination of so many endorsements, along with not knowing the territory, led me to cautiously accept Barry's offer.

Part II: Found

Day 1: Jade, Meet the Lost and Found. Lost and Found, Meet Jade.

Carlos is broken, so now I'm at the Lost and Found. Where do I even begin? Let's just say that this week should be interesting....

We drove only a few miles when Barry turned his truck onto a dirt road. Soon after, he pulled over, stopping the truck. We had just passed two women working by the side of the dirt road near the turn-off. They appeared to be making something with bricks and cement. Hovering over the dirt road, about 20 yards back beyond the bricks, stood two tall, rusted poles cradling a charming, rustic sign. The sign, worn by weather, announced "The L & F Ranch". With the desert backdrop, it was picture perfect.

Barry invited me to come and meet two of the "ranchers." This, apparently, was what one called oneself, if one lived here. We got out of the truck as they began to walk over.

"Jade, I want you to meet Reesa and Coco. They live at the ranch, too." It wasn't necessary to say who was who. Coco had beautiful golden brown skin. She was slightly plump with a lovely mop of dark ringlets. Reesa couldn't have been more different, with shoulder-length, straight, blond hair and a petite, but toned, smaller frame.

"Girls, this is Jade." He told them how he found me by the side of the road. "Her car broke down and it looks like she might stay a week or so until Ace has it fixed." Both girls took off their gloves to offer their hands to shake mine and said it was nice to meet me. I echoed the sentiment. They backed up Barry's claim that Ace knew his cars. Barry looked towards the pile of bricks near what they had begun.

"You guys working on the planter?"

"Yep. Almost done. Huey and the guys finished the drip system yesterday. In a month or so we'll have wildflowers. The mailbox was looking pretty bland. Flowers will color it up. Don't you think?" Barry and I both agreed with Coco. After a few more minutes of catching up, we walked back to the truck.

"Glad you're here, Jade. See you later," Reesa called as she turned to get back to work.

"Nice to meet you," Coco added. "See you at the Big House." I looked at Barry.

"You'll see," he answered the question on my face.

We drove less than a quarter of a mile until I could see the ranch. It wasn't at all what I expected. I didn't see any bales of hay anywhere near a building resembling a barn. There were no wooden fences or campfires. About the only thing that I did see that belonged on a ranch were a couple of bandanas and they were around the necks of an aging Golden Retriever and a not so aging, energetic, gray and black mutt. They were following, running behind the truck.

Barry pointed out the Big House and continued on a smaller dirt road to a smaller house. As he stopped, the dogs came running. I got out of the truck just as they caught up.

"Freeze!" Barry commanded, with his hand held up, as if to block them. The dogs stopped where they were and waited anxiously for Barry to change his mind.

"You guys stay right there. That's Jasper," pointing to the Golden Retriever, "and Pima," pointing to the other. "We have three more: Cairo, you met Shasta," who had already jumped out and was running towards the bigger house, "and Jamison. Cairo's brother, Casso, died last year." After a short pause, he added, "And last month we had to put down Tosh. Lilly took that pretty hard." Barry looked over at the dogs and gently reminded them to freeze. They did. "We have more than a few families here and many of us came with dogs. Now they're all just everybody's," he explained. Suddenly the dogs' attention turned to a woman slowly running toward them.

"Speaking of Lilly…" Barry trailed off with a blend of humor and sadness.

"How do you know it's her and not Diana?" I wondered out loud. Barry didn't take his eyes off the approaching woman.

"She's got a jump rope in her hand. How many 58-year-olds do you know who like to jump rope? Or hopscotch?" He was watching her. "Usually she is skipping. She's being shy." She approached us.

"Hi Barry. Nonnie told me you were bringing someone home." She went and stood near Barry and turned to face me. You could see that she looked at him as a protector.

"Are you her?" Lilly asked.

Barry took over.

"Lilly, I want you to meet Jade. She's staying here for a little while until Ace fixes her car." He turned to me. "Jade, this is Lilly."

Lilly held out her hand. I shook it. Lilly shook hands like a kid. Kind of an awkward exaggeration. It was odd and surprisingly noticeable.

"Hi, Jade." Lilly was a slim yet strong woman. You could see that she was in good shape. Her long, light brown, wavy hair was in a loose ponytail, exposing her toned frame. Her face was beautiful. Not classically. More of a pretty girl-next-door sort of way. Her features were soft, yet slightly worn. And her face did not look like a women in her 50s, nor like a preteen adolescent.

"Hi, Lilly." I wanted to say something else, but I was a little nervous. "Barry tells me you like to jump rope."

"Yep, I really like it. It makes me feel good," Lilly answered. It was very strange to see a grown woman behave like a young girl. I hadn't considered jumping rope as terribly therapeutic, but Diana, or Lilly, was clearly happy and healthy, so I believed her.

"You want to jump with me?"

"Lilly, let's give Jade a few minutes to settle in. You can visit with her later. Maybe show her around a little." Barry was running interference for me. I felt bad that he thought he needed to do this.

"OK," Lilly said, with a small hint of rejection. I turned to her.

"How about Barry shows me where to put my stuff and in an hour or so we can jump rope."

Lilly's eyes opened wide.

"Really?"

"Sure," I said. "If that's alright with Barry." I looked to him for an answer, thinking that, perhaps I should have checked with him first.

"It's fine with me."

He seemed relieved. "I brought you some honey sticks. I heard you tell Nonnie that we were out of them." He handed her the bag he had taken from the truck.

"Thanks, Barry. I'll take them to the Big House and come back later." She just turned and began her trek back to where she was before she found us. With the small bag in hand, she began to skip away, then she turned and hollered back to us.

"I'll be back later, Jade. See ya, Barry. And thanks again for the honey."

I turned to Barry a little anxiously. I wasn't sure if what I had done was the biggest mistake or no big thing. Barry could tell that I was thinking about something. He had to remind himself that being 58 and thinking you are 12 is very noticeable. It was clear that he had become so used to Lilly that her presence didn't bring him any pause.

"Please, please, don't feel obligated to spend extra time with Lilly. She's always around. So you'll see her... a lot." Barry went on to explain that, lately, Diana returned very infrequently and Lilly was a busy child who made her presence known. She just wanted to be a kid. The kid Diana never got to be. I could tell that Barry was trying to find a delicate balance between saying too much and saying just enough.

"So, there's no danger in jumping rope with her?" I tried to make light of my lingering worry.

"God no! Well, there may be a danger that she'll want to play with you all of the time," Barry smiled, sure of his words. "I'd be a little careful. You should let her know that you are not the ultimate game partner sent here by the game gods."

"It's OK. I like kids." There was an awkward silence. I had no idea why I said that. "Wow. That was weird." I took a breath. "I'm a teacher, so I like kids. I'm not teaching now, obviously. I'm taking a little break…," I said, trailing off.

"Well, it's good you like kids, 'cuz Lilly is usually Lilly. So…" taking his turn to trail off.

We both smiled. Barry grabbed my suitcase and I followed with my smaller bag. The house Barry took me to was similar to two others next to it. Barry called the three guesthouses "casitas." He explained that there was also his house, with Lilly, Nonnie and Poppie. Nonnie and Poppie were his in-laws, Diana's parents. The Big House was the communal house, too. Everyone usually ate together. He told me that I would get the lay of the land later. He didn't want to overwhelm me more than I already was. He showed me my room and told me I could unpack and make myself at home. Before leaving he reassured me that the ranch was easy, and that if it seemed too much to handle, it would pass quickly. He promised me and I'm not sure why, but I believed him.

"I am sure Lilly will be here sooner rather than later to take you up on your offer. You can always tell her you need a little more time to settle in, if you want."

I told him I would be fine and then he left, hollering that he would see me later.

"Thank you again, Barry, for everything. I really appreciate it. I'll see you later," I called out as he walked back to the truck.

"No worries," he hollered back. "And thanks for playing with Lilly. I really appreciate that."

A little more than a week was too long to live out of a suitcase, so I unpacked my clothes, put some stuff away in the dresser and hung a few things in the closet. I made a quick call to Jesse to explain my situation. He didn't pick up so I left a brief message. Then I called to cancel the reservation at my next stop. This conjured up a memory of a fight that Dean and I had in a hotel lobby about who was supposed to make the reservation that was never made. From then on I made all our reservations. I hadn't thought of that in years. And I wished I hadn't.

◦ゃん ◦ゃん ◦ゃん

"Who were you talking to?" I heard a holler from the front room. Diana, or Lilly, had found me. I walked out from my room, glad for the distraction.

"I was just checking in with my brother."

Lilly stood there waiting for me. "Are you ready to play?" As I said it, I knew it sounded funny. Asking this woman, who was a few inches taller and a few decades older than me, if she wanted to go play was weird. But it sounded much better than being alone in a quaint little house thinking about Dean.

"Yes! Are you ready? Barry said not to rush you." I could see that she was trying to hold back. It really was an odd sight.

"No, I'm ready. What do you want to do?"

"Let's start with jump rope. 'kay? I'm pretty good at it. How about you?"

"Well, it's been awhile, but I'm sure it will come back to me." I wasn't really sure.

"Barry said we could play today, and I can show you around tomorrow. 'kay?"

"Sounds like a plan. Let's go." I grabbed my sweater and followed her.

"These are our casitas. Yours is Casita 3, then 2, then 1." She said pointing to the next one over and then to the farthest. We were walking on the path she had taken earlier.

Before we went out to jump rope, Lilly took me to the Big House. She wanted me to meet Nonnie, who was on the back porch repotting a new plant. Barry had explained that while Nonnie was Diana's mother, these days she was more like Lilly's grandmother. Nonnie's five-foot frame was petite, wrinkled and topped with a gray braid coiled in a bun. I couldn't help but notice that her skin was dark, but not very. When she saw us walk closer, she wiped her hands on her apron and slowly got up from her knees to greet me. Lilly chimed in.

"Nonnie, this is Jade. She's the one that's gonna stay for a week. Maybe more," she said with enthusiasm.

"So very nice to meet you, child. Barry told me that you're staying with us for a spell. I can't tell you how happy that makes me. We love company. And we especially love company that jumps rope, right baby?" She reached up and put her hand on Lilly's cheek. She smiled with more love than I had ever seen in one smile.

Nonnie was a little old lady in every sense of the word. Her worn, slow moving frame, her silver hair, her earned aged wrinkles were all a little old lady's. And there was also her remarkable smile. Her eyes squinted from the brightness of it. And I would learn, very soon, that she rarely smiled without a tilt of her head and an ever so slight lift of her shoulders. It was as if her whole body joined in. And her smile radiated something I could not find the words for. I'm sure I wasn't the first to find comfort in Nonnie's smile.

"So nice to meet you, too." I reached out my hand. "And thank you." Nonnie by-passed my hand and came in for a hug. She felt small and soft.

"No thank you's, child. We love company and making new friends," she said as she held on gently, waiting a moment before starting to pull away. I felt the goodness of her lingering hug. "You stay as long as you want." She stepped back, still holding my shoulders and looked into my eyes. She held my gaze as if she were looking inside me. Then her face softened even more and she repeated herself. "You stay as long as you want." Whatever apprehension I felt faded some by meeting Nonnie.

"Thank you. I really appreciate it. Should I call you Nonnie?"

"Of course, child. Unless you're speakin' to someone else," she said with a slight Southern accent. She let go, but the feel of her touch stayed.

Lilly told Nonnie we would see her later and I followed her down the porch steps to the basketball court, hollering another "Nice to meet you, Nonnie." When we got down off the porch, Lilly tied one end of a longer jump rope to the basketball pole that had a metal loop attached to it and held the other end about seven feet from the pole. While she tied the rope to the pole, I noticed that she had matching light scars all the way around both wrists. This made me feel sad for her. I wondered about them, but didn't ask.

"Wanna jump first? We can take turns. Usually I play with P.S., but she just got home from school." I was going to ask who P.S. was, but Lilly started turning the rope so I started jumping. It seemed as though I was not entirely correct about that 'all coming back' thing. I tripped up more than a few times before I got into a groove, but my efforts provided Lilly with entertainment and her laugh was joyous. After a series of successes and failures, I improved significantly.

"Bliss and exquisite are my two favorite words," Lilly announced.

"Those are two great words," I said, wondering how that was related to jump rope. I kept jumping, still tripping up, but Lilly was encouraging.

"See, you're already better. Are you ready to switch now?" I was ready after the first two minutes! We switched. I took off my sweater first. This was a workout!

"You can turn the rope a little faster for me if you want." Apparently Lilly was turning the rope slower for me, being older than her, sort of. I thought it interesting that Lilly interjected her favorite words out of nowhere and then moved on. We kept jumping, taking turns and chatting.

I learned they had a rooster and lots of chickens, making it a smidge more ranch-like than my initial assessment. Poppie was married to Nonnie, but he hadn't been well lately. A dog that lived nearby was going to have puppies soon and she might get to watch. Outdoor games were her favorite. And she hated homework. I made a mental note to ask about that later. Did she go to school? Lilly learned that I had a twin brother, Jesse ("just like Casso and Cairo"). I am an elementary school teacher. I love movies and music ("just like Poppie"). My favorite candy bar always had caramel in it. I was on a trip and my car broke down. And this was how our chat went.

After about 20 minutes we switched to hopscotch. This came back to me a little faster. But not fast enough. Lilly beat me every time. I don't know how many games of hopscotch we had played when a bell sounded from the big house. I looked to Lilly to see what that meant.

"Aww, man!" Lilly said disappointedly. "It's time for dinner." I was more worn out than hungry, but mostly I was glad to be done jumping and hopping.

"C'mon. We'll wash hands and then go eat. Nonnie likes it better if we wash before dinner." I helped untie the rope from the pole and gathered it up. After putting it away, then washing up at the hose and drying with a towel kept on a post next to it, we went up to the Big House. A woman approached from the side of the house.

"Hi. You must be Jade. I'm Annie, Barry's sister-in-law. He told us that you would be joining us for a while. We're glad you're here."

"Annie is Michael's wife. And P.S.'s mom. Remember I told you how P.S. jumps rope with me? She'll be here in a minute with Michael. We'll save her a spot. She'll wanna sit with us."

"I'm sure she will." Annie gave her a reassuring smile. "So, I hear you have another jump rope partner." Annie was looking at Lilly, but then looked at me with what I thought was both gratitude and sympathy. I followed them to the dining room. I was a bit nervous and became even more so when I walked in and saw almost a dozen faces look up at me.

"Everyone, this is Jade." Lilly announced. She turned to me.

"Come sit by me?"

"Alright." I waved timidly to everyone. "Hello, everyone. Thanks for letting me join you." I didn't really know what to say. They all offered back various forms of sincere welcome. Michael and P.S. came in after Lilly and I sat down, then they introduced themselves.

With everyone now seated, Nonnie began passing bowls and platters around. As we filled our plates, we all began to eat and visit. I was passed a platter of barbecued chicken from my right.

"Hi, I'm Coco. We met earlier on the driveway. If you don't eat meat, there are always plenty of sides."

"Thank you. I'd love some chicken. And I remember meeting you. Did you and Reesa finish the mailbox planter?" I asked as I took the platter from her.

"Almost. We'll finish tomorrow." She moved back in her seat so I could see the little boy sitting next to her.

"This is my baby boy, Jack. He's almost four." She introduced him to me and then turned to him. He was a cherubic toddler with chubby cheeks and beautiful skin, like his mama.

"Say, 'Hi, Jade,'" she told Jack. He had food in his mouth but said, "Hi," anyway. It sounded like, "Ha, Jed."

"Hi, Jack," I said back.

It wasn't long before I began to relax and my tummy growled. So it was around the dinner table that I met many of the people of the Lost and Found. There was Michael, Barry's brother, and Annie, with their 11-year-old daughter, P.S., Nonnie, Barry and Lilly, Coco and Jack, Reesa and her 4-year-old son, Tawn, Kelly and Lloyd. A couple other regulars were away. I imagined it would be a bit before I remembered everyone's names, especially if more came and went. It was a bit overwhelming, so much at once. But they made it easy by being so genuinely welcoming.

P.S. was covered in freckles and long strawberry curls that went down well past her shoulders. She wore a headband, so she looked like she had a golden lion's mane. She was quiet and sweet, and later I would find that she sometimes got frustrated with Lilly, and for good reason. What other 11-year-old is thrown into a ring with their 58-year-old aunt who behaves like her 12-year-old cousin most of the time?

I was told that Poppie wasn't feeling well tonight, so he had dinner earlier at his house. The dinner count was never the same. Sometimes only four or five were around or sometimes everyone was around with guests and the second table was used.

Everyone was so disarming. Just like Barry had been on the roadside. I expected them to ask lots of questions but, to my relief, they didn't. We talked a lot about the ranch. The mailbox project, the egg collection from today (apparently it was good), the citrus tree fungus problem they were having (apparently it was bad), Nonnie's new coffee shipment and talk about Guthrie visiting soon. Guthrie, they explained, was one of Diana and Barry's foster kids who became an Air Force pilot and was injured recently, overseas. He had multiple injuries that put him in a wheelchair, for now, but he was rehabbing back east and trying to get well enough to come see Poppie. I gathered from the discussion that Poppie was more than a bit sick.

In between bites of chicken, roasted vegetables with faro and a choice of cobblers for dessert, I learned a little more about this group of people, all of who seemed genuinely delighted that I was staying for a week or so, despite not knowing me. Dinner clean up was easy since almost everyone took their own things in and rinsed them, before putting them in the dishwasher. There wasn't much to do with so many of us around. But I managed to find a few things to help. I remember Barry telling me that was how the ranch worked. You help out, you get a place to eat and sleep. After a little while, I said my goodnights, along with the others who were still there and headed for the door. Coco offered to walk me back to the guesthouse.

"It's dark and I don't know how well you know the ranch yet. I'll drop you off on the way to my house. Cool?" Reesa had already taken Tawn and Jack back to their house to get ready for bed while Coco, Kelly, Lloyd and I helped clean up after dinner. Michel and Annie took P.S. home, which was on the property just west of the ranch. All of these people were attached to one another and their common bond was Diana. I thought of the expression "it takes a village to raise a child." Everyone here was the village, and Lilly, this 58-year-old woman, was the child.

"Sure." We closed up the Big House and walked down the porch steps. I was glad to be with Coco. I wasn't too sure which path to take. I followed her to the right and it began to look familiar.

"I think Lilly is quite taken with you. It's nice. She needs lots of attention and you seem pretty comfortable with her. Pretty funky. Yes?" She waited for me to answer.

"Well, it's definitely different. When Barry explained the situation, I thought it would be weirder. Lilly is kind of a cool kid…." I stopped and thought about my words. We both laughed a little. "OK. Yeah – pretty funky." We kept walking.

"Most of us were Diana's fosters from the day. The day being when she was healthy and whole. So, you're hiding from something." It wasn't a question. Coco got right to the point. "It's OK," she was quick to add. "I don't need to know what it is. Don't wanna pry... just stating the obvious." I didn't respond. Coco waited.

"I'm not doing this right. Let me start over." She took a long breath while she closed her eyes and chose her words. "Everyone here has a story. And many of us have some kind of running in our story. So you're in good company. But luckily for us, our running is over. You seem to be stuck right in the middle of it." She paused. "But you know you won't always be."

"I hope so," was all I could think of to say. It occurred to me that Coco might think my situation was similar to those at the ranch. Not that I knew all the stories of the people there. But it didn't seem like any of them had heartache.

"I'm in the middle of a broken heart. I guess I'm running from a man. That's all." I hoped that would suffice as an explanation.

"That's all! That's enough!" confirmed Coco. "If you need help, holler. There's lots of help here. All you have to do is ask." She waited to see if I wanted to elaborate. When I didn't, Coco shared a little.

"I came here for the same reason. It was a woman though, not a man. But it's the same kind of love... so it's the same kind of heartbreak. She trailed off, beginning to remember. Then she stopped herself.

"It's big... that kind of pain. But even deep pain heals. Just takes a bit longer, that's all." We reached my patio. "You good for now?" She asked.

"Yeah. Thanks. I appreciate the help. I'll see you tomorrow?" I had no idea what the routine was. The who would be where, when and why. I figured I would take it a day at a time.

"Of course. Probably every day," she said with a smile. "Goodnight, Jade. Dream good. And if you ever want to talk..." She trailed off as she turned and waved. As she hit one of the lights on the path, I saw, again, how pretty Coco was. She was a bit taller than me, maybe 5 foot 6 or so, and wore a printed loose long skirt with a teal t-shirt and large hoop earrings.

"Good night, Coco. Thanks again." I turned to walk to my house. I went into the quiet casita and stood there in the main room. I looked around and felt temporarily comforted. These walls felt safe for some reason, but they still couldn't keep out thoughts of Dean. Heartache and fatigue swept over me, again. I showered and got ready for bed. First, I sat out on the patio, trying to clear my head. The cold air felt good, but it didn't work. The distractions of the day helped. The nights always made time for the pain.

In L.A., the night sky is just a very dark gray. But here, the stars littered the sky. More stars than I could imagine. I heard once that there were more stars in the universe than all the grains of sand on all of Earth's beaches. I don't know if that's true, but I used to think it impossible. But now, looking at a clear Tucson night sky, I started to think it might be. The stars filled the sky. Hanging up there twinkling and dazzling, as if this were their job. I went to bed that night with an ache, but it was no match for my exhaustion. I tried to write in my journal, but soon sleep found me.

Day 2: Note to Self… You're Not 13!

You know the saying, "You can't judge a book by its cover?"
Well, it's true. This book is named Huey. And he helped me forget,
for just a bit, about my aching heart and aching body…

I slowly woke, forgetting where I was. As I looked around the room, I remembered that I had left Dean. The pain didn't hesitate to move in. I laid there for a few minutes, trying to redirect my thoughts, willing myself to start another day rather than go back to sleep and attempt to forget.

I moved my body, hoping it would help my mind wake up. I turned slightly, in an attempt to get out of bed and the first ache was felt. I moved again. Bigger pain. I wondered if it was the jump rope or the hopscotch. I sat up slowly, and put my legs over the side of the bed. It had to be both. I ached like I had never ached before.

"Oh my God," I said to myself. "No wonder Lilly is in such good shape." I talked to myself often. I've wondered if it has to do with being a twin. Beginning, really beginning, life with company. "Ow ow ow!" I got up and limped slowly to the bathroom. After a hot shower and moving more, the pain level went from ridiculously hellish to moderately excruciating. I headed to the Big House. As I came in, the smell of freshly brewed coffee took my mind off my shell-shocked muscles, momentarily.

"That smells so good," I said to whoever was in the kitchen. I limped in and saw Coco pouring herself a cup.

"Yeah. We like our coffee here at the ranch. Want a cup?" she asked as she reached for another mug. "How do you take it? Cream or sugar? I use sweet cream. Want some?"

"Sure. Thanks."

Coco poured me a cup and handed it to me.

"Nonnie orders the coffee. She used to be a barista before they called them baristas. She loves her coffee hot in the winter and iced in the summer. She's in charge of the coffee stash. "Thank God for Nonnie," I thought to myself. It was excellent. Coco noticed my discomfort as I took a sip, moaned with relief and very slowly sat down on the stool by the island in the middle of the kitchen.

"Did Barry warn you about the games? Lilly will play you to death."

I looked at her with gloom.

"Yep. He warned me. What he didn't warn me about was that I should have trained first. That girl has some energy."

Coco offered me a sympathetic grunt and a word of advice. "I hate to tell you this, but moving around is gonna make you feel a whole lot better than sitting."

I wasn't so sure. Sitting perfectly still sounded just right to me. Kelly, Reesa and Tawn came in and greeted everyone. We moved to the table and began chatting away, like this was my normal.

"So, what's a typical day here at the ranch?" I asked. This was met with glances to one another and a little laugh from all three.

"Typical isn't what you find here at the ranch," Kelly answered.

"What Kelly means is that we always have things to do, and while we all have our jobs, a routine to speak of, let's just say flexibility is the key. Our jobs crossover. We expect the unexpected and we always wait and hope for Diana to show up," Coco explained.

"How will I know if Diana comes back?" I asked. I wondered if this should concern me or if I should know what to do in case this happens.

"She probably won't. But, you'll know," Reesa answered.

"They are different people. You can tell. Diana doesn't do ponytails," explained Coco.

"And her wedding ring," added Reesa. "Diana wears her ring on her finger. Lilly wears it on a charm necklace around her neck." I remembered seeing the necklace. It had a ring sandwiched between a tiny gold angel and a red lacquered rose charm.

"What do I do if Diana shows up?" I wasn't sure of the protocol. They explained that it rarely happens, lately. They assured me that if Diana showed up, she would know what to do. This didn't make sense to me, but it made me feel better knowing that I didn't have to sound alarms.

"OK, so there is no typical routine here. How does everything get done? Who does what?" They looked at each other, waiting to see who would field this question. Coco stepped up.

"OK. So, in a nutshell…" She gave me a quick rundown on the ranch. I knew about the family house and Coco's casita. She filled me in on Kelly and Lloyd, with Sunshine and Will, living in the other. Sunshine and Will were away but would be back soon. And I was in the third. If Guthrie came, he'd take the other room. Sunshine helped with the kids or greenhouse and Will helped Barry with the maintenance, but they also worked at a non-profit for Native American youth. Reesa and Huey took care of the kids. Huey didn't live there, but he might as well have. And, apparently, I was going to "get a kick out of meeting Huey." I wasn't sure what that meant, but I had heard it before. The kids being taken care of were Jack and Tawn, P.S., when she was here, and any other kids brought along by whoever else came by to help. This apparently happened often. Huey also did after school activities with the kids three times a week. Xavier came to help around the ranch and he often brought his eight-year-old daughter, Serita, and five-year-old son, Julio. And Ace's kids often came by. Belle was nine and Johnny Jr. was six (they called him J.J.). Kelly was in charge of anything green: greenhouse, garden, fruit orchard. She did this with Reesa's help sometimes, and everyone else's when certain crops were ready. Coco took care of household duties. This meant food shopping, coordinating schedules and keeping the Big House clean, stocked and running smoothly. Nonnie helped her with this. Coco also worked part-time in a photography studio in town. Lloyd and Michael helped Barry with ranch stuff – fixing things, renovations and whatever else came up regarding general ranch maintenance. Annie was the bookkeeper. She paid bills and kept the accounts and records. With all that being said, they reminded me that lots of things come up and so lots of things were often tweaked and improvised.

"There's way more to it, but that's the ranch 101 intro. It's a bunch to take in. There will be no quiz. And you'll catch on soon. You'll see."

Barry and Lilly walked in. I saw that Lilly had the necklace around her neck with the ring on it.

"Good morning, ladies," Barry said, as he grabbed a coffee mug.

"Hi, Jade," Lilly chimed in excitedly. We all exchanged morning banter while Lilly poured herself a bowl of cereal and cut up a banana to put on top before pouring her milk. She sat at the bar and ate.

"Barry said that I could show you around. Since you're gonna be here for a little bit, I can show you where stuff is and introduce you to people. You are gonna stay for a little bit, right?" Lilly was double-checking.

"Yep. I'm here for a little bit. My car is going to take a little while to get fixed. So I would love for you show me around." After we finished our nourishment (breakfast for Lilly, more coffee for me) we got started.

"This is command central," she said as she turned away from the sink, where she had just rinsed her bowl and spoon and put them in the dishwasher. I did the same with my coffee mug. She pointed behind me a bit to the right. Up on the wall was a very big white board showing the month.

The calendar was full of appointments, celebrations, library days, farmers market dates and more. Lilly explained that it was always changing. There was room on the far right for a list. If you were in for dinner, you put your name on the list. That helped them know how much food to make.

There were also three tablets attached to the side of the refrigerator. One was to add groceries or market items. One was for animal supplies and the last was for household, property and office stuff. When someone noticed anything running low, they put it on the tablet.

"OK. You wanna go explore the ranch? I'll give you the best tour ever." She skipped out the door and hopped down the steps before I could even answer.

"Just a sec, Lilly," Barry interjected. "We'll meet you at the greenhouse. Then you can show Jade around from there. But I need to talk to her for a minute first. OK?" he yelled to Lilly, who was already waiting for me outside.

"'K.'", was all we heard before we heard her call the dogs. I didn't think Lilly liked being alone. I wondered what Barry wanted to tell me.

"I imagine you have some questions," Barry kindly turned his attention to me.

"Well…" I hesitated. He smiled.

"Of course, you do. And I imagine you will think of new ones after you get answers to the ones you have now. I have to go into town. But later, after Lilly's done with you, I can fill you in a little more if you want."

"Barry, we can do that for you, if you want." Coco offered to help.

He thought about this and looked at me. He took a couple more seconds before telling Coco that he would appreciate it. He explained that he had told me a little about losing Hope and how it hurt Diana. He just thought that maybe they should fill me in on how all this came to be. How the Lost and Found Ranch was born. "We don't need to bombard her with everything. Just the ranch story." Barry looked at Coco with an intentional look in his eyes. Coco seemed to get the message.

"I agree. The Birth of the Lost and Found. Coming right up... after your tour. Do you know which way to the greenhouse?"

"Nope. But I know which direction Lilly and the dogs went. Can I just follow that way?"

"Yep. Just follow that path at the side and you'll find Lilly. If she doesn't come back to find you first."

"OK. Then I'm off for the greatest tour ever. Have a good morning, all. See you later." I headed out the door to find Lilly. Just as Coco predicted, she was coming out of the greenhouse, as I was walking up.

"I was just going to go see where you were," she greeted me with enthusiasm. She turned to the greenhouse, held up her arm like one of the ladies on a game show, presenting their potential prizes and said, "So, this is the greenhouse."

And that is pretty much how the entire 'greatest tour ever' continued. We would get to a point, she would hold up her hand (sometimes both) and announce what it was that we were looking at and then on to the next stop. Her commentary was minimal, but I did get the lay of the land. I saw better how the ranch was laid out. The Big House, just a little bit off the main road, was the meeting place, the hub of the ranch. And surrounding it was a greenhouse, tetherball and pole, basketball court, henhouse, gazebo, orchard and the Family House, where Nonnie, Poppie, Lilly and Barry lived. The three casitas were farther northwest. If you took a winding trail for a third of a mile or so, you would find a very small lake. Or a very large pond. I wasn't sure. Lilly told me we would go out there later. We didn't really stay in one place long enough to see it well, but I got my bearings and this helped. And the fresh air and walking helped ease the aches in my body. Coco was right.

"Today I have to go do homework before lunch. Nonnie makes me do homework every day during the week. She calls it homeschooling. It's almost time. Do you wanna play just a little while?" That answered the question I had earlier about going to school.

"Sure. But just for a bit. I'm a little sore from yesterday. I'm not used to jumping so much."

Lilly smiled. "Nonnie says a good life includes a bit of pain. It makes you appreciate when it's gone. So hopscotch, Chinese jump rope, jacks or tetherball?" she asked.

"How about tetherball, for a change."

Lilly smiled at this. I thought she was smiling because she was happy to have someone to play with. After about three minutes, I realized I was wrong about that smile. Although she took it easy on me, I didn't know then that I was being hustled by the 58-year-old woman/child ranch champ. Lunch didn't come soon enough.

Lilly's assignment was to interview Poppie. Nonnie gave her a list of questions to ask him and explained that it would be good for Poppie, too. It would give him something to think about other than Guthrie or his pains.

"So go on, child. Go visit with Poppie. And remember, this is homework. No goofing off, baby. I want your best writing and spelling always counts."

And with that, Lilly skipped out to go see Poppie, hollering her goodbye to all of us as she disappeared out the door.

Nonnie came over to where Coco, Reesa and I were in the family room of the Big House, sitting around the table. Lloyd had taken the boys for a while so Coco and Reesa could fill me in.

"Dr. Sabian thinks maybe this kind of thing will jog something or trigger something. Lord knows," she said, shaking her head. "It will be good for Marcus, too, to go down memory lane with her." I gathered that Marcus was Poppie's real name. "So, I know Coco and Reesa are going to tell you about the ranch. I wanted to first tell you how my Marcus and Diana met." She seemed so small standing next to the big table.

"Girls, come sit with me on the couch. It's much more comfy for such a talk. Jade, you come sit by me." And so we moved over to the couch. Reesa and Coco sat across from us in the love seat on the other side of the coffee table. Nonnie began her story.

"Diana had just turned 12 when Marcus found her. This was before I met them both." I hadn't realized that Nonnie wasn't related to Diana, but this explained the difference in their appearance. "They both liked Sabino Canyon. That is a magnificent canyon a little farther north, maybe a 20 minute drive from here." She spent the next five minutes or so explaining how they became a family. Diana and Marcus both loved the canyon and they went there often. "It's a great place for hiking and relaxing. After the snow melts on the mountain, the creeks fill and the bridges overflow. It's beautiful, really." I believed her from the way she described it. Not her word choice, but the way she said the words.

She explained that after the fourth or fifth time seeing her there, when Marcus knew she should be in school, they started talking. He learned that she had just turned 12 and was living with her fourth foster family. And this one was no better than the first three. Diana had been unlucky in all her placements. She had been, at the least, neglected and, at times, horrifically abused. Marcus's heart broke for her. Nonnie thought his own broken childhood helped him connect with her.

He learned that Diana was in the foster system because her mother had died at birth and her father, a mean, abusive man, seemed to blame her for this. Maybe the alcohol gave her father the bravery to do what only a scared, evil man can do. He began slowly with inappropriate touches that, "showed Daddy how much he loved her." As his baby girl got older, it turned into a horrible combination of rage and molestation. By six, when she started to resemble her mother more, the rapes began. And this continued for years before a teacher noticed her changes in behavior and the bruises that Diana, continually, made excuses for. She went into the foster system and he went to prison. "God help that child." Nonnie had to stop. Tears suddenly spilled down her cheeks. Her lips quivered. But she did not full out cry. She simply took a tissue, wiped her eyes and continued.

"Marcus had just retired from the Air Force. They both felt alone and soon came to realize that they needed each other. Slowly, they grew closer and he kind of became her mentor and then, eventually, her foster father. She wasn't always easy. Her early teen years were a little edgy, but Marcus knew her scars were deep. They got through them. I came in around then. We look back now and it seems so obvious that she was already broken. Her behavior was not like a whole child. But we did not see that then. We explained away the acting out, the erratic and unpredictable behavior. But even with all the difficulties, we became family. Right before her 18th birthday, she asked us to adopt her. Marcus and I had been married a few years by then. His first wife died from cancer after their seventh wedding anniversary. He'd been alone for so long and never thought he'd have a wife and a daughter." She smiled at this. "But his chapter two was wonderful. Diana and I gave him great joy. It was Diana who introduced us. I was a professor, doing a workshop for a study I was doing at Diana's middle school. She had been with Marcus for one year. Diana was taken with me from the start, and I with her. And soon after the study was over, I was taken with

Marcus, as well. So when we became family, I got close to Diana fast. Diana was the daughter I never had and I was the mother Diana never had." She paused for a long breath.

"We were blessed. Diana got a master's degree in social work and soon after establishing herself at a non-profit for foster children, became a foster parent herself. Some kids were long-term, some were a couple of days. She fostered hundreds of kids. Halfway through the hundreds, Barry came into the picture and swept her off her feet and they married and fostered together. We were all so very happy back then. It wasn't easy. Some of the kids came to them so damaged, but Barry and Diana had a way of helping them heal. It was hard at times, but life was good for a long while. There was a rough patch when Diana had several miscarriages in a row. The doctors felt that the abuse she suffered as a child affected her ability to carry a baby to term. But they did not give up. Then, miraculously, they finally had Hope. Life, truly, could not have been better. They took in a few less foster kids, but still continued to open their house to children who needed them. But," she hesitated, "when Hope was just a young girl, she was taken from us." I waited for more. I wanted to know more. But Nonnie was finished with her chapter.

"Now Coco and Reesa will tell you about Kelly. Our angel Kelly." Nonnie looked at Coco and Reesa. "You may know by now, that while other ranches have horses or cows, we have angels at this ranch." This was Coco's cue to take it from there. For the next half hour they told me about Kelly and what she did to create the Lost and Found.

Much like Diana, Kelly was a remarkable woman. She had no family other than those who fostered her and she was lucky that she eventually was put on a path that led her to Diana. Most of her foster placements before her were horribly negligent and one was abusive. By the time Diana and Barry got her she was malnourished and frightened of almost everything. The first month, Kelly would constantly be found checking the pantry and the refrigerator to make sure there was still food. Diana would find packages of food hidden in various places in Kelly's room. She didn't do anything about this, other than give Kelly the time she needed to realize that there would always be food. Little by little, her pantry visits became less frequent. Eventually, Kelly came to feel safe with Diana and Barry.

Kelly thrived in her new home, both physically and emotionally. With Diana and Barry's help, she was transformed from a slight, painfully timid girl who rarely spoke, to an active, healthy teen who had quite a bit to say. She lived with them for almost six years. After graduating high school, Kelly attended the university in Tucson so she could stay close to Diana and Barry. They were the only true parents she had ever known. She studied to become an agricultural engineer and while she was in school she met Lloyd, another engineering student. Together they graduated, married, found jobs and moved close to Barry and Diana. Soon after that, the horrible thing happened.

When Barry and Diana lost Hope, Diana crashed. It was Kelly who initiated the ranch plan. She sent out letters to everyone who Diana and Barry had kept in touch with after fostering, as well as colleagues and friends. She and Lloyd sent out almost 130 requests for help. They had 109 responses. Some came in without being asked. Word spread. Kelly solicited over six dozen local businesses and organizations for donations of goods or services. About half responded. They had donations from pet supply stores, furniture warehouses, office supply stores, nurseries, restaurants and more. They heard from past foster kids, family, friends, friends of friends and so many more. The response was overwhelming. It was a tribute to Diana. Some gifts were modest and heartfelt, some were exceptionally generous and heartfelt.

One couple in particular, a local businessman and his wife, helped Kelly the most with her vision. Kelly had hoped to find a property that had a house big enough to hold the family and some of the fosters who had committed to staying near Diana and Barry. Her thinking, after meeting with therapists, was that creating a home that Diana would make would assist her process of healing. She understood that becoming whole again could take a long time, so they could use the time to create a place where Diana would feel safe and familiar enough to come home to.

This businessman's wife had grown up next door to Diana for most of the years that she, and then Barry, took in foster children. She had a long history with them. They knew about Diana and Barry's horrible loss. The businessman, from humble beginnings, was very successful in real estate. He had accumulated quite a bit of property, including the ranch. He hadn't used it for years after renting it out, occasionally, for retreats and group events. He was both a businessman and a giver, so he thought that the ranch might be useful for Kelly's cause and a smart business transaction as well. He and his wife had no plans for the land, so Diana and Barry's extended clan could live there as long as they wanted. It was a win/win. The family would live at the ranch and cover all of the expenses. Things like property taxes, insurance, utilities, improvements or renovations and all of the maintenance. The L & F Ranch (Lois and Frank) soon became known as the Lost and Found. It came with the Big House and family house. The buildings needed upgrades and some repairs, but they had that to start with. The casitas went up first and then the other additions. It took a few years to get it mostly like it was when I arrived. And there were always more projects.

Kelly and Lloyd got things ready for Barry, Diana, Poppie and Nonnie. Soon after the casitas were finished, they moved in. Shortly after that, Jack and Coco, Reesa and Tawn, and Sunshine and Will followed. Michael, Annie and P.S. moved down from Portland to help. They wanted to be close, so they bought the house on the next property over. All this time, two doctors had been treating Diana, as well as her family. Slowly, the locals became more involved. Huey, Charlie and the others. What Kelly did with Lloyd's help was amazing. They had slowly created a safe, nurturing home for Diana to return to, when she was ready. It took a year to transition and smooth out the plan. That year was the start of Diana's healing. The ranchers developed a routine. And life continued. Mostly with Lilly and without Diana, but life continued.

After the story of how the ranch came to be, I understood a lot better why this place was so unique. It humbled me. My resentment towards my mother seemed trivial compared to Diana's tragic tale. And my broken heart seemed to pale in comparison to Barry's or Nonnie and Poppie's broken hearts. The story made me want to help, too. And if that meant more jump rope and tetherball, then that's what I could do.

～～～ ～～～ ～～～

"Jade, come meet Huey." I heard Lilly calling me from outside. After the chat with Coco and Reesa, I had gone back to the casita and called Jesse to check in. He was in a meeting, so I left another message letting him know I was fine. After, I called Deb to tell her I'd be delayed and would let her know when I'd be on my way. She said she felt badly about my predicament, so I tried to reassure her that it was more of a hiccup than a real problem.

"I'll be right out," I yelled back. So today I would get to meet the famous Huey. I went outside to be greeted by an enthusiastic Lilly and an odd looking young man. Huey was not what I expected.

"Jade, this is Huey." She made a sweeping motion with her arms and then added, "Huey, this is Jade."

"So very nice to meet you, Jade. I've heard about you," he joked.

"Nice to meet you too, Huey. I've heard a lot about you. You seem to be a popular guy around here." We shook hands. Huey took my hand in both of his when we shook. His hands were soft and his shake was gentle. And he looked straight into my eyes. This caught me off guard. It was very disarming. And Huey did not look disarming. He actually seemed like the kind of guy that mothers warn their daughters about. He had on a very faded t-shirt, jeans with lots of holes in them and untied combat boots. His wrists were wrapped with black leather bracelets. But it was his eyes that I was drawn to. His eyes reassured me. And they did this even though they were framed by moppy hair with a blue streak. And even though his nose and right eyebrow were pierced and he had two full sleeves of tattoos. His eyes were still reassuring. There was a calm there that I did not see in many faces. If you didn't notice the eyes, Huey would be the kind of guy that you crossed the street to avoid. But I noticed. I always notice the eyes. That was how Dean had caught my attention. He had magnificent eyes. Now that there was time and distance between us, I thought that Dean's eyes were probably his only honest feature. Even though Huey's eyes were serene, I still had some apprehension. But they were enough to give him a chance that I would not have offered otherwise. Besides, I really did want to see what it was that everyone loved about this man.

"Want to come to class with us? Huey is teaching solo today. Reesa has an appointment." Earlier, Reesa told me she had to be away and I had offered to help. She told me Huey always managed, but she was sure that he wouldn't mind the help. She left it up to me.

"The kids love Huey. He's fun to watch. He does class from 3 to 5."

"What does he teach?" I asked Reesa.

"All kinds of stuff. Huey has… an unconventional style." She looked at me with a grin. "He definitely has a gift. He's like the kid whisperer."

I saw evidence of this gift when Jack and Tawn ran from their house after seeing Huey. They both called out as they ran to him.

"Huey. Huey." He turned when he heard them call and a big broad smile formed on his face. As Tawn and Jack got closer, Huey bent down and swooped them up into a giant bear hug and swung around once. Now I know what glee is because they giggled with it. Watching this grown man full of ink and metal receive the boys with such tenderness and affection and seeing the boys run to him with such abandon and adoration was quite remarkable. When Xavier dropped off Serita, Belle, Julio and J.J., the same thing happened. They ran into Huey's waiting arms. Huey got them all gathered with

P.S. arriving last. She had just come from school, but always wanted to be with Huey, too. Then the learning began.

The two hours flew by. Huey began with pairing the older kids to help the younger ones practice their phone numbers and addresses set to the tunes of London Bridge or B-I-N-G-O. The music made it fun. They all broke up into groups and you could hear them singing their numbers. After this, we did a cooperative exercise to music. The music was instrumental and the kids partnered up. When the music began the pairs faced each other and one took the lead in moving to the music while the other mirrored their movements. They moved as if they were a reflection of each other. It was touching to watch as they began with a little reserve and eventually let go, getting bigger and bolder. Each pair exhibited their own style and form.

Math followed. Huey would tell a story and at the end they had to give the number answer to the question he posed. Varied silly stories and questions geared to their age kept their attention. After this, the kids gathered in the gazebo to learn about the Earth's layers, using different colors of homemade play dough. The inner core was one color, outer core another, the mantle another and so on. He talked about the make-up of the layers and then sliced them all in half so they could see a cross section of the Earth they just made. The kids didn't even realize that they were learning. They thought they were just having fun. He was more creative and he inspired the kids more than most of the teachers I've known.

"Who's ready for the dance off?" All of the kids jumped up and cheered. This was always his closer. He put on some pop music and they all got in a circle, dancing in place. Huey began in the middle and danced like no tomorrow. He did a little moonwalking mixed in with the twist and a little free-styling. He left the circle and tapped one of the kids, taking their place in the circle while they went into the middle and danced. Then that child would go tap the next, take their place in the circle while they danced until everyone had a turn.

They were having too much fun. After everyone had a turn, we all danced together. They all congregated around Huey and some even tried to copy him. The kids finished with flare and soon our time was up. Huey truly was a child whisperer.

After the parents came to collect their kids, Huey and I found that everyone else was leaving, too. Lilly went with Nonnie and Barry to see Poppie before going to therapy. Everyone else seemed to be going their own way. It was rare that no one was around. We went to the Big House and made some hot tea, then settled in, facing each other on opposite sides of the couch. Huey was comfy. It didn't feel like we just met hours ago.

"So Lilly has taken a real liking to you, I hear."

"I guess so. I'm not quite sure why."

"I can see it too. It's probably because you never knew Diana." Huey said this casually.

This thought had never occurred to me. I pondered it a bit.

"So you think that because I never met Diana, Lilly connected with me?" I asked for clarification.

"Yep."

"It's just a theory. No comparing. No missing. No resenting. Makes sense to me," he said almost whimsically. He started to sit up. "Are you hungry?"

"Sure," I answered.

"I'll be glad to fix dinner, if you're not picky," he smiled. With everyone else away, I was glad for the company. Thoughts of Dean lurked. Company kept them at bay. And again, Huey was comfy.

We went into the kitchen and I helped him make a roasted eggplant dish that was unbelievable. We sat down at the table to eat.

"So how did you meet Diana and Barry?" I began the conversation.

"I was one of their boys. Actually, I was first one of Diana's boys then later I came to be one of Barry's boys too.

"Wow, how did that happen, if you don't mind my asking?"

"No, I thought you might know already." And Huey told his story.

Huey's grandmother raised him. When he was around 12 or so, she broke her hip. Diana took him until she healed and rehabbed and while this was happening, Diana and his grandmother became true friends. The whole family came to be close to his grandmother. Huey was with Diana for about 10 months and then on and off for a few more. He had grown close to them, especially Poppie, and so they kept in touch and shared time now and then. When he was almost 16, his grandmother died. She had named Diana and Barry in her will as his legal guardians. So Barry and Diana took him back. Taking him in at 16 was a little more of a challenge because he was going through a serious Goth phase. They had three other foster kids when he got there with his eyeliner, studded collar and black nail polish.

"No tattoos yet, or piercings?" I took another bite of the eggplant. The savory flavors were an interesting blend of Middle Eastern with a mild garlic spice. I wanted this recipe.

"No, not yet. My grandmother had always said not until I was 18, when the law gave me permission, because she planned on giving her blessing when hell froze over." He was smiling.

"So here comes this eyeliner kid. How'd they deal?"

"Barry and Diana? They didn't really care about stuff like that. They were more worried about my loss. And they both made it clear that I could grieve in my own way, as long as it wasn't harmful to others or myself. They just wanted me to be happy. After a while we all saw that it was good. I was weird but got great grades. They let me be me and I didn't disappoint. "

"How great were your grades?"

"I had a 4.0."

"Wow!" I said a little too incredulously. "Was that hard to do?"

"No, I'm not a genius. I just tried hard. My grandmother taught me well." His smile grew at the thought of her. "She always knew I was different and she said that not everyone would appreciate it. But a skill and smarts... people appreciate that. She said that good worthy people judged hearts and minds. She said she already knew my heart was good, so all I had to do was work on my mind. And I loved my grandmother, so I believed her. And so I kept trying."

"She sounds like a wonderful grandmother."

"She was. She wasn't a knitting, tea sipping, bridge-playing grandma. She was a yoga, gardening, cooking classes kind of grandma. She broke her hip on a fall while hiking. And that pissed her off!"

"So what about your parents? You said your grandmother raised you," I trailed off, waiting for Huey to fill in the gaps. I wondered right away if I had crossed a boundary, but Huey answered with little hesitation.

"I never knew my dad. I'm not really sure how well my mom knew him either since he raped her as a teenager." Huey saw my reaction. I think he was used to it because he didn't hesitate. "Because I was a product of rape, my mom didn't want me. She couldn't love me and so she felt she couldn't keep me. But my grandmother wouldn't let her give me up, so she took me. My mom moved away and I never really knew her. My grandmother kept in touch with her, but always told her that if she couldn't be a mother to me, then she could stay wherever she was. So she did."

We continued talking while we ate and cleaned up. After seeing him with the kids, and sharing some time learning about each other, it appeared that this pierced, tattooed, blue-haired child whisperer housed a kind soul. Huey was a different kind of person. Just like they all had said. I was glad I had met him. And now I understood why everyone was so fond of him. Huey was the first man that I spent hours with that did not take me back to broken hearts, love or lies. He simply made me feel like I had made a new friend and I was grateful for the respite from obsessing about Dean.

Day 3: Birdland

Today I met Simon, the duck, and his girlfriend, Sasha.
And no, I'm not drunk. Lilly introduced me to Birdland...

I wasn't sure if the sounds were part of a dream, or if I really heard my name.

"Jade," someone whispered. I turned around in bed before I heard it again.

"Jade." I opened my eyes, but it was dark in the room. I thought that it must be a dream, when I heard the whisper again.

"Wanna go see the sunrise?" It was Lilly. She was outside the doorway to my room. She didn't come in, but she didn't go away either.

"What time is it?" I mumbled.

"I don't know," Lilly answered. "But it's early. I like watching the sunrise. Wanna go watch it with me?" I wasn't accustomed to watching the sunrise. But then again, I wasn't accustomed to being woken up by a woman/child, either. I was awake now and knew that I probably wouldn't get back to sleep. I used to never have trouble going back to sleep. In fact, it was quite easy. But not lately. Now when I wake, I remember and the hurt jolts me awake.

"Sure," I answered. "Give me a few minutes." I got up and walked into the bathroom, grabbing my clothes on the way. It took a few extra minutes because my body wasn't done punishing me for playing. After splashing my face, brushing my teeth and getting dressed, I went outside.

Lilly was patiently waiting for me.

"Is Barry going to worry about you? Is this OK to be out so early?" I still wasn't sure of the rules. I didn't want to do anything to make things worse.

"Yep. I do it all the time. Barry knows I like to watch the sunrise. He just reminds me not to go somewhere new in case he needs to find me. And to take one of the dogs. He knows where I go. He likes Birdland, too."

"Birdland?" I asked. We began walking away from the Big House. "Where is it?" I asked.

"At the lake. Come on. This way." Lilly had one of those big flashlights to illuminate the dirt path. We kept walking, getting farther from the houses. I followed as the sky began to get lighter. The sun was starting to rise and I thought we might not get to where we were going in time to see it when we turned a corner and right in front of us was a small lake. We walked to the east, turning right at the path before we found a big patch of grass. Lilly announced our arrival and told me we could sit here to watch the sun finish rising. From our view, you could almost see the entire horizon. As the sun grew higher I saw reeds and a big rock jutting out of the water, about 50 feet in front of us. The rock was more like a mini-island. A bee flew by and scared Lilly. Clearly, she didn't like bees. It buzzed close to her for a few long seconds, making her very nervous. She relaxed, only when it flew away. She took a few seconds more to switch modes.

"I call this Birdland. 'Cause of all the birds," Lilly said, in case I didn't make the connection. The lake seemed to be a haven. All kinds, all around. Throughout the next half hour, she pointed out the cute little finches, lots and lots of ducks appearing to wake and start their day, gray shimmery doves, a lone crow, a roadrunner farther down the edge of the water, quail, thrashers, dancing hummingbirds and bright red cardinals.

"That's the boy cardinal. The girls aren't as pretty," Lilly explained. At night, she said, you could hear the owls. But during the day you could hear everything else. If you listened hard enough, you could imagine the conversations. The questions and answers that followed. The gossip. Birds interrupting other birds. Even arguments and flirting.

We sat and watched and listened while we talked now and then.

"Once, when I was waiting for Kelly, I sat for 20 minutes and counted 119 birds. But maybe I missed some or counted some birds twice. They don't hold still while you count," Lilly explained. She pointed to the water.

"See those ducks?" she asked. "The two in the middle, next to each other, are Simon and Sasha. They're in love".

"How do you know they're in love?"

"Because they're always together. Sometimes they fight and sometimes they snuggle. But they're always together. Even after a fight. Just look at them." I looked. They looked like the other ducks, but they did follow one another. When one paddled right, the other followed. When one ducked under, the other did the same. Maybe Lilly was right.

"How do you know which one is Simon and which is Sasha?" Lilly explained the markings and I could see the differences, once she pointed them out. "Do you have names for all of them?" I wondered out loud.

"Of course not. That would be ridiculous," she said with such seriousness that it made me feel foolish to suggest such a thing.

"Can you keep a secret for me?" Lilly asked. I was surprised. I hesitated before answering. Secrets are curious things. They can make an honest man dishonest. They can create chaos from simply being shared or they can bond people for life. They can protect or they can hurt. They know no loyalty by themselves, just that of their keepers. While I had no big secrets of my own, I was hesitant to be a keeper of anyone else's.

"Sure you can," I answered, wondering why Lilly picked me to share her secret. I wasn't comfortable with secrets. They represented all that I had lost. Ever since I realized that Dean kept so many, I didn't trust people who had their own. I now associated secrets with trust and I just didn't have much left in me.

"See that reflection over there, across the lake?" she asked.

"Yes. The one of the trees?" I asked. The waterline was so still that it was barely visible. It took a moment to find where the real trees met their image reflected in the water.

"That's Diana and me."

"I don't understand."

"That's me in the water. And Diana is the trees. I'm not really real," she said slowly and with a hint of sadness. I was struck by her ability to be both innocent and wise. The innocence of a young girl co-existing with the wisdom of an experienced woman seemed to be Lilly's essence. Her analogy was sound. Diana *was* the trees. She was just a reflection of herself. I wasn't sure what to say.

"Do you want to talk about it?" I asked gently.

"I just did. That's all. I wanted to tell you." She seemed to have moved on. I waited, but she just watched the reflection of the trees across the lake. This time, with a little less sadness.

"Lilly, I'm curious. Why did you tell me this?"

"I just needed to tell someone. You know how sometimes you have something inside you and you just have to get it out? Well, I wanted to get it out to you."

"But why me? How do you know you can trust me?"

"Because I can."

"But how do you know you can?"

"I just know. Some people you can and some people you can't." She made it sound simple.

"But what if you're wrong? What if you trust someone who you can't?"

"Then I'm wrong."

"But when you're wrong aren't you disappointed? Don't you feel bad when you find out that the person you trusted really couldn't be trusted?"

"Well, of course I feel bad. Wouldn't you? But being disappointed is only bad when it happens. Usually after, you're better for it. After it's over you feel smarter because you know something new. And Nonnie always says that a good life includes disappointment. It makes you appreciate what's not disappointing." She was right. Nonnie was full of wise things to share.

"But I'm not wrong. I know I can trust you." We sat at the lake for a bit longer.

We headed back to the Big House and found Coco brewing coffee, Jack, Kelly, Reesa and Tawn eating breakfast and Barry on the phone with someone talking about bricks. Lilly went and got her cereal and fruit while I got my coffee.

"So, where did you go off to so early, Lilly?" Barry was off the phone now.

"I went to see the sunrise. I took Jade with me. We had a nice time, right Jade?"

"We did. Thanks for sharing that with me."

Lilly seemed pleased.

"So, did she introduce you to Simon and Sasha?" Kelly asked. She had a natural beauty about her. She had deep ice blue eyes, and freckles that lightly speckled her cheeks and nose. She was petite yet muscular, probably from all of the work she did around the ranch.

"Sure did. And I think Lilly might be right. They seem like a couple."

"They do, don't they?"

"So, what is on the agenda for today, girls?" asked Barry as he joined us at the table with his cup of coffee.

"Games and homework," piped in Lilly.

"I need to harvest about a third of the tomato plants. We need to get them ready for the farmers market tomorrow," Kelly answered. I offered to help.

"That would be great." Kelly seemed grateful for the offer. "Normally Sunshine would help, but they aren't back yet. I'm going to get started in about an hour. Is that good for you?"

"Sure. I'll meet you at the greenhouse in an hour."

Kelly took off. I asked if I could make myself some toast and was told that I didn't have to ask around here. I was to just make myself at home.

"Thank you. I really appreciate how easy you've made this."

A few of them answered at once: "No thanks needed." "No problem." "Mi casa is su casa."

I took my time with the toast and another cup of coffee, so I could just go from here to meet Kelly. Lilly asked if I would have time to play later.

"It depends on how long Kelly needs me." She seemed a little rejected, so I said we could squeeze in a couple of games of Chinese jump rope or hopscotch before dinner. This seemed to appease her.

Lilly finished her cereal, went to the kitchen to rinse her bowl and spoon, put them in the dishwasher and then skipped out the door yelling, "See ya later!" to whoever was listening. I had no idea where she was off to. I finished my coffee and toast and then went a bit early to find Kelly.

When I agreed to help Kelly pick the tomatoes, I didn't know what I was getting into. I didn't know that it involved over 80 plants. And while some plants, like the heirlooms, had six or seven tomatoes on them, the cherry and grape tomatoes had clusters that could be 30 or more.

"This is more therapy than anything else. I mean, look around. Isn't this wonderful?" Kelly was very enthusiastic about her plants. We stood in the middle of the big greenhouse. In every direction I saw colors framed in green. Shelf upon shelf, filled with planters or pots. I didn't know exactly what I was looking at, but I could make out some berries and herbs, here and there. It was very organized, with plants on shelves around the entire perimeter of the inside and double-sided rows of the same, filling most of the floor space. Near the storage room was a space left open for a big wooden island with a sink and a few wide, low benches. This was where certain tasks were done: germinating, potting seedlings, repotting and more. I didn't know much about gardening, but I knew I was in greenhouse greatness.

Kelly showed me around explaining, briefly, the plants and process she had developed. As we began to pick, she explained to me the difference between a "keeper" and a "market." The market tomatoes were boxed or put in cartons for the farmer's market booths to sell. They were the produce that was ripe and looked pretty. Kelly explained that people were picky about how the produce looked, so blemished produce stayed here, while pretty produce went to the market. Keeper tomatoes were kept at the ranch.

"They don't know that these taste just as good, or maybe they don't care and it's all about the look." She explained that they did all kinds of things with the tomato rejects. Nothing was wasted. Even the rotten produce was used to compost.

"When we moved here, we knew that Diana loved gardening. She always had a vegetable and fruit garden in her backyard. We thought that when she came back, she might like this. It started out smaller, but it grew, little by little into all of this. Now it sustains us and we can sell or barter the rest." So, the greenhouse was home to berries, tomatoes and herbs. All of the bigger plants or root vegetables, like melons, cucumbers, peppers, carrots, zucchini and corn were fenced into an acre behind the greenhouse. And another acre, to the side of the garden, was an orchard with 15 citrus and a dozen peach trees.

Kelly explained the color-coded baskets and crates: which were for larger or smaller produce for market and which were to stay here. It seemed like a simple and clear plan.

"If you help me pick and pack, then later I can trim up the fruitless plants to get them ready to grow more. I just need to get these picked for tomorrow. Usually Reesa or Sunshine help me, but Tawn has an appointment with his pediatrician. Shot time for Tawn," she said.

"OK. Where do you want me to start?" I asked. Kelly explained that we would start at the door. I would go to the left and she would go to the right. The tomato plants were on two levels surrounding the perimeter of the greenhouse. We would pick one level today and leave the next, which wasn't quite ripe, for the next market day. Tomatoes were the biggest crop in the greenhouse, so it was a big job. We would start and then meet wherever we met, and then we would be done. She made it sound simple.

Kelly reminded me that being a picker had its perks. I got to sample the goods. I tried one of the cherry tomatoes. It burst with flavor when I bit down. More flavor than I knew a tomato could hold. Kelly watched me with a smile. I looked around the greenhouse. I had never seen so many tomatoes. It was like a field of small, medium and large red balls.

"See what I mean? Nice perk, yes?"

"Oh yes," I agreed, still savoring the taste.

"Time to pick", announced Kelly.

As we picked, she explained the produce protocol. Her "Produce 101" speech.

"The veggies and fruits that are blemished or bruised, we use for juices, sauces, salsas and other things. Some of that we sell at the market and some we keep. Barry's favorite is fresh tomato juice." She motioned for me to follow her to the shelving in the back. They held empty cartons and crates.

"Here's what we need," she said to herself more than to me. She grabbed cartons with partitions. "This time of year is slow. We get our orchard fruit in the summer and winter. And more veggies. But we get some good stuff off-season." It kept the ranchers very busy, but it was a good situation.

It took us almost three hours to pick and box up the tomatoes. The small ones we had to put in cartons and then stack in boxes. The others were put into smaller bins, so the weight of the top ones didn't smash the ones at the bottom. We filled dozens of boxes. Then we broke for lunch before packing up the tomato baskets and cartons into bigger boxes, loading them into her truck and covering them, so all was ready to go early the next morning.

This took another couple hours, which left me with more than enough time for games with Lilly. She had checked in once, after finishing her homework ("math – yuck!") to see how we were coming along. I went to go find her, which didn't take long, since she was waiting outside with the dogs.

We began with a quick hopscotch game, then went to Chinese jump rope and ended with warming up our ball and jacks skills when the dinner bell sounded. We both knew the drill. We washed up and went into the Big House. Once I sat down, I realized how tired I was. Dinner smelled fantastic, reminding me that I had only had toast in the morning. I had skipped lunch and instead tried to reach my brother or mom. I just missed Jesse and wasn't quite sure where my mom was. I left messages for both. I didn't really mind playing phone tag. Although I missed Jesse's voice, it was kind of nice to keep the outside world outside.

Coco and Nonnie fixed pot roast with roasted vegetables and some sides. It was all delicious. My full belly and long day caught up with me. I was hit with a wave of exhaustion, so after helping clean up, I said my goodnights and headed back to my casita. I rinsed off quickly and then fell into bed. I jotted a bit in my journal and then sleep found me fast.

Day 4: Roadrunners and Dirty Sunsets and Corned Beef... Oh My!

Roadrunners really are speedy. And they don't go, "Beep Beep."
Today I met Freddie...

I told Kelly the night before that I would go to the farmers market with her early in the morning. I used to hate waking up early. After a couple days, it wasn't as bad as I thought. So here I was at 6 a.m., waiting for Kelly in the Big House so we could go early to set up the stall. Kelly walked in a few minutes after me.

"Good morning, Jade. I really, really appreciate the help. Tawn has a slight fever from his vaccinations and with you covering, Reesa can stay with him."

"No worries. I'm glad I can help." Kelly was wearing a "Kiss me, I'm Irish" t-shirt. I asked if she was Irish. She said no, but that it was St. Patrick's Day. I hadn't remembered.

"Just so you know, if you aren't wearing green, pinching is outlawed here at the ranch because one-year P.S. and Lilly got too carried away." I wasn't a pincher.

"But, I'm sure Nonnie will have a St. Paddy's Day dinner tonight. I hope you like corned beef and cabbage."

We grabbed our coffee in some to-go cups and walked out to the loaded truck. Lloyd had loaded everything we needed the night before so we could just take off when we woke. I expected a drive, but it only took about 10 minutes to get to the park where there was a weekly farmers market. The tent was easy to set-up. This was good, since I had no experience in the tent department. After we got our stall set-up, we began to unpack. Market regulars were already starting to congregate, waiting for vendors to finish setting up. The market included about two dozen stalls, with a variety of goods. Some were produce, some were jams and others were breads. There were also some cheeses and jerkies. I even saw the honey vendor that Barry stopped at a few days ago. His stall was three down from us.

"This is not a big load for us. We'll finish by noon, I'm guessing." Kelly explained the pricing system, showed me the cash box and declared us open for business. Soon, we were very busy. I think it helped that only two other vendors had tomatoes. I think it also helped that the locals knew the Lost and Found and wanted to support it. So business was good. There was a steady flow of people as the market filled with market sights and sounds and smells. I could hear one little girl hawking her family's wares.

"Strawberries. Get your fresh strawberries. Just $4 a basket." Her sales pitch mingled with other vendors explaining their products, asking people if they wanted a sample or if they wanted to "buy five and get one free." I smelled sweet, spicy, oniony, garlicky, peppery and kettle corny smells. These smells were all around, luring me, depending on the shift of the breeze. Some of the buyers were first-timers, taking their time at each tent, sampling, visiting and asking questions. Others were regulars who came prepared with shopping bags and a plan. The market was open from 8:00 until 1:00, but we sold our last basket of tomatoes before 11:30.

Instead of packing up, we decided to walk around and visit with the other vendors. Kelly knew many of them. We sampled our lunch. I had some salmon jerky that was fantastic, some cactus jam and cashew butter on breads that were as flavorful as the toppings. We got a few loaves for the ranch and we finished with a variety of cheeses that I had never tasted before. As we walked around the stalls, Kelly was greeted with affection and inquiries about Diana. Her response to one was similar to the next. A variation of "So good to see you, so-and-so. Thanks for asking, slow progress, but fine." I wondered if the ranchers ever tired of having to give updates. As if she read my mind, Kelly told me that as hard as it was to repeat the same thing each time, it comforted her that people still remembered.

We packed up a bit after noon, which was quicker without the tomatoes, and headed back to the ranch via the gas station, bank and the nearby nursery to pick up some fungus treatment for the citrus trees. It was after 2:00 before we turned onto the ranch road. The dogs greeted us as we pulled up next to the greenhouse, with Lilly not far behind.

"Hey guys, how'd it go?" Lilly was already by the door by the time we got out.

"Hi, Lilly," we said in unison.

"It went great," I added. We began to unload the boxes and tent to take into the greenhouse and storage.

"Lilly, could you take these bread loaves to the Big House for us, please?" Kelly handed the big bag of breads to Lilly.

"Sure. Are you gonna come up when you're done?" She waited for an answer.

"I'm going to do some stuff in the greenhouse, Lilly. But I'll see you later, alright?" Kelly told her kindly.

"What about you, Jade?" Lilly lingered.

"Sure, I'll be up as soon as I finish helping Kelly unpack. I'll see you in a bit, OK?"

"Great." And she was off with her bag of breads. "Dinner is gonna be late tonight. Nonnie said to tell you," she hollered as she left. I picked up a few empty boxes from the bed of the truck.

"You know she wasn't asking about me. I think you've really won Lilly over. She's had a little more twinkle in her eye since you got here." Kelly grabbed some boxes, too.

"That's what I've been told. I'm not sure why. Huey has a theory, though." We kept unpacking.

"What's his theory?"

"He thinks that she's become attached because I didn't know Diana. I met her as Lilly, so there is no history."

"Hmmm." She pondered this for just a second. "Huey always amazes me. He is really a smart guy. It makes sense," Kelly agreed. "But, Jade, you have something to do with this. I doubt that she would have bonded with just any stranger. The fact that you give her attention and time. And you're so patient with her. I think that has a lot to do with it, too." I thought about that while we unloaded the last of our load. As we were coming out of the greenhouse a roadrunner dashed in.

"Whoa! What was that?" I was startled by the size and speed of the bird.

"Damn! Freddie's back," Kelly cursed. She ran after the bird, chasing him all around the greenhouse like they were playing a game. She yelled to me to keep the door open.

"How do I help? Does he bite?" I wasn't really sure what to do so I just chased after Kelly, who was chasing after Freddie. The bird was so fast and it didn't really fly. It just kind of ran while flapping its wings. If someone were watching, I was sure that they'd be amused at the sight of us.

"Help me corner him. He's done this a few times before and he is really a pain in the ass," she moaned, panting, and already out of breath. I ran the opposite way from Kelly and we tried to trap him but, when we got him in between us, he darted between my legs. I freaked out again. So much so that I fell backward into the pile of boxes, knocking a potted plant over as I did. It fell on top of me and now I was covered in soil. At least the boxes broke my fall.

It would have been comical if it wasn't so frustrating. Kelly went and grabbed a broom to see if this would get Freddie motivated to leave. It didn't. We tried to corner him again, but this time he ducked under the ledge in the corner where we couldn't see him unless we bent down. So we bent down. Then that son-of-a-bitch bird attacked us. He just ran right into us and then backed up then off he went again. As he finally headed towards the door, we split up, corralled him out and slammed the door after his exit.

"Whew! Damn bird!" Kelly proclaimed.

"OK, was that normal? Do those birds usually behave that way?" I wouldn't have believed it if I didn't see it with my own eyes. I was out of breath, too, and my heart was still racing a little.

"No. Roadrunners are actually quite shy. But not Freddie. He is freaky-deaky. His first visit, Freddie accidentally got locked inside here and had a feast... and almost destroyed the place. He prefers the bugs in the soil to the fruits and veggies above the soil. And we get lizards in here, which is no problem unless you have a lizard-chasing roadrunner in the same place! Ever since then, I think he stakes out the joint and when he feels bold enough, he makes a move." We looked at each other and started to laugh.

"Well, that was fun!" Kelly said sarcastically.

<hr/>

I went to change my clothes before going to find Lilly. I knew she'd be waiting. After checking the house, Coco told me that Lilly and Nonnie were at the gazebo and that Coco had strict orders to tell me where they were. I headed over. The sun was slowly reaching the horizon and would be down in another half hour or so. Not that I had the energy, but I was sure that Lilly and I could squeeze in a round or two of hopscotch before dark. I hadn't noticed until now how beautiful the sky was. It was full of different shades of peach and purple blended into one another. It reminded me of the sunset I saw at the inn. I found Nonnie and Lilly sitting in the gazebo, watching the horizon.

"Hi," I said, as I approached. Nonnie and Lilly turned around to see me.

"Hi, baby," Nonnie greeted me.

"Hi. Where were you? You almost missed it," Lilly said with a hint of irritation.

"Missed what?"

"The dirty sunset. I wanted to show you your first dirty sunset."

"What's a dirty sunset?" I asked.

Lilly pointed to the sky. "That's a dirty sunset."

I looked to where she was pointing. The sky was even more beautiful than it had been moments ago. The colors richer and now some orange mixed in with the purple and peach.

"Why do you call it a dirty sunset?"

"When there is a lot of dust in the air, the sunset colors are more vibrant. Lilly and I saw that there would be one tonight, so we came out to watch it. Care to join us?" Nonnie invited me to sit.

"Sure." I sat down next to Nonnie and then Lilly came and sat down next to me. We sat there watching the sun slowly fall. It was so beautiful that it almost commanded your attention. I remembered other sunsets, with Dean. When we first met we watched many together. I wondered when that had stopped.

"Jade, why are you sad?"

"I'm alright, Lilly," I answered.

"But you look sad," Lilly answered back.

"Child, you've got to let people have their secrets. People will share when they want. You shouldn't be so nosey." I looked over at Nonnie and she gave me one of her beautiful smiles.

"But Jade is my friend. Aren't friends supposed to help friends? I don't want Jade to be sad."

"Yes, baby. They are. But friends also respect each other's privacy. If Jade wants your help, she'll ask for it. Until then, you just be her friend without the helping." Lilly looked at Nonnie and then me.

"Nonnie says that we are never done learning. Even her. So she's always teaching me stuff. And she lets me teach her, right Nonnie?"

"That's right, baby." There was a hint of melancholy in her voice. "Like these beautiful dirty sunsets. You taught me about them. Right?"

"That's right." Lilly sounded happy with herself. We watched until the sun set and then went back to the Big House for dinner.

Sure enough, we had corned beef and cabbage for dinner. Everyone ate and caught up. Reesa told everybody that Freddie had paid a visit. This was met with groans. Mine included. Barry had spent the day with Michael contemplating the next project. They decided on a new brick entryway. Huey had the kids this morning and Nonnie had spent most of the day with Poppie. I wondered if I would get to meet Poppie before I left. Lilly was excited because tomorrow she and P.S. were going to paint a new hopscotch board on the side of the court. We settled into a relaxing dinner.

"St. Paddy's Day reminds me of my friend, Dev. His birthday is on St. Paddy's day and we used to always celebrate. One year, his birthday included Lucky Charms, green beer, a biker named Mags and a broken nose." I was lost thinking about that day and didn't realize how absurd it sounded. I looked up and saw everyone looking at me. Some with grins and a few without. Barry looked at me with a huge grin and a raised eyebrow. He didn't ask though.

"But that's a whole other story," I added, blushing. Everyone laughed. Even Jack and Tawn. But they just laughed because everyone else did.

"Well, now you have another St. Paddy's Day story. No Mags, but we did have Freddie," Kelly was quick to add. This led to Freddie stories, which got me off the hook. Apparently, Freddie was quite the bird. Night raids, picnic crashing and taking on Shasta. Freddie stories took us through dinner and dessert. Walking back to my casita, it felt like I'd been here longer than four days. I walked along the path feeling very fortunate that Barry had found me. I liked being here.

Day 5: Perfection Doesn't Teach You What Mistakes Can. ~Nonnie

The day started with a she said/she said, spilled paint,
blame the other, hopscotch fiasco between P.S. and Lilly.
And, I finally got to meet Poppie. I think I'm in love…

"Lies are very uncomfortable for me. Forget that they are so much work and that you have to keep your lies straight. You usually wind up feeding them and they grow. And they get so heavy, girls. I'm telling you, they get so heavy they start to hurt. *Especially* if they're selfish lies." I overheard Nonnie talking to Lilly and P.S. It was a school holiday, so P.S. was spending the morning with Lilly. They had been planning this hopscotch-painting project for a while.. But, right after they started painting hopscotch squares, the paint spilled.

"Now, P.S., you say that Lilly spilled it. And Lilly, you say that P.S. spilled it. I don't really care who spilled the paint. I've spilled paint myself. And a bunch of other stuff. But you always need to take responsibility for what you do. Spilling isn't the problem. It's lying that is." Nonnie was kind in her tone, but she was firm, so she had the girls' attention.

"Now, until I hear some truth, we're just going to have to stop painting. We can get back to it when you both show me that you know the right thing to do." She reminded them that she loved them both and told them to go to the gazebo to figure out how to work together and find a solution to this problem. Reluctantly, they did what Nonnie told them to do.

"Jade, baby, come on out here and sit with me a bit while the girls work out their problems." Nonnie knew I was in the kitchen and could hear what was going on. I came out and Nonnie patted the couch cushion next to her.

"Hi, sweet child. Tell me, how are you today?" Nonnie wore such a disarming expression that I felt like actually telling her. I hadn't really spoken about Dean too much, aside from a brief explanation to Coco that first night. And while the pain seemed to be a bit less consuming, it was still there. The distractions were still just Band-Aids.

"I love being here. I can't thank you enough for letting me stay."

Nonnie seemed to be reading my mind. "That's not what I asked, honey. I want to know how you are. You don't have to say much. I just want to know that you're doing all right. And I want you to know that you can tell me anything. Everyone has a tale. You'll tell yours when you're ready."

She patted my hand while she spoke. Her hands were beautiful. They were small and soft and wrinkled.

"My heart hurts, Nonnie." Then the tears fell. Before I knew it I had told her all about Dean. It sounded cliché to offer up smells of perfume lingering on his clothes, the late work nights that I defended to my girlfriends and the changes in the way he touched me. And then the confession when he realized that I trusted my gut more than I did him. Nonnie didn't need to hear more. She simply held me while I cried. It felt good to be wrapped in a mother's arms. My mother had never comforted me the way Nonnie was comforting me now.

"There is nothing better than someone you love believing in the best in you. And nothing worse than someone you love hurting you so deeply that you're left scarred. And you need both to appreciate the difference." I hadn't really talked to anyone about this besides Jesse and my mom. And that felt more like informing than sharing.

"Why does it keep hurting? Why doesn't it go away?" I moaned.

"Baby, this isn't new pain you're feeling. It's the old pain still there. The same pain you brought with you when you came to us. It takes time, sweetheart," Nonnie said. "It takes time." Nonnie often thought that if it was important enough to say once, it might be important enough to say twice.

"Is it me?" I pleaded.

"Jade, honey, I can't tell you that. I don't know enough and I never met this young man who broke your heart. And to be fair, sweet girl, I haven't heard his side. And Jade, there's always another side. But I can tell you that when two people promise themselves to each other, and only one honors that commitment, much more than a promise can be broken. And it takes a long time to fix. I wish I could tell you something to make you feel better. But only time will do that. And distractions. And we have both of that here for you. So honey, if he gave you a big lie once, he may do it again. Unless your gut tells you to try again honey, I would put my energy into healing."

"But how am I going to trust again?"

"Oh baby, that's the easy part. You just do."

"But it hurt so much, Nonnie. I don't know that my heart is big enough to break again."

"But it is, child. It really is. God gave us so much when he made us. And that included big enough hearts to break over and over. And it will, baby. When your son loses student council elections or your daughter has her first broken heart. Yours will break with theirs. A woman's heart breaks all the time. We get our share of the pain, but we get the good stuff, too." She smiled at that.

"How will I know who I can trust?"

"Well, I wouldn't trust him again. But what reason do you have not to trust the next boy? This boy hurt you. Why would you let him keep hurting you by cheating you out of your next love?"

"Did you ever love someone who was bad for you, Nonnie?"

"Well, of course, child. Most of us have. But you can't stay with someone like that. That kind of love is toxic and it will just make you sick. Either in the belly or in the mind. But either way, it's not a healthy love. There is plenty of other bad in the world to make you ill, child." I thought about this for a minute. I thought I knew disappointment well. I considered it to be one of my best friends; we had spent so much time together over the years. But Nonnie was helping me see that I could pick a different best friend.

"Thank you, Nonnie," I said quietly. She reached over and gave me a final hug and rub. We could hear the girls coming up the steps.

"For nothing, baby. Anytime you want to talk, you just come and find me." She turned her attention to the door. Lilly and P.S. came in and stood there for a moment before Nonnie spoke.

"Well?" Nonnie asked, waiting to hear what resolution they came up with. Lilly spoke first.

"Well, Nonnie, the truth is that we both spilled the paint."

P.S. chimed in after that, "Yeah. We both spilled the paint." The girls weren't sure what to say next. They waited, but only for a second because they saw that Nonnie was waiting for them to continue.

"We were fighting over who got to paint first and then we bumped the crate it was on and it spilled," Lilly confessed.

"So, girls, what do you think should happen next? Remember what I told you before you went to work this out. You aren't done yet." The girls looked at each other meekly. Nonnie looked over at me and offered a subtle wink. She was good at that.

"Sorry," they mumbled to each other in unison.

"You surely don't think that was a proper apology. I know you both are smart sweet girls and so you can do better than that."

"I'm sorry, Lilly. I shouldn't have blamed you for this," P.S. offered first.

"Me, too, P.S. I should have told the truth to begin with," Lilly followed. "But I was so darn mad that the paint got spilled and that the board was ruined."

"Now, just wait one second, child. An apology is just an apology. Don't go decorating it with excuses. 'I am sorry' is all you need. And a sincere offer not to do the same again. And babies, the board isn't ruined." She said this as if they were crazy for thinking so. "It's just gonna be different now. You both are such creative girls. I am sure if you put your heads together you can find a way to make this board around the mess you made. Perfection doesn't teach you what mistakes can. Mistakes are how you learn. Why don't you both go out and brainstorm on how you can make this mess into a proper hopscotch board. I know you can." And off they went, again.

"Nonnie, you're good," I told her. "How do you know what to say every time?"

"Thank you, honey. You gotta remember, I've had a few more decades of experience with children than you have. And really, I'm learning as I go, too. Diana's is such a unique situation. All I can do is listen to the doctors, go with my gut and pray a whole lot. This is not something I was prepared to have in my life. But I'm learning. We all are. And we all do the best we can. That's all any of us can do. Right, sweetheart? We just do the best we can," she repeated. "Now let's go to the porch so we can see their imaginations at work."

I helped Nonnie off the couch and we went out to sit and watch the girls. They seemed to be in negotiations about what direction to take. I thought I heard Lilly remind P.S. that Nonnie always said a good life includes compromise. I looked over at Nonnie. She was smiling like a proud mom. Which, in reality, she was. She was Diana's mom. My heart skipped a beat trying to imagine how this must be for her. But her smile glowed with such brightness, that it didn't seem like she was missing Diana. It was more like she was proud that Lilly was remembering the things that Nonnie had taught her. It took hours of planning, negotiations and painting to get the hopscotch board painted. It was beautiful, really. It turned out much more colorful than their original plan. By the time they cleaned up, it was time for lunch. The girls would have been disappointed, except that they knew the paint had to dry before they could hop their first hop on their new masterpiece.

As usual, Lilly had homework to do after lunch. Nonnie asked P.S. if she could help and make it a group project, since the paint was still a bit damp. Today's assignment was to research the history of the hopscotch game. Both seemed eager to get to work. I helped Nonnie clean up before she went to go sit with Poppie for a while. I thought I would just sit for a bit and think about what Nonnie and I talked about. The day was beautiful. It should have been cool, but it wasn't. The sun was shining, but it wasn't hot. I got comfy on the patio lounge. Too comfortable. I didn't know I had fallen asleep until I heard Lilly saying something to me. I slowly rose from my unexpected nap.

"What did you say?" I asked, opening my eyes. Lilly startled me. I still found myself surprised, sometimes, when I saw her.

"Sorry I startled you. Did you know that hopscotch was first called Scotch-hopping and it was for boys only? Do you believe that? Just for boys. That is messed up." She seemed more incredulous than mad. And clearly proud to share her new-found knowledge.

"Wow. I did not know that. What else did you guys find out?"

P.S. sat down across from me. Lilly paced. She didn't sit still.

"Well, some people say the Romans started it to help soldiers train. Others say the Chinese invented it. The board was a path to heaven and the stone was your soul. I like that idea better than Roman soldiers. Don't you?" P.S. waited for me to answer.

"Yeah, I like that one better too," I said, nodding.

"I asked Barry if I could take you to see Poppie. He's feeling up for a visit. I checked. Wanna meet him?" Lilly had eager eyes.

"I would love to meet Poppie. When should we go?" I was eager to finally meet him.

"Barry said he wanted to explain some stuff to you first. He's in the kitchen. You can go talk to him, then we can go see Poppie. P.S. has to go home soon so we'll play a little while you grownups talk." I thought it funny to hear a 58-year-old tell me to go have a grownup talk. I was half her age! So I went inside and chatted with Barry for a minute.

He explained that Poppie had COPD, a respiratory condition. This, coupled with existing health problems was causing him to become weaker and he didn't seem to be able to bounce back this time. Hospice care would probably begin soon. The doctors said there was no way to know how fast he might deteriorate. He wanted to prepare me for all that I would see when I first met Poppie.

"I'm so sorry, Barry." He had enough to deal with. And the thought of Nonnie losing her husband made me ache for her. I realized that she had known all of this while she spent time with me and she never gave any sign of her impending loss. I guess she, like me, did not want her pain to be the clothes we wore every day. He said that he appreciated my good thoughts, but that everyone had been preparing for this. They just hadn't told Lilly how serious it was yet. They planned to explain when hospice began. I went out to find Lilly. P.S. had already left through the grove towards her home. She took the path between the two properties. Lilly was making Pima do tricks while she waited for me. Lilly signaled to Pima to dance and he got up and propped his front paws on her hips and walked in a circle with her. She saw me watching and gave Pima his treat. Then we went to see Poppie.

"Are you ready? He's really a nice man," Lilly explained without waiting for my answer. "Really, really nice," she added. While she guided me to their family house we chatted a bit.

"I'm ready."

"Good. He's gonna love you. Sometimes Poppie calls me Part-time Lilly. I know why." She said like a kid trying to sound confident. She barely hesitated before adding, "It's to remember Diana. I'd never forget Diana. She's why I'm here. My doctors explained it to me. But Nonnie doesn't like it when he does that. She rolls her eyes at him when he calls me that. Then she says, 'Good Lord, Marcus, Our baby's name is Lilly.'" She copied Nonnie's southern accent.

"Does that bother you? Poppie's nickname?"

"No. I think that Poppie needs to remind himself that Diana will come back. When she does, Poppie said that I always would be inside of her. Kind of like she is inside of me now. But we'll trade places. Poppie tells me that he loves me all the time. But I know he loves Diana too."

"Well, I am sure that he does. I'm sure he loves you both very much." Lilly and I smiled at each other.

"Yep!" Lilly agreed. I didn't know what else to say. We turned onto the path to the house.

"He's been a fun Poppie... till he got sick. We did lots of stuff. We had picnics and scavenger hunts and read-a-thons and games. And we put on shows. He would be the Master of Ceremonies. We got to play a lot." We arrived at the family house.

"Ready?" Lilly asked me again.

"Yep," I reminded her. We walked into the house and Lilly announced ourselves.

"Poppie, we're coming to see you," she hollered as she gestured for me to follow her back to the bedroom. We walked through a comfortable living room to get to Poppie's room. As we walked in, I saw that the room was set up for someone who was not well. Lilly walked up to her smiling Poppie, sitting upright in his hospital bed. She kissed him on the temple then hugged him tightly, careful not to tug at his oxygen tube.

"Poppie, this is Jade." She turned towards me.

"Jade, this is Poppie. There!" She seemed quite proud of herself. "I've been wanting you two guys to meet! We told Poppie all about you. Nonnie and Barry and me. About your car breaking. And how you jump rope with me. About how everyone likes you." She took a breath. "A bunch of stuff."

I looked at the man lying in the bed. He was looking at me, too, smiling, as if to say, "I know there is more to you than jump rope and a broken car." He pushed a button that raised his bed, pushing him more upright.

"Well, look at the two of you. Best friends already. Hello, sweet girl." He looked at me again. "It's so very nice to meet you, Jade." He said this deliberately and animatedly as he held out his hand to mine. I grabbed it and he held my hand in both of his. He looked at Lilly.

"Could you go get us some of that sweet tea that I like, sweetheart?"

"Sure, Poppie." She turned to me.

"Do you want some, too, Jade? I'll be right back." Lilly waited long enough to hear my "Yes, thank you," and left for the kitchen.

Poppie gestured for me to sit.

"You can sit if you want," he said softly. I moved the chair a little closer to Poppie and sat down. He was a very handsome man. He had a full head of gray hair and broad shoulders that rested on a tall, ailing frame.

"My daughter tells me that you are her new best friend. I'm glad. She doesn't have many friends."

"Sure she does." I began to protest. Poppie held his hand up weakly.

"Those are Diana's friends." His words felt like a defense, but I understood.

"I'm flattered, but I don't really know what I've done to deserve the honor."

"I'll tell you exactly what you've done," Poppie said quietly. "You've paid attention to her. Everyone needs someone to pay attention to them." Poppie seemed to want to say more, but he stopped himself. I waited and then thought about what he had said. He interrupted my thoughts.

"Thank you," he whispered.

"For what?" I asked softly.

"We all need validation. Even Part-time Lilly," he whispered back.

Lilly brought us our tea. She handed me mine, set his on his nightstand and pulled up a chair next to me. Poppie, slowly and quietly, told stories about some of the adventures that he and Lilly had had. He spoke about the time they fired a rocket with a little plastic parachute man inside. They had painted "Bob" bright orange so they could track him. They had looked for weeks, but it was a year before they stumbled upon him. He reminisced about the time they had a scavenger hunt for bugs. They had one hour to walk around the ranch with their cameras and take as many different pictures as they could of bugs. Lilly won: 14-16. This picture is perfect, I thought. A father reminiscing about past adventures with his daughter. But the daughter in this picture wasn't whole. I watched Poppie and realized that he had two sets of memories with this girl sitting next to him.

"Hi Poppie." It was P.S. She came over and kissed Poppie on the cheek.

"Well hello there, Pretty Sarah. How are you today? I heard you have a holiday." Even though Poppie seemed relegated to his bedroom, he appeared to be up on all the comings and goings of the ranch. I had wondered, but kept forgetting to ask, what P.S. stood for and now I knew.

"Yep. No school today. Lilly and I made a hopscotch board. But the paint is still drying. We can't use it till later." She turned to Lilly.

"Wanna go play tetherball?" Lilly jumped up and then stopped herself.

"Is it OK with you, Jade, if I leave you with Poppie?"

He answered for me. "I think that's a great idea. Maybe P.S. will beat you for a change." Poppie winked at the girls. They both kissed Poppie quickly on the cheek, yelled their goodbyes and were out the door. Poppie and I were alone now. Without the girl's chatter, I noticed quiet music in the background.

"The music is nice."

"Annie made this CD for me. She knows I love the saxophone. It has all kinds of great sax players." He beamed. The song faded out and another began.

"Ahh, this one is an oldie." He said this before he closed his eyes, seemingly to hear the music better. We sat and listened.

"So you're the secret keeper?" He had a subtle, kind grin across his face. He explained how Lilly told him about her sharing her secrets and how she liked having someone else to keep them for her. Poppie didn't want to talk about it. He only wanted me to know that he was glad, too.

Another song began. As it did, Poppie's smile grew into something bigger. It looked, oddly, like love and pride. Right there on his face. He listened for a few seconds as the saxophone began. He whispered to me, "This... is Guthrie." And then he invited me, "Listen." Guthrie seemed to be a topic that came up a lot lately. I had heard that he played the saxophone. I listened. The melody was haunting and beautiful. As I listened, the notes washed over me bringing me some sort of comfort. I understood why Poppie loved Guthrie's playing. It seemed medicinal. We sat and listened for a few more songs. Normally, the lack of conversation would be uncomfortable. But, for some reason, just listening with my new old acquaintance was enough.

Soon, Nonnie came in with Poppie's dinner. He ate early these days. I asked if Nonnie needed any help.

"Thank you, baby, but Marcus and I have a routine. Besides, we need our alone time too." She said this like a woman in love. That was my cue to leave.

"Bye, Poppie. It was so very nice to meet you." I held out my hand to his.

"I don't think Mary would mind if you gave this old man a hug." He winked at Nonnie and I could see Nonnie smile. "We like hugs around here. Do you mind?"

"Of course not, Poppie. I do, too." I went in for a hug. Poppie was fragile, but you wouldn't know it from his hug. He held me close and whispered in my ear, "We're glad Barry brought you home."

I whispered back that I was too. I stood to go.

"Come back again and we can visit some more." Poppie seemed to enjoy visitors. "When you have time."

"I will make the time. I'll see you later then." I told Nonnie goodbye and left them alone.

A couple days later Poppie summoned me, asking if I had time for another "little visit." And soon I began visiting on my own. I was lucky to be included in his days. So many wanted his time and council and presence. When I went to see him, sometimes it was with others, sometimes just by myself. We would talk about everything and anything. The one thing he didn't talk about was Diana. I never asked why. Most visits included music. He loved the oldies from his youth as much as the latest greatest. His taste was very eclectic. He played me Branford Marsalis and Charlie Parker, Eva Cassidy and Etta James, Louis Armstrong and Chris Botti. His all-time favorite was Sarah Vaughan. I didn't know then that this first visit was the beginning of mini music classes. I never did hear Guthrie's song again, sitting with Poppie during our visits. And often, I found that I was waiting for it. But one way or another, we found time to check in with each other. And every visit brought more love and admiration for this man.

I sat, with about 12 others, at dinner as the platters and bowls were passed around. Onion roasted potatoes, chicken and the most beautiful, eclectic salad I had ever enjoyed. They called it a "chunky salad." It had the usual, from carrots to croutons, as well as dried cranberries, pinion nuts, raw corn kernels, water chestnuts, jicama, chickpeas, sun-dried tomatoes, black beans and more. It was beautiful and quite tasty.

The food was good and the comfort of a cozy group after a long day brought me ready for a sound and deep sleep. But as soon as I put my head on my pillow, my heart felt bruised again. As I lay there, for too long, I thought of all the other nights I had laid waiting to fall asleep. Some nights laying there and thinking about the pain from a lie. Or others, awake, waiting for him to get home. Laying there as the shadows moved across the wall, not realizing that the night was gone until I noticed that the room was getting lighter. I hated that Dean had robbed me of so much time. With great effort, I finally wished myself to sleep.

Day 6: P-ball and Scorpions. Yeah, You Read That Right!

Lilly watched me as I came into the kitchen and got a glass of cold water. I had just finished helping Nonnie repot some plants on the family house patio. She saw me look at the aprons on the hooks.

"Do you like to cook?" I asked Lilly.

"Yeah. Sometimes, when I am really in the mood. Mostly I just help. Diana loves to cook though." I thought it strange that Lilly talked about Diana. I would come to find she did that often. Not so much talk about Diana as much as refer to her.

"Did you know the dung beetle is the only insect to navigate by the stars?" Lilly asked.

"Nope. I didn't know that." I really didn't. I was getting used to Lilly's random tidbits. She would normally be going to therapy this morning, but her doctors were out of town for a conference.

Coco, Jack, Lilly, Reesa, Tawn, Huey and I were in the Big House taking a snack break after a morning of chores. Even Jack and Tawn had chores. They helped water the patio plants. They spilled more than they hit their target, but it didn't matter. We were in the family room munching on fruit salad and cheese sticks, but for some reason some of the others were watching out the window. They predicted rain. I thought they were dreading it because they wouldn't be able to go outside and play their games. I was wrong.

It started with a few drops, like a slow drumming on the roof. Then suddenly it became bigger. Lilly looked at Coco at the same time that Coco looked at her. I caught something in their glance but neither one explained.

"Do you wanna?" asked Lilly. They all went to the window and looked up at the sky. It seemed sunny, but it was raining.

"We're in," answered Coco. Still no explanation. And just as quickly as the rain began, Lilly was off, running out the door.

"Where are you going?" I yelled after her.

"To get the ball," answered Coco. "and hopefully another player or two."

"What for?" I asked Coco, wondering what was about to happen.

"We're going to play P-ball."

"What is P-ball and why are we playing in the rain?"

"P-ball stands for Poppie-ball. Poppie taught us the joy of playing basketball in the rain. Hold on." She dialed Kelly and with one word: "P-ball," a game was being made.

In Poppie's voice (sort of) she added, "P-ball is strongly encouraged unless there is lightning or homework or if it's too darn cold." While Lilly was rounding up players and a ball, Coco explained that ever since she had known Poppie, a nice rainy day without lightning and homework often prompted a fun, wet game of ball. The number of players dictated the game. A couple meant two-square. More could mean four-square or basketball. Once they had so many people playing that they managed to play a game of volleyball. To this day it is still known as the Volleyball Game of '08.

As they went outside to find Lilly and her recruits, Michael and Barry, Coco told me that they don't play as often as they used to. It wasn't the same without Poppie playing, too, or at least cheering. But today was the perfect kind of rain. So I played my first game of P-ball. It was a sunny, rainy day when Diana and Poppie first met. He always felt that those kinds of days should be celebrated. Little kids ask their parents about the day that they were born. Lilly would ask Poppie about the day that he and Diana met. He would tell her over and over about the sunny, rainy day. Diana, I was told, came to think of that as her birthday.

Teams began to form. Michael, Lilly, Jack, Coco, Reesa, Huey, Tawn, Barry, Kelly and I were in. Soon, P.S. came running over to join us. She was out of breath. Lilly had called her. We divided into teams. Lilly ran and got Jack and Tawn the pompoms. They were the cheerleaders when enough grownups showed up. So teams were made and a game was picked.

Barry lowered the hoops so the girls could make some shots. Even though Lilly was bigger, she shot hoops like a 12-year-old. She was definitely much better at hopscotch and jacks than she was at basketball, but it didn't matter. Everyone was having a blast and getting soaked. Jack and Tawn were cheering, more to each other than for their teams, but they were having fun, too. We ran across the court and splashed each other. We sucked in water while running back and forth. I had to wipe my eyes so I could see. The drumming of the drops on the court was rhythmic. We played for about 15 minutes before the rain began to slow down and the sun became brighter. We played a little bit longer and then we all went to change into dry clothes and meet back at the Big House for lunch.

As I was changing, I thought about how fun P-ball was. It wasn't anything like the games my mother let us play. Loud or messy was a no-no. As I walked up to the Big House, I saw everyone on the patio looking up at the sky. I turned to see the most magnificent rainbow. It filled the sky from one end to the other. It began at the orchard and arched over to the greenhouse.

"Anybody home?" Someone yelled from the front of the house. We were all so mesmerized by the rainbow that we hadn't heard anyone come in.

"It's Sunshine and Will! They're home," Lilly yelled with great joy. She ran into the house to greet them. We all followed. In the living room stood a striking couple. Both were tall and slim, had shiny black hair and dark skin. Will wore blue jeans, a maroon button-down shirt tucked into them, separated by a big belt buckle. and a cowboy hat. His eyes were the brownest brown I had ever seen. Sunshine wore a dark purple tunic with a wide teal sash connecting it to a full colorful skirt that fell to the top of her boots. Her hair was thick and straight and down to her elbows. She wore it tied in a beautiful ponytail that climbed down her back. And she wore a modest turquoise and silver necklace. Everybody greeted them with joy. Hugs, kisses, handshakes, more hugs and kisses. They were clearly missed. After everyone got their hugs, Lilly introduced me.

"Sunshine and Will, I want you to meet my friend." She pulled me closer. Before Lilly could say anything, Sunshine hugged me.

"You must be Jade. I'm Sunshine. It's so nice to meet you."

"And I'm Will. We've been looking forward to meeting you." He gave me a hug, too. I was a little surprised, but the hugs felt good.

"How did you know?" Lilly was curious.

"Nonnie told us. She said that you had a new friend." Sunshine turned from Lilly to face me. "And she said that everyone around the ranch is just as happy as Lilly that your car broke down. So, I guess we are, too!"

"Sunny, Sunny." Jack came in through the door running up to her and she swooped him up. He held onto her tight while he mumbled his hello to Will. Coco followed and joined in the hug.

"Let me look at you, little man," Sunshine said as she put him down. "Wow, you've grown so much. You must be eating your vegetables, yes?" she teased. "You are so big now. Are you married yet?" she teased again.

"No, Sunny. I'm just this many," he said, holding up four fingers.

"Oh yeah, I forgot. You just got so big!" Sunshine bent down to give him a squeeze. After a few more ranchers came in and everyone said their hellos, Will asked where Nonnie was.

"She's with Poppie at the house," Barry told him. He said this with a slightly solemn tone, communicating to them that Poppie was getting worse. I didn't know how long they had been gone, so I wasn't sure when they last saw Poppie. "We were just going to start lunch. Why don't you and Will get settled, then come up and join us."

"I think we'll go see Nonnie and Poppie, first. We'll take our luggage to the house later. We'll see you soon, alright?" Clearly, Sunshine was eager to see Nonnie and Poppie.

"I think that's a great idea," Barry agreed. Will and Sunshine went out the porch door and headed towards the family house. Lilly and P.S. went to play on their new hopscotch board while lunch was being prepared. Reesa took the boys while Coco, Huey and I fixed lunch. The menu was a simple one today. Peanut butter and jelly on toast with leftover chunky salad and fruit. I had never had peanut butter and jelly on toast. So Huey and I made an assembly line by the toaster while Coco cut up some fruit. It wasn't long before Sunshine and Will returned and we all sat around and caught up while we ate lunch. I have to say, peanut butter and jelly on toast is really good. The peanut butter melts on the toasted bread and the jelly warms up. And, like all peanut butter and jelly sandwiches, milk was essential.

"Please don't tell me that we missed P-ball," Will begged.

"You did," P.S. answered, rather loudly.

"I knew it. When we saw the sunny rain, we said, 'I bet we're missing a game.' Darn! Darn!" Will said with a bit of flare. All of the kids laughed at that. Lilly, too. They filled him in on the game and soon everyone was engrossed in conversation. I gathered that Will and Sunshine had gone up north to the White Mountains. They were visiting family and friends on the Apache reservation for a few weeks. After lunch, Will and Sunshine took their luggage back to their casita and got settled. Lilly offered to help clean up, which surprised me until I had learned that P.S. had gone home. We were both in the kitchen when I picked up a napkin from the counter and felt a sting.

"Ow!" I yelled. "That napkin just shocked me!" Lilly ran over and picked up the napkin carefully. Underneath was a small light brown scorpion. As Lilly lifted the napkin, the scorpion ran for safety heading under the toaster. It was very fast for such a little thing. Its tail was up and ready to strike again, if needed. Lilly smashed it with a cookbook that she grabbed without hesitation then yelled to Barry, "Barry, Jade just got stung." I could hear him cursing as he hurried in from the other room.

"I'll grab the ice." He ran to the freezer and grabbed some frozen peas. "Come, sit down Jade."

"Ice and elevate," added Lilly, while she cleaned up the dead scorpion with (too many) paper towels.

"She's right. With scorpion stings, you need to ice and elevate. This helps minimize the pain. Hurt's like a son-of-a-bitch, doesn't it?" he asked with sympathy for me and disdain for the very dead scorpion.

"Yes. Wow! That little thing did this?" I asked, as the pain on my pinkie finger began to flow to the rest of my hand. As we put the peas on my hand, the pain was trying to shoot up my arm. I was afraid it would go into my heart. It really hurt!

"Have you been stung before?" I asked Barry.

"Yep, most of us. Welcome to the Southwest. I think the rain brought it in. That happens sometimes. It'll hurt all day, but tomorrow you'll be fine." He felt confident. My finger did not.

"Generally, they just hurt like hell. I see Lilly took care of disposal duty. Thanks, Lilly." He turned and smiled at Lilly. She came over and looked at my hand.

"No problem, Barry," she smiled back. "Are you OK, Jade?" she asked sympathetically.

"I guess so." I was sure I was going to live, but it really hurt. I kept the peas on for a while. Soon the pain from the sting was replaced with pain from the cold. I felt like a baby. The little bug had packed a punch. The pain radiated from my finger. Barry suggested I go lie down for a while. He said I was officially off duty for the rest of the day.

"All you're gonna do is feel the pain. So try and rest. Remember to put it on a pillow or two to keep it higher than your heart." Barry seemed genuinely concerned.

Lilly walked me back to the casita and helped me get settled. She seemed quite worried. It was touching. She got me aspirin before she left and told me she would check on me in a couple hours. I had no doubt. I laid down and tried to get comfortable. It was difficult because I had to keep my hand on the pillows. After, what I guessed to be about 15 or 20 minutes, I escaped to sleep.

"Jade," Lilly whispered. "Are you awake?" I lay there waiting to see if I really heard the whisper. "How are you feeling?" I opened my eyes and Lilly was sitting on the edge of my bed. I moved to sit up and my hand reminded me that a scorpion had stung me.

"A little better, but it still stings."

"Do you want to come up to the house for dinner?" I didn't realize that I had slept so long. But I didn't really want to get up. I just wanted to go back to sleep and wake up without a hurting hand.

"Do you mind if I skip dinner? I'm not really hungry. I think I would rather just stay in bed if that's alright with you."

"Of course it is. You just rest." And then she bent down and kissed the side of my forehead. She did this with such tenderness that it surprised me. "Dream good."

"Thank you," I mumbled.

Day 7: The Art of Root Beer Floats

My hand doesn't hurt, just a bit tender. That scorpion stung like a bitch!
Today, I learned a few of the Rancher's stories.
One by one, they share their piece of the ranch puzzle...

I woke with the sunrise. Something that was becoming increasingly easier to do. Falling asleep in the afternoon, yesterday, probably helped. Amazingly, just as Barry had said, my hand didn't hurt. It was a little tender where the scorpion had stung me, but this was easy compared to the pain I had felt last night. I was still fully dressed, aside from my shoes. I got up and took a long, hot shower. It felt good. I got dressed and went up to the Big House. It was early and only Reesa and Tawn were there.

"Hi, Jade," Tawn greeted me.

"Good morning, Tawn." He was such a friendly, happy little boy. He had his mom's curly hair and her eyes. They both had hazel eyes that, I noticed, got lighter and darker.

"Morning, Jade. How are you feeling?" Reesa came in from the kitchen with two cups of coffee and handed me one.

"Aah, thank you." I took a sip before answering. "Much better, thanks. Sorry I missed dinner."

"Don't apologize," she scolded. "I've been stung. I know it hurts. I'm just glad you feel better. Lilly was worried about you. She hasn't been stung. Diana has. But Lilly hasn't. Weird, huh?"

"Yeah."

"It's OK. It's good that Lilly was worried about you. We like it when she has normal reactions. And being worried about a hurting friend is normal. She's fine. We all reassured her that you would be alright." We sat and had our coffee while Tawn ate his eggs and toast.

"So how did you first meet Diana and Barry? I know that you were one of her fosters, but that's all." As soon as I asked, I realized that this might be too personal. "If I'm being too nosey..." She cut me off.

"It's OK, Jade. No worries," she said reassuringly. "We all got a story."

Reesa had come to Diana and Barry right before "the fall." She was a classic wayward teen. Classic because she preferred boys over homework, fashion over function and attitude over effort. Classic because she didn't conform, follow or concern herself with what others thought of her. She was Little Miss Independent who was in great need of boundaries and control. And classic because she was pregnant. With Diana and Barry's help, she had baby Tawn and soon after, earned her GED. That was one of Diana's last gifts as a foster mother. To see Reesa through her GED and help her see that Tawn could bring her a whole new kind of healthy love. But Reesa didn't really need much help. The moment the doctor put Tawn into her arms was the moment that Reesa grew up. She saw, in her son's eyes, a tomorrow that she had not ever imagined. And whether she got there or not, she knew, depended on the choices she would make. It was fortunate that Reesa understood this. It was soon after that Barry and Diana lost Hope.

Reesa felt very close to them and credited Nonnie, Poppie and the two of them with saving her, so when Diana broke into other selves, she didn't consider anything other than helping Barry any way that she could. At first, the household became her responsibility and she embraced it completely. She took care of the cleaning, the laundry, shopping and cooking. She did this while Barry was learning about what happened to Diana and getting what she needed to heal and while Kelly was recruiting "angels." With more help, they settled into a routine. Reesa took some child development classes at the community college. She moved to the ranch with Barry, which made her a charter member of the Lost and Found. Her main role, which she seemed born for, was to take care of the kids.

As if on cue, Jack came running in, with Coco not far behind.

"Hi guys," he said casually.

"Good morning. How's the hand, Jade? Coco inquired.

"Much better, thanks."

Coco grabbed some coffee after fixing Jack some toast and jelly and a few fruit slices and joined Reesa and me at the table. Just as she did, Lilly came storming in.

"There you are! I went to your house." It wasn't drama. It was concern. "Are you OK?"

"Much better. Thanks, Lilly." My answer seemed to calm her.

"Well, I've been thinking. Since your hand might still hurt, maybe we shouldn't do jump rope or ball and jacks today. But don't worry. I have a game for you that you don't need your hands for." I was glad that she was giving me a day off from jump rope and jacks.

"So what game do you think we should play today?"

"Hide and seek," she announced. And then she went to go get her bowl of cereal and the fruit choice of the day. I saw Reesa and Coco look at each other. I could have sworn that I even heard one of them whisper, "uh-oh." I looked at them, quizzically.

"Lilly is the best hide-and-seeker at the ranch. Just like tetherball, she is the Ranch Champ. Once it took us two hours to find her! She's really good at it." Reesa said softly, so Lilly couldn't hear. "So good, that some of us give up before we even start. It takes too long to find her and people give up. While P.S. is determined to take her tetherball championship away from her, she won't even play hide-and-seek with her anymore. Jade, you do know that you can tell her 'no,' right?"

"It's OK. It will be a nice change from hopscotch or jump rope."

"OK. Don't say we didn't warn you."

Lilly came into the room and sat at the table with her bowl of cereal. "So, what are you guys talking about?" she asked, with a mouth full of cereal.

"Coco and Reesa were telling me what a good hide-and-seek player you are."

"You guys wanna play too?" Lilly asked with a hint of hope in her voice. They both offered their excuses and wished us fun. I wasn't sure how this was going to work, but I was sure I would find out. If Lilly was as good as they said she was, the logistics weren't terribly relevant. We finished our breakfast and Lilly and I went out to the porch to "go over the rules."

Playing with Lilly had two benefits. It made me feel as though I was helping or contributing in some way. Others mentioned how they thought it was a good thing for Lilly. And I could feel the connection that they noticed. The other was that I actually enjoyed it. Aside from the aches and pains, I welcomed the distraction and Lilly was fascinating, so it was a win-win. She gave me a new lens to look through.

"OK, so here are the rules. The porch steps are home base. One of us hides and the other has to look for them. If the hider gets to home base before the seeker tags you, then you're safe. But I don't care if I win, Jade," she reassured me. "I just like playing. Since it's only you and me, we can just take turns hiding. Do you like jicama? I tried some at my friend, Kenny's. Any questions about the game?"

"I do like jicama. Do we have boundaries?"

"That's a very good question, Jade," Lilly answered in a teacher's voice. It was kind of cute. "Yes. We have to stay on the ranch and we can't go to the lake. Oh, and we can't hide in the casitas or my house." Lilly thought some more, then added, "or the greenhouse."

"So that means that we can hide anywhere outside from the greenhouse to the orchards and from the front of the Big House to the basketball court and gazebo. Right?"

"Yeah, but you forgot inside the Big House. You can hide there, too. Any more questions?"

"Yes. How long does the seeker have to count before looking and is there a time limit to find someone?" I was wondering if I was in too deep.

"Well," Lilly stretched this out while she pondered for a few seconds. "Sometimes we have a time limit and sometimes we don't. Do you want a time limit?"

"I think since this is my first time playing with you and since you know the ranch better than me, maybe we can have a time limit. What do you think?" Lilly thought for just a second.

"How about 30 minutes?" I wasn't expecting that much time to be offered as a solution. Remembering Nonnie's lesson on compromise, I countered with 15 minutes. It worked, since our negotiations led us to a 22-minute limit. Because neither of us wore a watch, Lilly ran in to get the kitchen timer telling me the seeker can have this to keep the time. She ran back out and told me that since I was company, I got to go first.

"I'll close my eyes and count to 30. You have to do it slow like this. One-thousand-one, one-thousand-two, one-thousand-three. Like that. K?"

"Got it. I'm ready."

She leaned against the porch rail, hid her eyes and began counting. I had already decided that I would circle around to the front of the house, go in and hide in the kitchen behind the door that covered the command central nook. I took off running. I could hear Lilly counting. As I turned around the side of the house she was on one-thousand-six, and almost to one-thousand-seven. I ran around the house, quietly let myself in and went into the living room getting Coco and Reesa's attention. I held up my finger to my mouth, motioning them to be quiet and pointed to the kitchen where I was going to hide. They nodded their heads, acknowledging that they understood. I stood behind the kitchen door and pulled it closer to hide me. From where I was I could still hear Lilly counting. She was only on one-thousand-16, so I just stood there and waited. Soon I heard her yell, "Ready or not, here I come." I think it took less time to find me than it did to count!

"How did you find me so fast?" I wanted to know.

"Squeaky front door. I knew you came in the front door so I knew you were in the Big House."

"Darn squeaky door!"

"Barry says we can't fix it 'cause it helps us know if the boys go out," she said hurriedly. "K, now it's my turn."

We walked through the house to the back porch again. On the way, I got looks of sympathy from Coco and Reesa. Looks that said, "told you." I gave them a look that said, "I know, you were right." Once out on the patio, I took the timer, hid my eyes and began counting. When I got to one thousand-30, I set the timer for 22 minutes and headed towards the gazebo because I thought I heard her head that way. She wasn't there. I thought that strategically, it made sense to start at one end of the property and work my way across. Still no Lilly. I went into the Big House and began looking, but Coco and Reesa only shook their head no, so I knew not to waste time there. I went back outside and began looking around again.

Apparently, I should not have negotiated the time limit, because 22 minutes was not enough. The timer in my pocket went off just as I was returning to the Big House. I climbed up the steps and hollered to Lilly that time was up. From underneath the steps, I heard her laughing. I climbed back down and bent to see where she was. Apparently, she had hidden in the crawl space underneath the porch. I didn't even know that anyone could get under there. This went on for three more turns. Lilly always found me, although I did get better. The last time I hid it took 18 minutes. But I never did find her. Not in the truck bed (didn't realize that was fair game), not underneath the patio table in the front courtyard (note to self: a tablecloth can hide a 58-year-old) and not underneath the gazebo (which I should have suspected). In the end, Coco and Reesa were right. Lilly was the champ. Our game was called on account of lunch.

Nonnie and Coco had set up a tortilla wrap buffet so everyone could make their own lunch. They had plates and bowls of cheeses and meats, diced tomatoes, lettuce, sprouts, shredded beets, hummus and a big bowl of fruit salad. The kids, especially, liked this kind of lunch. I followed everyone's lead and spread my homemade tortilla with hummus before lining up whatever I wanted on it, which I would soon learn how to wrap.

Because we played all morning, Lilly had to do homework before Huey came over, so I stayed and helped Nonnie clean up and do a few house chores. After sweeping and rinsing and filling and emptying, we sat with some tea and visited while Lilly finished her homework.

"Nonnie, where are you from?" I wondered from the moment I met her. It was obvious that she was from the south, but I wasn't sure where.

"Baby, I was born and raised in 'Nawleens.'" She said this the same way that people from New Orleans say it. And she said it with big pride. This was all I needed to ask for Nonnie to tell me of her beginnings.

Nonnie was a Louisiana girl, born in the middle of two brothers. She was raised on roux, gumbo, crawfish and the blues. It was Nonnie who introduced Guthrie to the saxophone. As a young teen, she would sneak out on the balcony, late at night, to catch some of the woeful tunes that she could take back with her to bed and lull her to sleep. She told me stories about growing up. She came from a poor family. Her mother, who was black, worked two part-time jobs, while her father, who was white, worked extra long hours. A maintenance man and a housekeeper didn't earn much, but they always provided. Three kids and hate made it often difficult. Being mixed race provided the haters an even bigger reason to act out. Growing up had challenges that were so frequent that it was all they knew. They were treated as people of color by white people and as outsiders by people of color. But, what they lacked in money and support, they made up in play and music and exploring and discussion. They shopped at second-hand stores and sometimes ate at soup kitchens, but they always had at least two meals a day and a roof over their heads. Nonnie told me that each kid had two pairs of shoes: one for church and one for everything else. They walked almost everywhere but, once in a while, they had to go too far to walk so they took the bus. In her reminiscing, she told me that until she was older, she and her family had to ride in the back of the bus. Segregation was alive and well in Louisiana. When she and her siblings were young, they didn't understand. They didn't always want to go to the back, especially if there were seats closer to the door. So before a bus would pick them up, their mother would remind her and her brothers that the pretty people sat in the back of the bus. And that there was hardly anyone in the world more beautiful than them. This always helped. I thought that, if I had known her, I would have loved Nonnie's mother.

Just because Nonnie came from a poor black southern family didn't mean that she wasn't worldly. It's true that they were poor and that there was nothing left over each month after barely keeping a roof over their heads, eating meager meals and wearing used and shared clothing. But Mary Eleanor Robinson made something of herself. She knew at a young age that she would get out of her too small home and see more of the world. At 16 she began researching scholarships and free or subsidized exchange programs. By 18 her perseverance and good grades earned her a scholarship to the University of Louisiana. By 22, she had earned a year abroad in Italy. She took a summer internship in Israel when she was 24 and chaperoned a youth trip to South America at 27. Nonnie's world was bigger than I had realized, but getting to know her, I wasn't surprised.

She had an old soul and she was too worldly to be limited to the borders of "Nawleens."

The phone rang in the house, interrupting Nonnie. I got up to answer it. It was Ace, calling to tell me the parts for the car were in and that he was starting to work on it now. I was glad things were on track. But I wasn't as relieved as I thought I would be. In fact, I hadn't even thought about Carlos for a couple of days.

Lilly came walking up the path, just as I was coming back out to the porch where Nonnie was still sitting.

"Hi guys. What cha doing?"

"We were just visiting, sweetheart. Did you finish your work?" Nonnie asked.

"Yep. Wanna see?" She came up the steps with a folder.

"You know I do," Nonnie answered with her beautiful full-bodied smile. It was hard to believe that Nonnie was both mother and grandmother to Lilly. She had such strong shoulders to carry this burden that had been handed to her.

"Poppie said if you want, you could go visit him." Lilly sat down next to Nonnie and handed her homework. Nonnie smiled at me, giving permission to go.

"I think I'll do that." As I began to walk away I asked Nonnie if she wanted me to bring him anything. She smiled as she complimented me.

"That is so sweet of you, child. And I do believe there is a bran muffin in the kitchen with Poppie's name on it. Just watch that he eats small bites and drinks his tea. His mouth is so dry these days." I went and got the muffin and wrapped it in a paper towel and headed over to see Poppie.

As I opened the door to the house, I knocked and yelled out, "Hi Poppie, it's Jade."

I was surprised to hear, "Hello sweet girl, come on over here and sit with me, will you?" He was sitting in the recliner in the front room. I walked over and gave him a hug since his arms were already waiting for one. It felt good. Just like I imagined a grandpa hug felt. "I see my part-time Lilly gave you my message."

"She delivered, just like you asked. Nonnie is going over her homework with her now." I unwrapped the muffin and Poppie smiled.

"I'm guessing that came with instructions. Let me guess. Small bites with tea in between."

"How did you know?"

"Baby girl, after watching her the way I watch her, you just know. And Nonnie worries about me. That ups her 'take care' game. Nonnie has a bag full of 'take care' stuff. It's filled with green tea, massages, distractions, music, tapioca and bran muffins."

The recliner that Poppie sat in was just like any other. It was covered in worn brown upholstery. Clearly loved and lived in. But Poppie had a sheet-covered cushion set in it that was big and poofy. So much that it seemed to envelop him as he sat. He explained that Nonnie had made it for him. It made sitting up longer much more comfortable. His body ached a bit from not moving around like he had for the first 80 years of his life. Maybe his body was tired and slowing down, but Poppie didn't look his age. Aside from the hospital bed and prognosis, he looked more like an elderly gentleman than a worn out old man.

Music, muffin and tea were today's trio, while Poppie and I visited. Today, he seemed stronger and that was nice. The music was his medicine. I could see the effect it had on him and was glad for it. It calmed and comforted him and I was beginning to feel it, too. The notes put together sentences that spoke to the listener. The soothing flow and affective infusion of notes. We listened and just enjoyed each other's quiet company for a bit. When the music stopped, Poppie asked me if there was anything new to share. I told him that

Nonnie had just told me a little about her early years and that I had learned some interesting things about her.

"My Mary, she's something special. Don't you agree?"

"Yes, I do. You both are." Then he asked if I wanted to hear a little bit about his early years, too.

"I would love that."

Marcus Quenton Hamilton was born 81 years ago last August. He was born never knowing his daddy because his momma didn't know who his daddy was. She raised his older sister the same way, not knowing who her daddy was either. His mother approached the edge of neglect many times, but never actually crossed over to it. She did the best she could, brought up in a situation similar to the one she found herself in. But she wanted more for them, so she tried. She couldn't ever give them a stable, consistent home but, in trying, she instilled a sense of worth in Marcus and his sister. They always felt they were worthy of becoming something. She died when his sister was 18 and he was 16. They survived, but with great effort and sometimes great hunger and cold. His sister made sure that he graduated high school and avoided trouble. After that, Marcus was left with two choices: the wrong one or the other one. One of the few pleasant memories he had from his childhood was going with a neighbor to the air show at Nellis Air Force Base, in Las Vegas, where he grew up. He remembered being mesmerized by the dance in the sky. It inspired him to stay on the good path his mother desperately tried to maintain and to try harder in school. Ever since that time, he had tucked away a fantasy of one day learning to fly. So, after high school, partly to avoid the wrong choice but mostly to get closer to the sky, he joined the Air Force. He met his first wife, Shari, and they loved each other for too short of time. They had seven years of great adventures around the globe before returning to the States six months before she died of leukemia. His sister died a few years after that. He had no other family. It was a difficult time for him. Sixteen years and 10 countries later, he retired from the Air Force. It wasn't the military that he loved so much. It was the flying. After his last station in

Tucson, at Davis Monthan Air Force Base, he retired and got a part-time job flying for a small airline. This kept him in the sky, which was all he said he needed. It was around that time that he met Diana.

Poppie and I visited a bit longer before Lilly came to get me. She wanted me to go to Huey's class with her. Since I think I had worn out Poppie, I told her I would for a bit. I said my goodbyes, gave Poppie a long hug and told him I would visit again soon. Part-time Lilly gave him a hug, too. We left to go find Huey and the kids for after-school class.

Just like the last time, Huey had the kids' complete attention. I don't know how he earned their devotion, but they all were in it. They all followed the rules. I guessed it was his creative lessons and hands-on fun. Memorizing states and their capitals, the verb or noun game, and an insect scavenger hunt was on the list of lessons today. Who doesn't like a good insect scavenger hunt? While they hunted for bugs, I went to help with dinner.

It was soup bowl night. Coco had gone to the bakery and gotten a couple dozen bread bowls and Nonnie had prepared turkey chili and chunky tomato and basil soup. Grated cheddar, Tabasco, tortilla chips and sour cream were toppers, with a spinach salad on the side.

Like most nights, we caught up on the day's happenings. After cleanup, some of us went out to the porch to visit a bit. It was a beautiful night.

"Who wants a root beer float?" Lilly's voice came from the kitchen. There were a few takers. Sunshine and Coco went inside to help. After a minute Lilly hollered, "Jade, don't you want one?"

"Thanks, Lilly. I'd love one," I hollered back as I got up to join the others in the kitchen. I didn't know it, but I was about to be introduced to the art of making the perfect root beer float.

"It's all in the technique," Lilly explained. I watched, trying to notice a particular technique. I wondered if it was the slow pour of the root beer over the ice cream. I think I enjoyed my root beer float almost as much as I enjoyed watching Lilly enjoy hers. Each spoonful, she would start by licking the underside of the spoon and then turn it over on her tongue to swipe the spoonful. It had a flow. Like she'd had practice.

Day 8: Broken Crayons Still Color

The morning began with Cayenne pushing out her puppies.
We watched. Amazing x 7...

"Nonnie says it's the miracle of life, but I think it's gross." Lilly was watching Cayenne have her puppies. Maya had called right after breakfast and invited P.S. and Lilly to come watch. Annie had let P.S. skip school that day so she could see the "miracle of life." Reesa, Huey and I walked them over to the property next door where Maya and Charlie lived. We wanted to watch, too.

When Maya greeted Lily, I found myself surprised. And I wasn't sure why. I knew that Maya was Charlie's long-time girlfriend. And Charlie was exotically beautiful. Maya was equally beautiful, but in a different way. She had magazine ad beauty. An enchanting cowgirl cover girl. As dark and straight as Charlie's hair was, Maya's was opposite: so blonde it was almost white with long messy waves. Lilly introduced us before we went to watch the miracle.

While Lilly thought it was gross, you could tell that she was also fascinated. I suspected P.S. felt the same. It took a while, but we all watched with wonder, feeling a little bit of discomfort each time Cayenne pushed out another pup, displaying her own pain that accompanies birthing babies. Luckily, everything went smoothly and Cayenne cooperated by presenting us with seven tiny, wet, squeaky babies. One of them was noticeably smaller. Charlie explained that this made him the runt of the litter. He would have to be watched more closely because runts were smaller and in animal worlds, smaller ones had it harder. Cayenne was a beautiful, sweet Golden

Retriever, who Maya bred for service dogs. She began doing this when one of her best friends got a service dog to help her the last few years before Muscular Dystrophy took her. She saw how much the dog had helped, both physically and emotionally. She witnesses that her friend's dog made her last years worth living, even though they were difficult.

This was Cayenne's third and last litter. Maya decided to try training pups from the dog shelter. She felt there were too many puppies put down because they didn't have homes. This disturbed her, so she was going to take a chance on finding pups that were compatible for this kind of training. She didn't want to stop training pups, but it was hard to justify breeding them with so many puppies out there already. She explained that a majority of the puppies she had trained were matched with vets who had returned from service. Some came home with broken bodies, others with broken souls. And some were broken altogether. Some of the puppies went to victims of accidents or disease, but most went to returning vets.

Watching this miracle of life, Lilly and P.S. had all kinds of questions.

"Why are their eyes closed?" ("Because they aren't done developing: the eyes and ears finish after they are born.")

"When will they open?" ("In about two weeks or so.")

"Can we hold them?" ("Not yet, maybe next week.")

"How old will they be when you give them away?" ("If they are going to be service dogs, about 18 months. If they are companion dogs, then maybe only six.")

"Will Cayenne be sad when her babies leave?" ("Yes, a little, but Cayenne knows she is helping people so she is OK with it.")

"How does the milk get in Cayenne?" ("I believe that God made it so all mommies make milk when they have babies. Isn't that so smart of God?")

"Did it hurt Cayenne to have her puppies?" ("Yes, it hurts to have babies, but it is a good hurt and mommies don't care because they want to have their babies.")

"Can we name them?" ("Not yet. Let's wait and see what their personalities are. Then you girls can help me name them.")

"Do you think Guthrie can have one? He's a vet." ("If Guthrie wants one, he can have one. That's up to Guthrie.")

The whole walk home, we could hear Lilly and P.S. comparing notes. They discussed the best part (they agreed that it was the nursing) and the grossest part (Cayenne licking off all the "puppy goop" when they came out) and their favorite puppy (Lilly liked the lightest one; P.S. preferred the one with the spot on his nose). They tossed around names like Honey, Choco, Hopscotch and Marlie (for Maya and Charlie).

As we got closer to the Big House, the girls ran so they could tell Nonnie all about it.

We found P.S. and Lilly in the kitchen helping Nonnie get ready for a tortilla making session. The conversation rotated between tortilla making and cutest puppy debate. Apparently, once every couple of months, Nonnie made tortillas. When she did, she made lots of them. And whoever was around helped. This was because everyone loved Nonnie's homemade tortillas and because everyone competed for the perfectly round tortilla prize, which wasn't really a prize, but more like an honor.

They made dozens, which would feed the ranch clan for weeks. I watched as Nonnie mixed up the ingredients, waiting on the sidelines to make up the little dough balls that we would eventually pat into flat round tortillas to cook. Nonnie demonstrated the tortilla making process. She patted and squished the dough and then patted the dough, back and forth between her hands until it thinned into a circle. She worked on the edges a little bit, the same way, patting.

You could tell the pro's from the rookies by the thickness and shape of their contributions to the tortilla bank. Mine were the thickest. The crew was ready by the flat stovetop, with spray oil in hand to use before each tortilla turn. After a little while, we got in synch. My tortillas, by comparison, were not very good. But this was my first time and my fifth tortilla was way better than my first. And my 10th was way better than my fifth. I was a quick learner, but still, everyone had me beat in all aspects tortilla: shape, thickness, evenness and size. This took hours, but it was also our late lunch. Nonnie made a pot of refried beans earlier in the morning and as we made our tortillas we sampled them with beans and cheeses, sour cream, chopped lettuce and salsa. The kitchen smelled wonderful and the tortillas tasted even better than they smelled.

When we finished, Nonnie gave Lilly her homework assignment for the day and since P.S. was home from school, she got an assignment, too. They set off to do their work, but not before Lilly asked me if we could go see Simon later at the lake. I told her we could and off the girls went. I stayed and helped Nonnie, Coco and Huey clean the tortilla mess. While we were doing this, Ace called and told me my car would be ready the next day and that I could pick it up in the morning. This news was met with mixed emotions. Everyone was glad that Ace was able to fix my car, but no one seemed happy about my being able to leave. It made me feel good, but it made me sad, also. I wasn't sure how I felt about leaving. Until now, I had little choice but to stay. With Carlos fixed, I could leave whenever I was wanted. But I didn't know if I was ready yet. Nonnie was watching me.

"You know, it's on Lilly's mind, too. I'm glad she wasn't here to hear Ace's call. We're gonna have to be gentle with this news." She paused for just a second. "Jade, you know that she doesn't want you to leave. Can I make a suggestion, child?"

"Of course, Nonnie. Always."

"I think we break it to her in stages. Tell her your car is fixed, but maybe you can stay just another day or two, so she isn't hit all at once." Nonnie seemed a little concerned. She explained further. "If she knows you can leave, but you choose not to, that may make it seem like you aren't ready to leave just yet. Now we all know that she is the one that isn't ready. But we can get her ready with a little time. Do you understand, baby?" I did. And I also understood that I wasn't ready either. Somewhere in the last week, I stopped waiting for my car to be fixed.

"Yes, Nonnie. I understand. When we go down to the lake, I'll tell her my car is ready, but that I'm not ready to leave yet. I'll ask her if I can stay just a little while longer."

"Perfect, child. Perfect." She seemed relieved. We finished cleaning up the kitchen and while Huey finished bagging tortillas, Nonnie went to take a few to Poppie.

Huey, Coco and I went to the henhouse, where I got a lesson on gathering eggs. Another first. To my surprise, the henhouse was really like a house. It was a little one-room house. Inside, the entire perimeter held two tiers of nesting areas for the hens. A ramp led to the second level. They weren't cooped; they were free range with a large gated area around the house for them to roam. A few of the hens were outside, but most were sitting inside. The doorway was big so it was airy, but it still smelled of chickens. And if the smell didn't remind you of where you were, the droppings sure did.

L.A. girls know little about chickens, but one catches on fast. Coco introduced me to Isaac, the rooster, and all of his "wives": Henrietta, Grace, Desiree, Jill, Evita, Clara, Georgia, Martha, Betty and Sophia. Huey explained that Isaac favored Sophia, but they all seemed happy with any attention Isaac gave them. Huey pointed out Henrietta. He thought she was beautiful. I thought that funny. But after looking at her, compared to her roommates, I kind of saw what Huey meant. Her markings were more distinct and her colors more vibrant. Then he pointed out Clara. He told me that she was the frisky one that interacted with him the most. She could get quite sassy, according to Huey.

I learned that the number of eggs laid depended on anything from the breed of the chickens to the number of daylight hours they had. The average hen laid five to seven eggs a week. Usually, the henhouse supplied the ranch with about five dozen eggs a week, give or take a few. This was usually enough to cook and bake with, so the ranch rarely had to buy more eggs. Coco showed me how to get the easy eggs first. She literally grabbed unguarded eggs. Then she showed me how to get the harder ones. She armed herself with a plastic garbage can lid and prodded one of the chickens still roosting. The chicken wasn't happy and became a little aggressive, which explained the garbage can shield. For the tougher ones, she used a stick to softly poke the hen so she would move enough to snatch her egg. All but Martha had contributed to today's egg collection and by Huey and Coco's reaction, today's egg bounty was good. Huey stayed back to clean the house and pen. Huey wore lots of different hats here at the ranch. About the only thing he didn't do was sleep here, although he might as well, with the time he spent here. As Coco and I walked back to the Big House with our eggs, Lilly came running up to us. She saw us with the egg basket.

"So how many did the girls give you today?"

"Nine," answered Coco.

"Wow! Not bad," Lilly said, confirming what Huey and Coco had expressed already.

"Ready to go to the lake? P.S. had to go home to do her real homework." She said this with some soft jealousy. "Wanna go?" I looked at Huey and Coco to see if they minded.

"Go. Have fun. Tell Simon we say, 'Hi.'" Coco answered my gaze. Lilly and I turned around to head off to the lake. On the way, Lilly told me her favorite chickens (Henrietta and Desiree, because they were the nicest) and her least favorite chicken (Clara, because she was the meanest.) We talked chickens all the way to the lake. The discussion included chicken poop, Nonnie's egg "pancakes" (I would learn that this was one single egg scrambled in a medium skillet, so it came out thin and round, like a buttery crepe), Isaac and his crowing (never at sunrise and always at any other time), how it was her idea to get chickens and how she helped Barry and Michael make the henhouse about a year after they moved to the ranch. The conversation took long enough to get to the lake, find our spot and begin watching for Simon and company. As we settled in, I waited a few minutes before speaking. Then, I told Lilly that Ace had called and that my car was ready. I know she heard me but she didn't say anything.

"Lilly, did you hear me?"

"Yes." She stared out at the lake.

"I was wondering if it would be alright with you if I didn't leave tomorrow when I go get my car. I was hoping I could stay just a little bit longer." This changed everything.

"Of course, Jade! You can stay as long as you like. I'm sure it's all right with Nonnie and Poppie and Barry. I'm sure everyone will be glad. So good. You're not leaving yet. Right?" She eagerly looked at me for confirmation.

"Right. I'm not leaving yet. Now where do you think Simon is?" I wanted to change the subject before she asked how long I was staying. I didn't have an answer.

"I don't see him. Maybe he is off with Sasha. That's OK. They like their privacy." So we sat and watched the birds. After a few minutes, Lilly asked if she could tell me another secret. Just like the last time, I told her she could.

"Sometimes at night, when everyone is sleeping, I can hear Barry crying. I know it's because of me. And I love Barry. He takes really good care of me. But I know he wants Diana back. And if I am here, then Diana can't be."

I didn't know what to say. I was expecting something else. Anything else. Maybe that Lilly broke Nonnie's vase or that she was mad at P.S. again. Cheating on her taxes was more likely than hearing her husband crying because the person she became had replaced the person who she was!

"I bet that makes you feel sad."

"Yep. It does."

"You know, Lilly, that Barry loves you very much. He just misses Diana. I think when Diana comes back, he will probably cry 'cause he will miss you, too, just like he misses Diana now. But remember what the doctors told you. Diana is in you and you are in Diana. It's normal for Barry to miss her."

"Right." Lilly thought about this for a minute. Just then, Simon and Sasha came into view. "Look, Jade!" They paddled nearby and we watched for a bit, happy to see them together. After they were out of sight, we walked back up to the Big House. As we approached the house, Lilly ran ahead and I could hear her telling whoever was inside that I wasn't leaving yet. She sounded happy.

⸻ ⸻ ⸻

After dinner and helping to clean up, I headed back to my casita. On the way back, I noticed it was a full moon. The night sky was brighter than usual. I heard something off to the side of the path and wondered if I should be concerned. It could be a javelina or a coyote. I had never seen either one, except on T.V., but their reputations scared me. I tried to see where the noise was coming from. I could see some small animals scurrying between the trees. It seemed like there was a ballet going on in the brush. Two cottontails were performing for no one in particular. They came out of the brush and one would leap into the air and as he landed, the other would follow. This went on for a few minutes and then they hopped away. It was, I thought, a lovely performance. I went inside and showered before getting into bed. I smelled like puppies, tortillas and chickens. The shower felt good and it reminded me of how tired I was. I got into bed and thought about the ranch.

Meeting Lilly had changed me. I was now pushed to see through others' eyes. I thought about Lilly and P.S.'s frustration with each other. On one hand, P.S. could be a bit harsh and had little patience. But when I remembered that Lilly was first her Aunt Diana, her behavior was understandable. I thought about how Barry left much of Lilly's care to Nonnie and the others. Then I remembered that this child was the love of his life, his partner who he had lost a child with, and how unbelievably difficult it must be to watch and wait, for years. This unpredictable waiting, hoping, living, planning semblance of a life was their normal. The ranch had to find a balance between living today and planning for tomorrow. And they did. And then it would change. Then they found it again. And it would change again. And so on. I wrote a bit in my journal before drifting off. That night, I dreamt of roller coasters.

Day 9: Feeling Good to Be Lost in the Right Direction.

It's funny how things turn out. Carlos is good to go,
so I could leave whenever I want. But, I'm not quite good to go.
I'm not ready to be done with the ranch. And, it seems, thankfully,
that the ranch is not ready to be done with me.

It was a cooler morning, so Barry and I grabbed coffee to go before leaving to pick up my Jeep at Ace's. As we were getting ready to leave, Lilly ran up to the truck, slightly panicked.

"You're coming back, right, Jade?" Lilly looked at me with questioning eyes.

"Of course. We're just going to get my car. I'm coming back. I'll see you later. OK?"

"Promise?"

"I promise." Barry and I both could see Lilly relax.

"K. Bye." She was satisfied.

Barry pulled the truck around the drive and we passed the ranch sign before we pulled onto the highway. I wasn't sure what to think. In a short time, I had grown very fond of Lilly and everyone else at the ranch. While they were an eclectic crew, they all had one common thread: their connection and devotion to Diana and Barry.

Lilly's worry made me feel both flattered and concerned. I felt good that Lilly trusted me and enjoyed my company. She made me feel like I made a difference in her days. But I was also concerned that my being there was somehow encouraging Lilly to stay. I did not know where the balance was between helping Lilly and hurting Diana. I looked over to Barry.

"I know we haven't talked about it, but I am wondering what to do. You all have been so wonderful. And I have loved being here. Xavier was right. The ranch is like no other place. But I don't want to overstay my welcome. I don't…" Barry cut me off.

"You know, Jade, if anyone would have told me five years ago that I would be living here, with everyone else who was living here, for the reason that we were all living here, I would have thought them crazy." He looked at me, offering a resigned smile. He wasn't complaining. He was just talking.

"If someone were to tell me how our joy… Diana's and my joy would have ended and Lilly and the others would have come in Hope's place, I wouldn't have believed you. I mean, really… who would?" he said calmly, yet incredulously.

"Barry, you are an unbelievable man. I can't begin to imagine what this must be like for you. I don't even want to. Clearly, Diana was an amazing person for you and everyone to do all of this."

"She *is* an amazing woman," Barry said.

"I'm sorry. I said that wrong."

Barry looked over and reassured me. "Jade, don't worry about it. I know what you meant. It's just that you never met her so you are not one those who are waiting for her to come back. Lilly is all you know. And speaking of Lilly, I'm sure that you have noticed that she's become quite attached to you."

"I have. I worry that I might have made things worse. I'm not sure whether my being here is actually good for her. Or good for Diana. I would feel terrible if I made things harder."

"Well, I'm a little glad you say that." He paused and I looked over to get a clue what he meant by that. Nothing in his face revealed where he was going.

"Diana's doctors are a little concerned." He looked over at me and saw my face. It must have shown dread.

"Not that you made it worse," he quickly reassured me. "The doctors think that there might be something to this connection that

Lilly has with you. That it might be meaningful in some way. They think that it might be good for you to stick around a little bit longer." Barry looked over to see if I was receptive to his continuing or not.

"What can I do? Do they think I can help?" I was eager to hear what Barry had to say.

"Well, they aren't quite sure. This is new for us. But they would like to meet you and maybe they could direct us somehow... I don't really know what they want us to do, to be honest. All I know is that they think Lilly's connection to you means something. They don't know what, but they would like to explore it. Apparently, the last few sessions they've had with Lilly, you are all that she talks about. You and Poppie. I know that this is a lot to ask. And you have no obligation, I want to make that clear," he said firmly. "This isn't your problem. But I have to ask anyway. I was hoping you would stick around for a little while longer. I know you only planned on another day or two. But I was hoping you could stay long enough for the doctors to give us some idea of how you fit in with Diana's healing. I don't know how long that will take, but if you can give us another week or two, I know that will help." He looked over to get a hint of what I was thinking.

"I'd be happy if I could help in any way. But Barry, if I am being honest with you, I didn't want to leave yet anyway."

"It kind of grows on you, doesn't it?" he asked.

"Yes. It really does," I agreed. "So do Lilly and everyone else."

"Yeah, Lilly is my angel. She takes care of Diana and protects her. I keep telling myself that Lilly is on watch while my broken wife tries to make herself whole again. Lilly guards while Diana heals. And I try to be glad for it. I'm counting on Lilly. That's a lot to put on her." He spoke this into the air as if it were for anyone to hear. Like a confession. He hesitated and then returned to me.

"If you would stay for a while longer, I'd be grateful."

"I want to stay. Barry, you and everyone have been so wonderful to me. I have thought more than once how lucky I was that you were the one to stop and help me. I'm the grateful one."

"Thank you." He seemed relieved. "You may think I helped you that day, but as it's turning out, you are helping us. Before you meet the doctors next week, I want to tell you the story, the whole story, of how Diana broke. I think you should know it if the doctors want you to help in some way." I wondered how horrible the rest must be. What I knew already was bad enough.

We pulled into Ace's garage and went inside. Carlos was as good as new, he told me. After we caught up a bit and I explained that I was going to stick around longer, I paid my bill, thanked him for everything and told him I hoped to see him around.

"You will," he assured me. "And Jade," he hollered as I was walking out, "thank you for helping Diana. I know you never met her but, if you ever do, you'll know how grateful we all are."

"Thank you for saying so, Ace, but I'm beginning to understand already. And I look forward to meeting her one day." While I wondered how Ace knew that I was helping, it hit me that what I considered absurd a little over a week ago, I now considered normal. I never would have imagined then that I would feel so at home in a situation that was so bizarre.

Needless to say, as we pulled up to the ranch, Lilly was waiting with the dogs. She ran up to greet me and hugged me quickly.

"You're staying for a while longer right?" she did not know about the doctor's request. She only knew that I wasn't ready to leave, which was true.

"Yep. You're stuck with me for a bit." I didn't say how long because I didn't know. Lilly didn't seem to need to know anything other than that I wasn't leaving. The sarcasm was lost on her.

"Barry, can we go tell Poppie that Jade isn't leaving yet? He's gonna be so happy, too."

"Sure you can. Give Poppie a hug for me."

Lilly and I headed to the family house. As we knocked and walked in, Lilly called out.

"Good morning, Poppie. Jade and I came to visit you."

We could hear him from his bedroom, trying to speak loudly enough so we could hear. "Well, what are you waiting for, my sweet girls. Come on back." Poppie was sitting up in his bed. He looked more tired than the last visit. But his smile didn't. Lilly walked over and gave him two hugs.

"This is from me. And this one is from Barry."

"Wow. A hug from Barry. This is a special day." He winked at me with his Poppie grin. "Where is my hug from Jade?" I walked over and gave him a hug. As I did, he hugged me back, holding me close while he whispered softly in my ear, "You are God sent, and I thank you with my whole heart." I guessed he already knew why I was staying. Nonnie must have told him. But he didn't show it when Lilly announced that I wasn't leaving yet.

"Well, isn't that fantastic! I am so glad. I know that I wasn't ready to say goodbye yet," he said, with gentle conviction.

"I'm glad, too. I wasn't ready to say goodbye either," Lilly echoed.

"Well, then it's unanimous. Everybody is happy. Today is a good day," I added.

"Yep, today is a great day!"

Poppie and I both smiled at Lilly's enthusiasm.

"I think you should go celebrate with some milk and chocolate covered graham crackers. This deserves a treat. Tell Nonnie I said so." Poppie looked at me. "Lilly has a special dunking technique that you might find fun. I am sure she will be glad to show you." He smiled at the two of us. "You both have happiness all over you. If you girls don't mind, I'm a little tired and think I might take a nap. But I would love another visit soon." I could see that Poppie wasn't up for a longer visit today. It worried me a little that he had less energy. I knew that he was fading, but knowing didn't make it easy to see.

"I think that's a good idea. Don't you, Lilly?"

"Yep. OK, Poppie. See ya later." She gave him a goodbye hug. So did I. And then we left him to take his nap.

We headed over to the Big House. A bunch of the ranchers were just hanging out. Lilly announced that Poppie said they could have some milk and chocolate grahams and asked who else wanted. There were a few takers, so Lilly and I went into the kitchen to pour five cups of milk and grabbed the bag of chocolate covered graham crackers. And then she demonstrated, a bit dramatically, her dunking technique. She broke the cracker in half, dunked half into the milk with the open side up so the milk soaked in, little air bubbles trading places with the milk. After a little wait, she ate it, explaining that the graham melts inside the chocolate. A wet delicious chocolate mush. She had me try it. I must admit, it was pretty good. Good enough to have too many.

We sat around and talked about the puppies from yesterday, how I learned to gather eggs, root beer floats and scorpions. It was cozy being there with everyone. We had an hour or so before lunch, so Lilly and I went outside to play. Today's game itinerary included Chinese jump rope and hopscotch. We played for a bit, had lunch and then Lilly went to therapy with Barry and I went to call Deb, in New Mexico and Jesse to tell them that I would be staying here for a little while. Deb didn't have a set date for me to be there, so we just pushed it back a bit and I told her I would be in touch. But Jesse was not as easy. He was already confused about my situation. He would have been alarmed had he not heard the comfort in my voice. He trusted it, so after about 10 minutes, he backed off from worrying. The call ended on a good note, but it was a journey to get there. It wasn't his fault. He was in big brother mode. I had to admit, the conversation was as normal as the ranch, which wasn't normal at all.

Me: (big explanation about how I had come to decide to stay)

Jesse: OK. So let me get this straight. Diana is Lilly who is 12, but really 58?

Me: Yes.

Jesse: And Poppie is the grandfather, slash dad?

Me: Yes

Jesse: And Barry is the husband, slash father?

Me: Yes.

Jesse: And Poppie is waiting to die until Guthrie gets there. And Guthrie is a vet from Afghanistan who used to be one of their foster kids?

Me: Yes

Jesse: And you are living on a commune with 12 other people. Sometimes more?

Me: Well, it's not really a commune.

Jesse: And you play games all day? Like hopscotch and jacks?

Me: Well, not all day. I also gather eggs from the henhouse, help Huey with the kids, I help in the greenhouse and other stuff too.

Jesse: You gather eggs from the henhouse?

Me: Yes. I gather eggs from the henhouse.

Jesse: And work in the greenhouse?

Me: Yep. Greenhouse. You Got it.

After a few more reassurances, he reminded me to be careful and to stay in touch. I promised him that I would.

Everyone was at dinner that night. We overflowed to the second table. It was nice. Everyone caught up on their day and the discussion turned to Guthrie. Nonnie got a call that he may be able to be released soon to come visit. The doctors said that he might be able to leave the hospital for a short visit to come see Poppie. Everyone knew, but it wasn't spoken, that they hoped he would get there before Poppie passed. We all noticed Poppie faded a bit each day. This worried everyone, especially Nonnie. But no one dwelled on it. At least not openly. So we concentrated on Guthrie and everyone told stories about his service and his saxophone, his childhood and the day he became a pilot. They kept the conversation positive, not talking too much about his injury or getting here in time.

I was going to meet the doctors soon. I wasn't sure how I fit in. I fell asleep wondering what I could possibly do to help.

Day 10: To Karaoke or Not to Karaoke? That is the Question.

bananas

There were always things to do at the ranch. Plants and animals to care for, places to clean, projects to plan and do, meals to prepare, things to fix, kids to tend to, crops to harvest or eggs to collect. Everyone seemed to have their areas to cover. And often they helped each other, so they knew more about the whole. All of them could use the help, so there was plenty to choose from when considering how to fill my day. And there was Lilly, who, I think, was becoming my "thing." And I think my job description included being the on-call game partner.

I think I lost a few pounds just from skipping rope and playing hopscotch. But my game got better. Especially with Lilly's patient tutelage. As competitive as she was, she truly wanted to teach me how to do better. I first noticed this when we played jacks and ball today. We were outside on the basketball court, and Lilly had just taken her first turn and got all the way through to eightsies. My turn came and I didn't even get to onesies. It had been a day or so since Lilly had played jacks. It had been a decade or two since I had. I had warmed up the other day, but that was about it. Clearly, I needed to up my game, so today I got a true lesson. I tried again and barely got to twosies. Lilly could see my frustration beginning to creep in. That's when the lesson began.

"Jade, you need to relax," she said in a calming voice. "Remember, it's just a game. Yes, you want to win, but that takes time and practice. Nonnie says that a good life includes patience.

You'll get better. Just relax and take a deep breath." So I took a deep breath, cleared my mind (which, I might add, was filled with "I can't believe I am being 'schooled' by a 58-year-old kid") and tossed the jacks. This time I made it through threesies. Lilly cheered with excitement.

"See, I told you that you could do it." She was so happy for me. Like I had just won a raffle or found a $20 bill on the ground. "That's great. Pretty soon you will be beating me." It took almost another hour to reach foursies. Although less often, I still found myself staring at this woman/child. Even playing jacks, her demeanor was that of a kid.

After lunch, Nonnie gave Lilly a few chores to do at the family house. Nonnie asked me to join her in the family room of the Big House. Next to her on the couch were two photo albums.

"I don't bring out the family albums that often anymore," Nonnie explained, it was too hard for Barry. And she wasn't ever sure how Lilly would react, so she didn't want to take a chance. I was sitting on the couch next to Nonnie. "I wanted to give you a little visual of our history. Especially since the doctors want to meet you. I know that Barry will tell you more before you meet them. But I wanted to show you. Do you mind, child, sitting with me and going down memory lane?" Nonnie kindly asked.

"I would love to, Nonnie."

"Marcus told me that he thought you were God sent. I think he might be right. Yes, I think he just might be right" She patted my hands with hers. They were soft and worn from living and doing.

Nonnie opened the first album. We slowly went through both with an explanation for each picture. Some pictures took a sentence to explain. Others a story. Over an hour later, I had seen pictures of stories I had heard and heard stories of pictures I had seen. I saw photos of a younger Nonnie and Poppie, Diana and Barry. There were pictures of so many fosters. And there were pictures of Hope. It broke my heart. She was a beautiful child with Lilly's eyes. From there the pictures changed to the ranch in various stages. I saw the condition of the property when they first moved there and the improvements that Michael and Barry and the guys had made throughout the years. It was fascinating to see the evolution of the ranch, but sad to learn more about why the ranch came to be. I think this took a lot out of Nonnie. I understood why the photo albums did not come out that often. She put them away just before Lilly came in.

"Can we go see the puppies?" Nonnie thought about it and told her that she would call Maya to make sure she had time for a visit. Nonnie called and they spoke for a few minutes and then Nonnie said it was alright to go over. Sunshine wanted to come, so Lilly went to get her. Nonnie told me, after Lilly left, that one of the puppies didn't make it. Maya said she would explain it to them. Nonnie wanted me to be prepared. Lilly and Sunshine were coming up the path so I met them and off we went to go see the puppies. Lilly skipped ahead most of the way. This gave Sunshine and I a little time to chat. She told me that Maya had called and told her about the puppy. I was glad that she was aware. And I think we were both glad that Maya would handle this one.

I had to admit, from the first time anyone met Sunshine, they would walk away feeling good. She exuded positivity. She was her name. Sunshine was always up, but not too up. Just the right amount of up. She talked much of the walk. She told me more about herself.

Her full name was Sunshine Yellow Deer. It sounded contrived but she reassured everyone that heard it that it was, indeed, her birth name. She was 11 years old when she first came to Diana. Normally, she would have stayed on the reservation, but no family stepped up and Diana had friends involved with the tribe. And so her story began. She was 26 now. She was slim and had long black shimmering hair. She was beautiful. That was the only good thing she got from her mother. Her mother never gave her Indian pride because she seemed to have forgotten that part of raising her daughter. Or it was lost somewhere in the bottle. In between her highs and drinking binges, her mother barely managed to provide food, let alone a sense of history. And her father never gave her Indian pride because he never gave her anything. He came and went. Mostly he went. For years her mother fooled people that she was taking care of her daughter. But after a while, most knew differently. Friends started making sure Sunshine had enough food and a few clean outfits for school. This helped, but those things didn't protect her. Everyone meant well by taking care of Sunshine, but no one intervened. Anyone who wasn't sure how bad it was had seven weeks to think about it while Sunshine fought for her life after her mom crashed the car while drunk. When she left the hospital, Sunshine went to Diana's. Her mother never won the battle over the bottle. In fact, when Sunshine was 22, the bottle won. Because she was Native American, the system took longer to place her, but because no one on the reservation stepped up, the Indian Council had to look elsewhere.

When Sunshine first came to Diana, all she knew was that she was an "Indian." It was Diana who researched and taught her that she was from an honorable lineage. And it was Diana who taught her about her tribe and its history. She was like that. Diana and Barry taught and shared the culture and heritage of the fosters in their home. It wasn't always easy. They often had a multi-racial household and sometimes others had a problem with that. Barry and Diana always made sure the kids knew it was the others who had the problem, and not anyone in their wonderfully blended family. Sometimes kids came to them hating. These took extra care, but intolerance was not tolerated. In fact, defending and standing up for each other was required. It rarely came easy, but eventually it got easier. Barry, Diana, Nonnie and Poppie made it so the kids wanted to be part of the family. And in the family, certain things were expected. It was rare that a foster did not eventually feel safe enough to connect. And safe enough to be who they were. Diana was the one to show them.

Diana took Sunshine to the reservation to participate in the rituals of the girls from her tribe. She continued to take her up to the reservation a few times a year. That is where she met Will. He lived on the reservation with his mother, father and younger sister. They became friends first and slowly, as they didn't see each other often, their friendship grew. By the time they were ready to go on their own, they had committed to each other. And they had been together since.

When we got to Maya's, all the puppies were nursing, so we watched for a little while. I wondered how long it would take Lilly to notice that one was missing. Two seconds. In two seconds Lilly asked where the littlest one was. This was Maya's cue.

She reminded Lilly about mentioning the runt of the litter when she saw them all after being born. Maya explained that sometimes, even watching to make sure that the littlest one gets enough food and warmth, it doesn't always work. Maya explained that this usually happened when the mommy really and truly knew the baby would not make it, but didn't want to prolong the hard part for her baby. I could see that Lilly understood and accepted this, but I could also see that she was very sad. Her eyes welled over, but no sound came with it. Maya saw this too. She reminded Lilly that this is how some animals are. And that they know what is best, so we need to trust that they do.

"Let's watch them nurse. Then you can hold one." We watched as they finished, all with full-distended bellies. Their eyes were still closed and they were still so tiny. After a bit, Lilly paid more attention to their cuteness than the loss she just processed. She thought it funny that they squeaked instead of barked. She laughed every time one of them let out a little peep. Maya let Lilly hold one of them for a little while. His little belly was so full, he fell fast asleep in her lap. After a little while, Maya put the puppy back with its sleeping litter. The puppy's mommy licked her clean before letting him nuzzle in with the others.

We headed back to the ranch and the dogs greeted us along the way, their noses stuck to Lilly's lap, smelling the puppy that had been sitting there 20 minutes ago. Lilly thought this was funny. It was like their noses were glued to her lap.

When we got back, I was informed that a group of us were going into town to Charlie's bar for karaoke night. They all assured me that it would be fun for all, but I told them that I didn't do karaoke. They didn't care. Dinner was almost ready, so I went to go shower and change so I would be ready to go with everyone after dinner. At dinner, I was encouraged to fill my belly, because they told me it would be filled with booze by the end of the night. I wasn't sure about this, but everyone was looking forward to it, so how bad could it be?

◦◦◦◦◦ ◦◦◦◦◦ ◦◦◦◦◦

When we walked into the bar, it was already crowded and everyone seemed to know someone. Regulars, I guessed. Coco hollered to a few friends. So did Huey. Charlie was behind the bar. She waved us over. After grabbing some drinks we sat at the table that Charlie has saved for us. The tavern was pretty big, with more than 15 or so bar stools around a big "L" shaped bar and about 12 tables around the stage. There was a small dance floor to the side. It was packed because it was 'karaoke night'. The dance floor became the "standing room only" section. We settled in while a rather large man belted out *Freebird*. Our first of too many drinks arrived in time for an *Endless Love* duet. By the time the next round of drinks arrived, Coco was up doing a bit of Marvin Gaye. She was really good. After Coco were a few friends of the gang. To say it was entertaining was an understatement. Really, tell me that one wouldn't be entertained by a biker dude attempting Train's, *Calling All Angels* or a mild-mannered, angel-faced girl belting out *Hit the Road Jack*. And I will never forget Maya and Charlie singing Katy Perry's *Roar*. The crowd joined in. Oh-oh-oh-oh-oh-oh-oh-oh.

The songs continued. And the shots continued. And all throughout they kept telling me it was my turn. But I was a karaoke virgin. I was a virgin not because of virtue or values. I was a virgin because I had never shared karaoke with tequila. When the night began, I had absolutely no intention of being part of the evening's entertainment. I had delegated myself as the loyal audience cheerleader. I would clap like no tomorrow. Cheer like no cheerleader had ever cheered. The group humored me but they knew, they told me, that I would eventually get up on the stage. They promised me, which worried me, just a bit. I had my guard up but they were not karaoke and tequila virgins. They knew that after a few shots, I would get up on the stage and sing. The first thing that they did not know was that it actually took five shots to loosen me up. And the other thing that they did not know was what tone I would eventually take up to the stage with me. Charlie and Sunshine bet on a ballad. Coco, Barry and Huey put their money on pop rock. Will gave me the only heavy metal nod. They all would have lost their bets, had they really wagered anything. There was no pop coming from my mouth that night. No one could have predicted and everyone was shocked when I got up for my karaoke debut with a way too animated version of Joe Cocker's, *You Can Leave Your Hat On,* in the key of "naughty little skank."

By the night's end, everyone had gotten up to either make a fool of themselves, impress everyone with their skills or something in between. The ranch crew laughed more than they had in a long time. Clearly, we needed it. "Last call" was announced and Huey got up to give the final performance of the night. Everyone was buzzing. Apparently, Huey was a regular (another facet of his multi-faceted life) and no one ever knew what to expect. What tune would go with tattoos and blue hair? What melody would come from his pierced lips? Who would have guessed that Huey was a *Hollaback Girl!*

"This shit is bananas, b-a-n-a-n-a-s." After the lights came up and we said our goodbyes, Will, our designated driver, rounded us up and took us all back to the ranch. The whole ride home we were

reliving and re-singing the evening's musical menu. Our bellies hurt from laughing.

I didn't really remember much after that. I had a foggy memory of walking to my house, falling into bed after taking my shoes off and, I believe, trying to write in my journal.

Day 11: Five More Minutes

In five minutes you can fix a sandwich. You can make a phone call.
In five minutes the coffee could be ready or an e-mail could be sent.
Or in five minutes countless lives can irrevocably be changed.
My heart ached for all of them.

Unfortunately for me and the rest of the karaoke ranch crew, the next day lived up to its name, "Karaoke Hangover Day." Almost everyone had one and whoever did was cranky and foggy. I had been hung-over before. But this was the bigger, better, new improved version. It hurt to breathe. When I woke, I lay in bed trying to remember why I felt like a truck had hit me while I slept and how my tongue had grown fuzz on it overnight. The fog slowly lifted and I began to remember. I remembered the club and the music, but then stopped. Just thinking of the music was even too loud. I moved to get up, but my moan must have hurt my head, too. So I lay there a few more minutes. I slowly got out of bed, slowly showered, felt a smidge better, but not much, so I slowly went to the Big House for coffee. The House was empty except for Coco and Jack, Reesa and Tawn, Lilly and Nonnie. I wondered how Coco was functioning so well.

"Water helps. Lots and lots of water before bed. I learned the hard way, but baby Jack keeps me in line now. I gotta tell you, last night rocked!" She lowered her voice. "I really feel like crap. Kind of like the way you look. No offense."

"None taken." I remembered that I forgot to brush my hair and I was sure my eyes were bloodshot. "And the water tip... duly noted." I went back to my coffee. Apparently, Lilly had been warned to keep it down because she was very quiet, but full of smiles. I appreciated the quiet. The coffee helped, but the thought of food made me queasy, so I just didn't think of it. Thoughts of going back to bed kept creeping in my head, so I was going to do just that. I excused myself and told everyone that I was going to go back to the casita for some quiet and would be back later. They all either wished me a good nap or just told me they would see me later. I went back and slept through lunch. I felt bad when I woke to see it was after one o'clock, but I did feel much better. I went to the Big House, after remembering to brush my hair this time, to see who was around. Everyone was off, either doing something productive or sleeping off a hangover, like I had. Only Nonnie, Lilly and P.S. were in the Big House.

"Are you hungry, child?" asked Nonnie.

"Not really. Thanks, Nonnie. I'll grab something if I want." Lilly and P.S. were playing shesh-besh. Lilly had explained to me that this is what Nonnie called backgammon, since she learned it in Israel and that's what they call it there. I sat and watched them play. Lilly beat P.S. that game, but it was close, so P.S. was happy. After they put away their game, Lilly went and asked Nonnie something very quietly. I could only hear "please," "Jade" and "yogurt." After Nonnie ever so gently scolded Lilly for whispering in front of company, she told her to ask me directly what she wanted. Lilly apologized. She didn't like disappointing Nonnie. She then came over to me and asked if I wanted to take her and P.S. to go and get some frozen yogurt. She explained that sometimes on Saturdays, Barry or Huey would take them into town to Smoothies & Stuff, their favorite place, to get frozen goodies. I had to admit that my stomach was ready for something, but just a little something, so I thought that might be a good idea. Nonnie gave me directions, explaining that it wasn't far. She offered me money that I refused and I asked if she wanted us to bring anything back for anyone. She told me Poppie loved their peanut butter and frozen yogurt smoothie, so we could bring back just a small one for him.

"Maybe it will put a little meat on those old bones," she said to herself, grinning.

The girls were so excited to ride in Carlos for the first time. They were almost giddy. We drove out to the main street and followed it west to the shop. Nonnie was right. It wasn't far. The drive between the ranch and the shop was beautiful. Cactus and desert trees were so much better than traffic jams and smog alerts. The cool air seemed to lift some of the fog. I was grateful. When we got there, the girls ran in ahead of me.

"Hi Anita," they both greeted the server.

"Well, hello, you two. It's been a while. I've missed you. Everything good?" She came around the counter to give them both a hug.

"Yep," said Lilly. "This is my new friend, Jade." She introduced us. "Jade, this is Anita."

"Our new friend," P.S. corrected her.

"That's what I meant, P.S." Anita and I greeted each other.

"So, what's it going to be today? The usual or you want to try something new?" It appeared that Anita knew them well. After discussing their options, Lilly decided on the usual (chocolate and peanut butter swirled frozen yogurt in a cup with gummy bears on top), P.S. decided to try something new (chocolate malt frozen yogurt in a cone with sprinkles on top) and I ordered a small berry and citrus smoothie. We sat and had our treats in one of the booths. We all tried each other's to compare.

"Tell Nonnie to remember that she gets a free cup on her next birthday. Nonnie's birthdays are so special to me and the next one will be extra special if I remember correctly." Anita called over to us at the booth. Lilly promised to deliver the message.

"What is that about?" I was curious.

Lilly explained that when you ask Nonnie how old she is, she'd ask you if you mean in days or years.

"Why?" I was curious. P.S. answered.

"'Cause she says every day is her birthday. Last year we came to get yogurt on her 28, 846th birthday. Guess how old in years that is?" She waited almost one second before she gave me the answer. "79."

"Wow," That's all I could think of to say.

"So were we right? Isn't this the best?" Lilly asked. She and P.S. were waiting for a confirmation.

"Yep. You were right. For real. It's the best."

"So you're gonna meet the docs tomorrow. I'm excited. I've been wanting them to meet you. You're gonna love them."

I ordered Poppie's small peanut butter smoothie, to go. Anita told us to tell Barry, Nonnie and Poppie hello from her and that she wished Poppie well. I told her I would and then we drove back to the ranch. After finding Nonnie, the three of us took Poppie his treat.

"Now how did you know that peanut butter is my favorite flavor?" He smiled at the girls.

"Poppie, you always get peanut butter, silly." P.S. always found Poppie funny.

"Well, thank you girls. I think this is just what I needed." He didn't reach for the yogurt. I wondered if he really wanted it.

"How about you two girls go on out to play so Jade and I can visit while I eat this delicious gift." The girls, never turning down an opportunity to play, hugged Poppie goodbye and ran out. I wished I had their energy.

"Thank you, Jade, for taking them. They clearly had a nice time and the shop knows Lilly well, so we are all comfortable taking her there. Did you meet Gil or Anita? They are the girl's favorites. They both put on extra toppings for them." Now that he mentioned it, I did notice that they both had lots of toppings.

"Anita was there. And she was very nice. She sends her best. If you aren't hungry, Poppie, I can put this in the freezer."

"I actually would like a bite or two before you do that. But sweetheart, I am a little weak today. Would you be comfortable helping me with that?" When he asked, I felt both honored and sad.

"Of course, Poppie." I took the lid off of his smoothie, which was quite thick, and fed Poppie a small spoonful. He closed his eyes and savored the flavor. When he opened his eyes, I saw both gratitude for my help and resignation that he now needed it. My heart broke again. Nonnie was right. A woman's heart can break again and again. I fed him a few more bites while I told him about what I could remember from the night before. We laughed together and I think I wore him out. After a few more bites he told me that was enough and I could put the rest in the freezer for later. He reminded me to come back whenever I wanted. I gave him a hug and he hugged me back, again whispering in my ear his thank you's. I left him to rest.

When I got back to the Big House, Nonnie, Coco and Will were finishing fixing dinner. Barry found me and asked if I minded that we ate dinner together away from the ranchers so he could fill me in a little in preparation for meeting the doctors tomorrow. We both grabbed a plate and took it back to my casita so the two of us could talk. We sat on the couch and began to eat while we made small talk. Barry thanked me for taking the girls to the yogurt shop. He asked me how I was feeling after last night. I told him all that I could remember. We laughed, but we both knew a serious talk was following close behind our banter. When we finished, he explained that before I met the doctors tomorrow, he thought it important to know all the details of Diana's break. And so he began....

People say that when your adrenaline has cause to increase, for unimaginable reasons, one can be found capable of superhuman feats. Fathers lifting cars to free a pinned child. Or a teen becoming bold and brave enough to go into a burning building to pull out someone bigger than himself.

Unfortunately, Diana found this to be true. She bore matching wristband scars to forever remind her of her amazing feat. Not that she wanted to remember. In fact, she wanted so desperately to forget that she made it so. She created an entirely different memory. Not just the event that created the feat, but an entirely different life to go with it. By becoming someone else, she could say, "I don't know," whenever strangers asked why she had thick scars surrounding both wrists. A young one didn't care if they were believed or not. And the puzzled looks people offered her were simply met with an innocence that disarmed the stranger and helped them to move past their wondering. They may have pondered the sight for a few moments more, but not for too long. Eventually, they would realize that the woman they were talking with was not whole. Their curiosity was eventually replaced with sympathy, curiosity or, sometimes, nothing. It was very rare that people talked about what happened to Diana. Once in a while, some relationships grew enough to require a simple explanation like the one I got the day that I arrived. Some of the relationships grew, deserving the whole story. And the story, if you were worthy enough to know it, explained why Diana created this different life. I had been deemed worthy.

Barry had a habit of, sometimes, closing his eyes when he got lost. Like he had to block out the vision of wherever his thoughts or words took him. His eyes closed and then he tilted his head up and to the side, just a bit. He was doing that now.

"Close to five years ago, our daughter Hope left this world. It was that loss that revealed what was probably there all along." Barry began to tell me Diana's story. I already knew that Diana's life had started out horribly. Nonnie had explained to me the other night how Diana's mother had died in childbirth. That had created such resentment in her father that he punished her in horrific ways. Hearing Barry's account was chilling.

At first, it was extreme verbal abuse and neglect. Constant, unpredictable rage and withholding of food or water. And beatings. He was beyond cruel. And then things changed. It started with the touching. And it ended with a broken soul. It did not take long to go from touching to rape, with too many other horrific things in between. Diana knew this was bad, but she also knew that she was "loved." That's what he called it. Her father's lies lasted too many years. Finally, a teacher realized that there were too many excuses for too many bruises or scars. She got involved and Diana's father was arrested. Soon after, she was put into the foster system. It wasn't better. She was still neglected and in one home another foster child repeatedly sexually assaulted her. She continued to withdraw from people, not attaching herself to anyone or anything. Nothing in her life was permanent and nothing in her life was easy. Looking back, it was a blurred line between severe PTSD and emerging alters, and so her behavior was seen as acting out or retreating. Aggressing or withdrawing. And she was never diagnosed with a condition that would explain at least some of her behavior.

As she grew closer to her teen years, she discovered Sabino Canyon. She would go there whenever she could, sometimes skipping school. It was her safe place. And that was where she met Poppie. They developed a friendship and, with time, Poppie began getting involved in Diana's life. He had lost his first wife and he was alone. They filled a void for each other. And eventually, Poppie became her foster father, and later, right before she turned 18, both he and Nonnie became her adopted parents. He had given her the safety, trust and support she needed to "fix" her life. He made sure she got counseling to help heal her soul, he gave her boundaries to make her feel cared for and he gave her unconditional love so she began to feel safe. And she gave him love and purpose, which he had lost and needed. With this rebirth, Diana went on to college, became a social worker and then began to foster children herself. She did not want children to live through what she had. So she worked and fostered and then she met and married Barry. And they became foster parents together, all the time trying to have their own child. After three miscarriages, most likely due to the sexual abuse and the grief and loss that came with each, they finally had Hope.

I knew that Hope had died. To me, that was enough to make any person break. But now, Barry wanted me to know the whole story. I could see that this was not an easy thing to talk about. Barry spoke with some detachment. I guessed this was the easiest way to recall what had happened. Already it was too much. And there was still more.

"The day after Hope was killed, Lilly took Diana's place. Our daughter was nine years old when she was brutally murdered." He paused. "God, words seem too small to describe what happened. I wasn't there. Some days, I pray that I was and some days I thank God that I wasn't." He looked at me. "No one should ever have to witness what happened to our child." He closed his eyes again and continued.

"I remember one night, years before it happened, Diana and I were watching one of those news shows. The topic was how entertainment plays a role in desensitizing youth to death and violence. There was all kinds of blame. Rap songs responsible for gang rape. Video games responsible for crime sprees. They spat out all kinds of statistics. I was agreeing when Diana turned to me and told me I was wrong. It struck me as odd, because she never did that. She explained that there were no rap songs to inspire the Spanish Inquisition. No video games to inspire slavery. She said that she believed people used the words evil and saintly too often. Not that they didn't exist, but more that the true extremes rarely occurred. Her explanation was that we all, throughout history, have been born with the impulse for both good and bad. And most, with strong souls, could fight the impulse for bad. And those without strong souls could not. This explained a Mother Theresa or an Adolph Hitler. And this explained why there could be two people with the same hopelessness and desperation, but one decides to strap themselves with a vest made of explosives and one rises like a Phoenix and becomes someone of value. She believed that extremes were rare. But one day she met one of those extremes. His name was Stan Lindon. He's dead now. Diana killed him." He made this statement with no emotion. He paused a few seconds, while I waited, speechless, and then he continued.

"Like I said, I wasn't there. But Diana told us what happened. She stayed long enough to tell us. Then she left.

"Mommy, can I snuggle in with you?"

Hope's cherubic face was peering from around the corner. She knew the answer. This was their routine. Before Barry left for work, he woke up his girls. As he left he would first kiss Diana on the neck. She always sensed him coming and so she would pull her hair away so she could feel his lips touch her skin. Then he would walk down the hall to Hope's room and snuggle her neck. Barry loved the smell of his daughter. He would pretend to munch on her neck until she woke. She would always wake with a smile and a "Hi, Daddy." He would tell her it was almost time to get up. Then he would go back out to the kitchen, grab his "apple a day" and then go out the door to the garage. The garage door closing was Hope's signal to hop out of bed and dash down the hall to her parent's room where she would ask to snuggle and then jump in bed with her mom for another 20 minutes or so before they started to get ready for the day.

"OK but only for 15 minutes," Diana always said.

"OK," Hope always said, knowing that five more minutes always came after the first 15.

It was early February. The sky outside was still not fully lit and the air was still cold, which made getting out of bed even harder. Diana, as always, agreed to Hope's request of "five more minutes?" They were lying there when Diana heard the door open. She thought Barry must have forgotten something. But when she heard the footsteps, she knew it wasn't him. She jumped up out of bed just in time to see a man in the bedroom doorway. He was holding a gun. And some rope. The panic in Diana consumed her. She moved in front of her frightened daughter and told her to stay where she was while trying to reassure her.

"Baby, I'm just gonna go talk to this man, you stay right there. OK, honey? Don't move." She took a step toward the edge of the bed as he stepped closer and swung his gun and hit her hard on the side of her head. When she woke up, she was lying on her bed and Hope was gone. She looked beside her and saw the empty space where her daughter last was. She began frantically screaming for her daughter. She heard Hope's cries from her room down the hall. She got up to go to her, but she couldn't. Both wrists were tied with the rope to the bed frame. She called out to Hope that she was coming. She tried to pull away but the rope was bound on both wrists and she couldn't move. She listened, as Hope screamed. The sound of her terrified daughter consumed her as she kept trying to break free from the ropes that were now cutting into her skin. As she kept struggling, she heard more screams. And she could hear Hope's bed squeak along with these gut-wrenching moans. Diana knew that this man was hurting her daughter and I don't know how long it took and I don't know how she did it, but she broke free... just as she did she heard Hope's cries stop. And the squeaking. She ran down the hall to find the man still on top of her daughter. One of his hands was just letting go of Hope's neck, leaving her lifeless. He started to get up when he saw Diana come into the room. But Diana had grabbed his gun that he had left on Hope's dresser. She shot every bullet the gun held into the chest of that man. She wrapped her daughter in the sheet and carried her, out of the room to call the police. When they arrived, she was found waiting for them sitting on the front step of their house, rocking and clinging to Hope's wrapped, lifeless body. Barry arrived shortly after. The police took statements while Diana held her daughter, rocking and trying to soothe her with words.

"It's OK, baby. Mommy's here." She just kept rocking until the coroner took their daughter and Barry took Diana to the hospital, to get

her wrists cared for. They were both bloodied, with much of her skin torn or rubbed away by the ropes. Diana was in shock. She cried endlessly, but silently. At the hospital, they gave her some sedatives to help her sleep, but she was inconsolable. So was Barry, but he had to get Diana through the night before he could face all that happened, himself. Finally, Diana fell asleep. When she woke the next day, she was Lilly.

"It took one week for Diana to disappear completely and for Lilly to move in. At first, we didn't know what was happening, although the doctors suspected. It wasn't until we were referred to another doctor who specialized in DID that we began the path we are on now. We were so ill-equipped for this. We were so grateful to find a team that took us on early. Therapy was intensive at first. Lots of hypnotherapy. That's how we found out there are other alters, other personalities she had internalized that we would later learn about and eventually meet. The therapy gave us a small, tiny clue as to what lay ahead for us. During that week, when Diana emerged, she was inconsolable at first. After lots of help, we got her calm a bit. She came and went. When she was with me long enough, I made her promise to try and get better. I was so afraid that I had lost her forever, but after she came and went a couple of times, I began to believe the doctors when they told me that she was still there, somewhere deep inside whoever she had created to protect her. The first five months were harder than the last five years. Learning and getting her the right help and not knowing how this would all turn out was hell. So now, we wait. I know she is still here, but she just isn't ready to take back her life."

I wasn't sure which was more painful, his telling the story or my hearing it. I couldn't imagine living somewhere in their story. Now I understood, better, some of the things that I hadn't before.

"Do you have any questions?" Barry was trying to read me, I could tell. I thought about it for a minute. I wondered about the other alters or how Barry hadn't really had time to grieve over Hope and what he must be feeling with that inside of him. I had lots of questions, but I couldn't put him through anymore tonight.

"No. Thank you for explaining this to me, Barry. I'm sure it's beyond painful talking about this. You must miss them both, terribly."

"I do. Very much. Every moment of the day. But to be honest with you, Jade, I'm not even sure what I would do with Diana now. I know when given the chance, I will be grateful. And I will say goodbye to Lilly and continue my life that paused years ago." I felt guilty. I never knew Diana, so I couldn't miss her. And I knew that I would miss Lilly. And I believe that Barry would, too, when he is finally given the chance

"I'm sure she will come back, Barry. I know it's been years, but she has come so far. And the ranch is ready for her. Maybe the doctors are right. I mean, maybe they see something meaningful."

"Maybe."

We said our goodnights, I cleaned up from dinner and got ready for bed. It took me a while to fall asleep. When I finally did, the last thing in my head was the vision of Diana holding Hope, sitting on the steps. And it woke me. And so the night went. It was the first night at the ranch that I did not sleep well.

Day 12: DID and Other Stuff

So, today was interesting. It started with collecting eggs and ended with lemon meringue pie. And a bunch of big stuff in between...

Coco and I headed for the henhouse after our coffee. I needed a couple cups to wake up. She carried the basket while humming a tune. Well, not so much humming, as da-da-da-da-ing. But it was a really beautiful da-da-da-da. Kind of jazzy and familiar. We got to the henhouse and Coco opened the gate. I hadn't even gotten all the way in when (who I guessed was) Clara came right for me. She didn't exactly attack me as much as bump into me intentionally. I have no idea what I did to set her off, but I was on her radar. Wherever I walked, Clara followed. Now I understood Huey's comment. Coco had to shush her away with the broom. Finally, Clara went to bother other chickens. Coco and I got right to it. We gathered eight eggs and took them back to the house. Huey said he would clean later, so all we had to do was get the eggs, which was nice, since Clara was in a mood. And while I surprised myself at some of the things I had done, I still found cleaning the henhouse disgusting.

It was just Coco and I in the kitchen. Reesa and Huey had the kids outside and Nonnie was in the Big Room with a pile of something. We were putting the eggs away and as I passed Coco the last one to put in the refrigerator, she closed the door and turned to me.

"So, are you nervous about meeting the docs?" Everyone knew I was meeting them today.

"More curious and anxious," I said. "I'm just not sure what they want from me. Or if I can help."

"Well, they're both really cool. And whatever comes, you'll be fine. We all just do what we can."

"Well, I'm glad the doctors are cool. There are two of them, right?"

"Yep. You're gonna meet Dr. Devorah. We call her Doctor Leslie. She is the lead. And the other doctor is Dr. Sabian. We call her Doctor J. Her name is Jenni. They are both like part of the family. We've all been to their clinic and they've both been here. They've been with us from the start. Almost five years." As she said this, she looked amazed. "Man, I can't believe it's almost five years. So many things have happened since then." She paused for just a second and then she shook off her ghosts. "Anyway, both are good people. Usually it's therapy as usual, but once in a while something happens that triggers an episode. That's when we really need them. And they've always gotten us through. You'll like them. For sure."

We went into the Big Room where Nonnie was. She was putting her piles away. She had one manila envelope on the couch, apparently the bounty she was searching for.

"Hi Nonnie. I'll be back in a bit. Gonna go check on the kids. Huey's running late this morning."

"OK, child. I'll see you later."

"So, Nonnie, what are your plans this morning?" I wondered if she was thinking about my meeting the doctors too.

"Child, I'm going with you," she said, as if she was surprised I didn't already know that.

"Oh. I thought just Barry was taking me."

"I hope you don't mind. I thought it would be best if you had us both with you. We all want to be on the same page and maybe you'll have questions for us. Is that ok, baby?"

"Of course, Nonnie. I'm glad you're coming. I'm really, really glad." Her smile grew into one of her whole body smiles. She was so beautiful.

"That's good, baby. Now I'm going to go see the kids and then check on Poppie before we go. Barry will be ready to take us in about half an hour. I'll see you then."

"OK, Nonnie. Give Poppie a hug for me." She told me she would and went out the porch door. I went and refilled my coffee cup and sat on the patio. I needed a little boost. I sat there for a bit, thinking about the upcoming meeting. I was lost in thought when Barry walked up.

"You ready? Nonnie will be up in a minute." I shook my head and got up to put my cup in the dishwasher. Barry followed me. "Jade, I really appreciate your doing this... whatever this is, for us. You know you can leave anytime. You just might want to after our meeting," he tried to joke. "Sorry, I'm a little anxious. I'm really glad you're meeting the docs. And I'm curious about what they're thinking." We went to meet Nonnie on the trail. And then we went to meet the docs.

The office was not what I expected. That's because it was actually a little house. Nestled near the university, the practice was housed in a converted quaint, charming Southwest stucco home. It was a house in every way, except for a few things. The front entryway had an information center, filled with pamphlets and brochures. Another difference was that the bedrooms served as an office and two therapy rooms. The two rooms were on opposite sides of the house, with separate exits to preserve the confidentiality of the clients. Mexican decor in olive greens, maroons, teals and mustards filled the house. The look was comfy, yet classy. We went to sit in the living room to wait. The ceiling was unique. I had to ask what it was. I'd never seen an ocotillo rib ceiling before. There were books on the coffee table, as well as a beautiful candle and an Indian woven basket. You could hear soft muffled voices from the next room. Barry just sat while Nonnie explained how she had always thought this house to be so nice. She shared how her favorite was the mirror above the bathroom sink. She made me go check it. She was right. It was magnificent. The border was made up of 35 or so imperfectly lined up ceramic tiles in an explosion of colors. Some solid colors mixed in with others with textured designs. The glazes were vibrant.

We could hear the door to the other room open around the corner. A client was leaving through the back door. As we heard the door at the end of the hallway close, we heard steps coming towards us. My heart began to beat just a little bit faster. From around the corner came an older woman, in her late 60s or early 70s, with white hair in a short pixie cut. She dressed sharp and stood tall. Behind her followed a younger woman, maybe in her 50s, with long brown wavy hair. She was dressed more casually than the other woman. They both smiled as they greeted us.

"Hello, Barry," Dr. Leslie held out her hand and he shook it with both hands. She then went over to give Nonnie a big hug. Doctor J followed.

"Dr. Leslie (he pointed to the older one), Dr. J., this is Jade. Jade, these are Diana's doctors." They both came over to shake my hand and offer their thanks for my coming.

"I thought that since this was not an actual session that we would just go sit around the kitchen table so we could talk over some coffee or tea and maybe some snacks. It might be more relaxing. Is that alright with everyone?" Barry and I nodded and mumbled our agreement.

"I think that is a sweet idea, Leslie. Lots of good talks happen around kitchen tables." Nonnie was always so positive. Dr. Leslie led us in the opposite direction from her office and down a hall that led to the kitchen. It was just as beautifully decorated as the rest of what I had seen. Nonnie thought so too.

"Oh, child. I tell you, this is one of my favorite houses. So full of color and life. You have to be happy in a room like this."

She looked around and commented on how clever they were to decorate like they did, citing big, watercolor pictures of fruits and vegetables on the wall, the crates on the counters that held produce, and all of the plants. They were everywhere. Big potted ones to little herb jars. It really was a beautiful room.

We all sat at the simple wooden table. A set of glasses and a pitcher of tea were already set out with plates and bowls of assorted snacks. Nuts, fruit slices, muffins, cheese and crackers. Dr. Leslie asked if any of us wanted coffee. Barry and I took her up on the offer, while Nonnie opted for some of the "tasty looking tea with all the lemons in it." While Dr. Leslie got us coffee, we chitchatted about me. Where from? Where heading? Where were my people? It was fine. We all knew it was just warm up for what was to come. She handed us our coffee and we each grabbed a chair around the table and settled in.

"I think the best way to start is to first see, Jade, what your understanding is, so we know where to pick-up. I know that both of you," referring to Barry and Nonnie, "have shared Diana's history and how Lilly and the others came to be." She turned to me. "So, if you don't mind just jumping in...," and she said this with much kindness, "Can you explain what you understand the situation to be?" Everyone was looking at me. Any other time, this would have unnerved me. But looking over at Barry, with his not quite-hidden sadness and Nonnie, with a face full of hope, I felt fine.

"Of course." I began. "Well, Nonnie and Barry filled me in on how Diana's final break gave birth to Lilly and some others. I don't know how many and who they were. Just that there were others. I understand Diana had a difficult childhood and that this is understating it. She experienced repeated horrific abuse, both by her father and in the foster system. Apparently, there were early signs, but they weren't recognized for what they were. I know how she eventually found Poppie. And then Nonnie. And then Barry. I know about the miscarriages before finally having Hope. And I know about the day that Hope was murdered and the week following when Diana left and Lilly came in her place. And then the others. I understand that these personalities all emerged to kind of protect Diana. And I know that you both have helped Diana absorb, or integrate the other personalities, but Lilly is still here. And for some reason, Lilly has connected with me and maybe, hopefully, there is something I can do to help." I stopped. I wasn't sure if they wanted a more detailed account or if I overshared.

"Well. I would say you have a pretty good handle on the situation. Everything you've said is correct. And it seems you are pretty comfortable with such a unique situation. Many wouldn't be." Dr. Leslie seemed impressed.

"You know the ranch," I said. "How can you not be?" Nonnie smiled at this.

"Very True. The ranch is amazing. I wish every client had the support system that Diana has. She has much to return to. OK," she said, as if to officially open the next round of talks. "Dr. J. and I are going to try to explain how we fit in all of this. Interrupt whenever you need. Questions? Clarification? Comments?" She waited for a second to see if I had any yet. I had a bunch, but I wanted to wait to see what they answered, first. She continued, "Because Dissociative Identity Disorder is so unique and it's treatment so multi-faceted, I don't want to bog you down with clinical, so we'll try to explain in simple terms. For example, you referred to the other personalities that were absorbed or integrated. These terms are both used, depending on schools of thought. Some doctors believe that the personalities are not really absorbed by the host. The host being Diana. But more that they become a part of her. The DID community has some differences of opinion on the exact process. But my point is, you are right. The other personalities are somehow controlled, integrated, absorbed. Whatever philosophy you support, the common goal is getting the host to regain control. So, we'll give you the 'nutshell' version, just to give you an idea of what's been happening. OK?" I nodded, ready to hear how they got here and, hopefully, where to next.

"When I first met Diana almost five years ago, she had four alters. Later, two more emerged. The four that were present were not obvious until the family looked backwards and could recall glimpses of things that were unexplainable. Notes in different handwriting, memory loss or Diana eating a food that she never liked. We have a list of things like that. Mysterious purchases or a sudden and short-lived desire to learn how to salsa. It actually goes further back, to her childhood, when the DID first manifested. What her father and her foster families took as unruly or rebellious behavior may have been alters that were protecting Diana. We probably will never know the full history of Diana's disorder. We do know that it usually presents itself in childhood and since her birth father and foster families were not that forthright with information, we are guessing that as a child, there were symptoms that went unnoticed."

It took the doctors 72 minutes to go from Lilly's emergence to this very morning. Dr. Leslie and Dr. J. took turns. A few questions and clarifications came up, but mostly they talked. They told me about the other personalities. The first to emerge, and seemingly the last to leave, was Lilly. They feel the fact that she is 12, the age when Diana met Poppie, is significant. After Lilly came Shannon, the mother of the group. Nurturing, attentive and caring. Then we met Simone, the promiscuous one. Asking for it meant that she wasn't the victim. She was the one in control. She was a problem. They had to make contracts with her to keep her out of trouble. This, I was told, was part of therapy. Negotiations among alters. But they each had their own unique purpose. Desiree was 40-ish and loved to socialize. She talked all the time, apparently. Then came Daniel. He was like an 18-year-old brother to Diana. Also, the son her father never had. He was a protector. All boy. Busy and physical. Baby Hannah followed. She was childlike and always very timid. Last was Jonah. He was a kind young man who was sort of a helper. He liked to please. Each alter was a piece of Diana's puzzle. And they spoke about them as though they were other people who had come and gone over the last five years. Some stayed for a while and others only visited. Multiples can push every therapeutic boundary that there is, but they had gotten through a great deal. Aside from Lilly, they thought that all of the other personalities had been integrated, although Daniel and Shannon have both come and left again. Nonnie took out an envelope and showed me pictures of Diana when she had transitioned to these alters. They were striking. Each picture was of Lilly, or Diana, but it wasn't. Each had their own essence. It was bizarre.

The doctors explained that they used a variety of therapeutic techniques to treat Diana. First was the diagnosis. After the first week, everyone agreed that Diana was suffering from more than a psychotic break. Each personality has their own characteristics and, in hindsight, the signs were there. But they were too subtle to reveal what was coming. Usually, the host leaves after severe repeated abusive exposure. Although the cracks began in childhood, Diana didn't completely retreat until she lost Hope and her sense of stability and safety. She was not a risk to herself or others, so she was released to Barry and they began intensive therapy.

The first step was assessing the situation and gaining trust. It's very difficult to build trust. The alters may test and try to trip up the therapist. Boundaries need to be set. It takes time. And after trust, come more alters. They sometimes competed for time. In most DID cases, about half of the alters come out during therapy. This can also help make them aware of each other. There are still tests here and there, but with time, a relationship is established and with hypnosis, psychotherapy and group counseling, progress occurs. The doctors explained why they try to stay away from pharmaceutical treatment. They believed it can hurt one alter while helping another. And it is hard to regulate with alters. So they continue hypnosis and therapy. And until now they have had slow steady progress. But a year or so ago was no different than last month. Lately, they've hit a plateau. And then I came. From the moment I arrived, they told me, Lilly's been different. She's been happier and sadder. She has been more flighty and more reflective. She daydreams more. This was the only Lilly I knew. But they were telling me that my arrival prompted some of this. Lilly also told them that I was her best friend. Everybody agreed that this was because I was one of the few that had never known Diana. I had become her friend, as opposed to Diana's. I guess Huey was on the right track. But the doctors felt there was something more. Lilly worried about me. The doctors told me that Lilly worried about where I would go, would I forget her, would I be happy? Apparently, Lilly gave me a great deal of thought. They thought that this was good and meant something, but really, were not entirely sure what it was. I looked over at Barry. He still had a sad look of resignation on his face. And he was twisting his wedding ring around his finger, something he always did when he thought about Diana. I wondered, to myself, if he knew that he did that. Considering that other alters had integrated, slowly, but steadily, over the years, everyone believed that it was just a matter of time before Lilly left and Diana returned. And the doctors had faith that this would happen, too. They just weren't sure how I fit in. They asked me if I had any questions. I did. While I asked my questions, Nonnie had some fruit salad. Barry just listened.

Q. Why do you think I can help?

A. For some reason, most likely because you hit it off so well and you didn't know Diana, so there was no competing against her memory, Lilly attached to you. And lately, she has been thinking about her mortality, significantly more than usual. Specifically,

Diana's return. You and her reflections may or may not be related. We really don't know for sure.

Q. So where do I come in?

A. We mostly want you to continue what you are doing. Stick around for a few weeks or more, until we see where this is going. Be Lilly's friend, confidant, playmate. We want you to keep us informed of anything out of the ordinary. And yes, I know how that sounds, but I'm sure you know what I mean. And by the way, you come up in group and Lilly is not your only fan. From what I have heard of you and now that I have met you, I can understand why Lilly has connected. Jade, you are a kind soul who has walked into a situation that most would walk away from. That speaks volumes. We would also like for you to start coming to our group sessions. We realize that you have places to go, but your giving us a little more time, we believe, just may prove helpful.

They all were, clearly, waiting for an answer. They didn't wait long.

"That's all? Just stay and keep doing what I'm already doing?"

"And join us for group," added Dr. J.. It was Nonnie's voice I heard next.

"Child, could you put off your travels a bit longer for us? I know this is a lot to ask. But sweetheart, we have all become quite fond of you and would be so happy if you didn't leave just yet." Her face was more serious than I was used to. I looked over to Barry.

"I know it's a lot. And we have already asked far too much of you. Jade, you don't owe us anything. If you can't stay, we would understand. But please know that the ranch is your home for as long as you want it. It's your call." I could see a hint of worry in his face, but he spoke sincerely and didn't want to pressure me.

"Of course I will stay. I have become quite fond of all of you, too. I was worried you were going to ask me to do something I couldn't," I was relieved. Looking at the four around me, I knew I wasn't alone. We chatted, confirmed an appointment for group next week and snacked for just a little while longer. Even Barry had some fruit.

❧ ❧ ❧

"Poppie's going to be so happy. Let's stop at the co-op and get a few pies for dessert." Nonnie was happy too. We were on our way back to the ranch, but Barry made a detour so Nonnie could get her pies. She insisted we all go in so we could each pick one. Barry picked Dutch apple. I picked a berry cobbler and Nonnie picked lemon meringue.

"Poppie loves lemon meringue. And so does Lilly. This is so nice. Don't they just smell so delicious?" Nonnie smelled hers. So I smelled mine. She was right. We paid for our pies and headed back to the ranch.

"Now Jade, I think when we get back, it might be nice if you took Poppie a piece of this pie and you could tell him the good news. What do you think, child?"

"Sounds good to me, Nonnie."

"I'll explain to Lilly. She will be very happy that you are sticking around. And she was excited about you meeting the doctors. I'm sure she will come find you."

"I'm sure she will," I agreed. There were a few seconds of quiet before Barry spoke again.

"Jade, I'm trying not to put too much into this, but I see something too. And I just want you to know I appreciate your being here to help us. Whatever happens, I'm glad I found you that day."

"Thanks, Barry, I..." Nonnie interrupted.

"Well, of course you found Jade. The Lord put you on Barry's path. You are his gift to us." This was a declaration, not part of a discussion. We pulled up to the Big House and Barry helped Nonnie out of the truck, while I grabbed the pies. We could hear chatter outside, but the house was empty. We put the pies in the refrigerator, minus one slice for Poppie that I was going to take to him. I went out the back porch.

"Hi, Jade. Whatcha doing?" Lilly called from the group with Huey. I guess he had gotten an early start on the afterschool class. "Is that pie?" she asked. Then she added, "Looks like my favorite." Nonnie knew her baby well.

"I'm gonna go see Poppie. I'll come find you later. K.? Hi, Huey," I hollered their way.

"Hi, Jade."

"'K. Come find me when you're done. I wanna hear how you liked my doctors."

"They're great. We'll talk more after my visit. Have fun." I took the path to the family house.

"Hi, Poppie. It's Jade. Want some company?" I hollered.

"Now, how did you know sweet girl? Come on back." I went to his room and walked over to the side of his bed.

"I brought you a surprise. Nonnie said you would like it." I took the napkin off the pie so he could see what it was. His face lit up.

"That Mary sure does know her man. That's my favorite. Always has been. Where is your piece?"

"I'm going to wait till dessert. Do you want yours now?"

"Sure do. I love dessert as an appetizer. Thank you, child. Now, come sit." He raised the upper part of his bed so he was sitting. He was listening to music, like most days. Rarely had I come to visit when he wasn't listening to music, resting or reading. He didn't have a TV in his room. He told me before that if anything important happened then someone would tell him. Otherwise, music trumped TV. He was a little stronger today so I handed him the plate and fork. He took a bite and made a face like he was in heaven. His eyes closed and he rolled his head a bit as he savored the flavor. "You know why I always love this pie?" he asked.

"Nope. I have no idea, Poppie."

"Well, then I'm gonna tell you. It's sweet, it's sour, it's refreshing and yellow. This lemon pie makes me happy. That's why I love it. It's happy pie." He took another bite and got lost again. "So tell me, sweetheart, how did your visit with the doctors go? Aren't those two ladies something special?" He kept eating his pie, which left an opening for me to answer.

"It went pretty good. I like the doctors. Both of them. They explained and kind of filled in the gaps. I knew some stuff, but not all of it. And they explained how my being here has affected Lilly in some way. So they asked if I could stick around to see how. So I guess I'm staying for a bit longer if that's alright."

Poppie was smiling.

"Well, that makes me as happy as this lemon pie." He took my hand. His skin was soft and cool. "Child, I believe you and Lilly got something going, too. Something that's gonna lead to something else. Plus, we all love having you here. You won us over pretty quick!" He patted my hand. "This is a very good day. I think we should put on some special music." And so he did. We listened to soft jazz horns while we talked about what I had learned from the doctors. I explained that I still didn't understand why I had an effect on Lilly. He told me I had an effect on everyone. Poppie was a bit of a charmer.

"Now, I'm serious baby. You got something good and strong and special inside of you. And it's bigger than you know. And it's growing here. You just never had a place to let it out. But it's in you, baby. It's in you." He patted my hand again and then resettled himself in the bed.

"So the docs told you about the others?"

"Yep. All of them."

"That Daniel, what did they say about him?" I thought about it for a second.

"He was the brother-like alter. The protective one, right?"

"Yep. That Daniel was my favorite. I didn't care much for that Simone. She was trouble. And Jonah, well he was very handy to have around, although I didn't really understand why he was here. But that Daniel." Poppie closed his eyes as if he were conjuring the sight of him. He opened his eyes again and smiled. "He was cool and confident. Energetic and in your face. He was clever and witty and watched over Lilly and Diana fiercely. He was either being a teenage boy or a protector. The first time he came, he was around long enough to make himself known. He made sure all was in good hands and then he left. He was at the ranch less than a couple weeks. The shortest stay for any of Diana's alters. But he came back."

"When did he come back?" Poppie lost his smile. He waited a minute before answering.

"One day Lilly was at the farmers market with some of the ranchers. She heard a voice. A man's voice and he said something like "This won't hurt or I won't hurt you" or something like that. Well, I guess it sounded too much like the monster who took Hope, so Lilly retreated. I guess she had to leave for a while. Daniel came in her place. I think it was too much for even my part-time Lilly. Daniel was covering for her. But I do miss that boy sometimes. He was a good boy."

Poppie and I chatted for a little while longer, engaging in a conversation that just seemed natural, but if anyone heard us, they would think it was not. We listened to the music in the background. It was nice. Even though Poppie seemed more comfortable and had more energy, after a bit he asked for a little time for a nap. I hugged him goodbye and he whispered in my ear, as he often did, "I'm so glad you are staying. Thank you."

I whispered back in his. "Me too." I left Poppie and went to find Lilly. It didn't take long. She was in the Big House waiting for me. She jumped up when I walked in. She ran over and hugged me tightly. A sloppy 12-year-old hug, that I had to stand on my toes to get!

"Nonnie told me the news. I'm so glad you are staying longer. And you're gonna love group. It's like a giant visiting session. Except the docs get to lead the visit. You'll see."

"We're glad too." Coco, Jack, Reesa and Tawn came from the kitchen. The girls had smiles on their faces and it made me feel good.

"Who's happy Jade is staying?" yelled out Coco. Jack yelled out, "I am." And Tawn yelled out "Tawn is!" I bent down and opened my arms and they ran into them for their tickles.

"Jade, wanna help me set the tables? We have extras for dinner tonight and everyone is home. We set both tables and then went to help in the kitchen. It was a full crowd tonight. We set 22 places; the biggest dinner since I had been at the ranch.

After another 20 minutes, everyone started coming up to the Big House. Introductions were made. Xavier came with his wife, Tina, and their kids. Serita ran up to me and gave me a cozy hug like she had known me for years. It was nice to see Xavier again. We hugged like we were old friends. Tina was a tall beautiful and sweet woman, who looked to be around her mid-30s. She hugged me and told me that she had heard all about me from the kids. Michael came over with Annie and P.S. The girls were already picking out their spots to sit at the table. It was kind of nice to have a full house. It was noisy and comfortable. Everyone helped bring out platters and bowls and baskets filled with food. Throughout dinner, our conversations mixed and mingled and crossed over table to table. And everyone told me how glad that they were that I had decided to stick around. I learned that, if one rancher knew something important, it would not be long before all the ranchers knew.

"This must be special for Nonnie to make her forbidden rice and roasted balsamic Brussels sprouts. That's one of Nonnie's happy meals." Coco teased. Dinner truly was tasty. And then Nonnie brought out the pies, which made everyone almost as happy as Lilly.

Before settling in, I called Deb and explained the situation. While she was disappointed, she understood. I went to bed that night feeling full bellied, safe and wanted. My mind wondered to Dean, as it did most nights. Tonight it was a bit easier to redirect my thoughts. I stopped thinking about Dean and thought about my day. Right before I fell asleep, I remember thinking that the thought of him stung a bit less.

Day 13: Side Effects May Include... a Sore @ss.

Today was a great day. Another of many firsts. This one included a handsome cowboy and a horse named Nesta…

Waking early at the ranch had its perks. It was full of fresh smells and colorful sights and eclectic sounds. I began to look forward to waking up. The morning brought more clarity, for some reason. With this clarity, I realized that I had quietly embraced disappointment and regret for so long that contentment felt different. So different that I didn't recognize it at first. But I was becoming used to it and, it grew to be very cozy. Before the ranch, quiet was painful. But, now, the morning quiet was perfect. It wasn't silence. It was just quiet. At some point, I noticed that contentment was slowly replacing disappointment. I still hit speed bumps. A reminder of some kind or a memory jogged. But for the most part, I could feel the holes in me filling.

I was especially looking forward to this day because Kelly and I were going to ride horses with Maya. Lilly was at therapy and Maya had invited us the day before. I was excited. I was a big city girl and had never been on a horse before. So I went to the Big House, had my coffee with Kelly, and off we went. On the walk over, She gave me riding tips.

When we arrived at Maya and Charlie's property, Maya was already getting the horses ready. She had her ranch hand with her to help saddle the horses. He was beautiful and looked like he came straight out of a Western movie, minus the chaps and chewing tobacco. He wore a big brown cowboy hat that sat on top of a mop of rich brown wavy hair. A typical Western leather belt separated his snug faded blue jeans from his snap down shirt with rolled up sleeves. His boots were worn and dusty.

"Cisco," he said as he put out his hand to shake mine. I took his hand and probably shook it a little too long.

"Excuse me?"

"Cisco. My name is Cisco."

"Of course it is," was what came out of my mouth. Or at least I thought it did. I might have lucked out and only thought it in my head.

"No, really. I was born Francisco Anthony. Folks just call me Cisco.". I guess I did say it out loud.

"Oh," I said, trying not to pay too much attention to the beautiful mouth that was saying the words.

"Jade," I said. "Just Jade."

"Nice to meet you, Just Jade." He grinned. And that was it. His grin was officially his best feature. I knew I would never think of cowboys the same. That he caught my eye was encouraging. I wasn't nearly ready for something else, but at least I noticed. It hit me that noticing would eventually lead to wanting. That was too big of a thought so I shoved it out of the way.

He asked if I had ever ridden before and I told him that I hadn't.

"Then you get Nesta. He's the tamest of the group. He'll take good care of you." I was hoping by "tame" he meant autopilot. He saddled Nesta, helped me up and then adjusted the stirrups to fit better. Kelly hopped up on Diego and Maya took Sedona, her own horse. After Maya gave me directions, which sounded very similar to Kelly's, we started walking our horses out of the corral towards the mountain a mile or so north of the ranch. Maya was excited to ride with a first-timer. She led the way. I was in the middle and Kelly followed. There were trails already there, I imagined from past riding adventures, so we followed them through the brush and cacti for about five minutes. Our horses began in single file until we got out to more open space. While we walked, Maya gave me more pointers. We stopped at the opening to an open field.

"Are you ready for your first ride?" asked Maya.

"Sure," I said. But in my head, I really meant "No." She told me to hold on to the saddle horn to start and could change to the reins when I was more used to the running. With that, Maya took off and our horses followed.

To start, if I'm being honest, I was holding on for dear life. We ran through the field, Kelly and I following Maya. It was a rush to hear the thump of the hooves, which itself was magnificent, but you ride it like a wave. Trees rush past. Just like that and you are even further away, so fast it was windy. It amazed me that the horses could see where best to run and maneuver so gracefully. We rode long enough to give up my 'white knuckle' status and then stopped for lunch near a creek. The horses could drink and nibble on the plants. There was a makeshift campfire pit that looked like it was a few weeks old, at least. Maya explained that about once or twice a year she, Cisco or Charlie found makeshift campgrounds around the creek. She explained that people didn't understand that it was private property, but as long as they cleaned up, she and Charlie decided against fencing off or posting signs.

We visited for just a little while longer before we got back on our horses and ran the long way home. It was a rush just galloping until we could see the corral again. We slowed to a walk for the horses to cool down. Cisco was waiting for us when we approached the corral.

"How'd it go, girls?" He helped me off Nesta as I gushed about our ride. I started to walk away, but my legs felt wobbly. Cisco noticed and called out that I would adjust in a few minutes. We went inside Maya's home and all sat for a bit over beers and hot wings. It was the perfect end to a new morning. Soon after, Kelly and I headed back to the Lost and Found.

When I got up, I felt it. With each movement, I could feel it. A kind of ache that was new to me. Maya and Kelly giggled as they watched me hobble. My legs ached as I stood, my butt hurt as I moved and my thighs burned, I guessed from gripping the saddle with my legs. Each movement I made was only because my body had practiced it so many times, every day of my life. Standing, walking, moving forward. As Kelly and I got closer to the ranch, the pain began to subside, but my butt still hurt just as much as it did at Maya's. I asked Kelly to offer my apologies to everyone at the Big House. I thought a hot bath might help.

I walked back to my casita and walked into the house just as my mother called. I debated answering the phone but thought it better to get it over with. I was surprised. We actually talked. It was odd. And nice. But odd. I think some of Nonnie's lessons were sinking in. I applied the 'pick your battles' principal, so I didn't react to her jabs. I am pretty sure I used the 'redirection' maneuver to neutralize her. And then I closed with a little 'tell me about you' punch that wrapped it up quite well. We had a civil chat. Well, as civil as we could be. But in the end, we caught up and it didn't ruin my day. I lay for while in a hot bath before heading up to the Big House. It didn't help. My butt still hurt.

As I approached the door, I heard unfamiliar voices. I walked in and saw a young man and woman visiting with Nonnie on the couch. They looked just a little older than me.

"Hello, baby. Did you have a nice ride?"

"Yes, Nonnie. I used muscles that I didn't even know I had. It wore me out, but it was a blast. I'm sorry, but I have to sit down, I think." I sat a little too fast and I think I let out a moan but wasn't sure. Our guests smiled at me, knowingly.

"Sore butt?" asked the man.

"Sore butt," I confirmed.

"Jade, I'd like you to meet Ben and Sari. They are good friends of the ranch. We know them through Coco. They are joining us for dinner tonight." Sari had dirty blond, shoulder-length hair, a soft and simple beauty with dimples, and Ben had long brown loose curls framing his short beard and kind eyes behind thick glasses.

"Nice to meet you both." I began to get up to shake their hands. They stopped me.

"Jade, please... just sit. It's very nice to meet you. Nonnie has told us a lot about you." Sari had a sweet, calm voice. I sat back down.

"So we hear you went riding at Maya's. Do you ride much?" asked Ben.

"Nope. First timer, which explains the sore butt, I guess."

We sat and visited a little bit before we all followed Nonnie into the kitchen to help fix dinner. We made glazed salmon with some great sides. Nonnie had a simple, but healthy and delicious food repertoire. Everyone started trickling in and soon we were all eating and visiting, catching each other up on our days. Lilly asked to sit by me since we didn't spend time together today. She asked me what seemed like 100 questions about riding at Maya's. After another question Nonnie interrupted her.

"Hush, baby. You gotta let Jade eat her dinner. She needs some food in her belly or she is gonna shrink to nothing."

Sunshine and Will filled us in about their work at the center. Reesa and Tawn had gone to the Desert Museum with Coco and Jack. Barry had taken Lilly to spend some time with the doctors. Kelly and Lloyd went into town after riding to get supplies for the greenhouse. All things considered, it was another good day for all. Except my butt.

After dinner cleanup, Jade and Coco brought out dessert. Carrot cake and a cinnamon apple iced braid was a great way to finish the day.

Lilly was saying her goodbyes after dinner. She was off to have a "slumbover" with P.S. They did this about once a month. P.S. calls it a slumber party and Lilly calls it a sleepover and because the two of them get competitive, the "slumbover" was born. P.S. had the next day off for school parent-teacher conferences. Lilly invited me, but I bowed out, telling them that I might another time. After all the goodbyes and hugs, Coco, Reesa, Kelly, Nonnie and I had tea while planning out tomorrow.

"That was good to skip the slumbover. It's fun, but you leave with parting gifts like painted nails and crimped hair," Nonnie said with one of her beautiful smiles. "They would keep you up all night primping on you and telling stories and playing games." She shook her head slightly with a smile. "Tomorrow, I'd like to go through the pantry and jarred foods. I think we need to organize and take an inventory of what we need for the animals and gardens. For some reason, things seem off schedule. Let's talk about it in the morning." I helped clean up with Coco before heading off to bed.

Day 14: Angry Nonnie... Just kidding!

Nonnie had a little talking to with Reesa, Kelly and Coco.
This was the angriest I had seen her and it sounded something like,
"Now, sweet girls, I know we can do better."...

Nonnie was sitting at the kitchen counter with Coco, Reesa, Kelly and me, having our coffee and planning out our morning. She told us that the doctors were coming for an informal quick group later in the day. They wanted to update the ranchers about my involvement and just check in with them. Nonnie explained that the doctors came to the house once or twice a month in a relaxed setting for group therapy. They also wanted to see Poppie. Nonnie asked if I could keep Lilly busy when they had group. Possibly P.S., too, if Michael and Annie made it over in time. I would start with the next one. Class was canceled with Huey since he always came to group. Every once in a while they liked having a session without Lilly there, for obvious reasons. I, of course, agreed. I was more than sure that we could keep busy for an hour or so.

"What time are they coming, Nonnie?" Kelly asked.

"I think around 3:30. But we have a few things to do first." Nonnie dove right in. She had a list. Reesa, Kelly and Coco looked at each other. They didn't seem to like that Nonnie had a list. It wasn't often that she did, but it usually came with some kind of firm explanation.

Apparently, Nonnie was a list person. She felt they were essential at times. I guess this was one of those. So Nonnie presented a list with areas of "concern" that she needed either clarified or remedied. And by each point on the list was the name of the one responsible for that item. And so she let Coco, Reesa and Kelly look at her list while Nonnie and I grabbed another cup of coffee. She whispered to me that soon the bickering would begin. I looked at her, surprised and she gave me a small knowing smile. We sat and waited, but not for too long. Apparently, the list looked like this:

1. mason jars ordered for next jarring day - Coco

2. next three dates for farmers market- not set on calendar - Kelly

3. low on dog food and not put on list/check other animal supplies - Reesa (Barry shops/Reesa - lists)

4. low on ink and last cartridge is in printer - Coco

5. filters changed in casitas and big house - Coco

6. schedule oil change on the van - Kelly

7. craft closet mess - Reesa

8. schedule Shasta and Pima shots – Reesa

A combo pep talk and kind scolding accompanied the list. Nonnie reminded them that things were getting a little sloppy around here and she wanted to reign it in before it got more chaotic. She knew there was much to be done and with things always changing, this was not the worst thing. After the girls looked at the list, sure enough, the bickering began.

"Reesa, you told me we had enough mason jars left from last time. That we didn't need to order more for now."

"That was before we had Jade and now we are getting more produce ready."

"Then you shoulda said something," Coco countered.

"And I can't know the dates if you aren't sure what we are going to have. Fresh stuff or jarred? The market depends on the product. You guys know that," Kelly chimed in.

Soon they were all talking over each other. Loudly. I looked at Nonnie. She took a sip of coffee and watched. I took her lead. After about 15 minutes one of them proclaimed that they were not getting anywhere. They took turns talking, but still blaming and excusing. After a few more minutes, one of them reminded the others that they still weren't getting anywhere. Then, they began strategizing. And soon they had a plan.

"I knew you girls could figure this out and help with my worries. You always do." Nonnie gave them a half smile, half grin. They knew they were being guided to the right answers, ever so subtly... again. "Now you three can go get started on your plan while Jade and I visit and plan our dinner." All three went their separate ways. You would never know that words were yelled and blame was thrown around. I looked at Nonnie, clearly with some astonishment on my face.

"This is the way it always happens. Every once in a while things get behind and I bring it to whomever's attention it deserves and they all fight their way to the right answer. But they always get it done with no ill will. They find their way. That's what we do here. Every day, we find our way."

A week or so ago, I would have asked her about what she meant. But, today I understood. The ranch was far from perfect. Although, compared to what I left behind, it seemed so. But it wasn't. Miscommunications happened. Bickering took place. Jobs slipped through the cracks. Kind of like real life. But they found their way, just like the rest of the world outside the ranch. The ranchers just had to be more flexible and collaborative to get it all done.

"So, my dear, what should we have for dinner? It will be a full table," she wondered out loud, more than asked. I waited while I watched her think. "Maybe we will just make it easy and make a big "chunky" salad with a big batch of rigatoni and meatballs. What do you think, Jade?" she asked. "Oh, and maybe some garlic bread knots. Everyone always likes those."

"Sounds good to me. And easy. We can make it all now and cook what we need to before dinner." Nonnie agreed. So while Reesa, Coco and Kelly went to take care of their tasks, Nonnie and I headed to the kitchen and got out ingredients for dinner. I watched as she got out the pasta, ground beef, fixings for the sauce (including some of the last jars of tomato sauce: hence #1 on Nonnie's list) and then put on her apron. I got out the veggies for the salad and two big bowls. I was learning that a big crowd required two of the big stuff, one for each table. It felt kind of good to know what I was doing.

We were just getting to work when the girls walked in. Sure enough, they had painted fingernails, with cute heart and rainbow decals. They asked what was up and Nonnie filled them in. She gave them an assignment of spreading the word around the ranch that a short special group was this afternoon at 4:00. After that, they were to return for their homework assignments. This, of course, was met with groans.

"You poor girls. Do I need to remind you that there are countries where girls are not allowed to learn?" Nonnie did not preach this or say it with any judgment. "If I were a mean teacher, I would give you that assignment again, so it's a good thing your Nonnie isn't mean." She winked at them and they winked back. A signal that they got her point. It took all of five minutes for them to run around and announce the afternoon plan. I had barely got out the cutting board and rinsed the vegetables before they were back for their assignment.

"I want the two of you to do a little research on the history of haiku and then write a few to show us when you finish." They looked at her, waiting for further instructions. Nonnie waited too. After half a minute of silence, Nonnie asked if they had any questions.

"What's a haiku?" Lilly asked.

"I think it's a kind of a poem," offered P.S. Nonnie answered them.

"That's right, sweetheart. It is. Now if you both go research what it is, then you can write some for Jade and I. In fact, they are so much fun to write that I would like three each. One silly one. One serious one. And one of your own choice."

They looked at each other with slight dread.

"Don't give me that look. If you don't know what a haiku is, then you don't know if you like them or not. Now, you girls go and find out. You just might love it. You never know." She gave them a gentle smile. "We'll see you later." And with that, they left to go discover the world of haiku.

Nonnie and I got to work, too. I began on the salad while Nonnie began on the meatballs. After I finished, I helped Nonnie. Just as we were cleaning up, the girls ran in, ready to share their research. They were quite enthusiastic and you could tell that they were proud of their work.

They explained what a haiku was and its history. Then they shared their poems. Nonnie and I complimented them on their creative pieces and posted them on the refrigerator, after asking the girls' permission. They seemed quite pleased that Nonnie thought they were "frig worthy." Nonnie was going to make the garlic knots with the girls, so she encouraged me to go and see if Poppie was up for a visit.

I knocked on the door and announced my arrival like I always did. I could hear Poppie call out faintly from his room. I went in to find him both happy to see me (smiling his big smile and gesturing for me to come closer) and also uncomfortable with his breathing (not sitting or speaking well and a faint rattle in his chest).

"I didn't know you weren't feeling very well today, Poppie. Can I get you anything?" I was worried. His voice was raspy when he answered.

"I'm not sick. I have good days and bad. This just isn't a good one." He smiled at me.

"Maybe you should rest. I can come see you..."

He interrupted. "No. Please, I want you to stay. Maybe we can just sit and listen to some music." I think he was bored and growing tired of these walls. He hadn't been outside for a while.

"Of course, I'll stay." I pulled the chair up to his bed and sat. I leaned over and reached for his hand to hold. Before I could connect with him, he reached up and held his hand to my cheek. He didn't move it. He just held it there for five seconds or minutes. I'm not sure. It felt so good I could only close my eyes and feel his hand. His raspy voice broke the silence.

"Let's listen to some jazz again today. Is that alright?" So that is what we did. We held hands and listened to jazz. A little Dave Brubeck, Pat Metheny and Chris Botti. After almost an hour, I told Poppie that I would be by tomorrow or the day after. I hugged him goodbye. He hugged back, but today's hug was a little smaller than the last. I hoped Poppie was right and he was just having an off day.

I went outside to find Huey and Lilly training with Shasta. I couldn't believe the tricks that he knew. Pima knew tricks too, but Shasta was the master. Lilly explained that cheese crackers work best. He loved cheese crackers so much that he could now speak, sit, fetch, play Frisbee and play dead. And he did other, non-doggie tricks. He sat up straight if you told him not to slouch. He told you a story if you asked him to. He barked, ever so quietly, when you told him to whisper. They were working on a new trick. He was learning to "sing." After we played and trained for another 15 minutes, 20 or so crackers and a whole bunch of enthusiastic "Good Boys", he was batting two out of three. All of the dogs at the ranch knew tricks, but none of them knew as many as Shasta. He stopped "singing" when the doctors arrived. Shasta and Pima alerted us by running to greet their car.

We all met up in the Big House. It was nice to see the doctors again. They both gave me hugs, just like they gave everyone. After a few minutes, I took Lilly and P.S. and we left them to their meeting.

The three of us voted between writing more haikus (my idea) and playing games (the girls' idea) and, not surprisingly, I lost.

I was relieved, but the girls were not, an hour later when the dinner bell rang. I was hungry and tired from a marathon of Chinese jump rope, jacks (I was stuck on foursies), and a few rounds of hopscotch. But now it was time to wash, sit, eat and visit. And so we did. I guess the meeting was fruitful, as the dinner conversation revolved around daily stuff, and not anything serious. Then came cleanup and goodnights. Almost everyone was tired. I think the last few days were catching up to me emotionally. So most of us headed back to our own beds, rather than hang out. Coco and I chatted while we walked back to our casitas.

"So, it looks like you've found your place at the ranch?"

"It's really amazing. And I'm learning so much. You all have made such a great place and the ranchers are all so interesting. Everyone here has a story, but I didn't know that everyone's was so different. Some are tragic, some are not. Some are complex, some more simple. Kind of puts things in perspective. Makes my story seem normal and small."

"Yeah." Coco was thinking about my words. "Some of the stories are more dramatic than others. But it's how the stories end that counts." I looked at her quizzically. And then she elaborated on her own story, as we sat on the bench that rested at the intersection of our paths.

Coco wasn't exactly one of Diana's fosters, although she just might well have been. Her best friend, Shari, was and this meant that Coco spent much of her time at Barry and Diana's. This was fine with Diana. She preferred for her "kids" to have friends at their house, as opposed to having them go elsewhere. And Diana loved Coco. She knew she came from a loud, often absent, drunk father and a quiet, meek mother, who had trouble standing up to her husband. This left Coco without decent role models. Despite this, Coco was full of life. Diana told Coco that she thought she had a hunger for life because she was starved as a child. Not literally, but spiritually and emotionally. She was left alone and neglected too often and so she craved company and attention and connection. All of which Diana and Barry provided. Coco explained that they accepted her unconditionally. While others told Coco that she was a beautiful girl, but if she lost a few pounds she would be even prettier, Diana and Barry encouraged Coco to love herself, curves and all. Others told her that if she wore more feminine clothing that she might find a nice boyfriend. Diana would take her shopping and let her buy whatever boxy t-shirt and plain jeans she wanted. Barry got her an afterschool job as an assistant to a photographer friend. She soaked up photography like a sponge. She took to it so fast that she went from being an assistant to handling her own jobs before a year was up. She had developed her own photographic genre and word spread that she had a unique style. Life was good for Coco, but after Shari graduated and moved to Flagstaff for college, Coco went into a funk. Eventually Thomas, a boy five years older than Coco, took Shari's place, much to Diana and Barry's dismay. Coco's own parents may not have noticed, but Barry and Diana knew that Thomas was not good for her. Slowly, Coco began missing work days here and there and eventually she got more interested in drugs than photography and more interested in sex than school. She barely managed to graduate, and only because Diana was so involved. She didn't know that she was pregnant when she got her diploma and when she realized it at three months, Thomas moved on to someone else. This threw Coco into a tailspin that led to Amy. Coco fell hard for her. Amy gave her a reason to stay clean. She called Amy proof that love at first sight was real. But it actually wasn't. Amy stayed long enough for Jack to be born before she realized that she didn't really love Coco enough to be a mom with her. When Amy left, Coco fell. She fell straight into a drug binge and barely made it out. The family got her through this. They took care of baby Jack while Coco fought her demons in treatment. Coco told me it was her darkest time and that Jack was her reward for coming out of the darkness. And right after, Hope was killed. And it was Coco's turn to take care of Diana.

As I got ready for bed, my mind began to fill. It conjured up scorpions, puppies, dirty sunsets and a roadrunner named Freddie. And eventually, I thought about everyone's stories. While they were mostly sad beginnings, it was the sadness that brought them to Barry and Diana. Coco was right. It's how the story ends that counts.

Days 15-16 - Because Sometimes You Just Have to Have Some Mango Slices.

Sprinkled with Chili Powder.
Who could have known that Huey met a hitchhiker from Vega!?
But, first, the 4th Avenue Street Fair....

Today was a day off for almost everyone. It was known as "Street Fair Day." Twice a year Tucson hosts a big street fair. Ranch tradition dictated that each spring fair, anyone who wanted could go. So, after a light breakfast ("Save room for the fair food") we filled three cars and headed towards the other side of town. The fair was near the university. The way it had been described, I had expected a giant farmers market, just with more food, more crafts and lots of music. Which it was, except that it was less of a market and more of a... street fair! It was one long, double-sided marketplace down this long street, over four or five blocks that were closed off for the weekend.

Lilly had described it to me with great enthusiasm. And it was Lilly who guided me through the maze of booths and street performers and food vendors. Seeing it through her lens made it that much better.

I had been told to expect some music and a street performance or two. I didn't expect triplet sisters harmonizing acapella pop songs like masters, a mariachi band dressed in red velvet suits trimmed with gold braided piping and a teenage magician who possessed more charm and showmanship than he did magic. I expected cotton candy and kettle corn. I didn't expect an assortment of salsas ranging from sweet and spicy to "blow your ass off." I thought maybe there would be ice cream and corn on the cob. I didn't expect sopapillas, deep fried pickles, or jalapeño cheese breadsticks with a variety of dipping sauces. And I expected the usual variety of crafts: pottery, jewelry, candles and wall hangings. But I didn't know they would be made from ocotillo ribs or recycled ironworks. It was wonderful, bursting with color, smells and sound. The fair included over 70 booths filled with all the food and fashion, lotions and potions, entertainment and creativity that had been promised.

At either end of the fair was a small stage with rotating local musical talent. In between these stages were crafts and products booths back to back so that you could walk a full cycle to see every booth that had a space. Right in the middle of the fair was a bigger stage that also rotated talent. On each side of this stage were food booths with way too many choices and temptations of fantastic smells coming from the tents and booths. We sat at our picnic tables, some of us filling up on mangoes on a stick dipped in spicy chili powder, roasted corn on the cob dripping in chipotle butter or shredded beef tamales. Others indulged in fish tacos, funnel cakes covered with powdered sugar or barbecue pulled pork sandwiches that required a minimum of eight napkins. And while we sat and enjoyed getting tummy aches from too much food, our group was thoroughly entertained, full and happy.

"Did you like the street fair?" Lilly interrupted my thoughts while walking back to the car.

"It was wonderful. Even better than I expected."

"Good. Maybe it will be a memory for you. Nonnie says that memories will keep you company when you are too tired to make more." Then she added, mimicking Nonnie's Southern accent, "That's why we have to make them now, child." I laughed at her Nonnie impression. She laughed too.

"That sounds like something Nonnie would say," I agreed.

When we arrived back at the ranch, filthy, full and a bit wiped out, we all spread out to our own homes to shower before meeting back up in the Big House for a group game and a light dinner, which Nonnie knew was all we would have room for. While we tried to muster up something resembling an appetite, we gathered in the living room to begin our game of Yes/No. Michael, Annie and P.S. had gone to their own house, taking Lilly with them for dinner and Reesa had kept Tawn and Jack back at their casita. They were exhausted from all the walking and dancing. Barry and Lloyd came down to join Coco, Sunshine, Will, Huey, Kelly and me for the end of our fantastic day.

"OK, Jade," Huey began to explain the game since I was the only one who hadn't played before, "this is the one and only rule: Tell the truth or not." He explained that we would rotate around the circle and think of a crazy, unexpected or wild thing that we had done (or not) then we would go around and each cast a vote on whether the player truly had done that before. He gave an example of him saying that he had attempted to catch a rattlesnake. Some quickly answered yes because that would be insane and they thought Huey was part insane, but in a good way. Sunshine, because she thought that even he was not that crazy, voted no. As it turned out, everyone got a point except for Sunshine. Huey had, in fact, attempted to catch a rattlesnake. "So that's the Yes/No game. Any questions, Jade?"

I told them that I thought that I had gotten it, but that it would be better to start across from me so I could get it better by the time it was my turn. And so the night went. Almost every turn gave us opportunity to laugh. By the end of the evening we had learned that Lloyd had, in fact, bungee jumped in Brazil but did not have sex for money. Coco had gone to Space Camp but had not hitchhiked across the US. Sunshine and Will did a triathlon and got arrested for protesting an oil pipeline. Huey had, in fact, picked up a hitchhiker who professed to be from Vega, another planet, but had not posed naked. Kelly really had entered a hot dog eating contest (placing third), but had not – and, I repeat, not – had a threesome with two other girls. I confessed my part in a seventh-grade shoplifting episode but had not really had an encounter with a shark while scuba diving in Mexico.

We laughed so hard that it was hard not to choke on the soup or the cornbread. Between the adventurous day, laughing hysterically and the warm soup, we soon began to fade.

Day 17: Seeds Need Room to Grow. Kind of Like the Rest of Us.

I wish I had Lilly's ability to go from blues to wonder.
It's a gift. And probably a survival mechanism.
If the blues kept her, they might swallow her...

"That's the perfect depth, Jade, but the seeds are too close together. They need at least a foot apart." Coco and I were helping Reesa plant the spring vegetables. She was referring to the zucchini plants.

"Zucchini plants spread out and need lots of room. They need space. Just like the melons." Some of the planting was in the greenhouse. Things like tomatoes and berries. But the bigger crops or the ones that needed deeper roots were planted in the garden. We were equipped with tools, seeds and seedlings and were ready to start our plot for Round 2 of our spring crop.

"Would you girls like a little help?" Nonnie had walked up to the gate to see if she could assist.

"Of course, Nonnie. You know you can dig in anytime," Reesa encouraged her. She seemed a bit surprised, along with Coco, but pleasantly so. She opened the gate for Nonnie and let her in.

"OK. Jade, you come with me and we can start with some of the root vegetables." She took charge. "Grab the onion, carrot and radish seeds and I can show you how it's done. Come with me, child." I abandoned the zucchini seedlings and did as I was told. She had me help her get down on her knees, kneeling on a foam cushion that she had brought with her. She showed me how deep to make the holes, how to make them spaced apart for the seeds to have enough room for each vegetable to grow and how to cover them properly.

Nonnie with dirty hands was different than Nonnie with clean hands. It did not matter if it was cookie dough or potting soil. When her hands were in something, her face changed. I was watching her with her hands in the dirt. She looked relaxed and content. And happy.

"I don't get out here as much as I used to," Nonnie told me. "I really should try harder. Just because it is not easy to make happen doesn't mean one should stop trying," Nonnie said as much to herself as to me. We made garden chitchat.

"What's the fence for?" I asked.

"For the javelina. Or rather it's for the vegetables. Those cute, mean piggies would have a feast. The bunnies too. We would have nothing if we couldn't keep out the critters. And some still climb or break through now and then. We keep the porch plants full, so if they are really hungry or thirsty, they can take those."

"Why keep repotting if they keep eating?"

"Well, sweetheart, they usually have enough to eat in the desert. But when it is really dry, especially before the monsoons, they will go anywhere there is something to help their thirst. I hate to think of them as parched, they are some of God's beautiful creatures." We continued our chat as we planted seeds.

And so it went for another hour or so before it was time for lunch. Nonnie looked sorry to be done for the day, but the bending over, I thought, would not be good for her to continue. I was glad she joined us, but I was also glad to get her upright and mobile. I would help Reesa more after lunch. We still had more to plant. I found that I liked gardening. I never thought I didn't. I just never knew I did.

The guys came in after us. They had just washed up from digging in the front. I think some irrigation lines for later. Coco had already prepared pasta salad and sandwiches and the kids had already started their lunch. Lilly had gone into town with Sunshine. She had taken her to the library earlier to borrow some books. Lately, Lilly had discovered the Encyclopedia Brown mysteries. Nonnie explained to me that Diana had also loved them when she was younger. I had no idea what was significant with Lilly. But the doctors told me to just keep doing what I was doing and to report to them once a week with updates on conversations and activities that stood out. They would be the ones to determine what was important or not. When we walked in Lilly ran up to me, hugged me and told me she missed me. I hugged her back. She was increasingly affectionate.

"After homework, can we play?"

"If I get finished helping Reesa, then for sure, we can play. She was happy with my answer and went back to the table to finish her lunch, sandwiched between Jack and Tawn. After lunch, Lilly went to do homework and we cleaned up before resuming our tasks for the day. I went back to the garden with Reesa while Nonnie went to spend time with Poppie. It didn't take us long to get into a groove together, one of us making holes the other planting and covering. We were done fast, so I went to find Lilly. She was at the Big House on the computer.

"What are you working on?" I asked Lilly, who was looking at the screen intently.

"Working on my homework," she answered without looking up. "I'm working on my 'Place of the Week'. It's Israel. That's in the Middle East," she said knowingly, as she looked up at me. She went on to explain that Nonnie or Poppie gave her a place each week to research. She had to find out where it was, be able to show them on the globe and share with them a few facts regarding the people, geography, customs, food and religions. "They always pick places that are in the news. They tell me it keeps me up to date on what's happening in the world. It's kind of an interesting place. Have you ever been there? Nonnie has. I think that's why she likes hummus so much!"

"Nope, maybe one day." I smiled at her. She seemed so child-like.

"I'm gonna take my notes to Nonnie and see if we can go play now, 'K?"

"Sounds good to me." I waited while Lilly, literally, ran to go find Nonnie and give her homework. She was back within five minutes, happy that she could play now. We went outside and began a jacks and jump rope marathon. As we began playing, Lilly got chatty.

"Moods are such strange things, aren't they Jade?"

"Yes." I wasn't sure where she was going with this, but clearly, Lilly had some reason for bringing up the subject.

"I mean, sometimes, you are in the mood for fun stuff and sometimes not. Why do you think it's that way?"

"I don't know. What do you think?" That was my go-to answer for many of Lilly's questions. "Are you alright?"

"Yeah," she said unconvincingly. She looked around to see if we were alone. She spoke softly now. "Sometimes, I get tired of being Diana." My heart sank. And again, I was left not knowing what to say. So I waited, trying to think of something.

"It's only sometimes," she added when she saw my discomfort. "I know that somebody has to be her. Especially since she doesn't want to be her either." Lilly's eyes held her tears. It was as if she willed them not to fall. I had never seen her like this. And it occurred to me that, under the circumstances, I wondered why she didn't cry more often. I mentally added this to the things I would tell the doctors on our weekly calls. This and her increasing physical affection towards me.

"I don't know what to say, Lilly. I wish I had something that would make you feel better." Lilly looked at me.

"Me too." After a deep sigh, she missed the ball, handed me the jacks and continued her conversation.

"I know that it will be OK. It's just that sometimes I feel bad. Everybody loves her so much. And that's good for me, 'cause that means I get loved too."

"Lilly, you're not going to go away. You will always be part of Diana. And I think that Diana picked you for a reason. I think she knew that she was safe with you. That you had so much love inside of you, that she knew you could handle her life until she came back to share it with you."

"Dr. J. tells me that too. Did you know that a duck's quack never echoes?" And she was back!

When I went up for dinner, Nonnie had a picnic basket packed and asked me to take dinner to Poppie. She told me that he wanted a little company and he was hoping for a little alone time with me.

"Of course, Nonnie." I was both honored and concerned. Poppie had never requested dinner alone with me. I walked over to his house, knocked on the door and walked in, announcing myself.

"Hi, Poppie. It's Jade." I hollered softly as I walked towards his room.

"Come on back, sweetheart," I heard him try to yell. He was weaker each day, but I could still hear him. I walked in with the picnic basket, having no idea what was inside.

"I'm so glad that you could join me for dinner. Come sit down. I see Nonnie packed us a picnic." I went and gave Poppie a hug before sitting down on the chair by his side.

"How are you feeling today, Poppie?" He thought about this for a minute.

"Well, I imagine that I feel better than some and worse than some." It made me sad to think that Poppie was not going to get better. He saw my sadness.

"Child, now don't go feeling sorry for me. Sad would be if I had an empty life. But this old man has had a long, full one." He paused and then added, "I'm a blessed man, Jade. Please, baby, don't be sad." I tried to hide my sadness. I asked if he was ready to eat.

"Well, let's see what Mary has packed for us." I opened the picnic basket and inside were two thermoses full of leftover soup from lunch and some rice pudding, I guessed, for Poppie, and a Tupperware full of salad, I guessed, for me. Soup was Poppie's choice for most meals these days. It was easiest for him to swallow things that went down easy. I pulled the tray stand over to the bed to put Poppie's lunch in front of him. I set up his soup for him and asked if he needed any help.

"Not today, honey. I like to feed myself whenever I can. Soon enough, I'm gonna need everyone's help. But tonight, I can handle my own spoon." He was in a good mood. We both had our soup while we chatted. I told Poppie about the garden and how nice it was to see Nonnie digging in the dirt. He seemed happy about that. And he told me about his day. The doctor had visited. And he told me about the nail-biting, edge of your seat episode of *Jeopardy* that he had watched.

"Do you believe the man who won the game had reached $43,000? In just one episode! Amazing. I love that show. Mary always said I would be a good contestant because I had too much useless information in my head and maybe that show could put it to good use." He laughed at that. And then he coughed. I watched him carefully.

"I think I'm ready for that rice pudding. I might just love rice pudding almost as much as *Jeopardy*. Especially if it's Nonnie's homemade rice pudding." I set out his bowl and we talked some more. He told me about some of the picnics in his and Nonnie's life. They had picnics at the park, on the road, in an airplane and even once at the theater, although they were asked to leave the basket home the next time. The subject eventually got around to Lilly. I had a feeling it would.

"Jade, honey, could this old man ask you a big favor?" He had a smile on his face, but it was a little more serious than the smile he had on earlier.

"Poppie, you could ask me for any favor. What could I do for you?"

"Well, there really is no easy way to say this, so I'm just gonna come out with it. I wanted to ask you to stay until I go." He saw the alarm on my face.

"Now before you get all mushy on me, let's be honest. I'm not going to make it through another month. And I know that Mary will take this hard, but she is a very strong woman, so I am not too worried about her. But I have to tell you, I have no idea how my part-time Lilly is gonna take it. She may be just fine, which I suspect is the closest to the truth. But just in case she has a harder time than I think she will, I sure would appreciate your being here to help out. I know it's a lot to ask. And if you have to be on your way, I certainly understand. Don't give me an answer tonight child. Just think about it."

I hadn't even thought of when I would leave since the doctors had asked me to stick around for a bit. And, really, I had no desire to be anywhere else right now.

"Poppie, of course I'll stay. I don't know how much I can help Nonnie and Lilly. They love you so much. But I will be here for whoever needs the help. But Poppie, you're having a good day. Maybe you're gonna have a bunch of them. You never know." I hadn't realized that panic had crept into my voice. He patted my hand firmly to calm me down. It caught my attention and I calmed myself.

"I'm sorry," I said meekly. He reached over and wiped the tear that had fallen down my cheek. I didn't even realize that I had started to weep. His hand touching my cheek made it harder. His hand was too soft and too cool and too loving. The tears welled up and I tried not to let them fall.

"Come here, baby." I stood up and sat on the edge of his bed and leaned over to hold him, while he held me. I cried softly in his shoulder and he just let me. We stayed like that for a few minutes. His arms around me felt so comforting. I wish I felt this way when my parents had attempted to comfort me. They didn't really have the ability to. They only had the ability to upset me, so that I would need comforting after they were done with me. After a few minutes, I wiped my tears and blew my nose.

"That's my girl," he said. "I didn't tell Mary I was asking you this favor. I know that you are a very good secret keeper. I hope that this can stay between us." I nodded in affirmation, still sniffling.

"Now, let's listen to a little jazz before you go. I have two new songs I want you to hear. So Poppie and I listened to a little jazz. He introduced me to *Nature Boy* by Miles Davis, a slow and slightly haunting, beautiful melody. After that, we listened to a more upbeat song. It began with a few instruments and just grew. "This is by Weather Report. It's called *Birdland*." I looked at him, a little surprised. He winked and we listened together. It really was a good song. Lots of horn, percussion and keyboard. It changed the tone for our "goodnight."

I walked back to the Big House with an emptier picnic basket and joined the others for dessert, just in time for root beer floats. Dessert and Lilly were welcome distractions. She was giving the dinner crew a mini-lecture on Israel and the history of hopscotch.

Days 18-20: Lessons From an 8-Year-Old

Lots to catch up on. My first ranch therapy meeting,
visiting with Poppie, Margaritas,
and a wise and dear little boy named Kenny…

"He has Down's Syndrome," whispered Lilly. I didn't know why Lilly was whispering. It was just the two of us going to find the kites. Huey was bringing Kenny over. Kenny was one of his "other kids" around town and he had a thing for kites. Today was windy. Perfect for kite flying. It was clear, by the way she talked about him, that Lilly was fond of Kenny. We were in one of the sheds looking for the string spools and kites. They hadn't been taken down this season yet, so they were dusty. When we got outside, we cleaned them by holding them up to the wind. This would be easy. The wind was cooperative.

As we finished getting everything ready, Huey came out from the Big House towards the shed, with Kenny in tow. Kenny was beyond cute. He had dark blonde hair, glasses that were too big for his little face and a couple teeth missing. He also had freckles all around his nose and cheeks. He was a surprisingly slim, lanky child. Kenny's mother kept him fit with exercise and healthy food. When Huey and Kenny came up to us, everyone sort of yelled their hellos fast, as the wind was growing. Kenny and Lilly hugged like they were best friends. She had to bend down, as Kenny was eight years old. Then he let go and turned to hug me. He, seemingly, was a hugger. The wind chimes danced chaotically. It sounded like a frantic symphony. You couldn't hear anything but the wind and the clamor of the chimes until you got further away.

We gathered up our stuff and walked away from the houses. Kenny and Lilly chatted loudly about everything "kid": the puppies, his new bike, the latest Tooth Fairy adventure and other extremely important details of their lives. It took four sentences to see that Kenny was a hoot. He liked to talk… a lot. Kenny couldn't speak without using his whole upper body. He punctuated his sentences with his hands and his arms controlled the volume. To say he was animated was an understatement. This little boy was a born storyteller. He could make a trip to the dentist seem like an exciting, nerve-racking adventure, just as well as he could make an explanation of a teacher's assignment a one-man show. His wit was evident when he began talking to his kite.

"OK, kite. This is how it's gonna be. I'm going to do my best to hold you in the wind and you will do your best to stay up. Now, I know it's gonna be hard, kite. It's really windy. You're gonna feel pulled and tugged. But I got you. You can do this. We can do this. OK, time to fly!" It was a fantastic speech. I would be inspired… if I were a kite.

Huey and I helped the kids get their kites up. It was easy. The wind continued to cooperate as if it wanted Kenny and Lilly to have a good time. Soon, they both were flying and giggling at the challenge. Huey and I watched them with awe.

After almost half an hour, Kenny asked for his snacks. He said he brought enough for everyone. He reeled in his kite and opened his backpack. He brought out a big baggie full of raw husked cobs of corn. There were probably a dozen pieces. And he had paper cups and a large thermos bottle of water with lemon slices. It was cute. The raw corn on the cob was sweet. I had never eaten raw corn like that. Another new thing for me. With missing teeth, it was a bit of a challenge for Kenny. He seemed up for it, though. After 15 minutes it was back to the kites. Huey and I continued watching them. The wind was a little loud, but it was quieter near the ground.

"So, you know about Guthrie?" He was still watching Kenny.

"Well, apparently, he is beloved and therefore, must be family royalty." I thought I heard Huey agree with a drawn-out "Yeah." I looked over at him. He met the question on my face.

"Everything you hear about Guthrie is true. He is beloved. And he is royalty. He went out and did some great things." He had admiration written on his face. I thought he was done, but I was wrong.

"He is a good, good man, a caring and loyal friend, a lover of children and animals, a musician, a decorated air combat pilot and, strangely enough, a Barney Miller fan, which I am, too!" He seemed amazed by this last fact. "Guthrie really is one of the good guys." Like an exclamation point, he added, "Really." He continued, "Right after you meet him, you'll see." He stopped, startled a little bit at a thought. He turned to me with slight panic. "Hey, you're still gonna be here in a couple weeks, right?"

"Yeah, I'm going to be here. I didn't expect you to get freaky-deaky on me about this."

"I just like having time to prepare for things like this. You leaving someday… just give me some notice. That's all," he stopped there. After their "five-minute warning," we helped the kids put the kite stuff away and the boys headed out.

"So, what were you guys laughing about so much. You seemed to be having a good time. And your kite skills!" I shook my head. "I'm not even going to go there! Respect, girl!" Lilly giggled.

"We were talking about a bunch of stuff." Then her smile faded. When I asked if she was alright, she asked me if we could talk about it later. I reminded her that she could talk to me anytime.

"Maybe after we wash up, Nonnie will let me and you have a special dinner in the gazebo and I can tell you what we talked about."

"Good idea." I wondered what was coming.

We met at the house and packed up a light dinner while Nonnie was getting it ready with Coco and Kelly. Reesa had just gone to get the boys from Lloyd. We asked Nonnie if it was ok to have our dinner out at the gazebo. Nonnie looked at me and I gave her a slight nod.

"Well, of course, child. I think once in a while doing things differently than you usually do gives you another way to see things. Go get what you want and have fun, babies." We each grabbed a bowl and filled it with our dinner. We filled the bottom with wild rice. Then layered roasted vegetables and shredded chicken on top. We grabbed everything we needed and walked to the gazebo. Lilly still looked sad. Nonnie saw it. That's why she stayed out of it. Lilly had asked for my company. So we sat in the gazebo and watched the sun start to sink.

"Are you all right, Lilly?" I asked. She was mid-bite. She shrugged. "You look sad," I asked again. Lilly was quiet. "You don't have to tell me," I told her. We watched the colors start to change a few more minutes, while we both took a few bites before Lilly spoke.

"Kenny is really, really smart. I know he doesn't seem like it, but he is."

"He seems smart to me." I still was not sure where this was going.

"He says a bunch of smart things whenever I see him." I waited. "He's told me that even bugs have families, so don't step on them. It's good for the bugs and it's good for us. He told me that kid manners make you a better grown-up. Once he told me that God hears your prayers better if he knows your voice. That kind of makes sense to me." She hesitated briefly. "And today he asked me what I wanted to be when I grew up." And then I understood why Lilly looked so sad. "Growing up" was not part of Lilly's future. I thought that it was interesting that Kenny looked at Lilly as a child. He related to her, completely, as Lilly.

"What did you tell him?"

"I told him that I didn't know." There was frustration in her voice. "I didn't really lie to him," Lilly said defensively.

"Of course you didn't," I answered her. "And I think I understand why this might make you feel sad." She looked at me. "You wonder about your future, so maybe thinking about it can be upsetting. It would be for me." I tried to sympathize. "You are how old, Lilly?" She answered that she was 12. "Do you know what you want to do when you become older?"

"No, but that's 'cause I don't ever get that far. I always remember I'm going away, so I stop thinking about it."

I realized, then, that I wasn't sure what I wanted to do when I got home. Did I really want to stay in L.A.? It's not that I never wanted to leave here. It was more that my world had opened up and with the opening came questions. Questions I knew not to rush.

"But Lilly, you don't have to. You can make a plan for tomorrow or next week and go for it and then on to another plan. Instead of one long journey, you'll have dozens of little ones. That can be just as good." She thought about this for a bit. "You don't have to decide what you want to be when you grow up. You get to decide what you want to be now." She nodded, ever so slightly.

"Yeah," she said with a new clarity. And then, you could see on her face, she stopped thinking about it. "Look at the purples now," she instructed, pointing to the sunset, which had, indeed, begun creating purples. She was fine after that.

The next morning, Poppie was barely awake when I took him his coffee. We took turns. That way everyone got a few minutes with him each week. Everyone was gone or busy, so this morning, I got the honor.

"You awake?" I whispered. I didn't want to intrude. He looked like he was asleep.

"Yes, I am," he answered. "Come on over, child." I handed him his coffee and he took a long sip. I guess Poppie needed his coffee in the morning, just like we did. He was more awake now. He gestured like he was patting the chair next to the head of his bed. So I sat and we talked. We discussed Kenny and his love for kites and his words of wisdom, Lilly and how she gets carried away with her homework, how he wished he could join us in the greenhouse and how frustrating it was getting past foursies. And we talked about meeting the doctors for a session later. It was easy to talk with Poppie. This must be what having a grandfather was like, I guessed. We finished our visit with a song. That was, now, our ritual.

I went out to find Coco to help, again, with the garden. We got carried away with chatter and dirt, so we were a little late for the meeting. We only missed the meet and greet, so we were there in time to grab a quick drink and find a place to sit.

The therapy session consisted of all of us sitting in the living room in the Big House, meeting to discuss anything noteworthy or pertinent to filling in the puzzle. Everyone here, except me, had been to these meetings and so I was not sure what to expect. This made me a little anxious, but only because I wasn't sure if something would be required of me that I didn't know about. I hoped that the meeting and the doctors would guide me. Usually, Lilly was present during these meetings.

"Barry will bring her back in an hour and we will begin our official meeting. So for now, let's brainstorm what's going on here," Dr. Leslie prompted us. "Anything (and she drew this out for stress) could be helpful. This is new for us. This is just information gathering so let's put it all out there and make the most of the hour. Let's go." Dr. Leslie took control right away. No one spoke, so she went first.

"OK, this is how it's done. For us, we've noticed a resignation in Lilly. Less questioning about what will become of her and more just talking about it. And a bit more focus on the here and now. This could mean something, in that she is beginning to accept her future integration." She continued, "You all know Jade is helping now. We've spoken and she has filled us in on a few things that confirm this. Lilly seems to share the most with Jade." Dr. Leslie looked over at me. "And we are glad that she does. It's given us more information. Thank you, Jade."

"I agree. There is definitely something different with her. But it's not Diana." Coco added, with a little bit of regret. "She is just different. That's all." she finished.

Sunshine and Will agreed. Sunshine added, looking at Will, "I think that her inner spirit is in dialogue with her unconscious self. They are in talks, so-to-speak." Dr. J. took notes on her computer as people gave their observations.

Slowly, more than a few others offered similar observations. "Her moods change fast." "She's more clingy." "She's more emotional."

"She's more flat." Nonnie, who knew her best, said that one. "Just a bit. But enough for me to see and feel." She closed her eyes and shook her head slightly. "Poor child," she added. Everyone agreed that they noticed something different. Questions, theories and opinions were tossed around. We agreed to keep in touch. Report anything. They warned us that there might be little cracks first. Tantrums, agitation, outbursts. We all agreed to watch for signs of trouble.

Soon Barry came in with Lilly. And Dr. Leslie, once again, "began" the meeting. We all were warmed up, so we got right to business. The comments, compliments and suggestions flowed. "The garden crew has really come through. We got a lot done this week." Dirty Sunset report (one in last week, two since last house meeting). The puppies at Charlie and Maya's were important, especially to

Lilly. When Lilly spoke, she talked with a pensive tone. She told no one in particular that she knew better than to ask for one of the puppies. It was odd because no one had discussed a puppy for her. Not even her!

"I know that I will go before the dog grows up," she said softly.

"And that makes you feel sad?" asked Dr. J.

"Of course, I'm sad. And I don't know when things will change just like you all don't know. It doesn't matter what I want anyway 'cause it's not up to me, either." Her voice was raised. I wondered if this counted as an outburst.

It was quiet after that, and Dr. Leslie knew well enough to wind up with that. She asked, "Lilly, before we go, do you want to tell us more about how you are feeling or more about you and Diana?"

"Nope. Sorry, but it's always the same anyway. I'm just saying that there isn't anything new. Diana gets to decide when things change. I'm not mad," she reminded us. "Just sad." Dr. Leslie didn't push. She thanked everyone for the session, reminded us about the next group meeting date and then everyone kind of scattered. The fact that the meeting was a little derailed by Lilly was further proof that something was changing. The rest of the afternoon everyone kind of did their own thing.

～～～　～～～　～～～

Coco, Sunshine and I had been drinking. Probably a little too much. Coco picked up the pitcher and poured the last of it into our raised glasses.

"Last call!" she yelled quietly, as she poured. It was getting a little late, but we weren't in a hurry to end our day. It had been bittersweet. It began early with a visit to see Poppie. Then helping more in the garden and greenhouse. We had gotten so much done before, Reesa asked if Coco and I could give her another three to four hours to get to some extra stuff crossed of her list, so we did. Apparently, extras included pruning trees, washing tools and equipment and cleaning out the old small shed that had become the dumping ground. The small shed was the hardest. A month ago I would have freaked at seeing a dead snake and lots of cockroaches on their backs. Somehow, it wasn't as disgusting now. It was just something that had to be done. Lilly wasn't the only one changing.

After cleaning up, we had our meeting with the doctors. Lilly had, sort of, torpedoed it and everyone had scattered, so as the day began to fade, Sunshine, Coco and I found ourselves in the gazebo for an early dinner. We were having margaritas, with a side of margaritas! Barry and Nonnie had taken the girls out. Poppie's doctors had encouraged Nonnie to switch to hospice care, which meant that comfort was the goal, rather than treatment, as his doctors had finally confirmed that there was nothing left to do to make Poppie better. Barry and Nonnie wanted to explain this to the girls, so they took them over to Michael and Annie's to talk about what this meant. They worried that it could trigger something in Lilly. Reesa, Jack and Tawn were hanging with Poppie. The ranchers understood that Poppie's time was limited, but they also knew to share him, as he "belonged" to all of them. Lloyd and Kelly had taken off somewhere and Will was doing some work.

The three of us had decided to drink our dinner outside. The weather was perfect. I think we had just finished our second pitcher. But they were small! Sunshine went in to grab another one. We waited for her. I think Coco and I were thinking about Poppie and his decline, but we didn't share our thoughts, so I wasn't completely sure. I felt both dread at the thought of this place without him and a jealousy of some kind, that everyone here had more of him than I did. I was glad they did. I just wished I had the same.

Sunshine came back and the talking and, eventually, laughing resumed. It was the end to another day at the ranch and it was quiet now. Except for the three of us. We were the opposite of quiet. The three of us laughed at jokes that didn't even get finished being told and answered questions with more questions. We tiptoed around

Poppie. There was a clear effort to avoid his medical status, so Coco and Sunshine tried to lighten it up with talk about Guthrie and his upcoming visit.

"Girl," said Coco, with some attitude, "You gonna love this boy. I am telling you. You gonna love this boy." She nodded her head as if she was agreeing with herself. Then she asked for confirmation. "Am I right Sunshine? Or am I right?" I might have been wrong about the pitcher count.

"Yep, Coco. You are right. Jade's gonna love that boy." Sunshine walked over and sat on the end of my lounge chair. "Jade, we're telling you the truth. Honest to God. For real. You are gonna love that boy. Nobody doesn't love Guthrie." She slurred this with great conviction. They both tried to mask their hints at matchmaking with their genuine love for the man.

"I'm sure I will. Everyone else sure does." I had no doubt that I would like Guthrie. Getting along fine? Sure. A match? Not so much. While the stabs had gone a way, the desire to try again had not returned yet.

We finished our drinks and decided to call it a night. Somehow, we managed to put our things in the kitchen, separate and find our houses and our beds and lay down on them.

"Come on over sweetheart," Poppie motioned me to sit by his side. I had gone to the Big House and Reesa, who had the boys, told me they were all having coffee with Poppie at the gazebo.

"Wanna cup to go?" Reesa looked at me, knowingly.

"Love one," I answered and waited.

"Thank you." She handed me my cup. I pretended to take a bite out of each of the boy's necks on the way out. I loved their giggles. I first found the girls painting a mini-hopscotch board for the boys. They had learned from the last hopscotch masterpiece, so this one was going smoothly. Also, it was half the size. I visited a few minutes, told them it was beautiful and that I would see them later.

Poppie was having a good day. You could tell. And it was so beautiful outside, so Nonnie had Barry and Michael help him out to the gazebo to sit for a few hours. He looked really good today. Stronger and more stable.

"It's nice to see you, baby. Sit with me. I'm so glad you came over to say 'Hi.'" Even though he looked good, he still seemed too empty for the size of him. He looked like a man that used to be bigger. I remembered the pictures of him. He was fuller and healthier. Even from the first day I met him I saw a difference.

"It's good to see you outside, Poppie. You look good." I sat down after giving him a soft hug. I didn't want to hurt him. It felt good to sit down next to him on the gazebo couch. He could feel me relax, so he nestled against me a bit more. Everyone buzzed around us. We just sat there for a little while, until his attention was required elsewhere. The boys had run over to see Poppie. I could see his face when he heard them call to him. He lit up at the sound of their voices. He turned to his other side and opened his arms to Jack and Tawn. I could hear Coco screaming for them to be careful with their Poppie.

"Be gentle!" she yelled.

Poppie was giving them some loving. They each got squeezed, tickled, poked and hugged before Nonnie called them over to her.

"How is the morning going?" Poppie whispered to me.

"It's going alright." I didn't want to tell him about my margarita hangover. It seemed so small compared to what he must be feeling. "Lilly and P.S. are painting a smaller hopscotch board on the side of the basketball court, for Jack and Tawn. They're busy with their masterpiece. I'm glad to see you outside. It's a perfect day. Not too hot, not too cold."

"P.S. came to see me earlier and told me about her plans. She was already anticipating problems. It's hard for her, being older than her 58-year-old aunt."

"It can't be easy. But they'll be fine. Or they won't be fine. I've learned that once they get into it together, they forgot what their argument was about anyway. I'll go back and check on them soon. But I have a little time. Is this alright to sit with you for a few more minutes?"

"Sweetheart, I know how much you are caring for my part-time Lilly. But you can sit with me for however long you want. I love your company. And so does she. You are almost all she talks about."

"What kinds of things does she say?" I was curious. I wasn't sure what things Lilly thought worth sharing. And I wondered if they were the things I would think worthy too.

"Well, let's see. She told me you like strawberries and music. She said you weren't very good at jacks, but had confidence that you would improve. She told me about your twin brother and that you always make time to play games with her. She also told me how she showed you her tree reflection. I wish she wouldn't dwell on that so much. But at least it's fleeting." He saw my eyebrows rise when he mentioned the reflection.

"She tells me secrets too. Aren't we the lucky ones?" he whispered with pride.

"I'm glad she talks to you, too. She needs to share," I said.

"Yes, she does. I'm glad you agree. No wonder she's become attached. She can see that in you, just like Nonnie and I do." He thought about this for a minute. Then switched gears. "And to be honest, I was never good at jacks, either. Even in my prime, I could never get past sixies."

"Me, too!" I was happy that I wasn't the only one. And I was happy to be there next to Poppie. After another 10 minutes or so, I said goodbye and went to check on the girls.

"Do you like it?" asked P.S. Lilly was still painting while P.S. was taking a break to mix more paint.

"Yes, I do. You and Lilly are doing a great job. I love the colors. Did you both decide which ones to use?"

"Well, Lilly wanted a black board with red numbers. Red is her favorite color. I wanted all different colors for the numbers and purple for the board. Purple is my favorite color. So we compromised." She said this with the maturity of a girl who had to grow up a bit faster than others. I looked at their creation on the cement court. Lilly had gotten her choice with the black board. And P.S. got her different colors for the numbers. They were almost done. They had three more numbers to do. Three more colors to create.

"I'm very impressed. Compromising is very mature."

"Well," said P.S., full of confidence, "a good life includes compromise." I looked at her amused.

"Nonnie?" I asked.

"Yep," she answered. I watched a bit longer until the paint fumes started to make me feel queasy.

I told the girls that I looked forward to seeing it when it was done and then I went back to my casita and climbed into bed, planning to take a short nap. Lilly would be going to therapy soon, so I felt that I could disappear for just a bit. Lying with Poppie was nice, but I didn't want to be in his way or take all of his time. When I checked on the girls, the paint fumes started to affect me. After last night, I just needed to lie down for a bit. After breaking out in a cold sweat and wrapping myself in a sheet and blanket, I was out. I continued to sleep and sweat for the next four hours.

When I woke, I felt much better. After taking a long shower, I went up to the Big House, just in time help finish dinner preparations. I had an empty belly, so I was hungry. Sunshine had explained my absence during the day to the others with either a margarita explanation for the grown-ups or a "tummy-ache" explanation for the younger ones. Everyone talked about how nice it was to have Poppie come out today. I watched Nonnie. She didn't join in. I think she just worried about the coming days. After dinner, everyone broke up and headed home or out. I guess I missed what turned out to be a long day. I headed back to my casita.

I couldn't sleep, having had such a long nap. I got ready for bed and sat on the porch and got caught up in my journal. It had been a few days since I had written.

Day 21: Swinging

I did not like today. I thought I knew deep raw pain.
I was wrong…

Someone had just gotten a hit. You could hear the moms and dads cheer.

The day was too beautiful to stay inside, so after breakfast, Barry loaded up the back of the truck with Jamison, Cairo and Shasta and the front with Lilly and I, and we headed to the park that had a dog run. We were just getting out of the truck when we heard the crowd cheer. Some little one just became a hero, I thought to myself. Barry told us he would be at the dog run while we went to play or walk around. He would check in with us in a bit. He grabbed the dogs, who were very eager to go ever since they had realized where they were.

Lilly and I headed across the road to the play areas. We looked around and watched some of the other kids play. It made me nostalgic. I remembered, as a young child, climbing monkey bars like real monkeys, hiding out in big cement pipes from the boys with "cooties" and making my brother mad by blocking his way down the slide. We watched a group chasing a younger boy who protested so much that he was practically demanding to be chased. Lilly was a bit amused. We headed to the outer edge of the play area. I got the sense that Lilly was a little self-conscious around kids her "age." But I could have been wrong.

Maybe Lilly just preferred swings, as that is where we wound up. There were three empty swings so we sat. Slowly, Lilly began to pump her legs back and forth. Soon she was in full swing and I just watched in awe of her abandon.

I watched Lilly, as she swung back and forth. Anyone who didn't know her would see a middle-aged woman enjoying swinging. I saw a young girl get lost in the lull of the back and forth, back and forth. She seemed content to just swing. At first I began to swing next to her, but I didn't have Lilly's energy, so I slowed, stopped and just watched for a bit.

The dog park section was just across the path from the play area. I could see Barry over there with Jamison, Shasta and Cairo, along with another dozen or so dogs. They had the most energy of the ranch dogs and he liked to bring them here once in a while to play with other dogs. This helped them get some of their energy out. Most were playing with each other in the enclosed area, while their owners visited and kept a watchful eye on them. I looked back to the play area near the swings. I could hear the children giggling and calling out to their moms to help them get down from the monkey bars or to catch them at the end of the slide. One little girl was running her dad in circles while he directed her, "This way, love of my life," or "Not that way, baby girl." I decided he was a good daddy. There was a little red headed freckled face toddler yelling at his mom, "No-no, mommy. I do it." He yelled this, I think, five or six times. I heard birds chirping and cooing followed by a bee buzzing past me and it brought me back to Lilly. Usually a bee elicited a reaction from Lilly and there was none. I turned to look at her face.

She continued to be lost in her swinging, but her face seemed different. She seemed lost in thought, too. I watched her closely to see if she was alright. The swinging just continued. No higher than the last swing, and no lower either. Just back and forth. You could hear the chain of the swing squeak as she pumped. It was almost like a melody. There was a pattern to the squeaks. One short squeak as she pumped back and then a longer squeak as she pulled forward. The squeaky song continued. But soon, I began to see Lilly's face begin to change. At first, I saw a sadness in her eyes. A sadness that wasn't there before. But now it began to change to fright. It changed fast and unexpectedly. I wasn't sure what to do. As a quiet moan joined in the swinging melody, I called out to her.

"Lilly, are you alright?" She kept swinging, but she didn't answer. Her moans began to shadow the squeak. I was becoming afraid, too. I didn't know what was happening. I called out towards the dog run.

I called for Barry and looked back at Lilly, who had begun to pump faster and faster. The swing song was now chaotic and dark, as it echoed Lilly's moans.

"Lilly! Can you hear me? What's wrong?" I said loudly, standing in front of her, but out of reach from her feet, so she could see me. She didn't seem to hear or see me. I called Barry again. This time louder.

"Barry. Barry. I need you." He looked over.

"Something is wrong," was all I could say. I was filled with worry. Lilly never ignored me.

"I'm coming!" Barry yelled back with a voice full of concern. By the time he ran over, the moans had changed to sobs. Barry stood in front of Lilly and watched for a just a few seconds.

"Diana! Diana!" He screamed. His voice, filled with fear, broke Lilly's trance-like hysterics. She looked at him and stopped pumping her legs. I thought she was going to stop, but she tried to get off while the swing was still moving, which sent her falling into the sand underneath. She didn't fall far, but she began to scream.

"No. No. No." That was all she could get out in between the sobs. Her eyes were closed tightly now and she was shaking uncontrollably. But she kept yelling "no" between sobbing. It was frightening and heartbreaking at the same time. I didn't know what was happening. I didn't think Barry did either, but he had grabbed her and held her close to his chest, trying to calm her. He began rocking with her while she buried her face in his chest and just cried uncontrollably. She held onto Barry so tightly that she pulled him closer with white knuckles. Crying with her, he wrapped his arms around his wife so tightly that it looked as though he was trying to hide her. I knew he wasn't. He wanted to fix her. To make it stop… whatever "it" was. He continued to rock her gently as her cries softened.

I didn't realize I was holding my breath until I heard myself gasp for air. Lilly's pain was so fierce, that it overflowed to both Barry and I without knowing it was happening. Barry and Lilly sat like that for minutes or an hour, I wasn't really sure. After Lilly calmed, he said, "Let's go home." I went and got the dogs and met them in the parking lot. He asked me if I could drive home. He didn't want to let go of his wife.

The ranch felt different that night. The comfort that usually blanketed the ranch was absent. Everyone knew what had happened. News at the ranch traveled fast. Where there were usually games or chatter, there was only worry and quiet. The doctors had come out to the ranch when we returned. They spent a couple of hours with Lilly and Barry. They called me in once to give my account. I told them everything that I thought could help. I had never witnessed such raw pain. After spending time talking with them, the discussion led to thinking that it was the swing that had set Diana off. The squeak had taken her back to Hope and the squeaking of the bed as her life was taken. And back to the pain that she had tried to escape. I didn't know what to do or say.

"I'm so sorry. I didn't know that would happen. I didn't know." I was almost crying. Dr. Leslie held me for just a minute before pulling me away and getting my attention.

"It was nobody's fault." She said this firmly. "There was no way to predict this. You handled yourself perfectly. Not everyone would have done as well. Thank you for that." That didn't really make me feel any better.

While everyone knew they should eat, nobody did. No one wanted to visit or catch up on the day's events like we usually did after dinner. That was fine with me. I didn't want to either. It was an early evening.

Day 22: Struggling to Get Past Sixies

Lilly felt bad about yesterday at the park.
I felt bad that she felt bad.
It wasn't her fault. None of this was...

Lilly returned the next morning with little memory of the day before. But being the insightful girl that she was, she knew.

"I'm sorry, Jade." Lilly found me having coffee on my patio.

"There's nothing to be sorry about, Lilly. Are you alright?" I asked.

"Yeah. I'm just sad that I made everyone else sad too."

"You know that this isn't your fault. None of it."

"Yeah, but still...." she trailed off. "Most people say their prayers before bed. At least I think they do." Lilly was explaining why she said her prayers in the morning. "Nonnie told me that Diana taught all of her kids to pray in the morning. She said that Jewish people did that and she liked it. She explained that it seemed better to wake up and thank God for another day than to pray at night and ask for another." This made some sense to me. "Some days I feel bad, though," she added. I asked why.

"'Cause sometimes I think I am taking all of Diana's day from her." She got lost in the thought.

"Diana will get her days. There are enough to share." I said this firmly, hoping that it might help. Being Lilly, she was ready to move on.

"Wanna go play jacks?" Lilly had set aside a time for jacks yesterday. I had gotten better, but just could not get past sixies.

"Today's the day, Jade. We are going to get you past sixies." She was so positive and so motivated, that I almost believed her. In all of our jacks playing, I had learned much. I had learned patience. Lord, have I learned patience. I learned that the throw of the jacks is crucial. And it depended on where you were in the game. I also learned that "every expert was born a beginner." (Shades of Nonnie.) But I still got stuck on sixies.

"O.K., I think I'm ready." I was about to toss the ball when Lilly interrupted me.

"Wait! Remember what I told you about jacks teaching you about life?"

"I remember." I pictured Lilly "schooling"me about not giving up, strategizing and practice making you better.

"I think I forgot to tell you the most important thing."

"What's the most important thing?" I wondered what she had left out.

"Don't forget to have fun. That's the most important part." And once again, this beautiful woman/child surprised me. I don't know if she recognized it or not, but I had actually forgotten that part. I was trying so hard that it had become a chore. So I let go of that and decided to enjoy the game.

I was sitting alone on the porch after lunch, remembering our morning jacks lesson, when the hustle and bustle of the moment got my attention. Coco ran out the door and headed towards Poppie's house. She seemed worried and in a hurry. Without thinking, I followed her. Apparently, Nonnie had called her at the Big House and told her something was wrong with Poppie's breathing and that she needed help. We both ran in the house and found Poppie struggling for breath. Not an emergency struggling, but a difficulty breathing that wasn't there before. Coco calmly, yet quickly, checked the oxygen equipment and said that it seemed all right but suggested that maybe we had a dud tank and thought changing it out would be the first attempt at a fix. She was right. I learned later that every once in awhile, the tank was not secured well or filled enough or a host of other problems, so starting with a fresh tank did the trick. Thank God this was the case. After a few minutes of oxygen, Poppie's breathing became more steady and we all began to relax.

"Well, now I know what a man's gotta do to get three beautiful women by his bedside," he said with a husky voice, as he winked at me.

"Marcus Bennet, that is not funny." Nonnie took a little longer to relax than we did.

"You're right, sweetheart. I didn't mean to worry you." This disarmed her and you could see her shoulders relax a bit. "But it is all good now. So no worries, my sweet Mary. I'm fine. We all know that Coco is a superhero. And once again, she saved the day!" He said this slowly, with steady but slightly labored breath. Nonnie gave him instructions to rest and he didn't argue. Coco and I left them alone and went back to the Big House.

"Does that happen often?" I asked.

"No, not really, maybe two or three times before. But Huey and I seem to be the oxygen tank experts, so one of us tries to hook up the new tanks or double check, once in a while, that the levels or buttons haven't been accidentally changed or bumped or whatever. It scares the hell out of Nonnie, though. So far, it's always been an easy fix." Coco let out a loud, deep sigh.

The rest of the day was spent doing chores around the ranch. Barry was going to play golf, which surprised me. I didn't even know he played, but Kelly explained that this was the one distraction he could run to when needed, and since Lilly seemed solid, or as solid as she normally was, he decided to keep his scheduled game. I was glad that he had a distraction. He probably needed more of them. He stayed close to the ranch most of the time.

I thought about Nonnie while I did chores around the ranch. I couldn't imagine how she must feel. I guessed it must be something like walking a tightrope or being on the edge of a cliff. Safe if all went well and fearful that it could easily not. The chores took the rest of the day and I was glad to keep busy. It wiped me out and after dinner and a quick game of shesh-besh with Lilly, I went to my casita and showered before falling into bed. I found comfort in this routine.

Day 23: Back to Where it All Started.

Today we went to Sabino Canyon.
It was the place where this family began…

Barry woke in a rare good mood. I wasn't sure why. I told Reesa how nice it was to see Barry smile so much. I could swear I even heard him whistle as he grabbed a piece of fruit.

"Yeah. I wonder what's going on? Maybe Gus is coming." Barry overheard us and called out from the kitchen.

"Good guess, Reesa. Gus called last night and told me he is coming in. Gonna land anytime. After a meeting, he's gonna stop by for the rest of the day. He has to fly out in the morning, otherwise he would stay for the meeting."

I asked Reesa who Gus was.

"He's an old high school friend of Barry and Michael's," she explained and then added with a whisper, "They'll be out late tonight. Probably the three of them. Reliving the past and avoiding the future. But he's good for Barry. Always a distraction. And as much as he gives off the 'stuck in hippie' mode, he's an extremely successful and philanthropic businessman. He's helped us here financially, too, but doesn't like people to know." She saw my surprise. "He's just very… unconventional." Barry walked back to where we were sitting.

I would learn later that Gus was a throwback from the '70s. If the tie-dye shirt didn't show it, then the pucca shells sure did. And if the pucca shells didn't do it, then the ponytail sure did. Barry was going to hang with him for the day while the rest of us had an adventure planned. Today we decided to go to the much talked about Sabino Canyon.

Lilly was the most excited for the day. Everyone in Diana's circle knew about Sabino Canyon. That was where Diana met Poppie almost 35 years ago. They knew the history of their meeting. They knew the various trails that led to different areas of the canyon. And they knew that I was going to love it as much as they did.

We all piled into Carlos and one of the vans. Twenty minutes later and a scenic drive filled with more greens and browns flying by, we arrived at the parking lot of Sabino Canyon. The lot was almost full. Annie explained that the better the weather, the fuller the lot. Beautiful weekends allowed the overfill lot to be opened.

On the way from the parking lot, there was much debate about whether to take the tram or not. P.S. and Lilly didn't want to, but Reesa explained that the hike was too far for the boys and that if we took the tram, we could get on and off when we wanted and that way the boys wouldn't hold everybody up. They reluctantly agreed. Will got the tram tickets and we all climbed on and waited for the rest of it to fill before the driver began his slow, narrated drive up the windy turns and hills that led to the end of the main three-mile canyon road. Lilly, apparently always, sat in the very back row. She liked to be as much in the open as possible. The boys and their moms sat with her. The rest of us filled the two rows ahead of them. P.S. sat next to me, which normally meant Lilly was on the other side. But not today. Along the way, the tram driver, who was both witty and knowledgeable, spewed out facts and figures, anecdotes and jokes, history and myths about the canyon. It was more interesting than I thought it would be. According to Ben, the tram driver, who's voice came over the speaker system, the Forest Service was created and began to oversee the Canyon over 100 years ago and tram rides began almost 40 years ago. The main road included nine stone bridges and the lower trail led to seven falls. (These weren't really waterfalls, but various sizes of pools of water that filled from the melting snowfall that ran down from the Catalina Mountains.) The canyon was filmed in over a dozen major motion pictures and was home to a long list of wildlife that Ben shared, including roadrunners. Freddie popped up in my head.

"So what kind of animals have you seen here?" I was curious, but also wanted to be prepared. Wildlife in Tucson was very different from wildlife in L.A.

P.S. and Lilly answered. They said that they had seen deer, snakes, tarantulas, lots of prairie dogs or pack rats, and once, from far away, a mountain lion. That explained the mountain lion warning sign at the tram stop. We continued the ride to the end of the road and got off. We planned to walk back, since it was easier to walk downhill than up. If the boys got tired, we could get back on the tram at any of the stops along the way. It really was a magnificent canyon. Everything about it was beautiful. (Except for the "Watch for Mountain Lions" sign, which I now had stuck in my head.) We began to head to a place they knew where we could park ourselves for a while and the kids could play in the stream. It was about a half a mile down the road we had just come up. I was walking with P.S.

"I like coming here. Before we moved to Tucson, whenever we visited, Aunt Diana would bring me here. She loved this place, too. Did you know this is where Poppie met Aunt Diana?"

"Yes. I know the story."

It was always strange to hear P.S. refer to Lilly as Aunt Diana. I know she really was Diana, but to me, she was just Lilly. And I thought it interesting that P.S. used the name of the person she was referring to. It made sense and everyone else did it too. Maybe it was her youth that made it more noticeable.

"I wish she would get better. She still likes to come here. Whoever she is."

I thought about this for a minute. The fact that P.S. understood and processed the situation was impressive. She was so young. P.S.

continued, "Do you know why Aunt Diana is sick?" She didn't wait for an answer, just like Lilly often didn't. "Mom said it was because something bad happened. That man killed my cousin, Hope. You didn't know Hope, right?" I shook my head no. "I don't think kids should die before their moms and dads do. Losing their little kids makes them want to die, too. And they do, just a little bit. I think that is what happened to Aunt Diana." Then she, like Lilly, changed the subject.

"Look, quick! A deer. Maybe we'll see another one 'cause mostly they don't like being alone." I could hear the boys in the back, along with Lilly, get excited about the deer that was off the road about 30 feet or so. Sure enough, you could see another one hidden in the brush a bit beyond the first one. They were beautiful, with a rich cinnamon coat and white little tails. Their eyes were so shiny and black, like beads. They just stared at us and then walked away.

While I learned a lot about the canyon on the tram, I was glad to be off, as I was able to take it all in much more. Now, instead of the engine and loudspeaker, I could hear the water in the creeks bubbling and the buzz of various insects and bugs. Instead of fumes, I enjoyed the fresh air smell of a canyon.

The cacti had more detail, some having holes burrowed in them. Lilly explained that mostly the cactus wrens did that. We kept walking down, Lilly and P.S. running ahead then stopping to wait for us, then running ahead again and then stopping to wait again. We did this until we found the path off the road that led to one of the more open areas where we would put our stuff and chill for a while. It was hard not to appreciate the beauty of the Arizona desert. The running cool creek, the rock formations, cacti full of personality, wildlife that made the desert move and make noise. After we got situated and the kids started playing in the cool shallow water, Lilly asked if I wanted to take a short walk. I followed her back up to the road. Just as the bridge hit the bank, there was a concrete slab digging into the side of the bank. We sat down on that slab. Our feet would have hit the water if the water had been deeper. Lilly explained that there were years that the water flooded the bridge. This was one of the areas where she and Poppie sat and talked and grew to love each other. There were two other places. Decades ago, you would find them at one of those three places every weekend. And some weekdays, until Poppie became more involved and refused to meet her if she was supposed to be in school. I felt honored that Lilly had shown me her spot. It wasn't really her memory. She explained that this is what Poppie had told her. Those were Diana's memories. We went back to the group and joined the kids trying to catch tadpoles and negotiating with the moms about bringing them home to watch them become frogs. The moms held strong. No frog pets.

We spent much of the day there. Laughing and exploring, eating and playing. It was a fun day. Everyone was nice at the canyon, too. An added perk. All said, "Hello" and asked how you were. Packing up took awhile, as it always does with young ones. While we waited, Lilly told me that each arm on the saguaro took about 100 years to grow. Not as random of a fact as usual, but still unrelated.

When we got home, Gus was there. He had spent some time visiting with Barry, Nonnie and Poppie. Everyone who knew him went up to say, "Hi." A hug or handshake or the kids jumping into his arms. He knew them all.

"Jade, this is Gus. Gus – Jade." We shook hands. "Lilly, do you remember Gus?" I could tell that Barry was looking for some sign of recognition.

"Hi, Gus. I heard the ranchers saying this morning that you're a friend of Barry's?" There was no sign of familiarity. I felt sad for Barry.

"Gus knew us both a long time ago." Barry took a chance, trying to jog something. It didn't work. Lilly, being wise beyond her 12 years, understood this and everyone could see her regret. It echoed Barry's.

"That's OK." Gus explained what he was doing. Passing through for a quick visit. "Gonna spend the rest of the night with my buddies and then head out in the morning. It was nice meeting you, Jade. And you, too, Lilly. Really." And then Gus walked out. He seemed slightly smaller. I found out later, that he was more than a friend. He was one of the groomsmen at their wedding. And he was Hope's godfather. It was painful to see that the woman he loved so dearly did not know him.

"So, what are you guys gonna do first? Before the settling in at the bar begins?" asked Will.

I think we'll try the driving range. If it's not crowded, we may hit a few buckets. We'll see." What some people found in church, Barry found on the greens. He left feeling a bit cleansed and at peace.

Day 24: La Noche de las Margaritas y Sticky Floors

Ace came by the ranch early. Once a month the ranch has a Monthly Meeting. When I first heard things like, "Saturday Night is the Monthly Meeting," or "Remember, Saturday. Meeting," I thought that they were having an actual meeting. But the meeting turned out to be a party. A really cool party for lots of friends and family.

Planning began a day or two before and the execution took all day. Preparing food, drinks, rearranging furniture, getting things stocked for the bar, the cups, plates and other party related tasks. It was a joint effort done to a party playlist. Ice chests were filled to rock and roll. Country music serenaded us as we decorated. The kids loved to help decorate. A babysitter was hired for them all, so the grown-ups could come and have some respite too. It was strange to have a babysitter for Diana, but it was a daughter of a friend, and she was more like a playmate chaperone. The playlist continued with the blues while we got out trays and dishes and serving things. Pop music helped us slice lemons and limes, get out salt for margaritas and cherries and olives for other drinks. Some guys came over early to set up for the music. They did a sound check then left everything where it was. This meeting had live music! We would all return by 8:00. It took most of the day getting ready. But it was worth it. Party mode looked good on the ranch.

⸺ ⸺ ⸺

"Our meetings can get pretty coo-coo-roo-coo. Yes?" Coco was handing me another margarita.

"Oh yeah." (The "oh" peaked loudly, for some reason!) "Everyone is happy. Even Barry."

"Yeah." We both looked at him across the room. He was laughing at something Xavier said. It really was nice to see him smiling and laughing. He didn't do enough of that. Nonnie had explained that it was hard to distract Barry from his situation. Sometimes golf worked. These meetings definitely did. And a friend could, occasionally, distract him.

"I'm glad Gus came. You can see that it helped, aside from the brief hangover, which really, when you think about it, is a gift too... sort of!"

"Coco, how in the hell would you call a hangover a gift?" The margaritas were making me loose with my tongue.

"Hey, girl. Don't forget that hangovers have gotta be earned. And you and I already have had a couple of good ones, right? Right? Right?" she repeated louder with a friendly poke accompanying each "right?"

"Yeah, I guess." I turned around the room trying to take it all in. "And I think we're in the middle of earning another." I was surprised at how many people could be crammed into the Big House. And every single one of them genuinely wanted to be here. It was loud and chaotic and fun. If you glanced from face to face, each one had a smile on it, a laugh coming out of it or a drink going into it. Some were dancing, some singing to the music, some telling jokes or stories. It was all good.

This was new to me. There was no polite toleration or pretense, which was too familiar from home. These people genuinely enjoyed each other. Sunshine was trying to get others to dance. It didn't take much convincing. Huey had a captive audience on the couch waving his hands animatedly for one of his tales. There was a group in the kitchen reminiscing about the last meeting and cheers came from the rec room, probably reacting to the muted ball game. The cheers were intermingled with pool balls clacking.

"If the floor is sticky, I'm guessing that is a good sign," Coco told me. We had gone into the kitchen to the margarita station. There was actually a margarita line. Charlie and Sally were in charge of the margarita supply. They did a good job. Which was amazing, considering that they had sampled each blender-full. They were smiling, too. Loopy smiles, but smiles nonetheless.

After a while, the stereo stopped and Barry and his friends took a corner. Barry sat with his guitar. Huey stood with his harmonica. Huey rarely sat anyway. Xavier brought out his tall conga drum. I didn't know it was called that until someone told me. And their friend, Dijon, played the bass. They began to play and everyone's attention went to them. I was impressed. Their sound was good and solid. They were very polished for a pickup band, with a rich sound led by Huey and Dijon, who happened to both be strong male vocalists with husky, sweet tones. Because they rarely played together, and some came and went, Sunshine said they almost always played covers, but with their own spin. They could make very uncool artists sound very cool. They played some good dance songs. And dance, we did. The rhythm guided us, along with the alcohol, and we had very little inhibition and an abundance of abandon. I guess booze makes anyone a good dancer.

Tina, Xavier's wife, was definitely looped. And so was her conversation. She was one of those chatty, happy drunks. I actually heard her say the following just a bit earlier:

"I love margaritas. Margarita sounds like a girl's name. I know this woman named Margaret. Sort of like margarita. Boy, did she love to knit. She was always knitting sweaters for people. Like this one I'm wearing. She didn't knit this one though. I got this on-line. I like to buy things on-line. Oh, and while I was looking for it, I saw this great food site. I went on and found this really good pie recipe. I was gonna bake it but I didn't have the apples I needed. I needed Granny Smith, but I only had Gala apples. Don't you love Gala apples? So I went to the store. Guess who I saw there? Maya. It was so funny. I never see Maya at the store. She is usually out riding. Hey, we should go riding. But wait, it's dark out. Horses don't have headlights. Can't go riding tonight. Oh well. I guess I'll just have another margarita. I love margaritas." Seriously. She said that all in two or three breaths. And she did that all night. I was impressed. Confused, but impressed.

I met more than a few new people. Friends of friends. And unless you were someone's guest, you knew who Diana was. All these people were connected to her in some way. I met Nick. He was a middle-aged, sweet guy, with his wife, Shawn. Coco explained, later, that he was the social worker who worked with Barry and Diana's fosters to help them transition out of their house and into the community. This meant housing, jobs, setting up health care and budgets. He had spent many days at their house, way back when Diana was more whole. They were lucky to have such a long-standing relationship. Back then, it was essential. He now visited when he could, to check in on everyone.

Joe, from the garage, was there with a friend. I met a sweet redhead who was Barry and Diana's old neighbor. Also, a man named Chris, who was a stray (like me) from months ago, who still kept in touch and was in town. I'm sure I met more, but I'm also sure I forgot them in the morning. Margarita memory was not my strength.

Every once in a while, a song played that everyone sang. There were a few that were, clearly, tradition. The music was eclectic, and because of the booze, so was the dancing.

I had paced myself with the margaritas. Especially since I had learned that they can be deceiving. So I was just the right amount of buzzed. Enough to dance with abandon and not care what people thought, but not enough to regret doing so. The night was long, fun, energetic, tasty, exhausting and thoroughly entertaining. You could tell people didn't want it to end. This was usually when the waiting for the next meeting began.

With so many people hanging around to clean up, it barely took 20 minutes after everyone left. I observed that it was tradition for each guest to take a bag of garbage with them. Your choice: recyclables or trash. This really helped. The sticky floors would wait until morning. And all the other finishing touches. At least the garbage was out and the food was put away. The rest could wait.

We all found our way home. While I downed a glass of water I saw the red numbers "3:18" on my alarm clock. They seemed to be floating in the air, but I was pretty sure those were the numbers I saw.

Day 25: Hang Overs, Wedding Vows and Halle Berry.

I will take a ranch meeting over any other, anytime.
In fact, all other meetings will pale, in comparison to whatever I
remember about this one. But first,
I had no idea that tetherball injuries were a thing...

Apparently, it was also tradition to sleep in on the mornings after meetings. And everyone was very good about following that tradition, including me and I didn't even know about it! We had more of a brunch than a breakfast. Slowly, everyone gathered around 11:00-ish. Coffee was made in double quantity and served with bagels and cream cheese, scrambled eggs and fruit salad. Slowly, we ate, which helped us wake up. I could tell it was going to be a lazy day. After breakfast, most of us pitched in to clean up the rest of the Big House. This entailed wiping things down, finding surprise garbage that eluded us the night before, mopping and rearranging the furniture. We did this slowly, as no one was in a rush to be anywhere. We even took some breaks here and there. During one of the breaks, Huey suggested we play a quick round of the question game. Everyone was definitely not in a hurry to start up again, so they let him explain it to me.

"We all go around once and think of a question that we would want to ask someone. We try to keep it light. Like, no 'Hey, Hitler, what's up with hating the Jews?' More like, 'Hey, God, how'd ya come up with the orgasm? And thank you.'" We all laughed. Apparently, that was Huey's go-to example. So we went around the circle asking our questions. Sometimes there was slight banter but generally, we went in a circle and shared our curiosities. Will asked the Dali Lama what inspires him. (For some reason, I found this ironic.) Sunshine asked Rosa Parks what gave her the courage. Kelly asked Eve what made her do it. (Random, but a good one.) Coco asked Halle Berry if she would come to the next meeting. (We all laughed. Apparently, she was Coco's first girl crush.) Barry passed, too hung-over to participate, but not too much to smile at the answers. Michael took the easy way out and asked Halle Berry to make it to *every* meeting. (Apparently she was Michael's girl crush too!) I finished with a question for Huey. Why the obsession with orgasms? I got a laugh or two. It was a good break from the task at hand.

We all got up and slowly finished whatever task we were doing before the game. We were almost done so it didn't take long. Huey went to get the girls while we brought out the leftovers. There was food left over from last night. We warmed up the mini-chimichangas, taquitos, green corn tamales, and set out some cheese, salsa, chips and beans. Just as we were sitting down with our plates, P.S. and Lilly walked in. P.S.'s eye was already swollen. She headed straight to the freezer and got a bag of peas. She knew the drill.

"What happened?" Nonnie and Annie both asked, with some concern, but not too much. I got the impression that this wasn't her first black eye.

"Tetherball injury," she answered.

"Huey or Lilly?" Coco asked.

"Huey. But he feels really bad."

"He usually does." Kelly turned to me and said with some sympathy. I wasn't sure if it was for P.S. or Huey.

I heard that Huey and Lilly were the tetherball champs. And they took this very seriously. So much that people didn't like playing with them. They usually had to pinky swear that they would chill while they played. But P.S. wanted to be a champ, too, and she kept challenging them. And kept getting (slightly) beat up. But, to her credit, she didn't give up and she kept coming back for more.

Huey came in, full of apologies for P.S. She kept telling him it was alright and not to worry about it. She said that she was fine like she meant it. The three of them filled their plates and joined us. P.S., with her frozen peas on the side. We all ate together and then Huey took the kids outside for playtime. He was amazing. He drank just as much, if not more than we did. How did he have energy and stamina? Or even the desire? He explained later that his secret was lots and lots of water before bed. I remember Coco saying the same thing after karaoke night.

"I'm gonna go see Poppie. Feel like going or got a message?" I asked.

Reesa said she would see him later and Coco said to remind him that it's his turn on the chessboard and she would be by later, too. So, after our usual greeting, I told Poppie that Reesa and Coco would be over later and that Coco was expecting to continue their game. I pulled up a chair to be closer to his bed.

"It's so nice to have so much company. And it helps Nonnie so much. She couldn't take care of me and everything else she does. So her little angels help. That's the way things work around here. We make it work. What do you want to talk about today, child? We could read poetry or play gin rummy. I'm feeling good. Do you want to just visit, baby girl?" Poppie could always read his kids. And we were all his kids. Every one of us, except for Nonnie.

He was feeling a little nostalgic. We began to talk about how when he had met Nonnie, she didn't want anything to do with him. She thought it unprofessional to get involved with a student's family. But he was relentless. And so was Diana. They both knew that she was perfect for him. And him for her. Time and perseverance showed her that they were right. She was a spunky, intelligent woman who Poppie found curious, at first. But he was just enough of a gentleman and put in just enough effort to keep her interested. And the interest only grew. How could it not? They really were perfect for each other. She was his missing piece that he didn't even know was there. This made him grateful every day that he woke to what he had found. And he was exactly the same to her. He told me about the vows they had written and spoke together. He closed his eyes and said them.

"We have earned the other's trust,

We have earned the other's respect.

We vow to never give the other a reason to doubt those gifts.

And we vow to greet these gifts with kindness and support.

And to remember love is something that you feel,

Just as it is something that you do.

We promise to love each other with both intention and abandon.

Always. Always. Always."

Poppie had a huge smile on his face. He told many people he married up. He always considered Nonnie a gift. He still did. We talked a little about the meeting. He told me a few stories about some of the more infamous meetings. One meeting there was a fight between two of the bandmates that involved a smashed guitar and nine stitches. Too much "silly juice," he explained. And another where someone got sick out back and it led to a five- or six-person vomit domino. That was a hard one to top. Poppie was laughing remembering it all. I left him happy and tired. He was ready for his nap.

As I was walking out, I found Barry, Huey and a new guy by the shed looking at some blueprints. I forgot that the entryway project started tomorrow. The guys were making last minute plans.

"Jade, this is Roman. He's our brick guy. We're lucky to have him helping us, so he's going to be around for a couple days." He turned to Roman, this balding, tanned, muscular little man. "Roman, this is Jade. One of the ranchers." My heart skipped a beat, but I doubt Barry noticed. Huey did though. He gave me, a "welcome to the club" smile.

"Nice to meet you, Jade."

"You too, Roman. See you tomorrow." I turned to Barry. "If you need any help, I don't know what I can do, but if you can think of something…" I offered.

"You are gonna be sorry you offered. We could use all the help we can get. We can put you to work doing something. We start early. We're all meeting in the Big House for coffee and muffins at 7:00 a.m., if you want to join us."

"I'll be there."

Days 26-27: Laying Bricks 101

What's that saying?
Something about one's journey of 1,000 miles beginning with a single
step. Well, the journey of 1,000 bricks
Begins with a single brick. And lots of helpers...

While I was at the ranch, I had seen, I think, three projects. First, was the brick mailbox planter that Coco and Reesa were making the day I came to the ranch. Second, was the new shed between the gazebo and the orchards. And then there was a drip system out front. Project #4 was a big one. Barry and Roman had planned a brick patio on the front outside entry to the Big House.

The house was full of a dozen or so of us getting our coffee and fuel while Barry went over instructions, passing out copies of the end product as well as a few drawings of the phases in between. He also broke the task into four phases. Readiness, bricks, sand, and sweep/clean up. We were all thrilled to see, when we went out front, that the dirt had already been dug up. And the wooden border was put in. The dirt was also laid out with staked string guides for lineage. We guessed that Roman, Barry, Michael and Huey had done this earlier.

Barry thanked all of us for showing up and explained how he appreciated that this was a team effort. He then introduced Roman to those who hadn't met him already. Roman, then, took over directing the brick layout. Roman gave his instructions and did a demonstration. He laid about 30 bricks, approximately 5 x 6. He manipulated them in the sand, using a level to make sure they were evenly flat. He began filling in sand between the bricks and then tapped, repeating this for a bit before sweeping it clean. He explained that we would work from the front door out. Roman would be cutting brick to fill in the corners and edges while everyone else was assigned a job and a place in the sequence for that job. Roman was very, very methodical.

"Questions? No? OK? Back to Barry."

"As always, the key to a successful project is a good playlist. The right music is essential for motivation and productivity." Barry was speaking to his crew again. "Our current project, a new brick patio, clearly falls in the realm of rock. So, as always, you will hopefully enjoy and if not, suffer through, what is now known as 'The Lost and Found Brick Rock Playlist.' OK, let's go." He pushed play and people started moving. Throughout the day I heard old rock, current rock and unknown rock. It was fun with the music. Everyone looked forward to what the next song would be.

I looked at the picture of the front patio entry that Barry had given us. It was a big deck, stretching from the edge of the driveway to the front door and from the edge of the kitchen side of the house across to the outside of the window in the hallway. They had a hibachi waiting, as well as the hammock that P.S. and Lilly were putting together. They had a patio set, too. The outer part near the driveway would have flowering pots lining it and the entry into the open patio was a vine-covered arch surrounded by beautiful flowering shrubs. They wanted a big front patio, for nights that the weather was nice and we could spill outside more.

It took two full days, from start to finish. Everyone kept busy and did whatever came next. It may have been raking sand, laying brick, grabbing snacks, sweeping sand, stringing lights or potting plants, but everyone kept moving.

Almost everyone resumed their duties for Day 2 of Operation Patio. Coco took Lilly to therapy so Barry could continue to help. We continued our tasks and the patio began to take shape. Finishing touches and then an inspection led the way to decorating and furnishing, which was all preplanned. By the time we had finished, the middle of the patio accommodated a coffee table with two patio love seats and a small patio couch circling it. There were three high cocktail tables with four stools each. And there was a picnic bench that sat six kids. In between the three bar stool tables and near the back couch was a hibachi warmer. There were new flowerpots greeting you at the front door. And there were planters, escorting you in, on both sides as you walked into the entryway from the driveway, full of a kaleidoscope of multicolored plants. The patio was cheerful and inviting. Everyone felt quite proud of themselves. Nonnie had watched on the sidelines, but was smiling the whole time.

The sun would be down in another hour. We ordered food to be delivered and all went to wash up. We were tired, dirty and hungry, so we decided to bring in nourishment. So, while we all went home to wash, lather and rinse our filth off, our dinner was being prepared, packaged and delivered. Life was good.

Forty minutes later we were all circling the deliveries like scavengers. Some hovered around the pizza row. Others were in line for the Chinese. The pizza aroma mingled with orange chicken was better than you would think. And when you threw in Lupe's ribs… heaven! The patio looked even more impressive at night with the lighting. The sparkly little bulbs looked like glitter flecks and there were enough to light up the patio perfectly. Everyone fit, everyone was comfortable and everyone was content. It got a bit better as Barry turned the corner pushing Poppie, in his wheelchair. As everyone noticed we all got up to greet him. After greetings, we parked him so he could take a good look.

He sat there, next to Nonnie, and looked slowly, and methodically around the new patio. As he did, his smile grew. So did Nonnie's. Watching him.

"Hooooo-weeee!" is what he first said. And then he said, "Well, ain't this the most amazing magical place you made us here?" He kept looking all around. He looked amazed. And he kept shaking his head in disbelief. "Man oh man. Who did this?" Barry explained that almost everyone did and that we were glad that he liked it. A few locals had joined in the patio breaking in "ceremony," but you could tell it was more to see Poppie than to see the new patio.

"And with that, Poppie, are you up for a little Topic Tuesday? We can break in the patio."

"I sure am." Poppie smiled big. And so that was how the first night on the patio went. Take out and Topic Tuesday with Poppie. At the end of the game we all knew that all of us had songs that took us back to our first broken heart; If given the choice between a good book or a good movie, it was split down the middle; and the three biggest hits were the sofa set around the table, the herb garden and the flowerpots lining the path. I won the worst roommate prize for my first semester with a crazy roommate who, sadly, actually had a nervous breakdown, thereby answering all of my wonderings if it was me or her. If given the opportunity to have lunch with a famous person, Will would share his afternoon with, surprisingly enough, Scarlett Johansson, Reesa with Harry Connick Jr., Poppie with President Obama, Coco with, of course, Halle Berry, Jack with Sponge Bob and Lloyd with Derek Jeter. Oh, and Huey would like lunch with Miley Cyrus. It was so grand to hear Poppie and Nonnie laugh.

When I left Los Angeles, I used to dread waking to each new day. I didn't want it to come, although I knew it always would. But here, I looked forward to the next day, and so, saying goodnight was alright.

Day 28: A duck with an arrow in its wing, homemade ice cream sandwiches and javelina. Or, as I call it... Wednesday!

Where do I even begin?...

"There you are, Jade," Lilly blurted out as she came in the door, winded from running. "Are you going up for coffee?" Before I could answer, she added, "'cause I need you." She had a very worried look on her face.

"What's wrong, Lilly?" I asked as I got up to go over to her.

"It's Simon. He needs us," she said a bit frantically.

"What do you mean, he needs us?" I had no idea what this meant.

"Come on. We gotta go." She started walking out and then turned to make sure I was following. It wasn't long before I realized that we weren't going to the lake, like I had assumed we would. Lilly led me toward the newer storage shed. When we got there, she looked around to see if anyone was watching. I didn't know why she did this until she took me behind the shed and I saw Simon. He was lying there on a blanket that Lilly had obviously brought, with an arrow through his wing. He was weak and a little bloodied.

"Lilly, what happened?" I was so surprised I didn't know what else to say. Lilly was kneeling down by Simon now, stroking his head, ever so softly, and making soothing sounds.

"I don't know, Jade," she whispered. "I went to see the sunrise and found Simon on the side of the lake just like this. So I ran home, got a blanket and then went back to get him," she explained. "We have to help him," she cried.

"Lilly, maybe we should…"

She cut me off before I could finish.

"No!" she cried. "Barry will make us put him down. Just like Tosh. I know it. So will everyone. But I know we can fix him. We have to try."

"But we're not doctors. Maybe he is too hurt to fix." I saw tears coming down Lilly's face.

"But maybe they can!" She was terribly upset.

"Lilly, Simon needs more than us. And the doctor will know if he can be fixed." She was listening while she kept stroking Simon's head. "Lilly, you don't want Simon to suffer. I know you don't. I really think we should take him to the vet. They know better than us."

Lilly thought for a minute, and between her sniffles, she said, "OK." Then she looked at me and declared, "I want to help Simon. And if you tell me that we have to go to the doctor to do that, then I trust you."

I went back to the Big House and told everyone what had happened and asked if I could take Lilly and Simon to the vet. After some discussion and commotion, Reesa said she would call them to expect us. Barry told me he would bring the truck around. I went and got Lilly and she helped me carefully lift Simon in my arms, still nestled on the blanket. Barry pulled up and ran around to help. He saw the tears in Lilly's eyes and went to hold her for just a second. Lilly climbed in and then Barry helped get me up and in and then buckled.

"Barry, thank you. I thought you'd be mad at me," she sniffled again. It was quiet in the cab.

"Lilly, I can't be mad at you for this. You're just trying to heal a soul's suffering."

"Yeah, I am. Do you think Simon will be OK?" She was trying not to cry.

"I don't know. But we're gonna find out soon enough." He pushed on the gas a little bit.

It took almost two hours for them to even come out, only to give us an update. They got him set up and sedated, they were almost finished getting the arrow away from the bones in the wing and were beginning to repair it, as best they could. The whole time Simon had been weak, but stable. So we waited some more. Eventually, they came out and said that Simon should make it, with some TLC and meds. They were not sure if flying would be affected, but he should survive the attack. We were told that we might be able to come back tomorrow and get him, with his long list of do's and don'ts for the next week or so. The vet explained that Simon really just needed to sleep and stay hydrated. Food would be good. But rest and water were the essentials. No pond yet. He needed to stay clean. So we left Simon, after they let Lilly kiss him a few more times, and went back to the ranch.

We had gotten back just in time for a possible distraction for Lilly. It was the Ice Cream Sandwich Project. After Lilly filled everyone in on what was going on with Simon, P.S. filled us in on what they were doing. I guess Nonnie, Coco and Reesa had baked cookies all morning. All kinds of mini cookies. Chocolate chip, sugar, peanut butter and oatmeal raisin. The kids had made ice cream with Huey earlier. They made vanilla bean, pomegranate and chocolate. We got home just in time to make our own ice cream cookie sandwiches.

"They are small," Nonnie said, "so they shouldn't spoil dinner." The choices kept Lilly busy for about three ice cream sandwiches. I doubt she would have even eaten any, except that we had missed breakfast and lunch.

"Do you think Simon is awake yet?" Lilly was behind me. I turned around and saw worry on her face.

"I don't know. But the vet won't let him hurt. They need to keep him calm and quiet all week, so it's good they are figuring out how to do this at the clinic. They'll make sure he is comfy, Lilly. Don't worry." I knew she still would.

"Want to go play a game?" I asked, knowing Lilly still needed a distraction. Games seemed to be the obvious choice. So we spent an hour or so playing games. Jump rope, jacks (and no, I didn't get past sixies), hopscotch and just as we were about to get into some Chinese jump rope, the dogs started acting strangely. They would go out a little, to the desert, and come back growling with their hair up. Lilly called for Coco to come see. She watched the dogs and without hesitating, grabbed the boys and told us all to come inside. She whistled for the dogs to come in. It took a couple times and some calling, but they came in. Coco clanged the bell loudly as we all went in. Soon after, Sunshine, Will, Kelly, Reesa and Lloyd followed. We all waited by the window. It was quiet and I wasn't sure what it was that they were expecting.

"What are we waiting for?" I asked.

"Whatever it is, the dogs were getting a whiff of it. Either a mountain lion or some javelina. That's my guess," answered Coco, with a calm that wasn't inside of me. We all watched outside. Slowly, from around the side of the house, came a family of javelina.

Until this moment, I had only seen them on TV. But real live javelina are sometimes cranky, always messy, never alone, wire-like haired pigs that were somewhat flatter than regular pigs. Like they'd been squished in. And there were a bunch of them. An adult, maybe the mommy, with four younger ones. We all watched them from inside the house. Which was good, because they came right up the steps to the porch. The dogs were hard to keep calm. They were barking so much and got so irritated at not being let out that we had to put them in the rec room and close the door so they couldn't see them.

"It's good Barry isn't here, huh Nonnie?" Lilly looked at Nonnie for confirmation.

"Barry wouldn't like it one bit," she agreed. We just watched while they ate one of the succulents from the big pot. They knocked over another.

"What would Barry do?" I was curious.

"He would bang things and holler and scare them away." She kept her eyes on the youngest one. And it wasn't that young, just younger than the others. "I never really like when he does that. They're just passing through. And look at how interesting they are." It sounded strange coming from a 58-year-old 12-year-old. I had to admit, though, they were very different and unique. Coco defended Barry.

"He just worries about the dogs." Which explained why they were put in the other room going nuts. "One year, Tosh wanted to play with one of the younger ones. And he wanted to play with Tosh, too. But his mama didn't think it was a good idea. So Tosh wound up with 38 stitches and a three-day high. They can be mean pigs." Coco didn't like them. "They'll go away after a little while." So the plan was to wait them out. She was right. They left after about 10 minutes.

No one really was in a big hurry to go outside, so we all helped Nonnie get ready for dinner. Since we had such a "sweet afternoon," meaning the ice cream sandwiches, Nonnie wanted to have something healthy for dinner. She gave everyone salad assignments: wash and tear the different greens, dice vegetables, open up cans of a variety of beans, shred and bowl some leftover chicken and break up some cooked and cooled tuna. We made a salad buffet and everyone helped. Kelly made a huge basket of crescent rolls. And dinner was (self) served! Everyone sitting wherever; the couch, floor, table, back porch (with a little peripheral attention to any returning javelina). It was a nice change. A very odd day, but a pleasant way to end it. It made me think back to when I asked what a typical day at the ranch was like. I remember the girls looking at me like the word typical was not a word they used often. The arrow through Simon and javelinas visiting helped me understand why.

Day 29: eegee's. If You Live in Tucson, You Know What I'm Sayin'.

My favorite flavor, I think, is lemon. But that could change.

I woke to the most beautiful day. When I stepped outside, the magnificent blue hues of the sky greeted me. Not like L.A. at all. It was a rare day that you saw these kinds of blue in the city. Usually, it was a gray-blue or a hazy looming blue. And this Arizona air had a freshness that actually had a wonderful scent. After coffee and discussing with everyone who walked in what a beautiful day it was, I helped Kelly in the greenhouse for a little while. It was pruning day. So the morning was spent picking off smaller, weaker leaves and limbs. While we did this, we tidied up stuff that had fallen or rotted. It was a little repetitive but easy. And we brought out some music and talked. The morning went by fast.

The day was good. Just a little cool and fresh. Some of us ate our lunch outside. After, Lilly, P.S., Huey and I found ourselves in a friendly game of four-square on the court. I could tell that Lilly was distracted. She was thinking of Simon, but the vet said to get him at 3:00. We had another 45 minutes or so. We played a little more and then went inside to get a drink before leaving to go bring home Lilly's patient.

⌒⌒⌒ ⌒⌒⌒ ⌒⌒⌒

"Do you need us to pick up anything while we're out?" Nonnie thanked me and said that she didn't but that we would probably have to stop at the pharmacy, depending on how the doctors needed us to care for Simon.

"Will do. OK, Lilly. You ready?" She was ready when she woke. I grabbed the keys and we went to go get Simon.

The vet was waiting for us with Simon in hand. He had a bandaged wing and looked a little loopy. The doctor explained what they had done, gave us instructions for care (keep him sedated for a few days, but make sure he drinks and try to get him to eat a little). He explained that while small fish, fish eggs, snails and worms would be what he is most used to, until he can go back to the pond, seeds, grain, berries, some plant roots from the pond mixed with just a little sand would do. He explained that the sand could actually help with digestion by providing some grit. He wanted us to leave the bandages as they were and bring him back in three days for a follow-up.

They had pumped him with antibiotics, so he was good to go, so to speak. Lilly took Simon carefully and cooed at him like he was her baby. If I didn't know it was Lilly, it could have been Diana. The way she sheltered Simon with her body and comforted him as a mother would. It made me imagine the mother Diana once was.

The assistant handed us a bottle of meds and a dropper. She explained the schedule for putting it in his food to keep him a bit sedated so he wouldn't want to move so much. Other than his drunken stupor, Simon looked great. Well, aside from the bandaged wing, too. So home we went, Lilly already planning on how to convince Nonnie to let her keep Simon in her room. The whole ride home, which wasn't that long, Lilly gently stroked Simon, who sat on her lap nestled in a bundled up towel.

When we got home, Nonnie didn't need too much convincing. She actually thought it was a good idea. It gave Lilly something to be responsible for and keep her busy for the next few days. So off Lilly went to make a little safe enclosure to keep Simon in her room for the next few days. Nonnie was right. This "project" was as good for Lilly as it was for Simon. She had to plan, strategize, take the lead and be responsible. Everyone knew she could do it. As unfortunate as it was for Simon, everyone knew he was in good hands. It was good for Lilly to have something significant to be in charge of. With Lilly busy, I went to go see Poppie.

Apparently, Poppie was having another good day. It probably was one of his best in weeks and this seemed to worry Nonnie. But, being who she was, she shook off her worry and made up her mind to participate in the day rather than wait for her worry to grow.

"Will you do me a favor, child, and take Poppie this milkshake I made for him? He asked for one today. First time in a long time." I think that was one of the things that worried her. She added, "He doesn't know I add protein powder. He's got no meat on him. I figured it couldn't hurt, as long as he gets his milkshake."

"Of course, Nonnie. Anything else you need me to take?"

"No, except maybe a hug." I promised to deliver, took the milkshake and headed off to see Poppie.

When I walked in, Poppie seemed more alert than I had seen him in weeks. In fact, when I walked in he called from the bedroom, "Helloooooooo" in a jovial tone.

"Hellooooo," I answered back and headed to his room. I walked in and he was sitting up waiting to see who it was that answered.

"I thought that it might be your beautiful voice that answered." He saw the milkshake in my hand. "And you come bearing gifts!" I handed him his milkshake.

"Nonnie said you asked for a milkshake, so yes, I come bearing a chocolate creamy cold gift. Enjoy." He was already sucking on the straw, his eyes closed as if he was in bliss. He took a few long sips, stopped and let out a big blissful moan.

"Sit, sit." He gestured for me to stay. I sat.

"So I hear that our healthcare facility has now grown. We have two patients here that need tending to." Word travels fast. He smiled and took another sip. We talked, for a little while, about Simon and tetherball, javelina and the brick patio, and of course, jazz. Today's artist was Ravi Coltrane. He drank his shake as we listened.

"I told you that Guthrie blows sax, right? Yeah... he will always be my favorite." I knew he was getting excited to see Guthrie. He just lied there, eyes closed, head swaying to the lull of the horn.

"Yes. I think we've listened to him. I look forward to meeting him."

Poppie looked over to me. "I'm glad, sweetheart. You know when you first came to the ranch, you had a pain in you and an anger that you wore under your coat. I doubt that anyone noticed," he softly teased. "I say this because I see it has become so much smaller. I see that you are lighter. I hope I'm right."

We talked for a bit. I gave him the nutshell version, confirming that I had arrived with a wounded heart and that the ranch had certainly helped it to start healing.

The playlist ended. He finished the last of the milkshake and thanked me for coming to visit. I think our chat, along with a full belly, made Poppie tired. I hugged him, then hugged him again, explaining that I had forgotten to deliver Nonnie's hug earlier.

I left Poppie so he could rest. I knew that Lilly was probably in the Big House by now, working on homework, so I peeked in on Simon. He was sleeping in his blanketed enclosure that Lilly made by turning chairs on their sides in the corner of her room. I walked back to the Big House and reported to Lilly that Simon was resting and reported to Nonnie that the milkshake and hug were delivered. They were both pleased with their reports. I went into the kitchen to wash out the glass and found Coco and Reesa.

"We were just going to head out to the feed store and thought we'd grab an early bite. Wanna come?" They were still jazzed from Nonnie's "scolding," so they were staying on top of supplies.

I asked Nonnie if she needed me for anything. She didn't. I'm glad because I would never have been introduced to eegee's, the greatest fast-food sandwich and slushy drink place in the city. The sandwich was the kind I could eat every few days. The fries and dipping sauce… yummy. And the slushy drink was not quite like any other. They had lemon, strawberry and pina colada flavors all the time. And then a flavor of the month. I tried the lemon and knew I was hooked.

We filled the truck with supplies, our bellies with eegee's and headed home to unload the feed to the shed. We caught up with whoever was left in the Big House, exchanging stories about our day. I wanted to shower and make some calls, so I headed back to my casita.

While walking back to my casita, it occurred to me that there was more life here among the broken waiting to be fixed than other places that had people who thought they were whole. It was strange how the odd felt normal now. The ranch was affecting me. When I met with the doctors, they stressed the balance needed to help this work. While the goal was to make a safe place for Diana to return to, it was for everyone else to feel safe as well. The ranchers needed to do outside things, both for their mental health and so that when Diana returned, they would be able to live a life without Lilly. And while they weren't quite whole yet, the broken lived quite deliberately. And I was learning.

Day 30: Operation Guthrie

When I said Guthrie seemed like royalty, I was teasing.
Not anymore. The way the ranch prepared for and anticipated his arrival
was like watching them get ready for a visiting prince…

Coco, Reesa, Nonnie, Sunshine and I were sitting in the kitchen for our morning coffee. Lilly was getting a head start on her homework at her house because she wanted to help, later, prepare for Guthrie's arrival. And she wanted to be near Simon. She was doing an excellent job of caring for him, as we all knew she would. Nonnie let her skip therapy "just this once for Simon and Guthrie."

Apparently, that was the agenda for today: getting ready for Guthrie. We would help, too, after we were given our assignments from Nonnie. For now, we were energizing over coffee and muffins. Nonnie explained that Poppie didn't have an easy night, so she would give assignments and then go be with him. I think we all were thinking about Poppie before we all startled.

Our worries were interrupted by the sound of wooden boards being dropped outside the porch, followed by Barry and Michael's voices. We went out to see what was going on. Michael and Barry were preparing to make a wheelchair ramp on the far edge of the porch, so the incline was not too steep. This entailed pulling away a section of railing and attaching a ramp to the porch that would make the house wheelchair accessible. Only the casitas were wheelchair accessible. The Big House from the front was, but not the back. For some reason, Poppie didn't want them to put in a ramp for him at the Big House or his own home. The Big House was the first structure on the property and a ramp was never really needed but, with Guthrie's arrival, it now was. They would build a smaller one for the family house, too, so Guthrie could visit Poppie. Huey was walking over with a massive toolbox, with Will following, carrying some larger tools. Michael and Barry went to get more wood from the bed of the truck. We went back inside, knowing that the ramp was in good hands. Nonnie was ready to give us our assignments. She presented us with a list of things to do to prepare for Guthrie.

1. Build ramps (large one for the Big House and small one for Poppie's).

2. Paint or stain ramps.

3. Food shop for Guthrie's favorites.

4. Prep his room: clean sheets, towels, stock refrigerator, flowers in room and welcome sign from kids.

5. Shop and plan for special "Welcome Home" favorite dinner: brisket, with potatoes, Caesar salad, garlic green beans with almonds and carrot cake.

6. Call Guthrie to confirm flight info, special needs for injuries or therapy, ask about appointments while here for rehab.

7. Check with Guthrie what special things he may need to make his visit easier.

The plan was to get whatever equipment Guthrie needed to do his daily rehab at the ranch. We were waiting for a list of what he needed. We weren't even sure if he needed anything, but we wanted to be ready if he did.

The first was being tackled as we spoke. The rest was divided and assigned so we could get to it. Everyone was excited to see Guthrie, so none of it was considered work.

Around noon, the railing was down and the ramp was starting to be put up. Both of the ramps would be permanent, so if ever there was a need, the ranch could accommodate. Reesa and Coco were back from shopping, so Sunshine and I took what we needed and headed to the casita to prepare Guthrie's room and the casita we would share. No one really knew how long he was staying. It appeared that Guthrie wasn't sure, either. I imagined it depended on Poppie.

We all kept busy with our tasks, snacking in between, which kind of served as lunch, and then met up mid-afternoon to see how the ramp was coming. Amazingly, it was finished. We could hear the girl's laughter, as they were testing it with a wheelbarrow. Lilly was pushing P.S. up and down the ramp in the wheelbarrow to make sure it was sturdy enough. It was. The girls had finished their "Welcome Home" banner and now were campaigning to stain the ramps. Coco and I volunteered to help supervise and so the tasks continued to get checked off the list. It took all four of us to get the job done, but after cleaning up, both ramps looked pretty good! We had an hour before dinner, so Lilly and I went to go visit with Simon. We snuck in a quick visit to Poppie, too. Like everyone else, he was getting excited for Guthrie's arrival, you could see. But he was weak. He was having Michael shave him, so he looked "more presentable" when his "grandson" arrived.

If Poppie had not become ill, Guthrie would have waited to visit until after he had finished rehab. But, sadly, that was not the case. Guthrie had his surgery on his leg at Reed National Military Center in Maryland. He had just started his rehabilitation when Poppie began to fade, so he changed his plans. He needed to come say hello, and now, goodbye. He would come to the ranch for a bit and then return to Walter Reed for the rest of his rehab. But for now, he needed to be with his family, who were all at the ranch. He could get his checkups and bandages changed at the local VA hospital.

After visiting Simon, we went up to the Big House for dinner. Everyone was hungry, dirty and exhausted, so a simple spaghetti dinner, with salad and rolls, was perfect. We ate, cleaned up and scattered. While everyone was excited to see Guthrie, they were tired even more.

Day 31: The Most Touching Moment
I Have Ever Witnessed.

Today I met Guthrie. I'm not really sure where to start...

I was in the Big House when the call came that Barry was on his way with Guthrie. I could see the relief on Nonnie's face. We had just finished lunch, but she had not eaten a bite. She knew that Poppie was holding on for him.

Guthrie was injured in Afghanistan. After being initially treated there, he was transferred to a hospital back in the states. Nonnie explained that he had recently gotten clearance to come home for a visit. Since Nonnie and Poppie were his PMOK (primary next of kin) and they needed him, the doctors had made an exception. He would finish his rehab later. His left calf and foot were almost healed from the burns, but still bandaged, and he was not able to walk on his left leg. His right leg was in a cast from the knee to his toes so he would be in a wheelchair, but at least he was coming.

I remembered Nonnie telling me how Poppie took the news of Guthrie getting hit. As she told me about Poppie's reaction, her eyes welled up. I wasn't sure if it was for Poppie or Guthrie. Probably both.

"When we first heard, I thought I saw the life go out of him. We didn't know how badly he was hurt and news was slow in coming." She explained that it had taken days to get answers. Marcus had called every connection he had in the Air Force. Within the week, they had found out that he had been on his way to his base in a Jeep when it hit an IED. He had gotten pretty beat up, but thank God, everything was fixable. For both him and his driver. They had broken bones, and scrapes and a few burns. Even though both needed several surgeries, it was a miracle that they hadn't been critically injured. She told me that after answers had come, Poppie began to breathe again and was able to eat and sleep. He had been waiting to see him ever since.

······ ······ ······

I watched from the window as Barry's truck pulled up. Shasta and Brody greeted them as they stopped. As the door opened, Coco, Will and Michael, who had been waiting as anxiously as Nonnie, went out to greet them and help. Michael went straight to the truck bed and opened the tailgate to get out Guthrie's wheelchair. He brought it around to the side where Guthrie sat. They put on the leg rests before Barry and Michael helped him get into his chair from the high seat bench. I saw Michael start to push him, and then Guthrie kindly said something that prompted Michael to let go so Guthrie could wheel himself. When he turned the chair to head to the house I saw his face.

Guthrie was beautiful. And as he wheeled closer, he became even more so. I guess since his injury, his hair had grown out because he wore shaggy brown curls that were speckled with lighter and darker shades. Not exactly the military cut I anticipated. He was still in great physical shape, aside from his legs, with broad shoulders and muscular arms. He wheeled himself towards the house, chitchat and hugs and tears prolonging the arrival to the front door. Surprisingly, I found myself nervous to meet the man that everyone so adored. It was his eyes. They were a light olive green that drew you to stare, which I'm sure I did. They housed an old soul, which I did not expect. Finally, he wheeled through the door. Nonnie, Lilly and I were waiting.

Lilly had heard lots of stories about Guthrie but only met him twice, shortly after she arrived, when Diana "disappeared" and then again, a year or so later, when he was on leave. The military gave him emergency leave when the "crisis" occurred and it was then that Lilly and Guthrie first bonded. Nonnie explained that Guthrie was so despondent about Diana being gone that he almost clung to Lilly, so in those two weeks, he and Lilly connected. Before he even got his wheelchair through the door, Lilly ran into Guthrie's arms. He held her just as tight as she held him and it seemed like they would never let go. I could hear Guthrie whispering into Lilly's ear, "Hey, my precious girl? I missed you so much." And I thought I saw a tear run down one cheek, which he quickly wiped away before letting completely go to reach for Nonnie.

"Hi, Nonnie. I wish I could stand to give you one of those bear hugs you love so much." This time I was sure there were tears on his cheeks. No sounds of crying, just tears that matched Nonnie's as she bent down to hold him. She didn't have to bend far, she was so petite and his arms long enough to reach her. They both held onto each other for a minute before Nonnie let go and put her beautiful wrinkled hands on both sides of his face and she bent to kiss each side, tears and all.

"We're all so glad you're finally here. Poppie's been waiting for you. He's resting right now, so let's get you settled, then you can go visit." She took a deep breath, as she stood straighter. She looked at me, waiting quietly, watching all the greetings.

"Guthrie, I want you to meet Jade. Jade, this is Guthrie." We shook hands. He took my hand in both of his and held them for a minute, as he spoke.

"Some of the family has told me about you," Guthrie said. "I feel like I already know you. A little." I think I blushed, but I'm not sure. The expression on his face was so disarming. And his eyes… close-up, were even more mesmerizing than from the window.

"What did they tell you? I'm sure it was all lies," I teased.

"I know that you love dirty sunsets, you moan when you watch a really good movie kiss, you're a quick study for hopscotch, jump rope and ball and jacks, you have a twin brother and a broken heart." He smiled questioningly. "Did I get good intel?" I nodded and acknowledged that he was pretty much correct. I countered.

"Well, I heard that you are a poker champ, you also love dirty sunsets, you prefer bang-bang shoot-em-up movies with special effects, you play the saxophone and you were hurt in Afghanistan serving your country. How was my intel?" He smiled and thought, for just a second.

"Pretty good. I have a feeling that our sources might be the same," he said, again with this beautiful disarming smile.

"Come on, I'll show you which casita is yours this time. Oh, and by the way, you and Jade are housemates." Lilly was not ready to let him out of sight.

"Fine with me," I heard him say as he went out to the porch and inaugurated the new ramp. I could hear Lilly and him talking about the ramp being new and how he wanted her to remind him to thank the "guys" for their effort.

<hr />

"You know, Poppie is going to die," Lilly said. We were sitting by ourselves on the middle step of the back porch. We had been sitting there quietly for more than 20 minutes, just watching the dessert. I learned that if you just sit and watch you can see more than you would expect. Animals gathering food, hummingbirds gathering nectar, cactus blooms, tarantulas crawling across the court, what seemed like hundreds of lizards. We came to a place, the two of us, where we felt no pressure for small talk. So we just sat, content, and took it all in. I knew that Lilly was already starting to miss Poppie. I didn't want to try to imagine the loss it would be for her. I had only known Poppie for a short time and it seemed that my own loss would be big enough. I didn't care to imagine anything more. But I was worried about Lilly and was a little relieved when she brought it up.

"Do you think you'd like to talk about it?" I asked, wondering if Lilly needed to share. She sat for a while. Her face didn't turn to me, but I could see enough of it to recognize deep thought. Lilly got lost for a moment, seeming to forget that she'd been asked a question. Then she answered. Her voice was whimsical and quiet.

"When Diana grew up and went to college, Nonnie told me about how that can be for a mom. She called it bittersweet. It's sweet because that's what is supposed to happen. If your baby leaves when it's time, it means you did a good job. But it's bitter because there comes an emptiness inside that lives all around the stuff that was still in there. And Nonnie told me that when Poppie dies, I would feel a bunch of new stuff. She said that I might have something deep and hard inside me that would make everything else feel like nothing for a while." Lilly stopped and considered her words again.

"I think Nonnie is very smart. But I think some things you can't explain. No matter how hard you try. You can even hear someone else say it in a different way, but when the feelings come, everything anybody said isn't the same. They were right, but they were wrong." Lilly slowed, "Their words came from feeling their life. I'm gonna feel mine." She paused to track a family of quail, the mommy leading six or seven babies in a quick chaotic parade across the dirt right in front of us. After a couple minutes Lilly began again as if she hadn't paused at all.

"I just wanted to make sure you knew that Poppie was dying." She said all of this with such clarity, such assuredness, that I forgot Lilly was just 12. Sort of.

Nonnie, as it turned out, was right to be worried about Poppie's good days. They turned out to be the rally before the end. You could tell that Poppie was holding on for Guthrie. All of his friends and family had done what they were supposed to do. They told Poppie that it was alright to go. They reassured him that Mary would be taken care of. And Diana and Barry. But he wasn't ready. Lilly was the one to point that out to everyone. "Why do you think that God is taking so long to take Poppie?" I overheard P.S. ask Lilly. "Oh, God is ready for Poppie. And Poppie is probably ready for God. But Guthrie didn't get to say good-bye. God knows that Guthrie needs to do that. And Poppie knows, too. So he's waiting," Lilly explained. "The ones who go with God will be fine. It's the ones who are left behind that God has to watch out for." This woman/child continued to amaze me.

⁓ ⁓ ⁓

Poppie was lying in his bed, weak and frail. When Nonnie had told him that Guthrie was coming up to see him, Poppie gestured to her. He wanted to tell her something. She bent down to hear his whisper. Yesterday the whispering had started. His voice seemed to just disappear. Or maybe it was the strength to use his voice. Nonnie listened to his request and then raised his bed so he was sitting upright. He watched the door for Guthrie. He seemed surprisingly alert. His eyes were watering and Nonnie gently wiped each tear as it fell to his cheek. I wasn't sure if they were real tears or if his eyes were just watery. It didn't really matter. Nonnie, Lilly, Barry and I were with him as he waited for Guthrie. I was watching Poppie, remembering our first meeting, when a small, weak smile appeared on his face.

I knew without turning that Guthrie had just wheeled up to the door. I turned and watched as he paused, taking in what he was about to do. He had been warned about Poppie's condition and knew that this visit was difficult and might serve as his goodbye. Poppie was so aware and showed so much attention to the situation that I thought maybe Guthrie's arrival would heal more than release. But I knew that this was just a wish. As Guthrie slowly wheeled in, Poppie raised his arm. It wasn't shaky or unsure. I thought that he was reaching out to Guthrie. But he was not. His arm extended out and then raised some more, and he bent his forearm so his hand could reach his forehead. Then his hand formed a rigid military salute. Guthrie looked at Poppie with all the love he had showing in his eyes. As his first tear fell, he saluted back to Poppie. I had to leave and go outside to find air so I could breathe again. Soon, Lilly and Barry joined me on the porch. Guthrie needed his time alone with Poppie. Before Poppie had no more time to share.

⁓⁓⁓ ⁓⁓⁓ ⁓⁓⁓

Lilly waited for Guthrie to come out. He looked visibly shaken but composed himself when he saw us. She ran up to him and gave him a big hug. I could hear her comfort him with, "I know, I know. It's hard." He let her hold on for another minute before he announced that he was alright. Then, true to Lilly's nature, she switched gears.

"So, Guthrie, did you bring your saxophone?" She looked at him with her eyes filled with hope. His eyes didn't hold the same.

"I brought it, Lilly, but I haven't really felt like playing lately. Maybe soon." I could see that Lilly was going to revisit this and I didn't want Guthrie to have to explain, especially since he seemed uncomfortable, so I interrupted.

"Lilly, how about showing Guthrie your new hopscotch board that you and P.S. painted. And the mini one for the boys. I'll bet that he'll think they're cool."

Guthrie looked at me with a hint of gratitude. I think he needed to move to something lighter. Lilly led the way to their courtside masterpieces. I watched as Guthrie wheeled himself towards the court with Lilly talking away about anything and everything. I went to go help get dinner ready in the kitchen.

A bunch of us prepared dinner and set up the two tables. It was solemn and quiet, but there was a comfort in being together in the Big House and knowing that we were all feeling similar things. I think the reality of the situation was sinking in. The ranchers filled

Guthrie in on some of the major things since his last visit. I just listened. And watched. After dinner and clean up, everyone went their own way, a few sticking around the back porch, not quite ready for the day to end and afraid for the next day to come. Guthrie went back to spend time with Poppie. I went to my own casita. I was tired and afraid for tomorrow as well. No one knew what the next day would bring and the worry and anticipation were exhausting. I didn't know how Nonnie did it. I was thinking about that as I fell asleep. I felt my pillow getting wet as the tears fell while I drifted off.

Day 32: I think It Was Buddha who Said that the Problem Is That We All Think We Have Time.

I asked Lilly about her daydreams today.
She thanked me for asking…

"So what brought you to the ranch?" I startled. Guthrie saw me jump.

"Sorry. I didn't mean to startle you. I saw you out here and thought I'd say hi before heading to the Big House."

"That's OK. I just didn't hear you. Usually, I go up for my coffee, but I woke early so I thought I'd start here. Can I get you a cup?" He said he would appreciate it, so I went in and came out with a cup for him. It was hard not to stare. And those eyes. I looked away.

"So, what brought me to the ranch?" I repeated his question. "My car broke down." I began to explain. Guthrie interrupted.

"And Barry found you. That much I know. So, I'm guessing that Barry offered you a place to stay." He smiled. "So you stayed. And your car got fixed, I'm guessing. And you're still here. You seem like a regular. How long have you been here?"

"A little over a month," I said. "But it seems like I've been here longer."

"You seem to fit right in with this crazy wonderful bunch." He nodded in approval. "From what Barry says, you've helped a lot with Lilly."

"I don't know. But we do have a good thing. If that's helpful, then I'm glad."

"I think it's great that Lilly has a friend all her own."

"I hadn't thought of it that way, until others said the same."

"Well, I agree with the others. You are hers. In a good way. And she needs that. So, thank you." I thought about it for a minute. Guthrie waited. It was too quiet.

"So, do you have a story, too?" I asked. Guthrie looked at me quizzically. "I mean everyone around here seems to have a story. What brought them here? Or to Diana long ago. How about you? Do you have a story?" I rethought my question. "Never mind. It's really none of my business. I shouldn't presume that everyone wants to share." He ignored the last part.

"I guess everyone has a story. Even me. It's kind of boring. No bestseller."

"The way everyone talks about you, it sounds like one." I wanted to know about Guthrie. I wanted to know his whole story.

"OK, I guess you would say I am the odd one around here." He looked out at the desert as he spoke. "I came from a functional, productive, loving family. My parents were happily married. I was an only child and was quite pampered and attended to. Life was great until they got in a car accident when I was 13. While they were in the hospital, I was placed with Diana so I could stay close to them. My people were all on the East Coast. I thought my parents would heal and come get me. But they didn't. My mother died after 10 days in the hospital and my father four days after her. And since none of my family claimed me, Diana kept me. So, I really have no scars from abuse or neglect." He stopped and then added, "Just a tired truck driver who fell asleep and crashed into my parents' car while I was home with a babysitter." He stopped and looked over at me. "A bit different from the others, yes?"

"Maybe. But all of your stories include loss and the pain that comes with it. I'm sorry."

"Thank you, but that was a long time ago and Diana and Barry became my parents." And then he added, "and Nonnie and Poppie my grandparents." A subtle, yet sad look came across his face.

When he lost his parents, Guthrie explained, he began to change. His mouth began to get him in trouble so Poppie introduced him to the saxophone and airplanes. This kept his mouth busy and his time taken. He talked more about how these things kept him out of the trouble he was almost climbing into. He considered these gifts from Poppie. We sat for just a bit more. It was both comfortable and unnerving. Neither one more than the other. We went to the Big House to get an update.

Lilly always wore her charm necklace. Coco had explained this when I had asked how I could tell if Lilly changed to Diana. You could always see it on her. Except when she was jumping rope. She tucked it under her shirt when she jumped. If she was still Lilly, then she had Diana's wedding ring on the chain. When she was Diana, the ring would find its way to her finger. When Barry found her early this morning, she was halfway onto Poppie's bed, nuzzled in his neck. They were both sleeping. Her ring was on her finger. Barry looked at it and he knew. He was filled with great relief and a little jealousy. He knew that Diana had come back to say goodbye to Poppie. He was glad. Now he didn't have to worry about her getting to see him before he died. She had come. His jealousy came from not being the one to bring her back. How he wished that she would come back for him. He just stood there and watched them sleep. As long as she had her ring on her finger, she was his. He didn't want her to wake. But she did. His heart broke softly as she stretched and without even thinking, rubbed her eyes, took her ring off and put it on her charm necklace.

Later, Nonnie explained to Barry that she had heard Diana with Poppie throughout the night. As much as Nonnie wanted to have some of her and share her with Barry, she stayed "asleep," as she didn't want to interrupt what she knew would be their last visit. So she just listened. Nonnie told Barry how Diana talked to Poppie through yes and no questions. Nodding was almost all he could do now, so Nonnie could tell his responses by Diana's reactions and questions. They "said" what they needed to say. They remembered the past. Sabino Canyon and Diana leaving Poppie for college. They talked about now. Diana told him how hard she was working to feel strong so he could be proud of her again. And she cried to him and he stroked her head. And they told each other what they did not need to. That they loved each other and were better from having the other. She promised Poppie that she would come back one day and be able to take care of us.

The ranchers were getting a sense that Poppie's time was close to spent, so out of respect, they let Nonnie and Barry have most of it. Lilly could have as much as she wanted, but a child of 12 doesn't really want to wait for death to arrive. So Lilly asked me if I wanted to go the lake for a bit. She told me she already fed Simon and gave him his medicine so he was resting.

Twenty minutes later we found ourselves sitting on the far side of the bank of the lake. We had filled a couple water bottles, grabbed some apples and nuts and a sheet to sit on. We looked for Sasha on the walk in, but we didn't see her. After a few minutes, Lilly stood and went and found a few stones to skip on the water.

"I'm not very good at this. I've only gotten to two skips. P.S. got to three. And once she got to four. I want to get to three. That's my lucky number." She kept trying to get to three and I kept watching for Sasha. I imagined she missed Simon. After a few minutes, Lilly sat back down next to me. She sat there very quietly staring out into the water. I thought she might be looking for Sasha, too, but she didn't seem to be looking at anything. After a minute or so I interrupted whatever was in her head.

"Are you daydreaming, Lilly?" I asked. I was watching her and it looked like her mind was elsewhere. She took a second to come back.

"Yes," she answered. She looked different.

"Where did you go?" I asked, not sure why I chose those words. She didn't really go anywhere. She turned and looked at me, seemingly surprised. Her face changed again. Now it held something in between sadness and melancholy.

"No one ever asked me that." She saw my reaction. I was worried I had intruded somehow.

"No. It's OK. It's good."

"Oh," I said, with some relief.

"I can't really explain where I go," she said whimsically. "I go to a place somewhere between here and there." It was an odd answer, but I felt I understood what she meant.

"Do you like it there?"

"Yes," she said. "Yes, I do. Daydreams are a great place to visit." She was serious. And then, softly, she thanked me for asking.

⁓⁓⁓ ⁓⁓⁓ ⁓⁓⁓

By the time we got back to the Big House, others arrived and brought lunch. Some were ranchers, some visitors from town and a few who came in from out of town, wanting to be near. I introduced myself to some and others introduced themselves to me. This would be the way I met many new people in the week to come. They were all gathered in the gazebo, the weather being too nice to be inside. It was a clear day with just the slightest of breezes. Just enough to notice. And the sky was that blue that I came to love, with puffy clouds sharing some of it's space. We spent most of the day in the gazebo and visited. Except for Lilly. She went to be with Barry, Nonnie and Poppie.

Coco was reminding someone about Poppie teaching them the This or That game. Before we knew it, everyone had joined in to participate in what evolved into huge This or That game. We went around the group, taking turns asking and answering who preferred the Beatles to the Stones (Beatles won), Star Wars to Star Trek (a tie), boxers or briefs (boxer briefs won, with a few "commando" holdouts), sweet or salty (surprisingly a majority liked the combo), Blues or Rock and Roll (a heated debate resulting in what I would consider a tie), scrambled or sunny-side up (another tie), soup or salad (all agreed it depended on the kind of soup or salad), chunky or creamy peanut butter (crunchy by a landslide), martini or margarita (margarita, but this may have been a regional thing), thin crust or thick (again, depending on what type of pizza), crushed ice or cubed (I'd say a 60/40 split) and more This or That's.

We found comfort in each other's company and the small distractions that we provided each other. But everyone knew we were also waiting. The chatter didn't really mask the worry, the games didn't erase the anxiety and the little things didn't really distract anyone enough to forget why we were all here. I watched Guthrie interact with the others. It was becoming more and more difficult for me not to watch him. I was glad that his friends were there for him, as he was for them. They had a history that offered him some comfort. This was not to say that they hadn't brought me comfort, too, and that I truly appreciated it. But it was not the same.

So the rest of the day echoed the start of the day: comfort in each other's company partnered with the dread of what was coming. Everyone ate when they wanted, came and went when they felt like it, hiked around the area, visited the lake, reminiscing, crying, holding each other and laughing at some of the remembering.

And everyone was also very cognizant and worried about Nonnie. Many made sure that she was eating and drinking, resting as she needed. They took care of things that she normally would so she could devote herself to sharing Poppie's last hours.

I felt a little bit like an outsider, as I didn't share these memories with the others. But I also felt like an insider, as I was able to help because I knew the ranch, where everything was, the tasks that still needed to be tended to and more.

So I faded in and out of the circle of friends, in between watering the potted plants, gathering the eggs and feeding the dogs.

After a little while, and after my "goodnights," I faded back to my casita to be myself. Not the outsider. Not the insider. Just Jade. A girl who broke down, was taken in and was better for it.

I never really enjoyed baths. To me, it was like washing in dirty water. There were rare occasions that I made an exception to the shower option. Maybe a sore body, or a solemn mood. Even a foreplay bath here and there. Sometimes, when I made the exception, I enjoyed it so much that I wondered why I didn't take baths more often. Tonight, I felt like a bath. I turned on the water and added some bubble bath. I found a few candles, lit them and placed them on the ledge by the tub. I turned the lights off and slowly got into the hot tub topped with a frothy layer. The water was a little too hot and I could feel the sting of the heat, but I got used to it quickly and comfort set in. All I could see was the flickering lights and the shadows the flames made in the semi-dark bathroom. And there was no sound except for the bubbles. It was odd. It was quiet because that was all there was. But it was also loud because that was all there was. The muffled sounds of bubbles leaving. I lied there for a while and just let my mind go. At first, it didn't go anywhere. It stayed right there, listening to the bubbles and watching the flickering flames from the candles. When my mind began to wonder, it went straight to Guthrie. It was hard to keep him out of my head. After leaving Dean, anything intimate was the farthest from my mind. The thought of another man only conjured up feelings of mistrust and betrayal. And while I let my guard down slowly, the thought of intimacy didn't bring the sharp pain that it once did. Time had helped. And now with Guthrie here, the pain seemed gone.

As I lay in the tub, the thought of him made me feel good. But as good as the thought of him felt, worry about Poppie and all of those who would lose him muted the comfort of knowing that I was healing in some way.

Day 33: We only get one life. But if we do it right,
then one is enough.

Death can be patient. It knows no loyalty
except to the one that it came for.
It hovers, waiting...

Lilly greeted me at the Big House, asking when we could take
Simon for his checkup. She wanted to reunite Simon with Sasha
today. Nonnie was with Poppie, along with Barry and Guthrie. I told
Lilly to get Simon ready while I talked with Coco, who was fixing
baby Jack breakfast.

"Do you think I should wait? Maybe Lilly should stick around?"
I looked at Coco. She had a sadness in her eyes that was bigger than
yesterday.

"I already talked to Nonnie. She believes Diana already did
what she needed to and now Lilly is here to do what she can't. So
take her, but watch for signs. This is new stuff for Lilly. For all of
us."

So Simon, Lilly and I went to the vet. He complimented Lilly on
her caregiving skills and, after an examination, discharged Simon to
be reunited with Sasha. We returned to the ranch with Simon in
Lilly's excited hands, eager to take him back to his home.

"Do you wanna go with me to take Simon?" Lilly asked with
hopeful eyes.

"I do, Lilly, but first I want to check and see if Nonnie needs
anything. Do you want to go see Poppie before we go?" I was
hoping that she understood what was happening and would want to
visit first.

"No, I'll visit with him after. He knows that Sasha misses Simon." And that was all. She waited for me to check in with the ranchers before we headed out to reunite Simon and Sasha. The whole walk to the lake, Lilly talked to Simon, as if he understood. She explained to him that he was better now, but that he had to take it easy. She told him that Sasha was waiting for him and that she missed him. All the things that you would think to say when you return a duck that had been shot with an arrow, to the lake, where his girlfriend waited for him. I just listened and worried that we needed to be back at the ranch in case Poppie called for Lilly's company.

After what seemed too long, we arrived and stopped by the edge where we usually watched the birds of Birdland. Lilly carefully placed Simon down on the ground. He stood there for a minute just looking around, shaking out his feathers and then slowly waddled out into the water. I could see Lilly hold her breath for just a second, as if she expected Simon to sink to the bottom of the lake. He didn't. He, slowly, swam out towards some of the other ducks and as they saw him, they slowly turned and swam towards him. We looked for Sasha, and sure enough, she came from behind and took the lead swimming towards Simon. When they met, there was no embrace or shouts of joy. After all, these were ducks. But they did nuzzle their heads for a second and then swam off together, the other ducks following. We watched for a few minutes and then I told Lilly it was time to go. She didn't argue.

"They call that the death rattle. Did you know that?" asked Lilly. We had returned from the lake and were sharing our last goodbye with Poppie. I wasn't really surprised to see only Lilly. I was just hoping that Diana would show up. I was worried that she would later regret not being there. Maybe it was just too difficult. Most of the others at the ranch had come and gone earlier in the morning.

Lilly, Barry and Nonnie were with Poppie. I didn't want to risk spending anyone else's time, in case Poppie did not stay long enough to take everyone's goodbye. So I waited until everyone had gone in and then come out. Now it was my turn.

"No, I didn't know that," I answered, wondering how she knew this. But Poppie's breathing sounded like her words. I walked towards Lily's side of the bed. Barry was on Poppie's left sitting next to Nonnie, who was holding Poppie's hand in hers. She was quiet and still. Lilly was on his right.

"Come closer. Do you want to hold his hand?" She let me step in front of her. "Here." Lilly put Poppie's hand in mine. I looked over at Barry, not sure if it was appropriate to participate in such an intimate and private ritual. Barry smiled sadly, recognizing that I needed his permission. I took Poppie's beautiful, soft and well-worn hand. It still felt like life, but I felt it fading. Like a candle burning down to the bottom of the wick. He coughed a wet soggy cough that sounded too harsh for his weakness. I looked at Nonnie, sitting in the chair, simply looking at her husband with adoring eyes. There was no fear or anxiousness in her gaze. In fact, it seemed like she was seeing him as she remembered him to be. And she knew enough to know that this last part was what she made it. Poppie had no power. Only Nonnie could make it easier or harder. And she would, of course, choose easier. She watched him for just a little while longer. Then she got up, walked over to Poppie and kissed him on his damp, unresponsive lips. She whispered something in his ear. His eyes fluttered. And then she left. I couldn't imagine the pain of watching this. Barry walked her out to Coco, who was waiting for her. He quickly returned.

"You need to tell him it's OK now, Lilly. That we will all be alright." Barry was looking at Lilly. But he didn't sound like whenever he talked to her. I imagined that this is how he sounded when he spoke with Diana. His face held the wish that she was. And it seemed, for a fleeting second, that Lilly's face held the regret that she wasn't.

Poppie coughed again. His whole chest coughed. But I didn't feel it in his hands. His hands were still. Not quite holding mine but not quite letting go. Lilly stroked his forehead, bent down and whispered softly in his ear. He calmed with her touch. But his breathing was still labored. And it still sounded wet. Lilly kept stroking his forehead. It was like she was the adult and Poppie was the sick child. Barry was sitting where Nonnie had been, his face close to Poppie's. I wasn't sure if I should stay or not, but I didn't want to interrupt Barry's thoughts to ask.

And then, slowly, Poppie's breathing started to fade. And with the fading came quiet. My heart raced and I felt panicked. I looked over at Barry. He was watching Poppie's face, waiting. We both waited for something that we weren't quite sure of. But Lilly, calmly, just kept stroking Poppie's forehead. For what could have been seconds or minutes, Barry and I waited and watched Poppie's face. And Lilly kept touching. With a small wet cough, Poppie began breathing again. Not faster, as it should have been, trying to catch up from all the breaths lost. It was as it was before. It seemed as if Lilly didn't even realize that Poppie had stopped breathing. Barry and I looked at each other. I thought Barry was going to say something when Poppie's breathing began to quiet again. This time Barry and I watched Lilly. If she noticed you could not tell. Her fingertips were gently caressing the side of Poppie's face. She didn't look sad or scared. She just looked content, standing by her father's side. Comforting him with the same touch that he had comforted her so many times. She didn't seem to notice Barry watching her.

Poppie's breathing stopped. Lilly kept stroking his head. Barry and I waited. And just like before, it began again. No one spoke. Barry and I sat there holding his hands and Lilly stood by his side caressing his face. There was no sound other than Poppie's breathing. It wasn't loud. It just seemed so because that was all there was. Until it stopped again. And then came the quiet. This time Lilly stopped caressing. She gently leaned over and kissed Poppie's forehead, her lips lingering on his brow. I waited for Poppie to breathe again. And Barry waited for me to understand what Lilly already knew. It didn't take long. I was just as amazed that Poppie was now gone as I was that she knew. Then she laid her head on his chest and cried for just a minute. Barry walked over to comfort her. I had never witnessed what I had just shared with Lilly and Barry. And it wasn't like I would have thought it to be. At first, all that I knew was that it was alright. And after a while, it began to feel like a gift.

⎯ ⎯ ⎯

Nonnie wanted the funeral to be the following day. "So many people have come so far. Poppie wouldn't want them to put so much on hold for him."

Coco, Reesa and Kelly had known this about both Nonnie and Poppie, so they started making arrangements as soon as they knew. I think it must have been discussed beforehand and everyone was glad for that. The waiting had been difficult and so the idea of honoring Poppie sooner rather than later was desirable for everyone.

Nonnie stayed at her house with Barry, Lilly went over to be with P.S. and the rest of the ranchers and some friends got ready. Everyone sort of just took charge of what they thought they should and could do to help. Some began cleaning the Big House, knowing that people would be over after the funeral, some tended to the animals, some the little ones, and others ran errands to buy food and supplies. Coco tended to Nonnie and Barry, making sure that they were fed and had the privacy that they needed. Huey made arrangements to get Guthrie to the Air Force base to make sure that Poppie got the proper military funeral that he had earned. It was a long day. And it was a sad day. But Poppie was at peace now and we all tried to take comfort in knowing this.

Day 34: Poppie always said...

Poppie was even bigger than I knew.
I did not know that love for another could grow,
even after they were already gone...

I had never been to a military funeral. To say it was moving is not adequate, but I cannot think of a word that would be. I sat with Lilly, Nonnie, Barry and Guthrie in the front row. Lilly's last connection with Poppie was during his last moments, which were extremely intimate and loving. She had handled herself with such grace, and she did not even realize it. She did not let it wound her. Lilly seemed solemn, like she was lost in thought. She didn't cry, which I doubt surprised anyone. What did surprise me was that she held both Barry and Nonnie's hands, sitting between them. I wondered if it was to find comfort or to give it. Guthrie was in his uniform and had shaved. I felt for him, watching him stoically stare out the window.

The chapel was full of family, other ranchers, friends from town and fellow veterans. The hall was charming and comfortable. The front of the room held a beautiful wooden podium with a microphone, standing between two American flags on each side. In front of the podium was Poppie's casket, draped with a larger American flag. On each side of the podium were stained glass window panels depicting the United States Air Force emblems. There were rows and rows of seats, and still the room brimmed over. An honor guard, consisting of four men in their crisp pressed Air Force dress uniforms, stood at attention, two on each side of the podium. Throughout the service, they stood, without moving, as the chaplain and others spoke.

The chaplain began with Poppie's history before his military service. It was brief, but it told me his story before he was recruited, and then he spoke about Poppie becoming and serving as a pilot, which was more impressive than I had known. You could hear a few people crying softly, but other than that, everyone listened in silence.

Nonnie was the first to speak. We all told her that she didn't have to, but we knew she would. She slowly made her way to where the chaplain was standing. She had no speech written. I think she had always known what she would say when the time came. It was inside her.

"Hello, everyone. Thank you for coming to say goodbye to my Marcus. To your Poppie... friend... brother or uncle." She said this as she looked around at all of us sitting there. "This is a sad day. Anytime you say goodbye to someone you love, it's sad. But it's not tragic. My Marcus had a rich, full, exciting, adventurous life. It could have been a small life. Instead, his life was a big, pack it all in, don't live the same day twice kind of life. And it would be sadder if he was finished with it. But, really, it was just finished with him. He could have been alone. But thankfully, he was surrounded by all of you." She waited a few seconds. "Poppie would not want us to be too sad. I want to tell my Marcus...," she looked at the flag-draped coffin. "I want to thank you, my love. I want to thank you for giving me my gifts. Thank you for your love and devotion, which never wavered, even though we had some trials and tribulations that some would not survive. Thank you for our adventures and all of the memories that came with them. Thank you for giving me all of my babies, all of you." She glanced, looking across the room. "Thank you for making my life more grand than I could ever imagine." She had to stop and compose herself. After a deep breath, "And thank you for my little girl. She is now my part of you. Our masterpiece." I looked at Lilly. She just sat and held Barry's hand while she listened.

Nonnie finished and slowly walked back. Will greeted her halfway to help her to her seat. The chaplain then turned over the podium to whoever wanted to speak. This is when I learned the most about Poppie. Person after person took turns sharing their stories. If I hadn't fallen in love with Poppie that first day, I would surely fall in love with him today. As people spoke, you could see heads nodding in agreement and you could hear short whispered comments like, "I remember that." or "That was so Poppie!" The words were spoken with such love and respect and reverence.

After the last speaker, the honor guard moved, in precise, slow, synchronized steps, to the flag resting on Poppie's casket. They moved with such precision, it seemed like they were one. Two on each side, mirroring each other, lifted the flag and took three steps sideways so that two could release the flag, while the other two, in equally slow and precise movements began the formal ceremony of folding it in a precise triangular series that ended with one soldier, with his pristine white gloves tucking in the end of the flag, completing the task. They did this in crisp, long movements. The soldier then, in the same, slow, crisp steps walked over to Nonnie and presented the flag to her with a short military thank you, for Poppie's service to our nation. Nonnie accepted it graciously and held it to her heart. The soldier walked back into formation and one of the other soldiers took out a bugle. He began slowly and woefully playing Taps. I later learned that this was a special honor. Not many military funerals have a live bugler because there are not as many available as there once were. For Poppie, they found one. Everyone knew he loved his horns.

Everyone came back to the house after the funeral. We made Nonnie sit and eat, while many kept turns, willingly, sitting vigil with her. People came and went, all offering their condolences, some staying for a visit, some leaving after a short while and some sticking around for as long as they could. Just like many visits after funerals, there were tears, laughs, sobs and silence. It all depended on the person who was sharing the moment with you.

Many left after Lilly began saying her goodnights. Coco was taking her and Nonnie back to their house, ending a very long, emotional day, which brought a long chapter of their lives to an end. Tomorrow they would start another, without Poppie.

"No more Poppie," Kelly sighed. The ranchers, some of the out-of-towners and locals who didn't want the day to end, were gathered on the back patio. It was full, with some sitting on the floor or on a friend's lap. Everyone wanted to be together. One began with a story and then another joined in and soon it was a Poppie-fest, filled with more laughter and tears. I sat there and listened to them, hearing one memory trigger another, which triggered another. People just took turns jumping in with their Poppie memories.

There were two stories, in particular, that touched me the most. The first was Annie's story, a foster for much of the '90s.

If you were ever one of their kids, you remained one of their kids for as long as you wanted. Even after I returned to my mother, it just meant that I now had two families. Tyler was another one of Diana and Barry's fosters. We both lived there when we were in middle school. One day, Tyler was on his bicycle riding home from school when a car, driven by a man who was high on something, struck him. The day Tyler died was the only day that I ever saw Poppie cry. After his funeral, Poppie invited all of Tyler's friends from school and he gathered them with the other kids in the house, and one by one, Poppie took them up to Tyler's room. He sat them down and told them all the same thing. He told them to look around the room. He explained to them how he wanted them to pick something of Tyler's to take with them. Something to help them remember Tyler's life. He talked about the man who hit Tyler and how, from that moment, his life would be a very hard life. He wanted us to look at our keepsakes: a t-shirt, a baseball, a poster. They were to be a reminder not to become that man. To never drive under the influence. It took half the day and it exhausted Poppie, but he didn't stop until he had given something to each friend.

Lawrence, another foster from the '90s, told the second story.

Diana and Barry's was my fourth and final foster family. I stayed with them until I graduated high school and went off to college. I wasn't an easy teen. I had arrived so damaged, but Diana, Barry, Nonnie and Poppie had a way with kids. I thank God every day that I was one of them. And when I left their home, they didn't stop sharing their ways. With their help, I got on a good path. I graduated college, got my real estate license and, with a lot of hard work, I began to make a name for myself up in Phoenix. After three years in the market, and doing very well, I had decided to go on a well-earned, overdue vacation. My first cruise with some friends. It was going to be sweet. I called the family to let them know that I was leaving in a couple weeks and the next morning at work, Nonnie called and said that Poppie was on his way up to Phoenix. He only wanted 20 minutes of my time and that he would meet me at my office. After calling Diana and being reassured that Poppie was alright, I waited for him to show up. When he finally walked into my office, he gave me a big smile and hug, which gave me great relief. We sat down and he began by telling me how proud he was that I was doing so well. He spoke about how happy it made him that my hard work had paid off and how I had earned this vacation and he wanted me to have a great time. But, he continued, he had a request that he thought was important. He told me that now that I was an adult and on my own, and now that I had enough money, especially enough to go play, that it was time to start paying back. He wanted me to make some kind of donation or pledge to some cause, any cause before I left. I asked him why he needed me to do this now. He explained that my vacation would be so much sweeter if I did this before I left. That because I had received help achieving my success, he hoped that I would consider doing something similar. He didn't care what size check and he didn't care where I sent it, but that I should take care of this before I went to play. He was right. It was a great trip.

Lloyd brought out a few of the photo albums. They were filled with pages and pages of history and proof that Poppie existed. Lloyd went back and got a few more. Soon, small groups were searching for their books. Their place on the timeline that was Diana. The pictures triggered memories of t-shirts and toys, hairstyles and old roommates. Or blanket forts and houses made of cards, stitches from jumping off the bed and talent shows. I got to see Huey's goth phase, with his mohawk and black nail polish, and Coco with Jack still inside her belly. And Nonnie, with raven hair, just as beautiful as her silver hair now. They showed me Poppie in all of it. A much younger Poppie cheering at the swim meets or his silly bowling victory dance. His love of planes and trick-or-treating, pinewood derbies and tea parties. Poppie was equal opportunity. It was nice sitting around and remembering. Lawrence took pictures of us on the porch together. I found some solace in knowing that I would be in one of these books one day.

The reminiscing went on for another couple of hours before some others left. A few more trickled away, but not everyone was eager to end the day we all said goodbye to Poppie. Eventually, I trickled too.

I was walking down the path away from the Big House, looking at the countless stars in the night sky. I should have been watching ahead. Down I went, tripping over a boulder. I scraped up my palms and elbows hitting the ground.

As I sat up, getting ready to stand, I heard it. What began as barely a sound grew unhurriedly into musical air. It, very slowly, grew louder, like it was stretching after a long sleep. And eventually, it stretched out into a long musical note. I stood and tried to hear better where the music was coming from. The note held for a few more seconds. And then another. And the next note evolved into a haunting melody. It was a slow and tragic story. It was a questioning melody; wondering who else felt this kind of pain. It came from inside someone. As the notes continued to reveal themselves, so did the maker. Guthrie was at the house. He must have thought that I was still with the others, so he blew with abandon. And I guessed that this was his way of dealing. His photo album. Not wanting to interrupt his reunion with his sax, I stayed sitting on the ground. I wanted to listen.

I had heard much about Guthrie and his sax. The consensus was that he usually had it on (strapped, turned to his back) or near. And that he played often. But he hadn't played. He hadn't even brought it out.

The song began to sound familiar. It was a moan I had heard before. As I stood, the notes got bolder. Not louder. Just bolder. I tried to remember where I had heard this tune. But nothing... just a familiar tug. I slowly began to walk away from the music back to where everyone was remembering Poppie. And then I stopped. I remembered. It was my first visit with Poppie. This was the song that Poppie had shared with me. Remembering this first meeting brought me both pain and comfort. I didn't want to stop Guthrie's playing, so I sat down on the ground and remembered Poppie while I listened to his woeful melody. I wasn't really sure who Guthrie was playing for. Maybe himself. Maybe Poppie. Or maybe for all of us. It didn't really matter. What mattered was that Guthrie picked up his saxophone. Still not wanting to interrupt his grief, I eventually made my way back to the group. As I approached them, you could tell they had all heard too. And you could tell there was relief in knowing that he still could play if he wanted to.

"What happened to you?" asked Lloyd.

"I tripped. They hit first." I held my arms up. I didn't realize they were bleeding.

"Let's go inside and clean you up." Kelly got up and waited for me to join her. I did. She waited at the door for just a second to hear Guthrie's sax one more time. "That's Poppie's favorite. Mine, too."

Kelly led me to the kitchen, grabbed a branch of aloe and broke it off. She took out a first aid kit from the pantry and cleaned my elbows by the sink and then rubbed the aloe over the scrapes.

"Thanks."

"No worries, Jade. Family watches family around here," she said with a sad tone.

"I know, Kelly. I just never belonged to a family like this."

She started to quietly cry. Tears fell.

"I know you know," she said, almost apologetically. I turned into her and hugged her. She held on and her quiet cry became a duet. We held each other for a couple minutes before she let go. "I guess we needed that. Thank you."

"No worries, Kelly. Family watches family."

She let out a small laugh and we headed back out to the porch. After a full report on my injuries, I headed back to the casita. The music was over. He was in his room when I came in. I went to mine.

Day 35: Different Shades of Blue

I wish we could all switch gears like Lilly.
But we couldn't. We were wrapped in the blues.
And everyone wore their own...

It was early morning when Lilly came bursting in the door, just like she had a week ago. "Wanna go see how Simon is doing? I got a cup to go, just in case." She had it in her hand. "A little sweet cream, just the way you like it," she whispered, not sure if Guthrie was awake and happy with herself that she knew me so well. It was a beautiful morning so it would be nice to start it out by the lake. I guessed this was Lilly's way of coping (or not) with Poppie being gone. I was glad she wasn't feeling the heaviness that comes with remembering he wasn't here. Diana would later.

"Sure. Sounds like a great idea." I had already dressed for the day. I grabbed the coffee from her and we headed out. We walked down the path to the lake. The coffee tasted good.

"It's Coco's favorite blend. Good?"

I told her it was perfect. While I walked, Lilly skipped. She talked about Simon, still worried a bit. We approached the turn to the grass patch and walked over and sat down to wait for a Simon sighting. It wasn't a long wait.

"There he is," she said, pointing to Simon near the side of the lake. I looked to where she was pointing. There he was, waddling into the water. Sasha was a few feet behind him. He looked healthy, aside from waddling just a bit, to one side. But he would only grow stronger. Lilly had saved him. We sat for a little while longer. Lilly's concern lessened each time she saw him a bit healthier. I could tell she was feeling better about Simon when, on the walk back to the Big House, she asked me if I knew that pigs couldn't look up at the sky. I didn't, but that's beside the point. I enjoyed Random Lilly.

By the time we made it back to the Big House, friends from outside had begun to gather with the ranchers, resuming their commiserating and reminiscing. Many of them, aside from their own grief, were worried about Nonnie. The afternoon was filled with more food, stories, tears and laughter. And more learning about Poppie and his history with these people. My love still grew. How could it not?

The ranch became a refuge for those who Poppie left behind. And the Big House was filled with all of this. Past fosters and newer friends, family and his military brethren. Both Poppie and Lilly's doctors visited. The ranch was filled with coming and going and sharing and eating and crying and laughing and everything else that comes with grieving. Nonnie let people dote on her. I think more for them than for her. Nonnie knew time would be her only healer. But, she also knew they needed to be needed.

As I watched the ranchers and visitors, I saw everyone react in their own ways. Lilly floated back and forth between being solemn and being 12. Nonnie, while sad, wore her strength like a cloak. Barry kept busy, but he seemed tired. Huey clung to humor. Kelly and Reesa were weepy. Sunshine and Will kept to themselves a little more. And I watched Guthrie. I couldn't help but watch him. He was somber and mostly listened, but I think he found solace in the presence of those around him.

I was sad, but I felt that the others had more right to their grief than I did, so I mostly watched and helped where I could. I did dishes, cleaned up after people, and took out the garbage, anything I could think to do to keep busy. I really did not want to stop to take time to feel my own loss. I knew it enough to avoid it. I didn't want to think about it today. Maybe another day, but today I just wanted to keep busy. And that is what I did until the last person left and we all went our own ways at the end of the evening.

Day 36: The Blues, continued.

So, today I woke and shared the sunrise with Guthrie.
And he shared some of his life with me...

I woke up just before sunrise. I had been doing that more, ever since the first sunrise with Lilly. I stretched as I woke. I always had. Jesse did too. He called it "pushing out the sleep." After I was warmed up I got out of bed and contemplated putting on a robe. I opened the sliding door to feel the air. I decided against the robe. It was going to be a beautiful morning, I thought to myself. I went out to the patio, which faced east, and sat down on the lounge chair to begin waiting for the sun.

"Good morning."

I jumped.

"God, you scared me!"

"Sorry. I didn't mean to." Guthrie was sitting on his patio, which was next to mine.

"It's OK," I said, a little embarrassed at being caught in my underwear and a t-shirt. "I'll be right back." I went inside and grabbed a pair of pants, put them on, checked my hair in the mirror and went back outside.

"You didn't have to put on pants for me." Guthrie was grinning. I felt myself blushing, which I found odd. I wasn't usually shy about something like this.

"I was a little chilly," I answered back, thinking that it wasn't too far from the truth. It felt something like a shiver. I sat down again.

"Do you often wake up before the sun?" I asked him, trying to redirect my thoughts. My eyes began adjusting to the dawn. I could see that he was wearing a very worn out t-shirt and a pair of baggy sweatpants that were easy to get on over his casted leg and bandaged foot.

"More and more."

"Me too."

"It's strange to come back to this. I wouldn't have wanted to be anywhere else. But it's strange to wake knowing Poppie isn't here. Or Diana," he added. "And sometimes I have these dreams and they wake me up. The ranch helps. It's just been some hard days."

I wanted to ask him about his dreams, but I didn't want to intrude. It seemed personal and we had only met a few days ago. But then I thought that if he brought them up then maybe they were on his mind. And I wanted to know more about him.

"Do you want to talk about it?" I waited.

"Really, I'm not quite sure why I brought them up. I haven't told anyone about them except for the doctors."

"Did you have a dream last night?" It just had occurred to me that he was still feeling it and that was why it was on his mind.

"Yes. I dream a lot."

"I'm a good listener, if you need one," I offered. I could see him contemplate for just a few seconds before he answered.

"It's not such a big thing, but I still have dreams about my legs. Like before the explosion. All kinds of dreams with my legs doing all kinds of things. And I know they will heal and I will be able to do almost everything I did before. But not using them for so long, they feel useless right now. Last night, I was swimming. And I know I was asleep. But I felt it." He said as if he were trying to convince me.

"I felt the coolness of the water, the resistance against my arms, the exhaustion and burning in my muscles. I even woke up hungry." He paused for another second. "Swimming always made me hungry." I felt bad for him. I didn't know what to say to make it any better.

"Swimming makes me hungry, too," was all I could think to say. He let out a short quiet laugh.

"Well, that wasn't so scary," he said quietly.

"What?" I didn't understand.

"Talking about my legs." He looked directly at me, with a hint of puzzlement. "I really don't do that often. In fact, not at all outside of the hospital." Then he offered me a small, soft smile and my heart melted. It took me a minute to compose myself.

"I guess I can understand that. But I'm glad it was easier than you thought." I tried to think of something else to say. "I guess it's that ranch magic."

"Or maybe it's you."

I think I was holding my breath. He saw my reaction.

"I mean, maybe I knew that you'd be a good listener and I'd feel comfortable with you." He stopped, clearly not sure what to say next. I waited. "I know we haven't known each other that long. I think watching you with Diana... Lilly..., it makes me think you have something in you that can handle the broken souls around here. Or in my case, broken legs." He let out a quiet laugh.

"Well, I'm glad you feel you can talk to me. I feel the same. And I have my own fears." He feigned surprise. "Yep. I recently decided that I need to redecide what I want to do," I proclaimed. "Maybe go back to teaching. Maybe not. Maybe LA. Maybe not. I don't know and that scares me. But, it's a good scared. I think my life needed a good spring cleaning. I'm lucky to have time to think about it. After I give it enough deep, honest consideration, I will redecide." My proclamation was over.

"Sounds like a plan." He smiled again. I wondered if he could hear my heart beating. Or feel it.

We sat together and watched the sun come up, talking about light things and heavy things. We talked about how he missed

Nonnie's cornbread and the U of A basketball team. He asked me about my family. I gave him the nutshell version. I found out he had been stung by a scorpion, too. And he had met Freddie before. After a while, I noticed that my heart didn't react every time he smiled. I wasn't sure if that was because I was just growing more comfortable with his presence or if my heart was now stuck this way.

～～～ ～～～ ～～～

The rest of the day was solemn, but a little less so than the day before. There was less company. Out-of-towners had gone for the most part and many of the locals wanted to give the ranchers some space. But sadness still hung over the ranch. You could see it in everyone's movements. You could hear it in their voices. And you could feel it in the air. Even the dogs felt it. Lilly, too. I wasn't sure if it was because she was feeling the loss or feeling everyone else's loss. Either way, I had to admit that I was a little relieved to see that she was in the moment, too. That, to me, seemed healthier than missing the process altogether.

Day 37: At Last

It seems as though Guthrie has moved into my head…

It was right before lunch. I was sitting on the steps of the gazebo, getting a little quiet time after spending the morning with Lilly.

"What are you thinking about?" Guthrie asked, noticing the look of contemplation. He wheeled up to just below where I was sitting. I looked down at him. He was so handsome. His beard was a few days old so he had a sexy, scruffy look going on. And those eyes…

"I was thinking about something that Lilly asked me earlier." He waited. "We were passing by the gazebo on our way back from visiting Simon when we saw you on the path. I thought you saw us, but it turned out you didn't." He looked down with a blend of embarrassment and amusement.

"Go on," he said, without looking up yet.

"Well, I know you didn't see us, but we saw you hit a rock and, expectantly, your wheelchair fell over." He looked up at me.

"Why didn't you say something?" There was no irritation in his voice. Just curiosity.

"I wanted to. I wanted to help, but Lilly grabbed me. She only said, 'Guthrie doesn't like help.' So we watched you get back in your chair, with great effort I might add, and then I thought that since you got back in alright there was no use making you feel uncomfortable. So we waited until you went by before we went to play." I looked at him. I couldn't tell what he was thinking, so I continued.

"I thought that was very intuitive of her to say that. I mean, she reads people so well. I guess that's the Diana in her."

"Well, she is right. I don't like help. Working on that, though. What did she ask?" he reminded me. "You said that she asked you something." I thought about her words. I wanted to relay them correctly.

"She asked me why I thought God took seven days to make the world when he could have taken eight and made it better." I looked at him while he took this is in. He had the same reaction I did.

"Wow. What did you say?"

"I said I didn't know. And that I thought it was a good question. I wasn't really sure how to answer."

"I probably would have said the same. I sure don't have the answer. What did she say to that?"

"She asked me which I wanted to play. Hopscotch or jump rope." He laughed.

We went up to the Big House to have lunch with everyone. Along with the salad and chili, was cornbread. I looked over at Guthrie. He was happy. And I understood, better, why he missed Nonnie's cornbread. It was homemade with real corn and it had a mild sweet taste to it. It was so moist that it barely left any crumbs and Nonnie always made honey butter to go with it. I looked over and saw Guthrie watching me eat a bite. He smiled a "told you so" smile and then went back to talking with Will.

Nonnie was cleaning up the kitchen with Kelly and me when Guthrie wheeled in.

"Hey, my sweet baby boy." She dried her beautifully wrinkled hands on her apron. "I think I could use a hug about now." She bent down, just a little, and Guthrie wrapped his arms around her. She was so tiny and he was so not, that his arms enveloped her. I could hear them both moan ever so slightly, as if emphasizing their hug. As she let go and stood upright, Guthrie thanked her for making the cornbread.

"Well you know, baby, I remember that was always one of your favorites." She smiled and then added, "You know, Guthrie, if you felt like playing your horn, I sure wouldn't mind." Kelly looked up from the sink, wondering what Guthrie was going to say. He hesitated just a few seconds before answering.

"Anything for you, Nonnie." Kelly looked relieved and happy at the same time. "I need to make some calls to the hospital back east before it gets too late. Can I play for you a little later?"

"Of course, child. Maybe you can play for us after dinner tonight. We aren't having anything special. We have a lot of leftovers from the past couple days and we're gonna have more cornbread. So maybe some music will make dessert a little sweeter." They agreed and Guthrie wheeled himself out of the kitchen and a minute later I could hear the porch door close behind him.

Kelly was staring at me and smiling when I turned back around. Apparently, I had been watching Guthrie leave and was taking my time getting back to the task of drying dishes.

"What?" I asked with an amused, yet defiant tone.

"Nothing," Kelly answered with the same amused, yet defiant tone.

We both looked at Nonnie and she was just pretending to tidy up, but you could see that she had a small grin on her face. Kelly and I helped Nonnie sort through the leftovers. We took out platters and bowls of food that friends and family had dropped off over the last couple of days. Nonnie directed us on what to keep and what to throw out. Whenever she gave a "throw it out" instruction it was always followed with a "Lord forgive me, I know it's a sin to waste" or something similar. Nonnie had us trim some fresh herbs and told us to go do our own things while she recreated a dinner from what we kept. Kelly and I both knew that she was just trying to keep busy and now needed a little alone time.

All of the ranchers still had a heavy heart, except for maybe Lilly. Michael had come to get Lilly after lunch to take her to therapy and then spend the night with P.S. They wanted to make it easier for Barry and Nonnie and this was something that they could think to do that would give them both a little respite. No one was neglecting their jobs or each other. It was just that there was still a heavy cloud over the ranch. It would take a while for the ranch to feel normal again. Whatever normal was at this non-normal place.

Kelly went to find Huey, who was with the kids, and I took a walk out to the lake to see Simon. It was strange. I had never been out there without Lilly. It was much quieter and a bit lonelier. I actually found Sasha first and then saw Simon not too far behind, paddling in the water. I was amazed that I could actually tell one duck from the others, but Simon and Sasha had become the main attraction for Lilly and I. And I guess helping tend to an injured bird for a week or more helps with the bonding.

I called Jesse from the lake, filling him in on what was going on. I had talked to him briefly the night Poppie died, but we hadn't really caught up in at least a couple of weeks. I told him about how Nonnie, Barry and Lilly were coping, as well as the other ranchers. He asked questions and I asked him about what was going on in his life. It was mostly chitchat, but it felt good to hear his voice.

"Are you really alright, Jade?" he asked, as if he thought I wasn't.

"Yeah. I am. Just sad still. You would have loved Poppie. I wish you could have met him."

"You sound like there is more."

"What do you mean, 'more?'" Jesse always knew when there was "more."

"You know what I mean. What aren't you telling me?" he wanted to know. I knew he could hear something missing, but I wasn't ready to talk about Guthrie. I wasn't sure what to say. It was almost as if I said it out loud then I'd have to admit that I was falling. I don't know why, but I just wasn't ready.

"I'm fine, Jesse. Like I said. I'm sad. We never lost anyone like this. This is new for me."

He let it go, knowing that I would tell him when I was ready.

After a relaxing dinner, we all gathered around the living room, filling the sofas and chairs. Coffee was made to go with a leftover dessert assortment. We settled in after a bit. Guthrie picked up his sax. You could see that he was a little uncomfortable. And it was a bit awkward in a wheelchair. He was used to standing while playing. But Nonnie asked him and he could never say no to her. Since he told Nonnie yes, everyone had been waiting.

He began playing a quiet, unhurried melody that slowly grew slightly louder and bolder as he continued. It never grew faster, just stronger, as if each breath filled him with a comfort or a confidence that had been lost but was now being rediscovered. I watched him as his mouth blew life into his saxophone and his fingers moved to make each note. I watched his mouth first. I got lost in it for a moment. And then I watched his fingers. As they moved, I wondered how his touch felt. The thought stirred something in me.

He played with his eyes closed, as if he were alone. But he wasn't. He was in a room filled with people who loved him and had been waiting to hear him play again. I glanced around the room, looking at everyone's faces. Each face looked content. You could see that Guthrie's music was therapeutic. No one spoke. No one requested a certain song. We were all just grateful to hear the music and didn't want it to stop.

I watched Nonnie now. You could see that the song Guthrie had begun was familiar to her. Her eyes were closed, too, but her face almost played along with Guthrie's saxophone. When he blew a higher note, her eyebrows lifted, when he blew a lower note, they fell back down. Her head gently swayed and her foot tapped ever so gently to the slow soothing beat.

He finished with Etta James' "At Last." It was drawn out and made you feel something inside. After a while, Guthrie opened his eyes and we knew he was finished. No one said anything for a minute. Nonnie stood up and went over to Guthrie and put one hand on each side of his face, cupping his cheeks. She kissed him on the forehead and whispered into his ear, "Thank you, child."

Everybody thanked Guthrie. He wasn't comfortable with the attention, but he was gracious. His music filled my dreams that night.

Day 38: A Day with the Dynamic Duo

Today was all about Lilly and P.S.
Games and puppies. The library and frozen yogurt.
Not a bad way to spend the day…

The trail between the ranch and P.S.'s house was well worn. It was about 1/4 of a mile directly west of the ranch. The trail, itself, was a beautiful walk with lush bushes and cacti escorting you from house to house.

Lilly and I had woken up earlier to go down to the lake. We had breakfast bars, orange slices and a banana while we watched Simon and Sasha, along with their friends. I wasn't sure if it was my imagination or not, but it seemed like Simon swam a little closer to us these days.

"Do you know who Emily Dickinson is?"

"Yes, she is a famous author who lived a while ago. Why?"

"I read the other day in my homework that she said that forever is made up of a bunch of nows. I think that's smart. It's kinda like you told me after we flew kites with Kenny a few weeks ago."

I thought about that for a minute. So did she, with a grin.

"I guess that makes you kinda smart, too."

"I guess so." I returned her grin. Lilly still thought about her future. It seemed as though I had said something after Kenny's conversation that had comforted her, so this statement was more of a confirmation of that than a confession that she was still unsettled with this idea. She didn't seem haunted. She simply was relaying something she thought relevant.

"Wanna go and see if P.S. is ready to go see the puppies?" We headed out to get her. Coco and Kelly thought Nonnie could use a carefree day, so we thought keeping Lilly busy would be one less thing for Nonnie to think about. She really hadn't given herself time to absorb it all. Or maybe she had and she was superwoman after all. I told them that I had it covered. They would watch Nonnie and I had Lilly.

As I came out of the clearing I could see the back of Michael and Annie's house. I wondered why it had taken me over a month to even get here. Their yard opened to a clearing with a flagstone walkway that led from the path to their back patio. The house was different from the ranch casitas, but it was also stucco and very welcoming. The porch had plants in colorful pots and a big Welcome sign angled to the side of the door. The sign looked like P.S. had made it. On both sides were creatively dessert-landscaped garden beds. Annie had arranged benches and circular wooden perches around some of the mesquites and cacti. There was a tire swing on the largest tree. You could see where Michael kept the brush away from the swing seat and arc of the swing. It looked like a little archway was trimmed out of the side of the tree foliage. Shasta greeted us halfway up the walk. Some of the dogs often shared their time at both homes. His happy whimper must have alerted P.S. She came bounding out the front door hollering her goodbyes to her mom.

"Let's go." She whizzed by.

Lilly and I just looked at each other and then followed. It took us a minute to catch up but when we did we found her, not so much angry, but impatient. She was excited to get to the puppies already. So we set off, P.S. with a little attitude, Lilly amused at P.S.'s attitude, and me amused at Lilly being amused. I wondered how Diana's 58-year-old body had the energy of a 12-year-old. I guess it was the same thing when one of her alters was a southpaw and another was a boy. This was what DID was. Each alter having their own, unique attributes. Lilly's was her energy and innocence. After some huffing and puffing (mine, not theirs) we made it to Maya's house.

Cisco was out in the corral. As always, he looked great. But lately, I had thought a lot less about him and more about Guthrie. He saw us and waved. We waved back. He knew we came to see the pups. Maya was on her way to the barn when she saw us. She was carrying a pail of water but she stopped to wait before going in to see Cayenne and her pups.

"Good timing. Right?" Her smile glowing, just like her golden locks.

"Are they awake?" P.S. was most eager to get her little paws on those littler paws. Lilly was right behind her.

"I don't know. Let's go see." She led the way. "Let's be quiet, just in case," she whispered, just before we heard the squeaks and purr-like growls that puppies make. "Never-mind," she added. We turned the corner to the pen where Cayenne lay with her puppies. She didn't get up, but she still wagged her tail when she saw Maya.

"Hey, pretty mama." She scratched the back of Cayenne's neck with a vigorous, circular raking, which, according to Cayenne's face, was the perfect way to scratch.

The six puppies were all spread out. Two were nursing, two were puppy wrestling, one was in the corner sleeping and one was at the edge of the pen trying to get to the girls, who had already begun their cooing. Maya grabbed the large shallow water pan, took it out and emptied it into a flowerpot. She came back in and filled it with fresh water from a hose before replacing it in the pen. One of the puppies put one foot in and then quickly pulled it out, eliciting giggles from the girls. Maya let the girls in the pen and told them to have fun, be careful, holler if they needed help and that snacks were waiting.

I walked with Maya to a picnic table just outside, around the corner. Close enough to watch, but not enough to compete with their verbal adoration and disbelief that such cuteness could possibly exist. Maya had a pitcher of ice, lemon slices and pink lemonade with glasses. Next to the stack of glasses was a plate with rows of apple and orange slices, cheese cubes, jicama and carrot sticks and banana bread. There was also a cup holding straws of honey, with a toothpick taped to each one. I finally learned what a honey straw was!

We sat and visited while the girls rotated their affections, each puppy getting multiple turns. They even gave Cayenne a little loving, too. They played for a while, picked out their favorites, giggled a bunch, cradled and babied them, then changed their favorites again. Maya and I watched them and chatted. She told me the story of how she and Charlie had met. I had asked.

We met almost five years earlier at an Ozomatli concert, at the Rialto, downtown. Their concerts are always fun. They're known for their energy and genuine joy. Everyone was dancing and getting into the music. After one of the songs, I felt someone smack my ass. I turned around and it was Charlie, who had seen me from behind and mistaken me for her date. After an awkward moment and an even more awkward explanation, we parted ways. Then, in the parking garage, I backed out and tapped the car behind me. It was Charlie's. We exchanged numbers. And the rest is history.

She laughed at this then continued to explain that the property and the horses were hers. They came from family. And Charlie had the bar downstairs at night and a one-room studio above by day. Before the first year, Charlie moved in with Maya. The bar business was a tough one, with long, inconvenient hours that were not very conducive for a new loving relationship. It was difficult, but they had made it work so far and I didn't have to ask about their future. You could see it whenever you saw them together.

So, Charlie kept busy with the bar and Maya kept busy with the horses and dog training. I learned that she usually trained two litters at a time. One litter would rotate out when another came along. I had no idea that she had these other dogs. She took me to what I thought was a giant barn, but inside was nothing like I anticipated. She called it "the Box." It was rectangular and, inside, three of its sides were lined with individual, large, kenneled areas where the dogs began their training. They were all happy to see Maya and let it be known, either through doggie greetings or wagging tails.

The middle of the room held three big, separate, freestanding rooms. One held older dogs that lived together. They had to reach a certain level of training before moving to that room. The other two rooms were training rooms. One had a studio (bedroom/bathroom/kitchen) set-up and the other had lots of props against the wall. Maya explained they also did off-site training.

We walked back to the pen to check on the girls. They were still lost in puppy bliss. We convinced them that they could play with the pups some more after they let them take a little nap (which they promptly did) and they had a little lunch.

"Did you bake some banana vinegar bread?" asked P.S.

"Banana vinegar?" I asked. Maya confirmed and the girls ran ahead to the picnic table. Walking back, Maya explained that the girls loved her banana bread so one day they came over so they could bake together. The recipe calls for buttermilk but she hated to waste unused buttermilk (since she only bought it for baking) so she substituted a tablespoon of milk with vinegar. The girls, she said, were utterly shocked that vinegar was in one of their favorite sweet treats. Ever since, they called it banana vinegar bread.

We all washed up and then sat and ate and talked. Most of the discussion was between the girls and involved their conspiracy to get Guthrie to take one of the puppies. Maya reminded them that, while she would gladly let Guthrie have any pup that was available, it was Guthrie's choice and wasn't something to push on him.

"Oh, we know," proclaimed P.S.

"We just have to figure out how to show him that he wants one," Lilly explained.

"Cause we know he does," finished P.S. They both were very confident.

I had to admit, that I hoped he did, too. It seemed like he needed something to ground him. He still seemed unsettled and maybe something to be responsible for would do that. And remembering what Maya had said about soldiers with PTSD and the comfort that dogs bring, who wouldn't want to endorse this matchmaking conspiracy? But it was Guthrie's choice to make. I had a feeling the girls would show him the light. I also had a feeling that they wanted a "piece" of a puppy. If Guthrie took one, it would be around the ranch and that was a win/win in their book.

The girls finished their lunch and headed back to the puppies. Maya asked if I wanted to watch her train for a short session. We told the girls where we would be if they needed us and reminded them that we would be leaving within the next half hour. We went back to the Box and Maya took me to one of the rooms, on the way picking up Isaac, a beautiful, older black lab puppy. She explained that I could watch through the window from the other side of the wall. She took out a cot from the props on the side and set it up in the middle of the room. She took out a pillow and blanket and set them up and then she dimmed the lighting slightly. She told Isaac, who was watching her do all of this to lay by the door. (She explained later that he would be trained to sleep with his paws against the door, seeming to block it from being opened. This helped calm the vets so they could sleep.) Isaac followed her command and she got in bed while she told him to stay. She lay calmly in the bed for almost a minute and then began tossing and turning slightly. She told Isaac to stay while she did this. She tossed some more and then began tossing and turning harder. After she did this she commanded Isaac.

"Up, kiss."

The dog promptly jumped up with his two front paws on the bed and started licking Maya's face. She gave him a treat from her pocket and told him how good he was while rubbing his neck. She did this two more times before coming out of the room and letting Isaac go back to his roommates. While we walked back to the girls she explained that the dogs would learn to do that to wake up the vets from nightmares or trances and fits. They trained them in the light first, and then in the dark. They trained them with the vet lying in bed, on a couch and recliner. Even on a park bench. Sometimes, using canes, or walkers and sometimes in a wheelchair.

"So, what do you think? Kind of interesting, yes?" Maya asked.

"It's fascinating. I can't believe all you have to do for one task. You're amazing."

She thanked me and told me there was a list of tasks the dogs performed to "graduate." Things like retrieving objects, proper positioning for public places and morning and bedtime rituals. I was in awe.

"I have to tell you, while it's a lot of tedious repetitive work, when I place them, each one of those days is a gift. It's really, really cool."

I gathered the girls and after hugs for each pup, Cayenne and Maya, we were off back to the ranch. On the way back, the girls talked more about their plan for Guthrie. I just listened. I didn't want to bother anyone, so we grabbed our game gear (jump rope – check, jacks and ball – check, Chinese jump rope – check, chalk – check) and headed for the gazebo. We played every game once and then I sat out and watched with Cairo and Jasper, who had wandered over at some point, while the girls did another round. As I watched, I imagined that they would sleep well tonight.

"Who wants to go to the library?" I was ready to move on to something else. I thought we could go to the library and read and relax a bit, then grab dinner before heading back home.

"We do," they said in stereo.

"OK. Go put the game gear back, grab your book bag and I'll grab my purse and keys. P.S., we can stop and grab your books on the way." We all walked back towards the Big House. I told Coco our plan. She thanked me, again.

The girls came in ready to go. We stopped to grab P.S.'s book bag and tell Michael the plan. We were good to go. The library kept us busy for an hour and a half, dinner kept us another hour and then a stop at Smoothie's and Stuff kept us another half hour. Anita was there. She asked me, away from the girls, how Nonnie was and asked me to share her sympathy, along with a few quarts, on the house. All of this time was filled with chat about what had become "Operation Guppy." They thought it very clever to combine Guthrie with puppy. Actually, it was. We grabbed our quarts to go after we finished our treats, thanked Anita and then headed home. I dropped off P.S. and then Lilly and I headed back to the ranch.

Our timing was perfect. They had just finished dessert when we walked in. Sitting around the table were Barry, Nonnie, Guthrie, Coco, Jack, Sunshine, Lloyd, Kelly and Tawn. Kelly was just getting the boys ready to take down to get ready for bed. I put the yogurt in the freezer while Lilly went in to see Nonnie.

"Come on over here, child. I missed you." Nonnie opened her arms to Lilly, who was already falling into them. They rocked for a minute and then Lilly kissed Nonnie's cheek before proceeding to tell everyone about our day, leaving out the details of Operation Guppy, of course. She told Nonnie that Anita sent her some frozen yogurt, "free!"

"Well, Anita is such a sweet one and it sounds like a most excellent day," Nonnie said with a cheery voice but an absent smile. "I want to hear more about it. How about we say our goodnights and you tell me more while we go back to our house?" Goodnights were said and Nonnie and Lilly headed out the door. Lilly abruptly stopped and turned around, and ran over to hug me.

"Thanks, Jade. It was a fun day." And then she ran back to Nonnie.

The rest of us cleaned up while we talked about our worries for Nonnie. We agreed that we would just wait and pay attention. See how she was the next few days. We left it at that and then I said my goodnights. I was wiped. The girls had lots of energy. I had run out of mine sometime between dinner and dessert.

Day 39: A Wonderfully Ordinary Day...
Which is Weird!

Guthrie, Coco and I spent the day in the park with the kids.
It was the closest thing to a normal day that I had had since I got here.
It was so normal, that it was a bit weird...

Guthrie, Coco and I were in the gazebo reminiscing about the day. In many ways, it was like any other. We all met in the Big House for coffee, we did chores. By mid-day, the eggs had been collected, the plants had been tended to, the squeaky shed door was remedied, the pantry was reorganized and Lilly's bedroom had been tidied up. But it really wasn't like any other. Poppie was not there.

We needed a change, so the three of us took P.S., Lilly and the boys to the farmers market at the park. It turned out to be a good idea.

The trip to the park, and seeing it through the eyes of the kids, was a nice change. They slowed us down and opened our eyes. Kids could do that to you.

⁓⁓⁓ ⁓⁓⁓ ⁓⁓⁓

The girls walked ahead of us with the boys. We were heading to the playground first. Lily held Jack's hand and P.S. held Tawn's. Watching them from behind was entertaining. Jack had his arm all the way up to hold Lilly's hand. They were about to turn the path that opened to the playground when P.S. abruptly stopped them to point out a big, complete spider's web between two bushes off the side of the path. We caught up to them and they were just mesmerized by the web and the dime-sized black and yellow spider hanging on, watching over its labor. The web was almost a foot wide. And it really was beautiful. Picture perfect as far as webs go.

"Did you know that some spiders spin their web every morning and then take them in every night? So if you keep knocking down their web they die cause they have no more stuff to make their web." Lilly continued to tell us how amazing spiders were. Some spiders spun organized symmetrical webs and others were "just a mess" and how you could identify some types of spiders by their webs. By the end of her chat, I had a bit more respect for spiders. It made me think about how much I had learned from Lilly. There were so many things that Lilly had shared with me. They made me feel bigger. Tawn reached for the web and Lilly, gently, grabbed his hand.

"Want pider," Tawn let out as he tried to grab for it again.

"No. Tawn," P.S. gently reprimanded him. "We don't bother other creatures unless they are trying to hurt us. That spider just wants to catch some lunch. He doesn't want to hurt us."

Lilly chimed in. "Guys," she sang, getting the boy's attention. Remember Nonnie telling us, 'Child, teaching you not to step on a bug is as valuable to you as it is that bug.'" She did this with an animated Nonnie voice that made the boys laugh.

"The spider's job is to spin its web. It wouldn't be very nice of us to bother him while he does his job." She looked at the boys who were watching her.

"Right?" she asked, sort of like a cheer.

"Right," they all yelled back. And then they moved on. Once the playground came in sight they ran ahead. The girls already had instructions to watch the boys, so the three of us found a cozy spot, close by, to watch them play. They were like little mothers, spotting them on the ladders to the slide, putting them in the swing and pushing them gently, chasing them around. Even letting them interact with other kids, in that kid sort of way, watching over the boys as they tried making new friends.

After a while, we told them they could go play themselves and we would watch the boys. They preferred to stay with the boys. We were surprised, but Coco had a theory. She thought that since they were some of the older kids here, they were more comfortable with the babysitter role. Guthrie and I thought that made sense. It didn't really matter. It was nice to have another 20 minutes, or so, to relax before going to the stalls. The kids headed back to the climbing tower. They went up the ladder, played with the gadgets and then slid down and then did it all over again. We noticed that each time they passed the bottom of the ladder they also passed a little girl who was just watching them. You could see them talk to her at first as they passed her. Then each time they passed, you could see them gesture to her to join them. By the third or fourth try, she did.

"She looks like Diana out there. Making sure everyone is included. Do you think that's the Diana in her or did we teach her to be that way?" Coco asked.

Guthrie said he had no idea, but agreed that it was like watching Diana. They both were a bit sad about this. We gave them a five-minute warning before leaving for the other side of the park.

The market was busy. Probably because it was so nice outside. The girls held onto the boys' hands and we followed them. After they picked their snacks we would pick up a few things before going home. We did the usual walk around to see the choices. After they picked what they wanted, they followed us to the flowers and baked goods section of the market. Soon we were heading home with a little pink in our cheeks, some fresh purple and peach Iris stalks and a few lemon poppy loaves that Nonnie loved. It was a really good day. Nothing exceptional about it, which was part of its charm.

The night air had turned a little cooler and we were ready to call it a night. We walked (and wheeled) together to the split where Coco went left and we headed right.

"Goodnight, guys. Good day. Thanks," she hollered softly without turning. We offered the same back and headed to our casita. As we entered our house my phone rang. It was Jesse. I was conflicted about answering. Guthrie encouraged me to answer my phone.

"Hi, Jesse. Hold on a second." I turned to Guthrie and he was already heading to his room. When he heard me tell Jesse to hold on, he swiveled his chair and told me goodnight and wished me sweet dreams. And then he gave me a smile that equally melted my heart and made me irritated with Jesse's timing.

"You, too. See you in the morning." Then I got back to Jesse. He was checking on me since we last talked after the funeral and we caught up for 15 minutes or so. Me telling him about the ranch, Lilly updates and about the puppies and him telling me about work, mom and his girlfriend troubles (same girlfriend, same troubles). He asked, again, when I was coming home and I, again, told him that I didn't know. While this frustrated him, he was getting used to the answer. He could hear that I was happy, so he accepted my answer. I missed him, but not enough to leave and go home. I wished, more, that he was here so he could see with his eyes what I had been telling him with words.

Day 40: She Took a Deep Breath and Just Let Go.

Everyone who lost Poppie grieved in their own way.
Some were private and some needed a crew. Some preferred distractions
and others preferred Memory Lane. Today I helped Nonnie clean out
Poppie's things. I guess this was her way...

Nonnie had her reasons for getting to Poppie's stuff so soon. And they were good reasons. I was just surprised. It had only been a week. After putting aside what she wanted to keep and what she knew Marcus wanted to give to people, she offered any and all of his things to the ranchers. Most of them took a token. Something to have that was his. A hat, tie, pocket watch, compass. Things like that. And some of the guys took a few of his clothes. Nonnie was so glad that they did. So much so that it made me wonder if they took things for her or for them.

"Someone else could be wearing his stuff. And I don't know much, but I do know that they could use it more than Marcus could right now. So better to pass this stuff along to ones that need."

So we spent the whole day cleaning out Poppie's stuff. Kelly had gotten boxes and Coco had arranged for the equipment – his bed, shower chair, wheelchair, and other things – to be picked up the day before. We began a bit after breakfast and finished after dinner. Kelly brought us meals while we kept going. It wasn't exactly hard labor, but Nonnie didn't want to stop until we were done. We didn't work straight through, but our breaks were few and we stayed on task. The constant packing, sorting and trashing were interrupted with tales and vignettes. Filled in each of the 15 or so boxes and bags were stories of yesterdays and quiet tears. Each one a piece of the life that was Poppie.

The sun crawled across the sky and with every box came a chapter in Poppies life. Lots of chapters. It was sad. Packing his things ached with the finality of his absence. So the pain brought tears but was then softened with some laughter. And other times the laughter was interrupted by the tears. And as the sun began to hide, Nonnie and I finished sorting her husband's possessions into a few different groups. Each possession was in the Stay Where It Was pile, the Share pile or the Donate pile. When the share and donate boxes and bags were put on the porch for the guys to take away tomorrow, the house seemed bigger, Nonnie looked lighter and I felt grateful that I could help. I guessed that she chose me because it would be too difficult for any of the others. And maybe having me made it easier for her, too. An assistant who could not mirror her grief.

Nonnie was exhausted and Lilly came in, so I said my good nights after catching up with Lilly for a few minutes and went up to the Big House to see what was going on.

Everything was cleaned up from dinner and a handful were chatting or watching television. I smelled coffee, so I headed for the kitchen. Walking out with a full cup, I saw Guthrie wheeling through the door from the porch.

"How is Nonnie?" he asked with concern.

"She's OK," I said. Sort of amazed by this fact. I explained that as hard as the day was, she handled it well, all things considered. "Everyone deals their own way. She seems to have found hers."

He seemed somewhat appeased. I took a sip of the coffee. It tasted so good.

"She'd be irritated by our concern. She is one of the strongest women I know. But still…," he trailed off.

"She's Nonnie. I put my money on her."

He agreed and asked how my day was. I sat down and explained how we went through and packed up most of Poppie's things. And how I had learned so much about him from all of the reminders and triggers of keepsakes and possessions. He asked about some of the stories. Some he knew and some he didn't. He told me a couple of his own and before we knew it, everyone was closing up and saying goodnight. We had been chatting for over an hour. Guthrie and I threw in our goodnights and headed back to our casita, taking our time while talking quietly.

When we got inside the house, for the first time, there was an awkwardness between us. Uncertainty led to hesitation on both our parts. I didn't have any reason to believe he thought of me as I thought of him. At least not until this new awkward hesitation. But we were both unprepared for this bump, so we said our goodnights and went to our rooms. If I wasn't so exhausted, I would have been more frustrated. But the day was heavy enough and I just wanted to wash it off me and crawl into bed. I eventually fell asleep. But, it didn't come fast. Tonight, I was unsettled at the thought of Guthrie sleeping in his bed two doors away.

Day 41: Topic Tuesday. For Poppie.

Topic Tuesday makes me laugh. It makes everyone laugh.
There may be lots of tears here at the ranch,
but there is a lot of laughter, too...

I guess everyone sort of took Nonnie's lead and realized that they needed to put some intention in their days. It was time to catch up on some of the things they had neglected the past week. And their lists had grown, so it was time to start crossing things off. Things were a little dirtier, a little drier, a little overgrown and a little overripe. But today everyone got to their lists. And there was movement. Barry took Nonnie and Lilly into town, we thought to see the doctors, but we weren't sure. Barry said they would be gone most of the day and would check in later.

I found much to keep me busy. Some of the dogs had gotten into some mud, so I gave Cairo, Pima and Jamison baths. Not as easy a task as it sounds. I swept the back porch and the front entry. I made lunch for everyone and cleaned up. I juiced most of the blemished tomatoes. Coco and I took out some beef and barley soup from the freezer and ran to the bakery to get some bread bowls for dinner. It was a two-table dinner, so we had to add to the soup. We threw in corn from six or seven fresh cobs and defrosted a large single-serving container of brisket and shredded it up. This with some simmering of bouillon helped make the soup grow to another pot. Lilly, Barry and Nonnie got back just before dinner.

Lilly was the one to bring up Topic Tuesday. We all agreed that after we cleaned up and Reesa took the boys up, that we could play for a while. That it might be nice to laugh. Poppie would surely prefer that. While we did this, Barry walked Nonnie home. She was tired. Fifteen minutes later Barry came to get Lilly. After a 30-second protest, he gave her 15 minutes of playtime before saying goodnight.

Since Lilly only had 15 minutes, we began with topics that she could get into. So this is how our first Topic Tuesday without Poppie went:

With Lilly:

Topic: Favorite character from childhood. Answers: Jonny Quest (two votes), any of the Fraggles, Don Johnson's character from Miami Vice, Batman (or Bruce wayne), Peggy from The Mod Squad, Marcia Brady, Cookie Monster, Fred Flintstone and Hannah Montana.

Topic: School uniforms yes or no? Answers: four yeses and five nos with one abstention.

Topic: Can you taste the difference in the colors of M & M's? Answers: No, by a large majority, with one holdout that insisted we were wrong, but only regarding the brown ones!

Topic: Which came first, the chicken or the egg? Answers: One "Who cares", three felt slightly better chance that the egg did, three felt slightly better chance that the chicken did and everyone's favorite: the rooster. This came from Huey.

Without Lilly:

Topic: What's your bliss? Answers: When you are watching kids play and they do something amazing and pure and with complete abandon (everyone agreed); helping someone (most felt this a good thing, but not bliss); an orgasm (which brought debate regarding the quality of the actual orgasm); when I hear my baby call me mama (the mothers agreed); a rainy night with a cup of tea, a cozy robe and a good book; chocolate lava cake (a few agreed, but most thought that it was just delicious); finishing a long hard project that turned out well (this seemed to fall into most everyone's "sense of accomplishment" category, but not bliss); a triple play in the bottom of the ninth, bases loaded, while your team is one up (all the guys agreed).

Topic: Funkiest place you had sex. (Huey came up with that one.) Answers: on a La-Z-Boy recliner that tilted over from all the motion, in a closet while my parents were asleep, a cockpit (yes, a real cockpit and that would be Guthrie), the beach (so not worth the sand), 2 said a teepee (that would be Will and Sunshine), a boyfriend's parents' boat, an elevator (I guess in the day, Lloyd was a beast) and (drum-roll) the 50-yard line of the University of Arizona Football field at 4 in the morning after Homecoming!

We laughed about the guts that some of us had and the guts that some of us lacked, asked further questions about the teepee and the cockpit logistics and asked Lloyd if he was aware that most elevators had cameras. He said that at the time he wasn't, but didn't seem to really care. We laughed some more and then called it a night. Everyone was ready for the day to end. It had been a long one and everyone was still missing Poppie, which was, itself, exhausting.

Day 42: Mt. Lemmon... Another One of Tucson's Perks.

*Tucson is a great place. Beautiful. Filled with kind people.
But, compared to L. A., Tucson is like a giant village. Today we went to
Mount Lemmon, one of this giant village's bigger attractions...*

After breakfast, it was decided that the day was going to be beautiful and warm, and everyone felt that they could use some other "walls" to look at. So, today I would be introduced to Mount Lemmon.

Before we headed out after breakfast, a few of the ranchers each took charge of food, drinks, supplies, games and sports or dogs. It seemed chaotic to me, but it all came together quickly. I got the impression that they had practiced this spontaneity many times. They definitely had a system. Gathered, packed and loaded, we headed up the mountain in a caravan with one truck carrying all the supplies and Cairo and Shasta (I was told they were the ones that would be easy and stay close) and two SUVs.

It was about a 45-minute drive up the Catalina mountain range, but every few miles you could notice a colorful change from brown sprinkled with some green to darker, more forest greens. Before we knew it we were amongst giant pines. There was not a cactus in sight. Just green. Any brown was the forest floor, pine needles, cones or tree trunks. It was a winding, mostly one-lane highway up and down, so the drive up was not exactly calming. There were 17 of us, the oldest being Nonnie, who parked herself in a lounge chair as soon as we stopped and found "our spot" and the youngest being Jack, who was almost four. Guthrie stayed close to Nonnie, as it was hard to wheel among the pinecones and needles. So, some stayed close to "command central," while others hiked and disappeared for short spells here and there. The kids and some of the grownups played catch with a baseball and mitts, others tried Frisbee, but the trees and lack of Frisbee skills made it a bit difficult. Some relaxed and some bopped till they dropped. Everyone kind of did their own thing, mixing their company up now and then. Everyone ate when they were hungry and the day passed too quickly.

I was most taken by the smell. The firs and pines had such a fresh, distinct smell. There really was nothing like it. And the crackling under your shoes of the pine needles seemed to fill the air with that fresh pine smell. All of this, together, summoned a repeated childhood memory of shopping for Christmas trees with a family friend. Of course, our house had a fake tree. A silver fake tree "because it was easy and not messy." But, every year, my friend's family went to a Christmas tree lot and they always took me along as their "tree advisor." This is the air I smelled each year. And I would pick up pine needles and take them home so my room would smell like pine. The same smell that elicited this buried memory. The air was, now, almost cold. But with sweatshirts and scarves, we were all prepared.

My afternoon was filled will a little of this and a little of that. I hiked a bunch with Lilly, Sunshine and Kelly. They loved the mountain and they loved to hike. We didn't go too far, but we kept coming and going or circling around. We also played some cards games on the picnic table. We even tried a new game that the little ones could play too. A theatrical follow-the-leader. This last one drew the most giggles and belly laughs. I sat with Nonnie awhile, when we had lunch. We shared some tuna fish, cheese slices and sliced tomatoes wrapped in lettuce leaves, over some discussion about how Poppie loved the mountain, too. She wasn't sad as much as she was melancholy.

After lunch, I spent a little time with Guthrie, just talking. He was melancholy, as well. I just sat, staring into his eyes, and listened.

I listened to him talk about his family. How his favorite day was when he graduated and Poppie saluted him for the first time. How he is haunted by a day he treated Diana very badly and never got a chance to apologize and how he was still waiting to do so. He talked about leaving Nonnie and how he was already planning on coming back as soon as he could. And how he hoped I would be here when he came back.

A horn honk interrupted – our signal to start packing up so we could make it down the mountain before dark. We packed up as methodically as we packed up before, only with less food and more garbage. It didn't take long. We loaded Nonnie last. She was so content sitting and watching her family float all around her. If all we had gotten from the day was this, making Nonnie happy, it would have been enough.

In the end, the day was good for all of us. One that was full of play and movement and a change of scenery and smells. It was a day that ended in pizza (which was rare), a shower (which was magnificent) and sleep (which was peaceful and sound).

Day 43: Packed. Loaded. Ready.

And not In a gun-ish kind of way!
Getting ready for the market is not an easy thing.
The list is long of things to remember and do. These guys have it down
so I just follow their lead, but even following was exhausting...

Friday was farmers market day and so we spent most of Thursday getting ready. We were taking three stalls, so we had lots to do. Sunshine and Will were working today and Barry was going to the VA with Michael and Guthrie, then to meet some friends. So that left the usual suspects to prep for the market. By a very long day's end, we had loaded everything into the truck so in the morning, we could add our last-minute stuff and be off. We planned to set up at 7:30 and take down around 1:00. We had a lot of produce to sell. We even had banana, zucchini and lemon poppy loaves that Nonnie had baked. She had slowly been baking and freezing 48 mini-loaves of bread, over the past week, apparently, without us knowing. She did this, I think, to keep busy. She took them out of the extra freezer so they would defrost by morning.

Yesterday was a carefree, forest filled, play like crazy, mountain air day and today we did hard labor. It actually was good for us. We all enjoyed being productive and working as a team. We managed this with simple, easy chitchat, for the most part. If we had not spent the day picking and packing berries, I wouldn't know that both Lilly and P.S. had broken their arms together last year. It involved a rope, a pole and a dare. I wouldn't have learned that Lilly knew Spanish much better than Diana did or that Coco was allergic to cantaloupe and peaches. I learned that two years ago, Lilly managed to help four of six baby birds grow from eggs to freedom. It was an amazingly big commitment. And I wouldn't have learned that Iceland was on Coco's bucket list.

"I've never been anywhere, sort of," Lilly announced. "Diana has. But I haven't. So I guess I was in Costa Rica on a honeymoon with Barry." She made a face. "Gross." "And I think we went other places too." I realized that this kind of proclamation wasn't as noticeable as it once was. "It's weird. This body was places, but really I wasn't even born yet. Isn't that weird?" She looked at Coco and I, not so much for an answer, but more for agreement.

"Yep. really weird," Coco agreed. She was more used to these kinds of discussions than I was. "But you've got your own memories that Diana doesn't have either. She didn't watch Cayenne have her babies."

"And she doesn't know me," I added. "She didn't help fix Simon." I looked at Lilly. She seemed settled with all of this.

"Yep." And without skipping a beat, she asked, "So if you had to guess how many berries we've picked, how many would you say?"

We crunched the numbers for a bit. We were estimating, using the average number of berries in a basket and the number of baskets in a crate and the number of crates in a box. We figured that we had probably already packed well over 350 berries and had at least that much more to do before finishing. This number amazed the girls. It amazed me too.

Later that night, after a relaxing dinner where we all caught up on each other's day, exhaustion hit me. I went to my casita and took by a long warm shower. As I was falling asleep, I was remembering us trying to count the berries. Who needed sheep?

Day 44: You Can See a Troubled Soul, Especially When it's Big.

We did good today. Market Day is second in physical work, only to 'Ready for Market Day'. I noticed that exhaustion in Tucson was different from exhaustion in L.A. This exhaustion was earned...

We left early, so we didn't see her, but we left Nonnie a note, thanking her for all of the loaves she made for us to sell. Coco, Kelly and Huey and I all signed it, each of us adding our own personal doodle. She was too dear.

We got to the market and half of the stalls were set up already. The other half were either still empty or in some stage of completion. We got right to it. This not being my first rodeo helped a lot. I could anticipate moves and understand requests much better. We worked well together and so we were able to set up fast. Two stalls were strictly produce, and the other was part sample station, part bakery and part cashier. Huey, Kelly and I worked the produce and Coco did the loaves and ring ups. We fell into a routine pretty fast. Sales were good and we had to keep refilling from our inventory in the truck. The ranch's reputation was a good one, so people bought our goods. The prices were fair and the community liked to help. We would be done earlier than we had thought. We just kept moving. At some point, we agreed that the day on the mountain had done us good and so we vowed to get there more often. It felt good to take part in a vow that was meant for later.

There was little downtime and by noon we were almost out of produce. The baked goods were long gone. We even raised the price of each loaf another 50 cents halfway, knowing they would sell. We had sold everything and packed up by 12:45.

Usually, people brought a goody for Diana, in a gesture of helping. I hadn't seen it before, but today we got a lemon poppy loaf (yes, ironic!) and a basket of various spreads, like jalapeño goat cheese, southwest chipotle and garlic sweet onion. Coco thanked them and graciously accepted their gifts for Diana. She gave them hugs and put everything in the truck. We each grabbed a couple quick tacos or chicken kabobs before heading out.

"Let's go." Kelly smiled and added that she thought we had a thousand dollar day. That was always the goal, but rarely achieved. They often came close, but today, we did it. When we got home and unpacked, we counted. We had a $1,185 morning! I was glad to be part of it.

Guthrie was sharing the details of his being on the phone most of the morning with the VA back East. After several hours, he got one answer to four questions. Baby steps. He seemed to prefer to talk more about the market. He loved farmers markets and was hoping to join in partway through, but he was on hold most of the morning. Had he known, he said, he would have hung up and tried again on Monday. We were at the gazebo catching up. I was sitting on the steps and Guthrie was facing me. Some of the guys were working on some project over by the shed. Lilly was in the gazebo with Jamison. She was trying to teach him another trick, so she was loaded with Cheez-Its and patience. I think she was working on "freeze," but my attention was more on Guthrie.

"So third best record. Are you competitive? You gonna want to beat your record?" He wore a curious grin.

"Yeah. Probably. If given the chance. I gotta admit. It felt good," I said with some intentional cockiness.

"Feeling productive is nice." His tone was melancholy. Then, suddenly, there was a loud bang. Both Lilly and I could see his immediate reaction to the sound the board made when it fell from the truck bed hitting the other boards. We were close enough that it was quite loud and made Guthrie startle. He turned white and broke out in a sweat. He was trying to calm himself by breathing deeply when Lilly ran up to him to see if he was alright.

"Guthrie, are you OK?" Lilly said this as a mom would ask a child. Softly and with true concern. His breathing was helping and the color was coming back to his face. Lilly knew to wait. She held his hand while she did this. After another minute, Guthrie took a deep breath and let it out slowly.

"I'm fine, Lilly. Thanks. I just get startled easy. That's all". It looked like Lilly was going to ask why.

"Lilly, can you go get my sunglasses for me, please. I left them on my nightstand. I didn't think it would be so bright," I interjected.

"Sure, be right back." And she dashed off. Guthrie looked over at me with a look of gratitude. He managed a weak smile. I smiled back and changed the subject.

"So how about that record?" I bragged. Guthrie smiled again. He seemed better.

"Yeah. How about that record! We may have to make a wager on whether you break it or not." So Guthrie and I made small talk until Lilly returned with my sunglasses. We both jumped in trying to teach Jamison to 'freeze.'

Guthrie got a call he was expecting, so he went to go deal with it. And it was time for Lilly to go do her homework. I thought, since I had a little time, I might go see Poppie, but I caught myself. This had happened a couple times already. I'm sure it happened to others, but no one said so. This made me sad, so I went looking for Nonnie, to see if she needed me to do anything. She was napping, so I went to find Coco, to see what Nonnie had planned for dinner. I thought I'd get a head start and help out. All Coco knew was that there was a lot of ground beef thawing, which usually meant tacos, marinara sauce for pasta, meatloaf, burgers or chili.

I decided to take inventory in the pantry. There were lots of lasagna noodles so marinara it was. I gathered my requirements from around the kitchen. Garlic, tomatoes, tomato paste, onions and oregano. I was learning a lot hanging around the kitchen. After seasoning and browning the meat, I added the other ingredients and let the sauce simmer for an hour while I made a cheese blend of mozzarella, feta and ricotta. Garlic lingered in the air as I layered our marinara, lasagna and cheese dinner in several Pyrex dishes. As I was doing this, I was listening to one of the CDs that Poppie gave me. It made me feel close to him. So I cut vegetables for one of those big "chunky" salads that I had come to love while I listened to jazz. I had just finished cleaning up and putting the salad in the refrigerator and lasagnas in the oven when Nonnie appeared.

"Oh my lord, Jade. What did you do for me?" she was assessing the situation. She caught me putting the last utensil in the drying rack, next to the salad spinner and you could already smell the garlic in the lasagna, so it took only rudimentary detective skills to figure out the situation. "Thank you, my dear sweet girl. Did you leave anything for me to do?" she asked with genuine hope.

"Yep. I figured the garlic bread would be better last minute. Thoughts?" I deferred to Nonnie's judgment.

"Good call. So, if you have nothing you were going to get to, we can sit with some lemonade and visit.

"I would love that, Nonnie. Sit. I'll get us our lemonades." I directed her to the sofa and then went to get our drinks.

"So how are you doing, Nonnie?" I just put down her drink, sat and got right to the matter.

"I'm doing pretty well, child. Considering. I do appreciate your asking. I hear most of the asking behind me, not in front of me. It's alright. People do the best they can." She stopped for a minute, thinking. "I miss my Marcus. It's as simple as that." She sighed and then added, "I know my man, and I'm sure he's getting madder each minute I'm stuck in the blues. But he knows we all have our own process. He'll be patient a bit longer." She offered a smile. Not her usual full body smile, but at least it was something. Lilly walked in, walked over to Nonnie and laid down on the couch next to her with her head resting on her lap. Nonnie knew what she wanted. She began stroking Lilly's head. Right over her ear, from her temple back around the ear and down. It seemed to calm Lilly. I wasn't sure how Nonnie knew what to do. This must have happened before, but I had never seen it.

"Do you want to talk about it, child?" Nonnie asked while she continued to stroke her temple.

"I just forgot that Poppie was gone. I went to go see him." Nonnie looked at me with pain in her eyes.

"I know, child. I miss him, too. And I've done the same thing, baby. A few times already."

"Me, too," I added. "Just earlier today." Lilly looked at me.

"Really?" she asked, stretching her neck, to see if I was telling the truth.

"Promise," I said. And then she turned back to Nonnie. She touched Nonnie's hand at the side of her head. "I'm sorry, Nonnie. That you forget, too, and then you have to hurt some more."

"Baby, that's the way life is. It starts, you live and then you die. It's that livin' that counts. And Poppie sure did live. That's the important part. But thank you for thinking of me, baby. That makes me feel so loved." And she took both hands and stroked both sides of Lilly's face, both tenderly and firmly. You could see all the love she had for this woman/child. It was coming from her eyes and her hands and, now, her smile too. It radiated.

An hour later we were all sitting at dinner. Hot lasagna, a giant salad and freshly made garlic bread. Nonnie liked making garlic bread out of egg bread. She liked this bread best for French toast, too. Everyone caught up with each other, including a full account of the market. We told Nonnie that we could have sold twice as many loaves as she made. They were such a hit. All we had to do was sample them and they flew. Nonnie was flattered but warned us that next time, if they wanted more, she would need some helpers. P.S. and Lilly, of course, chimed in and offered their services without hesitation. I offered mine as well. It was odd. I didn't know when the next big market day would be, and I didn't know when I would be leaving, but here I was, volunteering anyway. I wondered what that meant. But just for a minute. I much preferred enjoying the moment rather than wondering about it. Coco spent time at the office so she filled us in on the latest. Huey had the boys show off their new Spanish skills.

Huey: Hola Jack y Tawn. Como estas? (Hi Jack and Tawn. How are you?)

Jack: Bien. (Good)

Tawn: Y tu? (And you?)

Huey: Bien, gracias. (Good, thanks)

Everyone was amazed and gave them much kudos.

"Wow wow wow, muy bien, niños." (Wow wow wow, very good, boys), cooed Nonnie. Then we moved on to Sunshine's latest cause, Jamison learning to "freeze," Ace winning $1,000 in the lottery, and a finale that the girls loved. Nonnie and Annie announced that they were taking the girls to get mani – pedi's tomorrow. P.S. and Lilly squealed with delight. In the end, the souls brave enough to share part of a spa day with the girls were Nonnie, Annie, Kelly, Sunshine and me. After Huey offered to watch the boys, Coco and Reesa were in. A girl's day would be nice.

After everyone said their goodnights, Guthrie and I found ourselves out on our patio. Mindful of the moment, I was sure that he felt the night air, too, and heard the sounds of critters or an occasional owl, and that he smelled the honeysuckle on the other side of the wall. I laid in a lounge chair and Guthrie was "parked" beside me. Brakes on and sitting back. As best you can in a wheelchair.

"I love this sky. I consider it mine." I looked at him. "Not literally. I mean that I know this sky. When I see it, I know I am home. It's my sky. Someone in China has a different sky. This one is mine?"

"I know what you mean. I think I know this sky better than the L.A. sky. I know I do. I never looked at the sky there. Actually, I don't think we have one." I grinned and continued. "This sky calls you to look up." I looked over and he was just watching me. I waited a second before interrupting whatever it was that was in his head.

"And your thoughts about the stars?" I asked.

"Yes."

"Yes, what?"

"Yes, there are stars. Yes, there are many. And yes, they call down to you to look up. How's that?"

"Are you mocking me?" I was pretty sure he wasn't.

"No. No. No," he insisted. "I was just agreeing with you. I, too, have a deep and unbridled love for our night sky." He was smiling, having fun. "So L.A. doesn't have a sky. Does it have a house or apartment? Any pets? Does it have an "other?""

"An other?"

"You know, an "other." A person.

"Oh." I thought about it for half a minute. "An apartment, no pets and not anymore." I saw him thinking about this. I made it easy. I told him I had an apartment waiting, with no pets in it. And then I explained the last part of the answer.

"A couple of months ago, I found out my fiancé was cheating on me. I couldn't deal and so after a week or so, I ran away. Two days later I broke down about five miles from here. Barry found me and you know the rest." I shifted in my lounge. He was so quiet. I looked over and he was looking at me with the most tender eyes, full of empathy for me. And I was not sure why.

"I'm so sorry he did that to you. You must know it couldn't be you." Such a statement startled me. It took me by surprise.

"I mean that it had to be his problem. He would have to be crazy to cheat on you. Aside from it being a chicken-ass thing to do to anyone." The tenderness was replaced with criticism, but it still touched me. I told him that I truly appreciated his condemnation on my behalf, but obviously something was missing from what I had with Dean. Otherwise, he wouldn't have wandered. I explained that when I had gotten here I was a bit broken, so Lilly's attachment was a good distraction.

"And time and Nonnie helped me."

"Yes. The old 'time and Nonnie' combo. Almost foolproof. I'm glad both did their magic. You seem alright. I know I don't know you that well, yet. But you seem far from broken and I can't imagine you not being enough."

I was stuck on his word "yet." I hoped it meant something.

"Thank you for that. But none of us are perfect. Even this record-setting girl from the big city."

He laughed and we talked a bit more about the peace here that heals. He knew what I meant. I explained that, for me, it was an evolving thing. So I go with the flow and take it one day at a time.

"So, what's your plan? I know you get your cast off soon. That will be nice."

"Yeah, I get it off next week. They say I may need a week or two of in-house rehab and then home rehab for a month or so after, depending on my progress." He looked at me. "So next week I'm going to leave for a week or so and then come back and finish rehab here. Will you be here?" His question was simple enough, but it seemed like there was much weighing on it.

"I should be. I don't have any plans to leave and so far, the doctors still want me here. So I should be here when you get back." I wanted to be as clear as he was seeming to be. His shoulders dropped slightly. Relief? He looked away and explained the different scenarios. He could come back in a wheelchair part-time. He could have a walker or a cane. It was different for everyone.

"So you'll surprise us. Maybe we'll make a ranch pool," I joked.

"I think there is one already, it's for whether Lilly convinces me to take one of Maya's pups." I looked into his eyes for a clue. Nothing, and I didn't want to pressure him. We sat there for just a few more minutes before going to bed. We wished each other 'good night' and went to our rooms.

"Dream good, Jade," I heard him say as his door closed.

"You too, Guthrie," I said to the door.

Day 45: Sunshine with a Side of Ladybugs

*Did you know that if you listen hard enough, you can
hear the sunshine calling you?*

We had all finished lunch and the girls were being lazy, just
waiting to get their nails painted. They were watching T.V., while
Nonnie and I sat at the big table.

"Do you hear that?" Nonnie asked.

"No," said P.S. and Lilly, cocking their heads, trying to hear
what Nonnie was hearing.

"I don't hear anything, Nonnie," said Lilly.

"I do. Listen." Nonnie paused as if she heard sounds coming
from somewhere. It was quiet.

"I hear the sunshine. And she is calling the both of you."

Lilly and P.S. looked at each other with resignation as they
rolled their eyes. They got up and turned the T.V. off. Lilly turned to
me, offering an explanation.

"Nonnie says that when the sunshine calls, you gotta go see
what it wants. She thinks she can really hear it. She says sometimes
it was hollering so loud that the calling was all she could hear. I'm
not so sure if she really hears it or not." Lilly and P.S. were heading
out the door.

Nonnie and I chatted about the day and watched Lilly dominate
P.S. at hopscotch. Nonnie called the salon to confirm our
appointment and remind them that we were more. We would just
rotate between the mani's and pedi's. Nonnie called the girls in after
letting the others know to get ready to go.

"What do the words 'color,' 'fingers' and 'toes' have in common?" teased Nonnie. The girls were halfway to the car.

Wild Cherry, Quiet Blush, Passion Fruit… too many choices. In the end, we all picked different colors. The girls got ladybugs on their thumbs. First, it was butterflies. Then, hearts. And, finally, it was ladybugs. There were so many of us that we almost took over the salon. Reesa brought treats and it was like a private spa day. By the time we were done, the afternoon was gone.

Nonnie knew the boys would come home, later, with bellies full of beer, possibly tequila, chicken wings, nachos and onion rings, so we picked up eegee's on the way home. It was the only fast food Nonnie let the girls have with her. I was thrilled. Orange Dream was the flavor of the month.

I had just scooped out the last slushy sip of my drink when the boys stumbled in, with the help of Huey and Ace, the designated drivers for the night. Guthrie's version of stumbling in was wheeling into walls, which I quickly remedied by telling him that I needed to burn off my slushy, and I would wheel him back to the house. Barry asked if I needed any help, which was a bit funny because he called me Jadester and Jadedog. Barry was blasted too.

Ace escorted Barry to his house and I escorted Guthrie to ours. He was so drunk that I knew he wouldn't remember ending the evening. He was a happy drunk with a quickly diminishing consciousness. I barely managed to get him out of his wheelchair and onto the bed before he mumbled something that sounded like, "Thinks for doonthis." (Thanks for doing this.) "You've orange tongue." (You have an orange tongue.) "I really, really like you." and then ended with something like, "Ahdon no wadidoo which outya." (I don't know what I would do without you.) The snoring signified that the chitchat was over. I was partially successful in trying to get him to drink a glass of water before he crashed. I pulled off his belt and tugged at his shoes and socks before I covered him and got a washcloth to wipe his face and neck, which smelled of wings and tobacco. I liked taking care of him. That's what I was thinking as I drifted off to sleep.

Day 46: Jacks, Ozzie and Doodles

Lots to write about. I finally succeeded in getting past sixies.
But I'm going to start with this morning, when Maya brought a few
of the pups over to play. Success is a relative thing…

Lilly was excited. Maya was bringing over three of the pups that weren't assigned yet. She was going to drop them off for an hour while she ran an errand. Lilly and P.S. were going to puppy sit. Lilly still didn't know if Guthrie wanted a dog.

"If he just sees them, how could he not want one, right?" she explained. We all just went along, feeling just a little like Lilly was setting an ambush for Guthrie. But we figured that if he wanted one, he would take one, and if he didn't, then he wouldn't. Besides, we loved seeing the pups too. We had visited them a few times already. On one of the visits, Maya let them name the pups. Lilly named two of them. She picked the names Chaz and Diego. P.S. named two, picking Nacho and Sophie. Maya was bringing over Ozzie, Kelev and Sophie. The puppies were almost six weeks old now.

We had no way of knowing, but Ozzie attached to Guthrie instantly. I wasn't sure if it was because he was closer to the ground, being in a wheelchair, or if he sensed a need in him. But for some reason, Ozzie shadowed Guthrie for almost the whole visit. When he wasn't playing with the other dogs, or licking P.S. and Lilly's faces, he would just sit by Guthrie's side. It was strange because the puppies usually had lots of energy. Sophie and Kelev were full of energy. Ozzie seemed to be calm around Guthrie. When he played with the other pups, he had lots of energy, but whenever he came back to Guthrie's side, he was calm and relaxed by his chair. When

Guthrie went into the Big House for a few minutes, Ozzie waited and whined at the door until he came out again. Guthrie was enjoying the pups, although it wasn't love at first sight. It wasn't until Maya came back that things changed.

As Maya pulled her old truck up the path to the back of the house, it backfired. Guthrie wasn't prepared and the noise shocked him. Just like before, he turned white and began to sweat. Ozzie was sitting by his side when this happened. He looked at Guthrie and became very alert. He turned around excitedly in a few circles before jumping up, putting his front paws on the side of his wheelchair so his face was closer to Guthrie's. Ozzie nudged Guthrie's hand with his nose, which was gripping the armrest. You could see Guthrie's hand loosen a little. Then licked his hand. It seemed to help relax Guthrie a bit more and his breathing slowly evened out.

Maya watched from the truck. She saw the whole thing and didn't want to interrupt what was happening. She got out and walked over. Kelev and Sophie greeted her enthusiastically. Ozzie didn't move from Guthrie's side. No one else saw this, except for Maya and I. The girls were too busy with the other pups. After giving time for Ozzie to calm Guthrie, Maya, with great resistance, rounded up the pups and said she would bring them back another day. I watched Guthrie's face as she drove away. While his color had returned, he was lost somewhere else for a bit.

〰〰 〰〰 〰〰

Lilly had set aside a time for jacks today. I had definitely gotten better, but just could not get past sixies.

"Today's the day. We are going to get you past sixies." She was so positive and so motivated, that I almost believed her. In all of our jacks playing, I had learned much. I learned that the throw of the jacks is crucial. It must be strategic depending on what number you are at. I learned the art of tossing up the ball. I learned about readiness after the ball toss. But I still got stuck on sixies.

"You know, jacks are like life," Lilly proclaimed.

"How so?"

"Well, jacks can teach you a lot about how to live. There are lessons everywhere. Nonnie taught me that." She said this like she was passing along some pearls of wisdom. She proceeded to "school" me. "Jacks teach you that when things are hard, you don't give up. They also teach you that practice makes you better. And you have to take turns." Lilly was quite serious. She continued, "Sometimes losing makes you better. You know what not to do next time. You can't quit if you want to stay in the game." She paused for a minute to think of what she was forgetting. "Oh, and you have to strategize. That's always important. Having a plan." Once again, I was amazed at this beautiful blend of woman/child. "And don't forget to have fun. That's the most important part"

We kept playing and, amazingly enough, I got past sixes. I couldn't believe it. I did it! It felt like quite the accomplishment. Not like finishing med school or volunteering in Africa. But still an accomplishment!

After dancing around and whooping it up, we decided to go sit on the front porch and just relax a little. Lilly got out the book she was reading and I got my journal and just started doodling. The air could not be more still. The coolness just hung in the air.

"Diana used to do that." We were sitting on the porch, waiting for dinner to be ready. It was a quiet afternoon. Lots of the ranchers were going out tonight, so it would be a quiet dinner with just a handful or so of us. Barry, who had just come out from inside the house, came up to where we were sitting. He watched me sketch a picture of a brick flower planter full of different plants and flowers. "Do you draw much?" he asked.

"Nah." I stopped drawing and looked up. "In fact, this is the only thing I draw. I just draw it over and over again." He looked at me with quizzical eyes.

"It's good, Jade. But why the same thing every time?" he asked. "It looks like you have had instruction."

Nonnie had come out to see what we were doing. She looked at my doodle and nodded her approval as she sat down next to me.

"It started in college. When I was bored with the lecture, I would start to draw this. Or if I was doodling at home while I was on the phone. I think I have drawn this same planter over 50 times. It has evolved over the years. And I can do it faster now. But, for the most part, that's all I draw. Maybe it's habit," I offered.

"Well, I love it." Nonnie was sitting quietly in between Barry and Lilly. "Nobody taught you, child?"

"Nope," I said. "Well, maybe a little, I guess. Actually, someone did show me a few drawing techniques." They waited for me to explain. "So, my mom's friend, Devorah, would let me visit and she would let me draw or play with clay. She showed me simple drawing tricks, like imagining a face in 2 x 2 circles so I would know where to put facial features. Or how to draw a little bit with perspective. One day she told me she could show me in three minutes how to make a beautiful clay rose. I told her she couldn't and we made a bet. She won. She always told me I could do anything and was very patient and a good teacher. And she paid attention to me. I always felt heard when I was with her. So, I guess I did have a mentor."

"Jade, sweetheart," Nonnie said with a trace of wonder. "It would appear that you had your own Diana." I looked up at her smiling face and realized that she was right.

We all went in for a quiet dinner. Well, sort of a quiet dinner. Lilly spent the first 10 minutes either bragging about my getting past sixies or asking me about how I did the planter. She was so enthusiastic that she convinced me to give her a drawing lesson sometime. I promised I would and then it grew more quiet. It was a nice change from the usual wonderful, noisy dinners we had. Afterward, as we were cleaning up, some of the others had returned from their dinner out. Lilly said her goodnights and everyone went their own ways. Only Guthrie and I stayed up in the Big House for a while.

"So, I hear from Lilly that you're an artist. Well, actually, Nonnie mentioned it, too."

"Nope, just a doodler." He looked at me as if I was being humble, which I wasn't. I explained the story of the brick planter to him and he understood my protest a little bit better. It was nice to be alone with him. We talked about his day and mine. We talked about Ozzie for just a bit. He confided that Ozzie did, in fact, help. He was surprised. Still no commitment, but it seemed like he was warming up to the idea. Eventually, it was time for us to end our day, so we, reluctantly headed to our casita. As we said our goodnights, there was some hesitation, but neither one of us was secure enough in what we were feeling to do anything else but push through it and go to bed. I laid awake for an hour thinking of what I could have done with that hesitation before I fell into a restless sleep.

Day 47: You're welcome and thank you back.

Everyone was happy that Ozzie had picked Guthrie. Especially Maya. She was hoping that Guthrie would take to one of the pups, but she explained that you never knew who connects and who doesn't. She knew that Ozzie would be good for him. She brought him back to spend more time with Guthrie and it was as if they were best friends separated for weeks. Ozzie saw Guthrie and ran up to him with a quiet, excited whimper and a wagging tail. After a few minutes, Ozzie calmed down and stayed by Guthrie's side the rest of the visit. Maya spent some time with them, explaining to Guthrie about Ozzie's training and how Guthrie, if he decided to take Ozzie, would need to be trained, too. She showed him the hand commands that Ozzie was beginning to learn and explained the dos and don'ts of a companion dog. It was nice to see Guthrie distracted and happy. Happier than he would admit, but you could see it. They spent a couple hours together, discussing the benefits and responsibilities that go with choosing a canine companion like Ozzie.

While Maya was with Guthrie and Ozzie, Lilly was helping Nonnie around the Big House when she got this "great idea."

"How about we do a campout?" Lilly asked Nonnie with great enthusiasm. "It would be so great."

"Child, you think this old body can do a campout? These bones don't remember how to lie in a sleeping bag. And besides, it's a school night and P.S. can't join you. Maybe you can plan one for next weekend or the one after."

I saw the disappointment on Lilly's face. While she went out to water the porch plants, I went in to ask if I could do a campout with Lilly.

"That's up to you, baby. They are lots of fun, but they are lots of work, too. Especially if it's just the two of you. That child will talk all night and beat the love of games right out of you if you don't be careful."

I knew what she meant, but I wanted to do something for Lilly. It seemed like Lilly's talk of her limited "nows" was starting to affect me. I thought some of this came from a place that acknowledged that her time was, indeed, limited. Besides, she seemed so excited about the idea. So we agreed that it would be OK if it was alright with Barry. Nonnie called Barry on the phone. He was out with Xavier, but he gave his OK.

"Do you really wanna go with me?" I went out to the porch and told Lilly that Nonnie and Barry said it was alright to go camp out by the lake. She was so excited. "We're really going to camp out? Just you and me?"

A night out with the moon and stars sounded good. Before long, Lilly had it all planned out. We would make roasted corn and hotdogs over the campfire and then roast marshmallows for s'mores. We would play games and tell stories and "girl talk." Lilly thought she might bring her telescope. There was a full moon, which was perfect. I was actually looking forward to it. I told her that she had to finish her chores and homework, then we would have a couple of hours before dark to pack up everything we needed. I don't think she had ever finished her chores so fast. Nonnie gave her a "homework light" assignment, so it wasn't long before she began gathering what we needed.

While she did this, Guthrie and I met by the gazebo to visit a bit. He told me about Ozzie and Maya's chat. He seemed a little torn, so I asked him about it. It was the first time that he opened up about his experience.

"It's really strange," he explained. "Being over there is so different than being home. Over there, we would have either hours of quiet or hours of blasts and gunfire. Even though I wasn't in the middle of it, being in the air most of the time, I was in the middle of the sound or the quiet when I was grounded. Over there, we always had someone watching our back. We knew there were other eyes watching for us. Here, both the quiet and the sounds are unsettling. Here, I can only see what's in front of me." He seemed a little lost in his head thinking about it. Like he was trying to find another way of explaining so that I would understand.

"I can't imagine what it was like for you over there, Guthrie. But, I think I get a bit of what you're saying. I've heard soldiers talk about the bond that comes with knowing that you were all in together. It's a different world over there. In almost every way possible. And returning isn't as easy as switching gears."

"Yeah. But it's strange. It seems that Ozzie gets it. How can a puppy bring me the same sense of safety that a fellow soldier could?"

"So, have you decided?"

Before he could answer, Lilly came running up to us.

"I got everything packed. Do you have what you need?" she asked, out of breath.

"Nope. I have to go grab a few things. Are you sure you have everything?" She went down the list. It was a long list that made Guthrie and I laugh. She hadn't left out a thing. The only thing I needed to grab was my jacket. She had everything already packed and ready at the Big House. She even had the backpacks packed and a cooler on wheels to pull behind us. Guthrie wheeled back to the Big House with Lilly while I grabbed my jacket. Once I got up there, Nonnie was going over the rules with Lilly. We each grabbed our packs and our sleeping bags. Lilly insisted on pulling the cooler. With everything ready, we headed out to the trail that led to the pond.

It didn't take us long after we got there to set up our campsite. A fire pit was already there, made of boulders in a circle, and Lilly and I gathered sticks and twigs to make a fire once it got darker. This took a little while, but eventually, and right before the sun set, we had a big pile that would last us hours. I lit the campfire while Lilly got out our dinner. You could tell that Lilly had done this before. I just followed her lead.

With our bellies full, our tic-tac-toe pad covered with wins and losses, our curiosity about the night sky satisfied through the lens of the telescope and marshmallow and chocolate wiped off our faces, we set up our sleeping bags and began to just relax and talk. We laid there, next to each other, one bag as the bottom and the other as a cover. It was a beautiful night. Not too cold. We laid there watching the moon. At first the conversation was about Ozzie and Guthrie and how happy she was that they might stay together. Then Lilly took a turn and began talking about the future.

"Everyone is supposed to do something with their life. I haven't done anything. Diana has. But I haven't. And I'm afraid I won't have time. Aren't I supposed to do something?" Lilly ended her question emphatically. She looked at me for an answer. She waited.

"I don't know what to say, Lilly. You're just a child."

"But I'll always be a child." She said this with such sad resignation that my heart broke for her.

"What do you want to do?" I asked, truly curious about what it was she wanted to accomplish.

"It doesn't matter, does it? I'm part-time Lilly, remember? I'm not gonna grow up." Then she went down the list of things that she would not do. College, getting a job, living anywhere else and even donating blood, "like Coco did." She continued. "I doubt winning at hopscotch is nearly as good as winning student council elections. There's nothing I can do?" Again, she waited as if she expected I had an answer.

"One time when I was young, I was staying with my grandfather. A friend of his had just died and I had to go with him to the funeral. There were hundreds of people. I told him that his friend must have been loved a lot. He told me that he wasn't. But that he had given away lots and lots of money to charities. He was the boss of a big company. All these people were there to pay respect, but not to share their love. He told me that, really, he was not such a nice guy. My grandfather told me that the measure of a man is not how many people come to their funeral. He said that it was how many would be better from having known you. From having you in their life. this is what made you a worthy person."

Lilly sat there and watched me.

"OK." She hadn't connected the dots.

"Well, my life is better from knowing you. Not Diana. You." Lilly was getting it now. "I mean it, Lilly. You make my life better," I said with true conviction.

"Thank you, Jade," Lilly answered calmly and quietly. "I think I needed to hear that. Thank you for telling me." Then, without hesitation, she got a smirk and asked, "Wanna play one more game before sleep?" Her eyebrows raised high.

We added wood to the fire and got comfy in our sleeping bags. Lilly wanted to play one last game, so we picked This or That for a little while before dozing off.

"OK, you first," I prompted.

"OK. Toffee bits or caramel syrup?"

"Caramel syrup. Cartoons or silly movies?"

"Silly movies. They're longer. Spaghetti or pizza?"

"Spaghetti. Mt. Lemmon or Sabino Canyon?"

"Sabino, of course. Tetherball or shesh-besh?"

"Shesh-besh. Chocolate or peanut butter ice cream?"

"Both." We laughed. "I remember. OK. Enough?"

"Enough," Lilly answered.

"Goodnight, Jade. Dream good."

"Goodnight, Lilly. You, too." Sleep came fast.

When I woke up I didn't see Lilly lying near me, as she was when we had fallen asleep the night before. I wasn't alarmed at first. I had come to be very familiar with Lilly's independence. I sat up and inhaled deeply. The morning smelled good. It was cool and fresh for the moment, but I knew that the sun would warm up the day. As I began to take in the sunrise, hoping to get a clue to where Lilly might have gone, I saw him.

I didn't recognize the man standing next to the tree. But my eyes were not quite adjusted to the rising sun behind him. It was difficult to see his face.

"Hello there, honey," he said. His face didn't matter. I realized that I didn't know this man. And I knew that I didn't think I wanted to. I looked around to see if I could see Lilly. She wasn't anywhere in sight. I sensed that the man slowly walking closer to me was not a good man. Then I saw the knife that he was holding. His eyes followed my gaze to his hand. His grip on the knife tightened.

"I won't hurt you, honey," he said with too sweet of a voice. He was lying. I looked around again for Lilly.

"There's no one around here… unless someone is hiding. And who would hide from you? You're such a pretty little thing." With this, I knew where Lilly was. I was filled with both fear and relief. I was grateful that the man would not find Lilly if she did not want to be found. And fearful in knowing that this man was going to hurt me. He moved closer.

"But I'm afraid," I cried to my mother. "He's mean. And when I make a sound he tells me to be quiet. I hate him!" I had always feared going to the dentist. From the first time I met Dr. Meeding, I didn't like him. It didn't help that it was abundantly clear that he disliked children, making it a sure thing that they would not like him back. My mother never validated our

fears. Jesse told her the same thing. But she did give us the one tool that helped us cope. "Let me tell you a little secret." She whispered to me. It will help you when you find yourself afraid.

His breath smelled like stale beer and it became suffocating as he moved his face close to mine. I was frozen, even my glance couldn't look away from his, but I could see his knife from the corner of my eye. I was amazed at the realization that I could almost feel the knife, even though it wasn't touching me. But his smell was touching me. His breath was against my neck. I wasn't sure which made me feel sicker. The smell of him or the gleam of his knife. I knew that I would never forget either one of them.

"Whenever I am really afraid, I picture a place to go to in my head. My mom taught me that. When I was afraid as a little girl, your grandma would show me her favorite calendar picture. It was a huge open field of hundreds, maybe thousands, of yellow tulips. There was this wooden windmill in the background of the picture. She told me to put myself there, with her, in that field. Walking hand in hand through all of those beautiful tulips."

His hands were exploring as he leaned onto me. He became frustrated with my clothing so he cut my shirt and ripped it open. Then he cut my bra. I didn't feel the jerk of the knife as it cut or hear the sound of my clothes as they ripped. All I could feel and hear was my heartbeat. It beat so loudly that I began to wonder if Lilly could hear it from her hiding place. I hoped not. After he put his hands on my skin I could feel his frustration lessen and his hardness grow. He reminded me that he didn't want to hurt me, but I knew that he would.

After my mommy described her place to go to when she was afraid, she explained that I could make my own place. "You don't have to decide right now and you can change it or add to it as you go. And after a while, you get so good at it that you begin to smell and feel what is in your picture. Grandma used to call it 'changing the channel.' Whenever you needed to get away from the fear, you could change the channel to get to your safe place." My mom explained that she used this secret lots of times. She visited her tulip field whenever she became afraid. "I can help you get started. Where do you want to go?"

I could feel his legs spreading mine, prying them apart. I thought about fighting the man. But I was too afraid. I couldn't decide if I was more fearful of what he would do if I didn't fight or of what he would do if I did. And I was afraid for Lilly. He began to struggle with his own pants but kept the knife near my face to remind me how he didn't want to hurt me.

I picked the beach. My brother running ahead, towards the water. Me following, with each step crunching the sand. It was a fall day, not too hot. Both of us had our pants rolled up to our knees. We always tried to stay dry. But we rarely did. We would walk to the waves and then run from them, like they were chasing us.

He climbed on top of me promising me that I would enjoy what he was going to do. I thought I heard a whimper. I looked around for Lilly. It wasn't until I heard the sound again that I realized it was coming from me. It made me think of hurt animals. I stopped. I didn't want the man to know how he was hurting me.

The waves were coming and going. The sounds were too loud. I couldn't hear anything else. They were much stronger than the last time I visited. Instead of soothing, slow waves, they were faster and not very calming at all. I tried to slow them down, but I couldn't. I tried to walk away from them, but they pulled me. I was caught and felt as if I was going to drown. Each wave became bigger and bigger. The next wave loomed over me like a giant. I knew that it was going to crush me. It began to fall and I took what I thought was my last breath.

Then, the fear lay still on top of me slouched to one side, his head bleeding. I was frozen. As his last breath came out of him, I gasped for air. He blanketed me, lifeless and bleeding. I could feel his hardness go away. And then I saw her. Lilly had a bloody telescope in her hands.

It was hours before I could sit down and process what had happened. After Lilly saved me, everything went so fast. I wrapped myself up in a blanket, grabbed Lilly from the campsite and ran all the way back to the big house. No words were spoken. Just me pulling her to get away from where we were. She followed without resistance. Barry was there with Sunshine and Coco, having coffee. They looked up as Lilly and I ran in. They saw the blood on me and jumped up. From that point on it was a blur.

I explained what had happened and Barry took Lilly aside to make sure that she was alright, while Coco called the police and the doctors. Soon everyone was awake. Chaotic flurries of people running around, sirens in the background and people in uniforms got all tangled up at the ranch. I was still in shock and didn't realize that Barry whisked Lilly away somewhere.

Soon Dr. Leslie came. After she spoke with me, she talked to the police about Lilly and insisted on being present when they questioned her. It wasn't long before Coco, Barry and the police returned to the Big House. Barry explained to me that Dr. Leslie was taking care of Lilly and that the policemen wanted to speak with me again.

"Do you want me to stay with you?'" Barry asked. "I can see if they will let me."

"That's OK, Barry. You take care of Lilly." I went over the waiting policeman. I was still numb. Throughout the chaos, I realized that I hadn't thanked Lilly for saving me. For some reason, I felt that I should do this very soon. I went over to the gazebo and sat with the officer who had talked with Lilly. Lilly had stopped the man before he could hurt me badly, so the medic had just cleaned me up and bandaged my few cuts. It seemed surreal. Like telling a story, not an experience. But my worry about Lilly reminded me that this was real. And while the sounds and the sights were blurred, I was focused on finishing the story so I could find Lilly.

After the officer was done with my statement, I escaped from the mess and ran over to find Lilly. I noticed that, even though I felt safe again, I hadn't stopped shaking yet. I didn't want to disturb Lilly and her doctor, but I wanted to make sure that everything was alright. As I stood by the door, hesitating, the door opened. The doctor was coming to find me.

We almost ran into each other and Dr. Leslie could see the anxiety on my face. She motioned for me to be quiet with her finger to her mouth. She stepped outside and quietly closed the door behind her.

"Is she alright? Can I see her?" The doctor could see how upset I was.

"First, Jade, how are you? Are you alright?"

"I'd be better if I knew that Lilly is too. Can I see her?" I was getting a little more anxious.

"No, Jade. Not right now. I gave her a sedative and she is resting for now. That is what she needs right now. She needs to just turn off for now. You can see her later."

"But I didn't thank her." I was desperate now. "I have to tell her. Please. I can't wait. She needs to know. And I have to make sure that she is alright. You don't understand."

The doctor could see how frantic I was.

"Jade, come sit with me for a minute." She led me over to the sofa on the porch. She almost had to push me into sitting.

"I just need to make sure she's alright," I whispered to the air.

"Jade, look at me." The doctor touched my arm, like a prompt for me to follow. She made sure that I was looking at her before she began speaking.

"This will take some time to sort out. But I don't want you to worry."

"I won't worry if you just tell me that Lilly is alright!" I was raising my voice. Dr. Leslie pulled me to her and held me. She felt me shaking and instinctively began rubbing my arms and back. My shaking slowed. I pulled back, calmer, and looked at her.

"I think so."

"What do you mean, you think so?" My calm was fading.

"Jade, breathe. The reason I said I think so is because I didn't see Lilly. By the time I got here, Diana was here."

"What?" I didn't understand. "What about Lilly? Do you think that this will hurt her? Will it change her again? How will we know?" I was getting agitated.

"Jade," the doctor said in a firm voice. "I think Lilly is OK," she said slowly. "Apparently, when you were in danger, Daniel, her brother-like alter, emerged as her protector, and yours. I can't say if Lilly came back before leaving or if she just returned to Diana. This makes sense to us, as Daniel has always been the protective alter. It wasn't really Lilly who saved you. She couldn't: she's just a child. But your situation inspired Daniel to appear." She stroked my arm, trying to calm me.

"But who is she now?" I asked, with just a little less desperation.

"Right now, she is Diana. I say this because she gave me a message for you." She could see that this got my attention. I waited, motionless, for her to continue.

"She said to tell you that it's OK. She said, 'Tell Jade that everything is OK.' And there is more. She wanted me to tell you,

'You're welcome and thank you back.' Does that make sense to you, Jade? She said to tell you 'You're welcome and thank you back.'" She repeated it like it was supposed to make more sense the second time. But, for reasons that I couldn't explain, I understood the first time.

"Does this make sense to you?" The doctor asked again. I nodded yes. I couldn't speak. Because I knew what it meant. I just wept. Dr. Leslie didn't push. She pulled me close again and put her arms around me.

I whispered, between sobs, "She means that we saved each other." The doctor looked at me with a sad smile. "And that Lilly is gone." She knew I was right. I cried in her arms.

From around the corner, Guthrie appeared. He looked desperate as he wheeled to the base of the ramp. He stopped and watched while the doctor comforted me. He had been out earlier and I hadn't seen him. He must have just gotten back, and so he knew what had happened. I could see that he was fighting the urge to move closer, not wanting to interrupt. He waited until I saw him. He looked at me with pain in his eyes. My pain. I hugged the doctor, not knowing exactly why. Then, I stood and walked slowly down the ramp and stopped in front of his wheelchair. He opened his arms and I crawled onto his lap and continued to cry.

Barry approached, giving Guthrie the time and space for me, and headed to the porch where Dr. Leslie was. He seemed desperate to get some answers from her.

"What does this mean?" Barry was on the porch now, pleading for answers A bit calmer now, I listened.

"I don't know, exactly. I'm just not sure, Barry. We will see when she wakes and we will go from there. I'm sorry I don't have more answers."

"I'm going to stay until she wakes up. I think you should be with her. When she wakes up she will want you there."

"I will help Coco and the others. We'll try to get some semblance of the familiar. First, I need to meet with the officer and finish my report. He's been waiting for me. I want to make sure they fully grasp this situation. Unless there's more to know, my understanding is that Lilly did nothing wrong. I don't expect there to be major problems, especially since there are no conflicting reports. Jade's account matches Lilly's."

"How is Jade? Is she alright?" Barry spoke softly, looking in my direction.

"Right now... fragile. But she'll be alright. I left her in good hands. He's taking good care of her." She smiled a little. "Did I miss something since my last visit?"

"Only that they've figured out what we've all known for a while."

"I'm glad," she said.

"Me, too," Barry agreed.

I held onto Guthrie a little bit tighter.

Guthrie wheeled me back to our house. I just sat on his lap, clinging to him. I was drained. He put me to bed and I asked him to lay with me. I didn't want to be alone. He climbed into the bed beside me and held me, as I fell into a sort of twilight sleep. He thought I was asleep as he began whispering softly.

"You don't know it yet, but we are going to be together," he whispered. "I knew the moment I saw you." That was the last thing I heard before falling into a true sleep.

When I woke up the next morning, I noticed something. The day was different. I noticed it the second I awoke. So strong was the feeling that it was as if it woke me up. I took a quick shower and went out to the patio. Guthrie was already out there.

"Hi."

"Hi."

"How are you feeling?" Guthrie was trying to find a balance between prying and giving me space.

"Weird. I was just thinking about that when I woke up. How different today feels. And I'm not exactly sure why."

"Jade," Guthrie chose his words carefully. "You know why." He said this softly. "Yesterday happened." He gave me a minute. When I didn't respond he asked me, "Do you want to talk about it?"

"No. Not yet."

"OK." He wheeled closer to my lounge chair and took my hand and held it with both of his. It warmed all of me and I wanted for him to never let go. I leaned against his shoulder and we sat there, with no words, for a little while. Eventually, we knew we had to go to the Big House.

Days 48 - 49: Falling back into life.

I see a lot of Lilly in Diana…

When we got to the Big House, the whole ranch felt different. Everyone knew. Maybe not everything. But they knew that Diana had returned and Lilly was gone. Just like that. I hadn't spent even a minute thinking of how it would be when Lilly left. Why she would go. But if I had, I doubt I would have thought it would be anything like this.

The whole ranch was anxious over Diana's return. She didn't come out at first, but everyone was waiting. It was bittersweet. Waiting for Diana and missing Lilly was almost too much.

On top of that, Guthrie was leaving, reluctantly, the next day to finish his medical follow-up and finalize his discharge before returning to the ranch to continue rehab at the VA here.

The ranchers did little tasks while they waited for Diana to emerge from her house. They did not know if it would be hours or days. So they waited. It wouldn't be until the next day that Diana would come out of the house. When it came to anything Diana, the ranch was as one. She needed a day with Barry and Nonnie before she could face all that was waiting for her. There was a nervous energy and everyone kept busy, wanting and waiting for her to appear.

Guthrie kept his eye on me the whole day. I found comfort in his attentiveness. At the day's end, we laid together another night before he left early the next day. I tried not to cry as he got ready for Will to take him to the airport. He saw this and tried to comfort me.

"I'll be back," he promised. "And I will be stronger and better for you. Just promise me that you will be here." I promised, as one single tear fell. He wiped the tear and held my face in his hands. He looked at me as if he could see all that was inside.

"Thank you," he whispered and he was gone.

I went to my casita and began to wait for him.

Two days after the morning that Lilly left and Diana returned, Nonnie and Barry came into the Big House, where we were having coffee and waiting. They told Coco and I that Diana was coming down from the house. I could see the longing on Coco's face. When Diana walked in, I caught my breath. I could see that she was not Lilly. Coco got up to greet her, slowly, waiting for Diana to give a sign. When she smiled Coco raced to her arms and they held each other.

"I missed you, Mama D," Coco cried, with tears running down her cheeks.

"I missed you too, sweetheart," Diana said back. Lilly was gone.

They let go and Diana looked over at me. I didn't know what to do. I wanted to do what Coco did. Get up and run to Diana's arms and tell her that I missed her. But I didn't miss her. You can't miss what you never knew. Barry could see my uncertainty.

"Diana, I want you to meet..."

Diana interrupted. "You must be Jade," she said with a smile that brought instant comfort. I stood up and walked over to Diana, who opened up her arms. We held onto each other for what seemed like a long time. I felt warm tears running down my neck. They were Diana's.

Sunshine and Will walked in and I let go of Diana so she could continue her reunion. A few others followed and soon there was a small crowd, waiting for their turn to greet their friend who had finally come home. Everyone was calm and quiet, not wanting to put too much on her too soon.

Her family, and soon the doctors, too, were all eager to spend some time with her. Diana made time for everyone. I watched for a while, and then went down to the lake. I watched Simon and his friends. After a while, I realized I was trying to count the birds in Birdland. Lilly was right. It was hard if they didn't hold still. I don't know if I started crying because I kept losing count or I because I missed my friend. I stayed at the lake for hours, not even realizing that so much time had passed. My stomach didn't tell me that I missed lunch. I kept an eye on Simon and Sasha. I wondered if they would miss Lilly, too. Birdland was hers, not mine. She just shared it with me and so the lake did not seem the same without her. Just like I imagine many things would not be the same. I sat there, alone, and cried for my lost friend and all that would be different because she was gone.

After a while, I returned to my casita. I grabbed an apple and called Jesse to give him an update. It was good that he didn't answer. I left a message that I would talk with him soon. I headed up to the Big House to see if things were returning to a calm. As I approached, I could hear laughter and teasing and relief coming from the house. I wasn't really ready to laugh yet. I sat on the porch steps and turned to the sunset.

✦   ✦   ✦

"Do you miss her?" Diana came up from behind me. She sat down next to me on the steps of the porch of the Big House. The sky was turning. So many times I watched the sky turn with Lilly. Yes, I miss her terribly, I thought to myself. Then she handed me one of the two root beer floats she was holding. She had noticed the sunset, too. The purple and orange blending in the sky was spectacular. I looked at Diana. It was then that I noticed her eyes. How could her eyes be so different? The innocence was gone and it was replaced with experience and time.

"It's understandable, you know," she added. Then she was quiet. I got the sense she was waiting for me to say something.

"I guess I do miss her. It's an odd thing." I stopped. "How do you explain something like this?"

"I imagine with great difficulty." I guess I didn't have to explain. After all, this was her life. Diana licked the ice cream off her spoon. Just like Lilly used to. The bottom of the spoon and then turning it over on her tongue to get the most of the spoonful. I found respite from missing Lilly in the ritual that I knew so well.

"Yeah. I guess it's weird for all of us."

"Yes. All of us," Diana agreed. "But for you, it's different. For everyone else, it was me who was gone. For you, it's Lilly."

I had a kind of déjà vu feeling, like when Lilly was talking about Diana. But reversed.

"I guess that's true. But just like you were in Lilly, Lilly is in you. I find comfort in that." Diana didn't say anything.

"I hope that doesn't make you feel bad," I thought to add.

"I'm glad you find comfort in that. It doesn't make me feel bad at all. From what I understand, you and Lilly made a good team. I'm glad she was here and connected with you. And grateful. I just wish my healing didn't cause you pain. Especially since you helped facilitate it. I can't tell you how grateful I am. You didn't have to stay. But you did." She looked at me with such tenderness that it made me miss Lilly just a little bit less. She smiled at me and then we finished watching what was left of the sunset.

"Come on, sweetheart, let's go inside." Lilly never called me sweetheart. And I didn't know it then, but Diana always would. "I want to show you something." We went inside and found Reesa and Coco looking at a scrapbook. They were entranced by it. The book was one of those big ones, full of pages with mementos and ticket stubs and flower petals glued to the pages. It had stuff sticking out from the edges. Coco and Reesa were talking about what was on the pages. Movie stubs from a "date" with Huey. Newspaper articles about Diana, Barry and Hope. Pictures of Nonnie and Poppie, a tag from one of the dogs that had died, a silly note from P.S., cartoons she thought funny. They were turning the pages in anticipation. Diana led me to the other sofa.

"Lilly seemed like an amazing soul. Everyone loved her. They told me," Diana said as she sat down on the sofa, leaving room for me. "And I knew," she added.

"She was," I agreed, too. "And she was devoted to everyone here. I guess for you. I felt my eyes start to swell. I told Diana about the first time we met, how she met us at the truck near the casita and she almost hid behind Barry before she realized that I would be her new best friend.

"It can't be easy. All of this, I mean."

I thought about it for a minute. Diana didn't rush me. Neither did Coco or Reesa.

"I'm OK. Really, I am. It's just that she is all I knew of you. And that meant something to her," I said. "At least, I hope it did."

"Oh, Jade, I know it did," she reassured me. "Have you ever seen her scrapbook?" she asked as she reached for the book from Coco. Coco passed it to her. It had a fabric cover with birds all over it. They filled the cover of a very full book.

"No. I didn't even know she had one. She never showed it to me." I was surprised. I thought I was her secret keeper. But there was one that she, apparently, didn't share with me.

"She didn't show anyone here at the ranch, I believe. Dr. Sabian said that she only showed it to them. I want you to see something." She opened the scrapbook to the last five pages or so and put it on my lap. I was surprised at how heavy the book was – for such a little girl. The thought lasted only a second as I looked at Diana. She wasn't a little girl.

Lilly had included so much of her existence in this book. It was open to a page that had the date I arrived at the ranch. Underneath the green, child-like script was a beautiful drawing (for a 12-year-old) of a woman and a Jeep. The Jeep was obviously broken. It had smoke coming from under the open hood and the girl had a sad face. She also had blue jeans and a USC T-shirt. It was me and Carlos. On the bottom of the page was the empty jacks-and-ball bag from the set that she gave me that first time we played.

I remembered that day. Lilly laughed at how bad I was but cheered me on. She had the confidence, even if I didn't, that I would eventually get past sixies. I heard myself let out a soft, short laugh. I wanted to go back and play with her again. But the pages were pulling me. So I sat back and took in all that was left of Lilly. It was all there like a diary. Everything was labeled with titles and dates. It had the receipt from the yogurt shop, a photo of me gathering eggs and another of the two of us playing hopscotch. I didn't remember that one being taken. But I was so very glad that it was. There was a tea bag from our Tea Party. The empty seed packet from when we planted melons. A feather from Simon. Rose petals. A picture of Lilly and me drinking our root beer floats in the gazebo. One of my planter sketches that had mysteriously disappeared. Scorecards from some of our games. Another drawing of a hopscotch board with, who I guessed to be, Lilly, P.S. and I. One of my hair ties that I had given her. All kinds of things to record our history. To make sure that people knew that we were real. On the last page was a poem, printed in Lilly's handwriting. It was decorated with a colorful flower border she had drawn with crayons. In the middle of the flower frame was the last thing Lilly put in her scrapbook.

She told me I'm important.

She told me I'm her friend.

She told me in her heart

I won't ever end

I trust her with my secrets.
She'll always play a game.
I know she'll remember this
When things are not the same.

She said that I'm a blessing
But really I think she's mine.
At the Lost and Found
What was lost you find.

I sat there staring at the poem. I didn't know I was crying until I felt Diana wipe my tears. I looked at her and leaned into her arms and began to weep. She held me while she whispered soothing words. "It's alright sweetheart." "I know. I know." Soon Coco and Reesa came over and joined in. They came behind the sofa and enveloped both of us. We sat there holding on to each other for another minute or two.

"So you see, you did mean something to her. Apparently, you meant a lot. The doctors say that, while they couldn't tell exactly how or why, it was clear to them that Lilly's pages showed that she had connected with you in a different way than she had connected to anyone other than Barry, Nonnie and Poppie." Diana paused for just a second. "And your arrival began a change. It's all in here. Her healing. And, I guess mine, too."

While Guthrie was gone, we talked every day. We chatted about his rehab and how it was going. But he didn't want to talk about himself. He wanted to know what was happening here. I gave him daily accounts. We talked about missing Lilly. I told him about the police coming back out and how Diana was settling in. Reporters wanted to come and interview everyone, but Barry wouldn't let them. He was in protective mode. I told Guthrie that Diana was still grieving Poppie and how Nonnie would hold her and comfort her. This must have been difficult for Nonnie. She kept trying to reassure Diana that Poppie was proud of her and knew that she would eventually find her way back. I explained to him about the relief everyone had each morning that Diana woke up. I told him that we both had to get stronger. And hopefully, by the time he returned, we would be ready to take it from there. He kept reminding me that the day he left was the day he began waiting to return.

"Me, too," I reminded him, every time.

❧ ❧ ❧

Diana had so much to catch up on. She wanted to see everyone and do everything. She did not want to "take it easy" or "slow down," as most were advising her to do. Barry had a hard time with this. He had, for too long, been the guardian of Lilly. It was an adjustment for both Barry and Diana. But they managed. Diana would give Barry a reassuring look or touch and Barry would relax.

Barry thought it was too much and too soon for Diana to have a party. But Diana wanted to celebrate and it was her birthday, so Barry went along. He wanted her to be happy.

"We'll call it a rebirthday party!" Diana had been handling the change of events better than anyone else. Some were still waiting for Lilly to return. Some were convinced that she was gone. Dr. Leslie and Dr. J. both told them that it was too soon to know for sure. But, somehow Diana knew.

"Come on, Barry, I don't want you to worry. I want everyone to be here. I almost need them to be. Nothing fancy. Just some good food and some good music with some good friends." Diana didn't know it, but she was talking about having a Meeting.

"It's your birthday." He kissed his wife. And so Diana planned her party. It would be a week from then, but Diana had much to do besides getting ready for her rebirthday party.

She wanted to do all the things that she hadn't been here to do. She marveled at the gardens and explored their bounty. She cooked with Nonnie, she rode with Maya and took on Freddie. She met her doctors, but this time as Diana. She played with the kids, amazed at how they had grown. She had seen them so infrequently over the last few years. She took long walks with Barry. And she still liked games. Just different ones.

Days 50 - 51: Bittersweet: bittersweet | ˈbitər͵swēt |
adjective • arousing pleasure tinged with sadness or pain

I'm so glad Diana is back. Everyone is the same but different.
They aren't waiting anymore. But I miss Lilly. And our games.
And her random facts. And…

It is an odd feeling to both want the day to come and go and yet
also wish for it to stay as long as possible. I had such mixed
emotions. I was missing Lilly and Guthrie, terribly, but I was also
eager to know, better, the person who Lilly was protecting all these
years. The sun was arriving. It began with a dull glow, announcing
its impending arrival. It was like a candle that was just lit and then
grew to a bigger flame. Slowly, it evolved from glow to real daylight.
It took a while, but I watched it all. As I watched, I felt the air turn
warmer and began to hear the morning's sounds. I remembered my
childhood, which never included watching a sunrise, and I found
myself wishing it had.

꘏꘏꘏ ꘏꘏꘏ ꘏꘏꘏

River had been one of Barry and Diana's kids, too. They saw
him through high school and from there he worked as a DJ assistant
and eventually became a popular local DJ himself. When Diana had
broken, River couldn't handle it. He tried visiting the ranch a couple
of times, but he always took it very hard, and then never came back.
He called Barry every week or two to check on Diana and the family,
but he couldn't visit and see Diana not be Diana. When River called
this week, Barry had the news for him. He told River about the party
and invited him. He said he wouldn't miss it and asked if he could

DJ the party. Barry knew that Diana would love it. She was always proud of River and his accomplishments.

This is how most of the next few days went. Word had spread fast that Diana was back and everyone was eager to see her, so most of the time was spent receiving calls or making calls. All included an invitation to her rebirthday party, and almost all said they would be there. Some wanted to come over right away, but we encouraged everyone to wait. After all, it was only a few more days out of too many years. They all understood.

And there were deliveries. Lots of them. I think there must have been at least a dozen flower deliveries, most either gerbera daisies or sunflowers, which everyone knew were Diana's favorites. Fruit baskets came, baked goods arrived and so did a couple of teddy bears, which Diana also loved. These people never forgot her. They all just waited from afar, just as the ranchers waited here, close by.

So Diana's days were split between planning a party and getting back to her life. Things like collecting eggs, feeding the dogs, watering the plants and cooking all helped Diana find a place in the space they had saved for her.

Day 52: The Wait is Over

Nonnie and Diana went into town for the morning. They had planned to do a little shopping. Diana could really use some newer clothes that were more fitting for a woman, meaning no butterflies or sparkles. They had an appointment to both have their hair done and then get a mani-pedi before going to lunch. While they did their thing, the ranchers and locals were busy.

Starting mid-morning, everyone was busy in the Big House. Some in the kitchen, cutting and mixing and cooking. Others in the big room, rearranging, and cleaning and setting up a sound system with River. Out on the front patio, Kelly and Maya were with the kids making decorations. They made color paper chains to hang and colored pictures to lean against the flowers in vases that had been delivered.

Coco, Sunshine, Lloyd and Kelly were busy in the kitchen making all kinds of food that they could set out later. They had so many baked goods sent that all they needed to bake was Diana's rebirthday cake.

Everyone finished their jobs by mid-afternoon and then we each went our own way to rest a bit and get ready. I heard the dogs greet Nonnie and Diana, so I knew they had returned. They went to their house, too. We all wanted to look nice. After all, how many rebirthday parties does one get invited to? And I wanted to look nice because Guthrie was coming home.

⸺ ⸺ ⸺

"I would like to make a toast." Diana hushed the group. Everyone waited quietly while Diana searched for the words she wanted to share. She looked beautiful. She had on a new bohemian maxi dress and her hair was trimmed a bit, lying in loose waves down past her shoulders. It took a moment for her to gain her composure. She was a bit overwhelmed. In a good way. Not from too much stimulation or noise. It was from so many of her people remaining together and joining her tonight.

"There have always been two things that I have thought essential to a person's well-being. First, to be important to someone. Anyone. A soul needs a connection to another soul. And the second thing is to have hope that tomorrow has a chance of bringing goodness. And I have been so blessed to have all of you. You have all made me feel so very important in your lives. And in doing so you have given me back my tomorrows. From the bottom of my heart, I thank you." Diana began to cry. Through her tears, she managed to add, "It would take forever to truly express my thanks. Well, I may not have forever, but I now have time." Everyone clapped and wiped their tears. Then they raised their glasses, or bottles or root beer floats and a chorus of "To Diana" was heard.

The music began and almost everyone began dancing. It didn't matter if you had a dance partner or not, joy was everyone's partner tonight.

A new song began just as the car pulled up. Diana went out to greet them. Everyone else kept moving, both enjoying the celebration and keeping an eye on Diana as she went out the front door. They were waiting, too. The song continued and so did everything else. Diana was greeting Guthrie, who Michael had picked up from the airport. I could see Diana run up to Guthrie as he got out of the truck. They held each other tightly for a long minute before letting go. I could see them both wipe their eyes and then hold each other again. The song ended and Diana came in without them. She explained that they would take his stuff to his room and then come up to the Big House. I was nervous. We had been talking every day about everything except for this moment. And it was here now.

Another song came on and everyone began dancing. Except for me. I was waiting. I was about to go get another drink when another song came on. I recognized it from the first few notes. My first thought was that I used to hate that song. My second thought, after listening for another few seconds, was that I now loved this song. *"Long ago... and so far away... I fell in love with you...."* The song moaned pleadingly. I looked over, I'm not sure why, to the back doorway. Guthrie was standing there. He held a cane. He was watching me, not moving. I looked into his face and slowly walked over to him, stopping right in front of him. We stood there for a moment, just looking into each other's eyes.

"Say something," he said with that beautiful smile on his beautiful face.

"You're taller than I thought you would be." He responded with a bigger smile but said nothing. He hesitated, and then sheepishly asked if I wanted to dance. He held out one hand and without taking my eyes off of his, I took it. He pulled me gently outside the door to the porch. He had a slight limp. He leaned his cane against the bench and turned to face me. With one hand on mine, he put the other around, resting on the small of my back, gently pulling me closer. He pulled his hand holding mine up against his chest. And we began to dance. Everyone stayed inside while we danced out on the porch by ourselves. Or maybe they were there and I didn't see them. All I could think of was that there was no place I would rather be than here on this porch dancing with this man. My head rested on his chest and all I could hear was his heartbeat and the music. And I knew it would never be long enough. After the song ended, I knew I had to share him with everyone else. They had waited long enough.

"Should we go inside?" I asked.

"Just for now."

We walked back in, reluctantly, knowing that we would have to share each other with everyone else. For now. Half the crowd came to greet him with almost the same amount of joy that I felt. He was gracious and attended to everyone who greeted him, all the while keeping an eye on me. I mouthed to him that I was going to get us a drink and he nodded in approval.

The night was magical. There was so much love and joy in the Big House that it felt like the house was not big enough to hold it all. But it did. The Big House had held a lot these past years. This was easy. River kept the music going, people kept drinking and dancing and laughing and crying. Guthrie and I managed a few more dances, but I still had to share him, so I waited and watched while he caught up with everyone.

People didn't start leaving until after 2:00 in the morning. They didn't want to leave Diana.

※ ※ ※

"OK, so we all agree that tomorrow the ranch sleeps in." Barry wasn't asking. If he was not by Diana's side all night, he was watching her. Not the same way he watched Lilly. He watched his wife like a man who had missed his wife terribly and was grateful to have her back. It looked good on him. Everyone laughed and agreed that there would be no early risers.

"If Barry's sleeping in, then we all sleep in," yelled out Will. We all knew that Barry never slept in. Our bellies were full of reunion and joy. We would all sleep well. Everyone grabbed the cups and plates and put them in the trash or sink. A few wrapped up the food and put it away. The rest, we would do in the morning... or the afternoon. No one touched the decorations. They stayed where they were, aside from blowing out any candles that were hanging on by a flicker. While Barry and Will took out the last of the trash bags, Guthrie whispered, "Are you ready to go?" I looked into his eyes, my heart fluttered and I nodded yes. He took my hand and we headed to the back door. "Goodnight, everyone," he yelled back, as we began walking out.

"See you all later. Sleep good, everyone," I added as the screen door closed. Once we were outside and down the steps, Guthrie stopped to face me. I was surprised, again, at how tall he was. I was so used to seeing him look up at me from the wheelchair. I knew I would get used to it fast.

"Am I what you want?" he asked. I was surprised by his words. He saw this. "I don't want to assume anything." I didn't know what to say. I knew, most definitely, that he was who I wanted. But now, with his question, I didn't want to assume either. He saw this, too.

"Let me be clear. I want you. I have wanted you from the moment we touched hands that first day I met you. But I know you have been through a lot. Especially these past couple of weeks. And I don't want to make anything more difficult. But I need you to know that I want you and if you want me too..." I stopped him with a kiss. I reached up and pulled his face to mine and kissed him. After a wonderful moment, he pulled away. He looked at me again, then slowly bent down to rest his forehead against mine. "Are you sure?" he whispered.

"I've known since that first day, too. I just didn't know I knew." This time he kissed me. A bigger, longer more tangled kiss. Then he wrapped his arms around me and held me tight. He whispered quietly in my ear, not so much to me, but more to himself, "Thank God."

We walked back to the casita hand-in-hand. That was something that we had never done. He opened the door for me and I followed him to his room. We were still holding hands. We stopped once we were inside the room, with the door closed. We faced each other and moved closer together. Finally, our mouths touched, brushing each other's open lips. But we didn't kiss yet. His mouth found my ear and he whispered softly, "I have been dreaming of this."

We stood there and undressed each other, dropping our clothes to the ground while we looked at each other's faces. Then he took a step forward, his hands found the back of my shoulders and he pulled me gently closer to him. His mouth went down my neck while he moved one hand to the back of my head and pulled me even closer. He bit the side of my shoulder very softly, and it made me want him even more. His breath fueled me. He lingered on my throat, brushing his lips gently. I let out a small, soft moan. As he felt me respond, his open mouth found mine. His mouth was soft, but his kiss was not. It was like he was thirsty and I could quench him. He wrapped his arm around me. Without letting go, he guided me to the bed. We laid there and kissed some more. He leaned over me a little and stroked my cheek. The light from the front room was still on so the bedroom was lit just enough to see each other but not enough to take away the dark. He propped himself up on one elbow facing me as I laid next to him. His fingertips started with my forehead, across my face and down my cheek circling my face all the way around and down my neck never lifting up, continuing slowly down to one shoulder and then across to the other. Then his fingers opened as he rested his palm on my neck, ever so lightly, while he bent down and kissed me again softly. He pulled up and moved his fingertips again, slowly down to my breast. He watched his fingertips, seemingly mesmerized at being able to touch me. I kept looking at this amazing man. His physical beauty was classic. But it was his other beauty that I noticed now. There was a difference in his look from the time that I first met him. It was peace. I didn't really notice it until I watched him touch me.

After he brought his hand up to my cheek I grabbed it with my hand and held it there. I closed my eyes and leaned into his palm. Then I opened my eyes and took my fingertips and touched his mouth. As he kissed them, my other hand pulled his mouth closer.

He slowly moved his fingers down my neck, passing my shoulders and down my arm to my hand. He took my hand and brought it to his lips. He closed his eyes and kissed the inside of my palm. I pulled his mouth to mine and let it brush over me. His hand moved down to my neck and waited before moving down some more. My body moved to meet his touch. I turned my head so he would kiss my neck. He sucked gently.

"I love your neck," he whispered, huskily, in my ear.

"My neck loves you back," I answered. Then he pulled me on top of him and we slowly and gently, yet urgently, touched and moved and explored until we were spent.

I wanted this night to last forever. Hours after we began, we laid in each other's arms, more comfortable than I thought possible. And we slept. Tangled together. I meant to sleep in, but I woke as the sun was rising. As I began to stretch, I felt him by my side and a wave of peace swept over me. I turned to my side and watched him sleeping next to me. I was remembering the night before. It was perfect. I would not have changed a thing. Not a word. Not a touch. Not a move. Nothing. I laid there, listening to him breathe.

He must have sensed that I was watching him because he soon woke and looked over at me. I wasn't sure what he would say. He didn't say anything. He didn't hesitate to pull me closer so our mouths could touch. We kissed tenderly. Each kiss exciting us more. This time with some familiarity. And with that, came even more want. More desire. We began exactly where we had stopped. It was as if we have simply pushed pause. So we un-paused for an hour then napped again before showering and getting ready to go up to the Big House.

"What are you thinking about?" We were almost done getting dressed. This beautiful man that I met in a wheelchair, with the magnetic eyes and a saxophone was staring at me.

"I was thinking that I noticed I haven't thought of Dean for a little while now. But he just popped into my head just now."

"And?" Guthrie looked at me like he was waiting for the end of the story.

"And I thought that I was grateful to him. I used to want to smack him. A bunch. I was thinking that now I just want to thank him. That's all." He smiled at this.

"Me too." We held each other a moment. Then we went out to another day at the ranch. Without Lilly and Poppie. But with Diana. And with each other.

Days 53-56: We are all unfinished.

So much to write about. I've been busy. But it's different now.
No writing about hopscotch and homework. Simon and secrets.
Or DID and daydreams...

April's arrival brought the Lost and Found babies and blossoms. It seemed that it was a (re)birth for many. All around there was new growth and new movement. Tangled in between the new bursts of color was new life. If you watched closely, you could see baby bunnies hopping behind their mothers. Or baby quail playing follow the leader with theirs.

Not everything at the ranch was perfect and finished. Guthrie still had his rehab. Diana still had her therapy. Freddie showed up again and Coco came down with the flu. It felt as if life was somewhat normal. Whatever that was. We still did what we did at the ranch. It just felt different. A good different. But the routine was very similar and some tranquility came from that.

Next week, I would go with Guthrie back East to help him pack up his apartment on base. My New Mexico visit was put on hold and my friend was thrilled to hear why. While we were there, we would think about where we would go and what we could do. We did not question that we would figure it out. Maya told him Ozzie would be ready to go in another month. We had to return so Guthrie could do the training with his new canine friend. Jesse said he might meet us here if the timing was right. He wanted to meet the people who became my family and I was eager for them to meet him, as well. I knew they would take him in as they did me. That was the Lost and

Found. Nonnie and Barry reminded us that we could just stay at the ranch. It was a possibility. If even just for a little while.

Leaving the ranch would be bittersweet. But it was time to go. At least for a little while. I knew that we would come back for Ozzie and that we could stay if we chose to. I also knew it would never be the same.

Time now moved at the ranch. The waiting was over. Diane and Barry had plans. They were going to take a little while to readjust to their new reality. And after they were strong again, they planned to make the ranch useful. They were thinking maybe an afterschool training center for wayward teens or developmentally delayed adults. Or maybe they would try foster care again. They had time to decide. There were always tomorrows.

"How will I be able to leave, Nonnie? To say goodbye?" She smiled at me, that beautiful, whole body smile, just like the first time I saw it.

"That's an easy one, child. You just put a one-foot in front of the other and walk. And saying goodbye... you just add 'for now.'"

Epilogue

*It is said that writing comes more easily
if you have something to write about.*

~ Shalom Asch

I woke before the sun rose. Thank God the sun didn't need my permission to rise. I never would have given it. We were leaving today. I watched Guthrie sleeping for a little while before I got out of bed, grabbed his shirt and put it on. I also grabbed my journal and went out to the patio to watch the sunrise. As the light came over the horizon, so did the morning sounds. Bugs chirping and buzzing and critters waking up or going to sleep. The breeze was just strong enough to know that there was one. You could feel it if you stopped and tried.

I thought about the last months here. I had arrived broken, to a family that opened up their home and hearts to me. So much had changed since that day when Barry first found me on the side of the road. And I would forever be grateful.

As I sat there wrapped in the smell of Guthrie, I felt only blessed. I could hear the birds begin their morning greetings. The sky was lighter now and I could see the mountain ranges nearby. I loved this place. It had changed me. We would be leaving today, but I took comfort in knowing that the Lost and Found would be my home whenever I needed it to be.

I got out my journal and I began to write:

I've never said it out loud, but for too long, I felt like I had a story inside of me. What's strange is that I can't remember a time when I didn't feel this way. But I never knew what to do with it. Until now...

About the Author

Moving from Pennsylvania to Arizona as a young child, Jami Ober Gan was raised the only daughter in the middle of four brothers. She grew up in a busy, noisy, wonderfully chaotic and happy home in Tucson. After receiving her Master's Degree in Deaf Education from the University of Arizona, she taught in Phoenix and Las Vegas for 5 years before returning to Tucson to teach and consult for another 22 years.

Jami has one daughter and two sons, who she still considers to be the three best things she ever helped make. They also grew up in Tucson and eventually grew up and out, which, she keeps reminding herself, is supposed to be a good thing!

Like many parents, after the kids leave and after retirement, she filled her time with joining boards, volunteering in the community and enjoying her hobbies. Discovering clay and glass became one of her favorite creative outlets, eventually turning this hobby into a small business. She enjoys doing artisans markets and fairs.

Her other favorite creative outlet is writing. While *The Lost and Found* is her debut novel, she has had decades of experience writing song lyrics, poetry, daydreams and musings. She calls all of these things "word doodles".

It was when she was working a part-time job while in college that Jami met a woman with Dissociative Identity Disorder (DID). She was intrigued by her interactions and observations of the woman with multiple personalities. This was when the idea for her novel was born.

Currently, Jami is still living in Tucson, Arizona with her dog, Gus (or *Guster*, if he is having a bad day!). She still makes glass and pottery works, writes word doodles and volunteers.

JamiOberGan.com (website)

facebook.com/AuthorJamiOberGan

Instagram.com/JamiOberGan

Twitter.com/JamiOberGan

34512824R00205

Made in the USA
Middletown, DE
27 January 2019